SEPTEMBER THOMAS

Wind and Reign

First edition

ISBN: 978-1-7342545-2-5

Editing by Fiona McLaren
Cover art by Natasha MacKenzie

This book was professionally typeset on Reedsy.
Find out more at reedsy.com

To Josh.

Together we can conquer anything.

Chapter 1

The crowd reeked of sweat and sin. A drunken laugh sounded from my left and I narrowly sidestepped a boy roughly my age hoisting a girl whose long, golden legs were wrapped loosely around his waist. He maneuvered their bodies, noses brushing, her dozens of braids snapping when he pressed her back firmly against the wall of a nearby bar. Their mouths fused in a sensual dance.

Ah yes, the third scent: sex.

I moved away from the couple while still lingering in the shadows at the mouth of the street. Loud, electric signs promising a range of alcoholic beverages and live entertainment jutted from storefronts. Above the businesses, balconies with wrought-iron railings strung with white lights and colorful fabrics overlooked the tumble of bodies packed on the street and sidewalks below. I scanned the crowd, not seeing the hundreds of faces but identifying magical signatures and their bright flashes of accompanying colors instead.

Humans outnumbered the fey, but not by much.

Like nearly everywhere else I'd visited over the past three months, Bourbon Street reflected the rise in fey embracing their newly rediscovered magical abilities. Up until last year, magic had been but a memory, lost over the course of the past two thousand years. Now, with magic back and better than ever, an adjustment period was necessary. However, I'd never seen so many types of un-glamored fey in one space like this: from bulky shifters to oil-eyed pixies. Even a gaggle of minute goblins darted around legs and feet, cataloging pockets and purses to pick.

I sighed, lightly patted the silvery, braided crown wrapped around my head, and tugged the hood of my jacket lower over my brow. Of the signatures I could detect, my own remained the strongest. That was bound to happen considering I, Zara Ramone, was the God of Water: a magical being at the top of the food chain. Only three others could match my might, and the fact that none of them were within sight, scent, or touch meant I'd successfully stolen another day of freedom.

"You're so hot, it's unreal." I glanced back at the couple who'd nearly crashed into me in their zest to devour one another whole. The girl speared her fingers through the boy's dark hair, ruining the styled, gelled perfection. "We should get out of here. Is there anyone you need to talk to?"

He only had eyes for her, but she wasn't watching him. Her gaze was fixed firmly over his shoulder, locked on me. Marigold eyes glittered as she scrutinized me, nostrils flaring as she attempted to gauge my veiled magical signature. The succubus smoothed square-tipped nails over the back of the boy's head, legs clenching tightly, claiming him as she pressed her lips to the fragile shell of his ear. I lazily batted away the reaching tendrils of her feathery, dark magic and her cheeks hollowed with surprise. She broke our stare-down long enough to glance at her conquest, then back to me, her inner quandary scrawled across her face: keep her prey or face a potential threat.

I tipped her a half-smile. "Don't drain him dry," I tossed out with a two-fingered salute.

The girl's face tightened as the human boy turned, but I'd already entered the throng. Fey acting on their base instincts were no concern of mine.

CHAPTER 1

And I was running late.

Ensconced in the crowd, I moved with quick confidence while keeping my head bowed, purposefully avoiding eye contact. It was a tried-and-true combination that I found drew the least amount of attention, which was exactly what I desired. None of these creatures needed to know *what* I was or *who* I was. Discovery only caused me trouble.

I squeezed between two human men fisting plastic cups of cheap beer. A girl in icepick heels stumbled, and I snagged her shoulder before she crashed into me. I set her upright and handed her off to her friends.

I rolled my eyes at the short skirt that barely skimmed the tops of her thighs. It was a balmy start to the evening, but it was still winter and it never ceased to amaze me how willing people were to throw practicality into the wind. Some dudes had shrugged on jeans and jackets, but most of the women rubbed goose-pimpled arms between sips of liquid—both clear and colorful.

I was definitely an odd one out with my knee-length, forest green jacket, skinny black jeans, and boots with knee-high, battered buckles. An added bonus of having more than Water magic: the combination of Fire and Air magics heating my blood meant I couldn't feel the mild chill settling in.

Two wolf shifters chortled as they shoved through the blurred glass door of a club. Someone had painted a mural of a woman with snakes for hair on the wall beside it. The shifters stumbled into my path, their eyes reflecting an opal hue in the spotlight. The smaller of the two reached for me, but I intercepted his hand and gently returned it to his side. His snarl ended in a whine when I shot him a hard look, my aquamarine eyes flashing in warning.

His jaw clenched as his friend tugged him away, acting on the urgent need to escape the impending danger I'd grown used to tossing around.

I tugged my sleeves over the heels of my hands, ignoring a burst of laughter from a group by the curb, waiting until they faded into the sea of the crowd before moving on. The tension binding my shoulders and back tightened, and I hooked a hand around the back of my neck before picking my way down the sidewalk, carefully cataloging each sign I passed beneath. My destination had to be close. My throwaway flip phone didn't have internet or GPS, but my contact had told me the bar would be here, right in the center of the block.

An oily curl of shadow unfurled in the recesses of my mind, along with a subtle scrape of nails along the backs of my eyeballs, and I massaged my temple. That wasn't good. I estimated I had about ten minutes before I found myself in serious trouble.

A burst of static tickled my inner ear, and I clenched my jaw, scanning the businesses one more time before finally spotting the sign. Among the bright displays of glitter and light, the outline of a crow burned into a swinging plank was deceptively muted. The entrance tucked around the corner in an alley, swathed in darkness, didn't help either.

As I passed beneath the sign, I tapped the bold, all-capital letters beneath the bird that formed the single word that held special meaning for all fey: Iridescence.

Chapter 2

The door groaned as I shouldered through it, and I inhaled a heady combination of incense and whiskey. Despite its name, which basically meant the ability to see and detect magic, Iridescence was as low-key inside as it appeared outside.

A bar stretched the length of the wall at the back of the room. Behind it, someone had painstakingly stacked an array of bottles in all shapes and sizes on a pyramid of shelves. Two dozen stools lacking padded seats and backrests lined up like matchsticks under the lip of the counter. Between the door and the bar, mismatched chairs circled a half dozen round tables. A troll slumped in one of those chairs beside the door: body-builder arms, blue-tinted skin, scruffy beard, and all.

He scanned me skeptically, his scowl deepening. Despite the ache threatening to crack my brain in two, I kept my face stiff, half-convinced he would toss me out before the door fully closed. With a wet sniff and a swipe at his nose, he growled, "Identification."

I thumbed a rectangular piece of thin plastic out of my pocket and passed it over, drawing back my hood enough for him to see my face. Iridescence may cater only to fey, but it had to abide by human liquor laws.

The troll brought the ID close to his nose. I didn't mind his skepticism. I was about three years younger than the legal drinking age, and that piece of plastic was a fake. Albeit, a very good fake. He scratched a cracked nail over the grainy picture, then lifted a shoulder and passed it back. I lowered my hood again and frowned when he plucked a long stick from the table at his elbow and held it out.

"Signature."

I hesitated. I'd heard about devices that measured a fey's magical abilities and identified their affiliation, but I'd never actually encountered one before. I didn't mind the idea of them, but I wasn't keen on submitting to a scan myself.

"Lloyd, let her through. I can vouch for her." An imp seated at the bar waved me over. Some amber liquid in a tumbler he clutched sloshed over the rim, but he paid it no heed. "Ms. Ramone, I'm glad you could make it."

I grimaced but shuffled past Lloyd who tipped his chin, pinpricks of eyes screwed up in concentration. My last name was less recognizable than my first, but it wouldn't be long before the fey realized where he'd seen my face or heard my name before. A pair of vampires playing cards froze as I walked behind them, conversation stifled.

Yeah, they'd already placed me, magical signature or not.

Good thing I was ready to leave this city tonight, anyway. If the blue flicker of cell phone screens at the makeshift poker table meant anything, I was about to be inundated with requests for help and bombarded with both criticism and praise alike.

My phone buzzed in my pocket. I ignored it and dropped onto one of the uncomfortable stools. "You're really testing my patience, Mayor."

"Sorry. I forgot you wanted privacy." Mayor Rory Oakland's tone was anything but apologetic. He threw back a large gulp of what, judging by the burn of its scent in the back of my throat, was top-shelf Scotch. "Though why you don't want everyone to know what you've done for this city is beyond me."

"What'll it be?" The woman behind the bar swiped a pint glass from beneath the counter and set it down with a snap. The motion showed off full sleeves of tattoos left bare by the cut of her shirt with a high collar so stiff it brushed her jawline. She styled her short hair in swiping spikes that exaggerated the jagged lightning bolts shorn in her sideburns. Rings set with tiny gems circled the cusp of one ear all the way to the lobe, which was pierced twice. Suspicion lingered in her azure eyes, her expression hostile.

I smiled up at her, relishing the first flare of cold heat that marked her magic. It smashed into me in waves, pounding and crashing like the ocean during a storm. Oh, she was powerful.

Despite my misgivings, it seemed this side trip might prove fruitful after all.

"Coke. Or Pepsi. Whichever is fine."

The imp scoffed. "Ignore her, Lee. This is a day of celebration. Bring the girl some Kraken."

I bristled, wondering if he was intentionally baiting me by referencing the Great Beast that helped guide me, but kept my face smooth, expressionless. "Only the soda, please."

The witch's gaze slid between us, settling on the imp's smirk, and, with the glass still in hand, she ambled over to a collection of bottles filled with dark liquids. She moved carefully, deliberately, defenses raised, aware of my attention.

I turned back to my companion, the one who'd invited me out tonight. "You truly are trying my patience," I growled. "But I'll let it slide. Overall, the fey in your city have been nothing but pleasant."

I dipped my hand into my pocket and withdrew a pouch of deep violet, squeezing its dwindling contents. At the touch, a blast of resentment that wasn't my own shot through me, and I swallowed hard against an accompanying swoop of nausea. Kaleal, the ancient and original God of Water who inconveniently lived in my mind, was waking up. Already she fought to assert control over me.

"I think you've got it backward, Zara." The mayor spun sideways on his stool, oblivious to my inner turmoil. With a grimace, he tugged a stained handkerchief from the pocket of his slacks and blotted at the moisture beading on his forehead and upper lip. Imps typically ran uncomfortably hot, their internal temperatures reflected by the reddish tint to their skin—like an ever-present sunburn.

"This city owes you its gratitude," Rory continued. "Shoring up the levees, holding back the Gulf, buying us another one-hundred years in this climate… it's nothing short of a miracle. Science was only going to hold back nature's might for so long." He sucked down the rest of his Scotch. "But getting a blessing from a God, getting a blessing from *the* God of Water nonetheless, it's incredible. More beings than myself should know about it."

Sure. I also wondered how much my *contribution* would add to his numbers at the polls once word about my involvement got out.

"You were the one who called me here." I glanced at Lee, who added the finishing touches on a tray of martinis for the table of vampires. "Don't go thinking—"

The mayor flicked his fingers at me, grin sloppy, past hearing me in his drunken haze of gratitude. "What you're doing for the fey, by going out and personally offering your assistance to all who ask, no matter how big or small the project—it's the most selfless thing I've seen in some time." He tapped twice on the counter, hard. "This time around, the Gods are truly here to help those around them, a true mastery of power I thought I'd never see."

Lee set two glasses in front of me with a thump: one a tumbler with nutty brown liquid that smelled like lighter fluid, the other a pint of the Coke I'd requested. I grinned at her again, the expression less teeth and more sincerity than before. She arched a brow and nodded at my arm as I reached for the soda. I followed her line of sight, and the Kaleal-induced headache I'd beaten back with a barbed baseball bat snapped right back into place.

The sleeve of my jacket had ridden up, exposing three delicate, black bands circling my wrist. They were only a few of the dozen or so designs that looped around both arms up to my shoulders. I wasn't ashamed of the oaths, but I kept them hidden because of their meaning and the power they emitted all on their own.

Oaths were binding, visible promises fey swore to one another—typically in return for favors or debts owed. They weren't exactly common, but I'd collected more than a few from the fey I'd assisted over the past few weeks. I refused to accept money for my services, dealing instead in offers of food, lodging, and, of course, promises that I never intended to cash in.

I snagged the soda and drew it toward me, condensation trailing behind it like a swipe of paint from an artist's brush. The motion also drew my arm back into my sleeve, covering up the oaths once more. Silently, I dared the witch to say something.

She didn't.

The mayor couldn't be more wrong about my intentions. Three months ago, I'd left Geneva in the dead of night, slinking away from my friends and my destiny in the name of self-preservation. At a meeting with several members of the United Nations, I'd had my name, my magic, and my obligations tossed in my face. Afterward, I'd forced myself to confront my primary weakness: my lack of understanding of both the human and the fey universes.

I helped the fey so I could learn about them, not because of some saintly mission to protect the voiceless and vanquish their oppressors. If anything, my actions were more selfish than they'd ever been. I'd left the Gods of Earth and Fire alone to deal with solving our ultimate destiny—preventing a nuclear apocalypse—while the God of Air figured out how to fix the church that had once devoted itself to serving us.

I'd abandoned my duties so I could understand myself and the world. There was nothing selfless about that.

"Put it on my tab there, Lee girl," the mayor said, his speech slurring around the edges. "And bring me another Scotch."

The witch eyed his tumbler, the glass cloudy with fingerprints. "You're two sheets in already, Rory. Are you sure you wouldn't rather have water?"

Taking advantage of their distraction, I reached for my pouch, straining against the weakness in my limbs, the ebbing control I claimed over my body as it turned traitor for the parasite that resided within.

How dare you subdue me, Zara, Kaleal rasped from a cluster of shadows I never dared to explore in my mind. *How dare you hold me back? This body is mine, too, you know. This magic is* mine.

With effort, I upended the green powder into the soda and swirled it in with jerky motions that drew the witch's attention. I was past caring. Kaleal was close, too close. Gritting my teeth, I lifted the glass and drained it, the rush of sugar on my teeth a refreshing departure from the bitterness sweeping my body.

You'll regret this. Repressing me will only spell disaster for you. I never took you for a coward. Kaleal's voice faded, her hooked talons relaxing their grip on my mind, on my body. *I was wrong. You are not the God I thought you were. I never would have picked…*

Her voice died as slumber forced by the powdery drug swathed her again. I scrubbed at my forehead, giddy with relief. I couldn't keep doing this. When I'd gained the ability to control Air in addition to Fire and Water, the ancient God had grown exponentially stronger. She made it no secret that while she and I were allies, we weren't friends. I also knew she wouldn't hesitate to overtake me if given the opportunity.

I wondered how much of the struggle showed on my face. If Lee's raised brow was any indication, it wasn't something I'd hidden very well. "Vitamins," I said with a cocky gesture at the glass and the herbal remedy I took twice daily to repress the ancient God. "Daily supplements recommended by my doctor."

The witch's eyes drilled straight to my soul, but I didn't give her so much as an inch. She could make an issue of it if she wanted, but she remained silent and snagged the glass to get a refill. I turned back to the mumbling mayor.

"Are you sure there's nothing I can offer you for your help?" he asked. "You wouldn't accept a room to stay in these past two nights."

"I'm fine." I found it easier to sleep near the water, anyway, despite the playful thievery of the water nymphs. Doing so had helped me connect with the Gulf and understand its natural predilections while asserting my desire to keep it at bay. I could have forced the issue and commanded the water to stay back, but that might have created catastrophic consequences. Nature didn't always appreciate being ordered around, especially when already suspended in an unnatural state. I added, "You've helped me enough."

The mayor held my gaze, unblinking.

It was true, information was far more important to me right now.

And he'd provided me with the most valuable information of all in my most desperate time of need.

"Even so, there's more this city can do for you." As Rory mulled over his words, eyes sharp with intent, the tiny hairs on the back of my neck prickled and my stomach dropped as *deja vu* swept over me.

"Zara Ramone, God of Water," he said, his voice raised. "The city of New Orleans owes you a tremendous debt."

I scrambled up, knocking over my stool in my haste. Behind me, the vampires went quiet. Lee crossed her arms, lips thinning. Even the incubus in the corner nursing a dark beer turned toward us. This was bad. I needed to leave. My phone buzzed for the dozenth time as I tossed a few bills on the counter with shaking fingers, barely noticing the denominations.

"For what you've done for this city, I, Rory Oakland, fey mayor of this beloved city, offer our people and resources should you ever require assistance."

I nearly tripped as I whipped around, arrowing toward the door, trying to ignore the burn swelling around my upper arm as the words of Rory's oath spun tight around me.

I hadn't asked for this. I hadn't wanted this.

"On the holiest of oaths, I swear our fealty to you."

I couldn't stop the gasp that slipped from my lips, the oath searing deep into my skin and muscle, hot as molten metal. I could deny this foolish mayor's oath, and would have were we in private. But out here with witnesses, the fey already braced with fingers on the screens of their phones, things were different. Few took public rejection well, and even if the mayor himself were cordial about it—I risked offending the very fey that lived in this city.

Rejection may very well earn me more enemies than friends.

"How say you?" The imp stood so straight and tall I wondered if his drunkenness had all been an act. He enjoyed being affiliated with me. Enjoyed the power that came with it. This was icing on his political cake.

I flung the door wide and spun on my heel, ignoring the gaping jaw of the troll who'd finally put two and two together. With the laughs of bystanders at my back and the wary stares of those at my front, I realized I never should have come.

But I'd needed his help, his information.

And I'd gotten it.

"I, Zara Ramone, God of Water and First of Four, accept your oath," I called back to him, anger simmering in my voice. "But hear me now, Rory Oakland, I pray the fey of New Orleans will never be called to task."

The burn turned to ice as the magic sank deep.

Then I vanished, a livid specter vaporizing into the night.

Chapter 3

I licked my middle finger and stuck it deep inside the velvety pouch, probing each corner, then tasted my skin again. I squeezed my eyes shut and resisted screaming. I was officially out. The magical powder created by a witch in Bolivia to suppress Kaleal was gone, and I had no way of creating more.

My head dropped back against the brick of the building, and I squeezed the soft material of my jacket bundled beneath me. Hours later and I was still mad at myself for falling for the imp's trick. Word of my most recent work holding back the Gulf had already spread. His name and mine twined together on the tongues of the city's fey, as Rory had intended.

But I couldn't hold back the tides of Kaleal's immense influence anymore.

Not by myself.

My plan had to work.

I drew a bottle of water out of my bag and took a swig before dashing some into my cupped palm. To the small pool draining between the cracks in my fingers I said mentally, *Out with it already, I know you probably have something to say.*

A low grumble and the Kraken touched my mind. *Does your plan not feel risky to you, little one?*

Everything feels risky, I replied. *But if I don't convince this witch to help me bind Kaleal inside that room*—I paused and spilled more water in my palm—*the cost to me and possibly to the world is too great.*

You've always been so skeptical of her motives, Zara. I imagined the Great Beast spinning Its long tentacles in the darkened water, house-sized eyes drawn wide as It implored for me to see Its reason. *Have you not considered the aid Kaleal could provide?*

I inhaled a shuddering breath through my nose. An owl swooped low overhead and landed on a board jutting from the side of the brick building. The alley behind the bar wasn't the cleanest, but it was quiet. I'd slipped back here after making my escape from Iridescence, not wanting Lee to slip from my grasp. It was 4 a.m., but I still had some time. The witch had to come out, eventually.

Calm again, I replied to the Kraken. *Four weeks ago, Kaleal gained control of my body and attempted to lock me away in the smallest, darkest room in my mind. She wasn't remorseful or conflicted. No, she wanted me shut away. She wanted me gone so she could play.* I recalled her honey-sweet tone as she'd fitted the key in the lock, her shriek of surprise when I'd nearly shattered several bones in my shoulder crashing into it, forcing a hole wide enough to escape.

I don't need to know her motives to know they aren't pure, I whispered to the Kraken. *I don't want to deal with her brand of crazy any longer.*

The Kraken went quiet for so long that the water nearly drained from my fingers. *Do what you must. But weigh all the outcomes.*

The connection between us snapped as the Kraken withdrew. The back of my head cracked against the brick wall again and I shuddered through my teeth. I knew the Beast well enough to know It was upset with me, though I couldn't fathom why. It should be in *my* corner. Not Kaleal's. I'd never understood what the Beast saw in the ancient God that It found so redeemable.

I stared up into the starry skies until my pulse evened. Only then did I thrust my hand into my pocket and withdraw my lighter. With a click, flames flared in my palm, illuminating the band of fleur-de-lis wrapping around my left elbow. I stroked the magical brand with my thumb, then ran it slowly down the length of my arm and up the other, mentally ticking off similar oaths of varying widths and patterns, remembering the ways I'd gained them, the fey I'd helped.

Twenty.

Well, twenty-one with today's unwanted acquisition.

I'd stopped in nineteen countries, met hundreds of fey, saved several towns, and still felt no closer to understanding the world or my place in it. I stayed no longer than a day or two in one place, my desire to stay hidden driving me faster and harder than anything else. I was well aware my friends dogged my every move. Sometimes I didn't mind it. It felt like a playful game of cat-and-mouse. But other times... I wondered how upset they were with me.

It wasn't like they didn't need me as they worked to solve the nuclear crisis.

And I'd left them all in such a lurch.

Staying in New Orleans for three days was a mistake, but a calculated mistake. It had taken more time to shore up the city's levees than I'd wanted, and Rory had staunchly refused to give me the name and location of the witch I had been looking for until I finished the job. I had to hope Ryder wouldn't sniff me out in the next hour or two.

I already sensed he was in the city.

I could practically taste the smoky, cinnamon scent that clung to his skin.

The doorknob rattled beside my head and I shot to my feet, crumpled jacket and canvas bag in hand. Finally. Lee was locking up. I slipped backward a few steps, silent in my boots. The door opened and the witch emerged, her spikey hair unmistakable despite the darkness.

"You aren't as clever as you think you are, Water God," she drawled, turning a spidery key in the lock before pocketing it with a pat. "I sensed you the moment you appeared on Bourbon Street."

I slipped my arms through the sleeves of the jacket. "I thought I noticed a few runes decorating doorways." Unlike how I manipulated the raw essence of magic to get what I wanted, witches channeled theirs through a complex alphabet of runes and symbols. "That's the only way you could have sensed my signature."

"Your defenses are ironclad." Lee glanced down the alley. "Then again, they'd have to be after what I heard happened in Mexico City. Someone told me you got some nasty scars from that scuffle."

I resisted rubbing my thigh where the very scars of which she spoke were engraved, long and red and deep. "You should see the other guys."

The witch snorted out a laughed. "No doubt." She moved past me. "I'm not sure how I snagged your attention, but I'd prefer you forget it just as quickly. I don't need nor want anything from you, or any of the other Gods for that matter. I've seen first-hand what happens to those who get involved in Godly affairs, and let me tell you, it rarely turns out well for the little guys."

"You're hardly little." I folded my arms, eyeing the tattoos curling out of the back of her shirt and under her short sleeves. They were black and brutal, not a hint of color to be found. Perfect for the woman who wore them. "Rumor has it you're one of the strongest witches in the world."

"That what the rumors say?" Lee presented her back to me as she strode swiftly down the street. She had no reason to worry, not with her level of power. "I'm not part of a coven anymore. I stick to myself and deal with *my* problems. My business is none of yours and I decline to help anyone I want." She paused. "Especially Gods."

"You sure about that?" I called.

"Sure as the demons that lurk on All Hallows Eve."

My skin heated as I followed her, my magics rising to the surface. "That's too bad because you're the only one who can help me. And with what's at stake, you won't be able to turn me down, Kristalee Salvada, daughter of Taratova Salvada."

I had only a moment to shield before violet lightning shot from her fingertips. The crackle of electricity grazed the back of my neck as I tumbled to the ground. A wall exploded, sending chunks of red brick raining down. A surprised burst of laughter tore through me as I straightened in time to see the witch whip around a corner and out of sight.

Well, *that* I hadn't expected.

I'd barely caught sight of the pen in her hand, completing a partial rune in the ink on her arm.

This fight just got infinitely more interesting.

I kicked through muddy puddles leftover from the afternoon rainstorm, humming low in my throat as I turned a corner. The labyrinth of the city slowly unfolded before my mind's eye as I moved, allowing instincts to guide me as my magic branched out along storm drains and pooled in gutters, searching until it found a specific set of feet splattering through the streets of the French Quarter.

She had maybe two blocks on me.

I'd be on her in—the world exploded. A tsunami of bricks crashed into and *over* me, flinging me across the street where I slammed into another building. My ribs cracked as I curled into a ball while simultaneously throwing up a rough pane of air, blocking the worst of the wall showering down, encasing me in a tomb of jagged edges. I buried my nose in my sleeve, coughing through the haze of red dust.

A rush of water bubbled over me and I blasted a tunnel outward. I clawed through the debris, and, on trembling legs, balanced on the rubble of a ruined flower shop.

"You witch," I gasped to no one, surveying the wreckage with disgust.

Sirens blared in the distance. Lee's antics had probably woken the entire neighborhood. There was no hiding the damage. Luckily, no one but me had been trapped beneath.

Chest heaving, I dropped from the pile, careful to avoid the splintered glass, and knelt beside the gutter, clutching my stomach until I was sure I wouldn't hurl. On the curb beside my clenched fingers, the stench of the magical signature marking it unmistakable, was a quarter with a rune drawn in Sharpie.

Lovely.

Just lovely.

I straightened and whipped up a whirlwind of air, attempting to create the lift I needed to fly. After a few moments, I cursed and gave up. Air was the orneriest of my magical abilities. I was better off with Water. It also didn't come with an added risk of burning anything to the ground.

With my bag weighing heavily between my shoulders, I bounded down the street again, ignoring the twinging in my ribcage as Water magic healed the cracks in my bones. That blast had cost me considerable time and distance, but Lee hadn't moved beyond my sights yet.

Now knowing her preference for magical markers, I dodged two more attacks by encasing the quarters in bubbles of air and water, containing the damage. I moved swiftly, eyesight keen and attention focused. As I gained on the pounding of the witch's feet, I failed to notice the black mark scribbled on some plywood boarding up a closed restaurant until I'd already triggered the trap.

I stumbled when a shadow the size of a motorcycle leaped from a window on the upper level and landed in a crouch, the panther's lean body stretching sinuously as it took me in. Blackened lips pulled back against sharp, glossy teeth and a rumble shook its immense chest. Twin curses. She had a familiar?

"A black cat?" I yelled, an insult in my tone. I knew I was close enough for the witch to hear me. "Could you be any more cliché?"

I didn't have time to sense a response because the cat leaped at me, all teeth and claws. I ducked beneath its lithe form and shoved my hand into my pocket for my lighter as the beast scraped the wall and bounced off, snarling. A circle of flames burst to life around me, and the familiar shot back mid-swipe, ears pressed flat against its skull.

"I don't want to hurt you," I told it, wondering if it understood me. "But if you continue this—"

It jumped through the wall of flames, eyes flashing, tail curling. Ice tingled against my palm as my favorite sword slipped into my grasp. I lowered my center of gravity, raising the weapon so the blade bisected the creature's face in my vision. "Well, I guess that answers that."

I attacked in a flurry of motion, my sword nipping and darting at the familiar which nimbly avoided my advances as I drove it back through the wall of flames that flickered so brightly they illuminated the spots disguised in its dark fur. I dropped the circle of fire and drew it inside me instead, flinging balls of flame that pushed the cat deeper into an alley.

When I thought I finally had it cornered, surrounded in by a screen of choking, black smoke, the creature hissed and… vanished, vaporizing in a shower of mist.

I tapped the tip of my blade on the cobblestones and blew the smoke aside. "What the—"

Four-inch fangs flashed as an anaconda with inky scales darted from behind a trashcan. The sucker moved fast, surrounding me with its body. It was so close I could see its body expand and contract as it breathed. I brought my sword up barely in time to catch its fangs, but the ice shattered under the impact, my resolve weakened by surprise.

I moved backward but tripped over a foot-wide coil of its body. Before I hit the ground, the familiar wrapped tight around me, muscles constricting, and my flustered mind went blank. Hissing filled my ears and what remained of the air in my lungs left me in a burst. I clawed at the slick scales, scrambling for purchase…

Then remembered who I was.

With a choked shriek, I thrust magic out in a blast. The balmy evening air went frigid, the temperature dropping to near-glacial lows. The puddles beneath the snake hardened into pools of ice. The familiar swayed, muscles relaxing as its cold blood reacted to the abrupt shift. Red eyes glazed and its thick coils fell away, landing limply on the ground with soft thuds.

I collapsed on my hands and knees, free of the suffocating squeezing, and choked precious air into my bruised and battered lungs. The surrounding air warmed as I released my grip on the element. I didn't want to kill the creature. Familiars were rare, and I'd never heard of one shape-shifting before.

As I rose, still clutching my sides, the anaconda curled in on itself, scales falling away as its massive body folded, leaving behind a kitten with triangle ears and a tufted tail. Its chest shook as it pressed against the wall, spine arched.

The familiar didn't have enough strength to give me any more trouble, but I locked it in a cage of air, regardless. The nature of the element would keep it contained while still allowing it to breathe.

As the kitten cowered, I scanned the alley. The edges of my vision grew hazy and a tar-like substance coated my tongue, its gasoline scent clogging my nostrils. Early signs of Kaleal rousing from her slumber. I was running out of time.

I darted to the main road as the world took on a reddish hue, throwing out my senses until I found her once again: the witch pounding toward a building with large glass windows and vines twined around an upstairs balcony.

"Enough," I growled, sending a blue pulse through the streets separating me from Lee.

She skidded on the sheen of newly formed ice and landed hard, her chin cracking as she slipped down the street. I almost felt bad for her when she crashed into a light pole, bones snapping in a series of ugly crunches. Chains of ice sprouted, lashing around her wrists and ankles as she struggled. Her Sharpie went flying.

I glided along the ice, moving faster than I ever could have run, pausing only when I reached the bundle that was her body. Lee's blue eyes widened as I stalked closer, a dagger of flames in one hand.

"Are we done?" I asked.

Chapter 4

Lee's bonds evaporated at her surly nod. Pinned and prone as she was, there was little else she could do.

Wincing, she rolled upright, massaging her wrists where shards of ice had dug deep. I repressed a sigh when the sharp bite of sulfur filled my nose. This time, when the bolt of purple electricity shot my way, I was ready. With a raised hand and a shake of my head, the particles distorted. The lightning sputtered and died.

The witch hadn't stopped to watch her strike move home.

Gravel flew beneath her shoes as she sprinted for the door of the shop and all but ripped off the top of the mailbox bolted to the wall. Triumph flashed across her face as she emerged with another permanent marker, her body in motion as she reached for the beginnings of a rune sketched on the doorframe, ready to complete what I was positive was some sort of shielding spell.

With a tsk, I snapped out a gust of wind and slammed her against the door.

Lee floundered, yanking futilely at her arm, but went limp when I plucked the pen from her frozen grip and shoved it into my pocket with its sibling. Reining in my temper, I examined first the black slashes of her handwriting, then her face, dark with resignation and fury.

I was tempted to scorch the mark right off the door, but knew better than to mess with whatever magic she'd started. Instead, I propped a shoulder against the wall, a picture of patience now that my anger had washed away. Her breathing evened and the hate in her gaze lost some of its heat. Only then did I step back and relinquish my grip on the weight pressing against her.

She slid to the ground, shaky on her knees. If the prickling of Water in my palms told me anything, she was in more pain than she let on.

"You're not natural," Lee bit out. "Water, Fire, *and* Air? Never happened before. Not in the history of the world. I don't like it one bit."

I tucked some fly-aways back into my braid. None of this was news to me. "But you have heard of someone with both Water and Fire?"

Her glare was icy. "What do you want with me?"

"I need a witch."

"Good for you. We're a dime a dozen. Can't walk through the grocery store without tripping over at least two thumbing through the basil." She rubbed her jaw where the beginnings of a purplish bruise bloomed. "Surely one of them would be more than happy to help. You know, without all this drama."

I couldn't help but grin. "I would, but any old witch won't be able to handle my request. I already told you, *Kristalee*." Her scowl deepened, and she almost held back a wince. Almost. "I've heard of you. You're as strong as they come."

"Stop calling me that," the witch snapped. "That girl is dead. Gone and buried along with Mama and the rest of the past." She spat at my feet. "History. Right where they belong."

I understood the feeling. "Then it's a good thing I'm not searching for a War Witch." I paused for effect. "I need the woman you've become."

"I—" Lee stumbled over her comeback, clearly not expecting my volley. "I don't understand."

I ambled to the window of the tattoo shop and rapped my knuckles against the glass, right across the word written in a big, scratchy font. "Auxilium. Latin for help, assistance, support. Power. Wouldn't the owner of an establishment with such a name be obligated to offer... assistance? Especially to her God?"

Lee's hand flew to her throat. She gasped when she discovered her stiff collar had gone limp, exposing the thick, swooping lines of Water's crest burned in black on her neck and the underside of her jaw. Understanding dawned in her face as she stepped back.

"You're sworn to serve me, Lee." I shoved my hands into my pockets and toyed with the markers. Her markers. "You may not be a War Witch for the Palace of Oceans anymore, but that doesn't negate the basic fact that you're sworn to do my bidding."

"You—"

My expression hardened. "You should be grateful I'm willing to overlook the roles you and your *mama* played in allowing the Order to destroy my temple." Lee's face went ashen under her dark skin, her throat bobbing as she clenched her fists at her sides. "In fact, I'm willing to go so far as to forgive you for working with Geoffrey, for telling him when my home would be at its weakest, for boarding his ships, for blasting my castle into the depths of the North Sea."

The goosebumps popping along my arms had nothing to do with the sudden dip in temperature. I may have been an infant when my world had collapsed, but it still burned thinking about it. Knowing what had happened.

"Yes, Lee. I know all about that time. You may have left your coven, but your sisters are still out there and they most definitely still talk." She tripped over her feet and went sprawling, nails digging grooves into the oath now glowing blue against her skin, reacting to my proximity, my power. "Just like I know your mother manipulated you into helping her. You were a child. Ten? Right?"

Her eyes had gone glassy, watching some other horror play out.

I lowered to a crouch and my voice softened. "Your old best friend, Ann, she's the one who told me. She also told me you never wanted to learn warfare, and that's why afterward, you poured yourself into learning the healing arts, to mastering your runes. To making them sing for you in a way they do for no other witch."

My words were bringing her back, her blue eyes focusing on my face. In them I saw the reflection of my own glowing eyes. "But warfare and violence are still ingrained in your blood. It's why you're able to imbue as much violence into your magic as you are." I ran a finger down the side of her face, my rage carefully netted behind my blank stare. "And that's a good thing, because I need you to combine those magics to help me."

For the first time in a long time, I allowed my mask to drop.

"I need you to save me."

Lee straightened, one arm hooking around the bend of her knee, leaning in closer. Seeing all I allowed her to see. "You're afraid." Lee reached out, nearly touched the crinkles fanning from the corners of my eyes, evidence of the strain and sheer amount of willpower it took to not lose what remained of my bloody mind. "You're terrified. I never would have guessed."

I closed my eyes against the raw compassion reflected in hers. "Gods know fear, too."

She braced her hands on my shoulders and nudged me aside as she slowly rose to her feet. "What could you—a God who's faced the Order twice and *won*—what could you possibly fear?"

"That's a complicated question." I moved from the circle of light haloing us to the edge of the shadows, desiring their dark comfort. "I fear a being far more powerful than I am. A being that lives in my mind. A God who can overcome my will at the slightest signal of weakness, a creature with intentions I don't understand and can't comprehend. I fear losing myself to her. I fear losing my mind."

My breathing turned quick, jerky. Inside, I was a raw mixture of boiling lava and blasting cold. I'd finally done it. I'd finally admitted my deepest secret. My most sacred of fears.

And I hadn't been struck down.

Kaleal hadn't shredded me where I stood.

Maybe I had a chance.

A hand brushed the back of my arm, and I turned back to the witch, my only chance at saving myself. Her tongue darted out, wetting her lips nervously. "What do you need me to do?"

I inhaled deeply, silently hoping the Kraken could forgive me. Maybe one day It would understand why I needed to do this so badly. "I need you to bind her back, to lock her away in my head for good. Trap her behind a door that neither of us can open." I shoved my hands in my hair, disrupting the coils wrapped at my crown. "I can't keep living like this, wondering if… or *when* she'll rise up. When I won't be able to hold her back."

Lee didn't respond for so long that I feared her answer.

If she refused to help me now, even a direct order as her God wouldn't be worth anything. I couldn't force her hand. A witch's spell was only as strong as her resolve. A witch forced to do something she didn't want to do created magic that was not only ineffective, but had a nasty habit of backfiring.

"I'll help you," she finally said, her eyes flickering as she completed some internal debate. "But I need something of equal importance from you."

My body went stiff. "I already offered—"

"I don't want your forgiveness." Lee's hand curled at her chest. "I don't want it, either. Frankly, it wouldn't make me feel any better. I made many mistakes back then. Many, many mistakes. And I pay penance for those mistakes every day I live and breathe."

Her eyes turned flinty, assessing. "But my sister is in trouble. She's sick and I'm not sure if she'll get better on her own. She's the only person I truly value on this world. If you say you can save her…" Lee pursed her lips, ground them together, and nodded. "Then I'll save you."

The word spilled past my lips before I could think it over. "Done."

Chapter 5

I pushed the belt back into Lee's hands. "Keep it. I don't want it."

The witch clicked her tongue, but dropped the strip of leather on the stainless steel tray at her elbow. "I'm telling you, this bravado thing you've got going on is cute. But once the ink touches your skin and I pour my magic into it—and honey this will be some of my most powerful runework if that God of yours is anywhere near as nasty as you say she is—it's going to hurt like demon's teeth."

I blinked at her and lifted my shoulder as I lay on the chair.

I'd nearly drowned. I was shot in the gut. I had been fried to a crisp. I'd been suffocated with sand. I'd blasted out of a glass wall in an explosion. And I'd survived.

I could handle a tattoo gun.

"Let's do this," I said.

Lee dragged her fingers across the bolt in her hair but didn't press the issue again. Instead, she picked up the twisted bundle of metal that would change my skin forever and rolled her stool closer to the padded chair—one of four in the studio. "You're sure I can't mark you between the brows? Your chakra is most open there, you know. The spell will take easier and it won't hurt quite as much."

I gnawed my lips. "I'm fine with you marking up my face, but between my hair and my eyes, I already get enough strange looks without drawing a literal target on my forehead."

Lee snorted. "I don't know. Being who you are, you might start a trend." She rolled forward, angling so she lined up with the left side of my body. My nostrils flared. She smelled faintly of baby powder. "Then the temple it is. No sedatives that might muddy the magic. No leather. Just you, me, and a whole lot of magic."

The witch flipped a lever and the fine hairs on my arm prickled at the soft buzzing that filled the empty studio. I held up a hand when Lee drew close. "Promise me that when you start, you won't stop. For anything."

Her face went blank as drywall.

"Promise me, Lee." I'd felt Kaleal stirring earlier and though she'd quieted, there was no telling what the God might do next. "Or I'll take the choice from you and insist on it through the oath."

The witch quirked a brow. "I doubt it, but I'll humor you because we're wasting time." Her navy eyes bored into mine. "I promise I won't stop even if you somehow die under my hands."

I sneered and dropped my head, pressing my cheek to the cool leather, lying still as the needle drew close and then vanished from my periphery. I closed my eyes…

Only for my lids to flash back open as raw lightning drilled into the side of my skull. The scent of burning flesh and ozone filled my nostrils, but when I tried to thrash, I found myself bound in place by another of Lee's clever little runes. Inside I flailed, wanting to scream but strangely unable to as the slender needle bored into me like a jackhammer.

I knew the exact moment Kaleal awoke.

I felt her lurch from her four-poster bed, guttural curses dropping from her lips like grenades, her fingers curling into claws as she took hold of my soul and pried it back from the Velcro holding it to my skin. Lee's eyes flickered as she caught sight of the Ancient God glaring out from my eyes before she buckled down.

"Get her back, Zara," the witch hollered, pinning my head to the table firmly. "Or this won't work."

Kaleal took control of my mouth. "You dare—"

I flung myself at Kaleal, wrapped my arms around her, tight as the Kraken, and wrenched her back. She shrieked as we fell, souls twisting as we tumbled into the deepest recesses of my mind—into hallways I rarely ventured anymore. I hit the floor with a grunt and threw myself sideways, barely avoiding the fist that crashed into the stone where my head had been.

Damn it. Kaleal always landed on her feet.

"What is this?" she shrieked, her long, violet dress swirling around her legs as she spun on me.

I shot to my feet, bobbing backward as a violent shudder rattled the corridor. Lee's magic prickled, a faint thrum through my veins. But Kaleal screamed, a sound so shrill it could pierce a siren's eardrums. She thrust her fingers through her dark hair as her back arched, gripping the sides of her skull with nails filed into points.

"You worthless wretch of a girl." Her voice shook with abhorrence. "First, you drug me. And now you—what are you doing with a witch, anyway?"

The last bit came out as a shriek as she launched herself at me again. I took a step back, intending to brace and instead pinwheeled when my foot found nothing but open air. I tried to call magic to me, but came up empty as I plummeted into nothingness—

Only to have my shoulder wrenched from its socket when a hand snagged my wrist.

"Not so fast." Kaleal's amethyst eyes burned so hot they were nearly white as she hauled me up. "You're not getting out of this that easily, girl."

"How kind of you," I puffed, ignoring the way my heart thrashed about my insides like a trapped bird. My good arm connected with the stone floor and I tried inching myself back onto solid ground, fully aware of my dangling legs as Kaleal wrenched mercilessly at my busted limb.

Another vibration, this one less violent but longer, shook the passageway, and I would have toppled back over the ledge had Kaleal not shifted her grip to the back of my neck, pinning me in place.

I didn't understand what she was doing, what she was after, or where this giant gaping pit had come from.

Was it her construct in *my* mind?

"What are you—" My voice cut off as Kaleal's hands closed around my throat and I gagged. She shook me, madness brimming in her eyes. I gasped only to find my air supply cut short. I snagged her arm, sinking my nails in deep, trying to draw her back.

But she held firm.

"You're trying to seal me in here," she said. "That's what you're doing. It's the only thing that makes sense."

I choked, drool trickling down my chin as I flailed against her. Black spots flecked my vision. I had no idea where my magic had gone.

"You think you're so clever," Kaleal continued, shaking me again. "Getting a witch to help you out. But there's no one powerful enough to—"

She gasped sharply and suddenly she was gone.

Elation crashed through me. I could breathe.

Beneath me ground had formed, sold and firm and wonderful. I assumed that meant I'd regained control over this portion of my mind. I slouched forward on my hands and knees, trembling as I hacked and coughed. Spittle flew as I reclaimed my tenuous hold on life while ignoring Kaleal's angry screams.

Only when my head stopped swimming did I look up to see what had made the God release me so quickly. I would have smiled were I not in so much pain.

"Well, look at you," I crowed, massaging my sore throat. "All trussed up and nowhere to go."

"To the underworld with you." The God's face burned red as she struggled against thin, silver manacles twined around her wrists and ankles. They bound her so tightly she couldn't move.

Lee must have finished the rune for constraint.

And if she'd gotten that far—my stomach curdled, my momentary glee evaporating. Lee was almost done, but Kaleal wasn't where she needed to be.

"If you know what's good for you, you'll release me now." Kaleal's yell speared through me, but I dismissed it as I dragged her down the hallway by the chain between her wrists. Ahead, I spotted the hunk of iron that used to be the door to her room. A room I'd once tried to trap her in after realizing how powerful she'd become with the addition of my Air magic. A room that had contained her for all of two minutes before she'd blown my plan to smithereens—forcing me to rely on drugs to hold her back.

I fell to my knees, dropping Kaleal unceremoniously when the ground shook so violently I wondered if a 737 had crashed nearby. I was running out of time.

"Give up, Zara," Kaleal panted when the rumbling leveled out again. "Give up already."

I looked her square in those awful purple eyes I hated so much. "Not today."

Her face tightened.

I dragged her the last few feet before shoving her into the darkened cave that was to be her prison—for good.

This time when I left the room, my magic came easily. The door flew into place and I bent it back into shape using a mixture of high heat and invisible hammers. Inside, the God cursed me, cursed my friends, cursed the world.

"You will regret this."

I didn't care.

She would not win.

I wouldn't let her.

As I carefully melted the door into the frame, I watched as runes popped up along the path.

No.

Not many runes. One rune repeated over and over again. A new rune, one formed from two old runes: protection and constraint. Two runes now bound into one.

I pressed my ear to the door, closing my eyes at the silence that met me.

Chapter 6

Silence.

Pure, downy, *lonely* silence.

I ran a fingernail along the longest of the inked lines.

My thoughts were my own. Finally. I'd never realized, until this singular, crystalline moment, how much Kaleal's conniving, her negativity, her ominous *being* had weighed me down… until she was gone.

I traced the second, slightly shorter half of the X. Its leg was maybe half as long as it would have been in true letter form.

My aquamarine eyes blinked back at me in the mirror, bright and bold in the dim light of the tattoo studio. They were remarkably free of the strain and exhaustion that had purpled my irises ever so slightly over the past few weeks.

I felt *free*.

Kaleal was gone. Not so much as a snide whisper or a wink of judgmental thoughts. Lee's magic had worked, her art a masterpiece.

I tapped the three-toed crow's foot formed by the inverted arrow on the upper right leg of the rune, blinking back the film of tears that glazed my expression.

"If you insist on touching it, use gloves at least." Lee tossed a pair of blue surgical ones at me from her spot beside the padded leather chair. I snagged them, and, rather than put them on, backed away from the mirror. "Until I get it covered, anyway. You may heal quickly, but that's no normal tattoo."

"Thank you." I sank into a crouch, luxuriating in my newfound flexibility, the lightness that made me practically weightless. "You did it, you seriously did it."

Lee snorted as she sanitized her equipment. "We'll see." She straightened and rolled her head, her spine popping as she worked out the kinks. "Now remember, for the spell to hold, you *must* apply yourself to maintaining it. Judiciously. That means your will must remain firm and the marks physically unmarred. A weakening of either will mean disaster."

I sat as she peeled a piece of clear plastic from a sheet, lined the edges with a sticky substance, and delicately applied it to my face.

"You should also know, that creature in there, she's... you're right to be afraid." Lee flexed her fingers, unwilling to say Kaleal's name out loud. I didn't blame her. "I felt her and it's good you found someone as powerful as me. Though, I hope you're ready to face what she might do to you if she ever gets out."

Me too. But I kept that thought tucked deep inside. "You have my gratitude, regardless."

Lee squinted at the mark. "I'm curious. How were you keeping her back to begin with?"

My knee bounced. I folded my hands carefully together. "Your friend—Ann—I ran into her in a small town in Bolivia. A landslide had wiped out half the homes on one end, and I helped clear some debris, reroute one of the nearby rivers, you know." I lifted a shoulder, uncomfortable talking about myself like this. "I got to know Ann as we worked. She talked a lot about you. She seemed to respect you despite you disbanding their coven last year.

"As a thank you for helping the villagers, she gave me some medicinal powder to keep Kaleal back and sent me here where she last heard you'd settled down."

And the mayor had finished the job.

"That sounds like Ann." Lee fiddled with her phone, the face illuminating briefly as she scanned an incoming notification. Her entire demeanor changed, trading confidence for wariness, satisfaction for fear. She stank of it, the worry radiating from her in waves. "I, uh—"

"Time for me to pay up, huh?" I tugged my sleeves back over the heels of my hands and stood. "Let's go see your sister."

"Are you sure you're feeling up to it?" Lee eyed me carefully. "I know how much it took out of me doing that, but it took a lot out of you, too. I don't want you to do something if you can't—"

"A deal's a deal." I *was* weary, right down to my bones, but that didn't matter right now. This needed to be done. "I said I'd help her. At least let me look at her." I paused. "Why exactly is it, again, that you can't heal her yourself?"

The witch ran a shaking hand across her face, pinched her nose, then released it with a huff. "It's easier to show you."

Color me intrigued. At my nod, she hooked a finger and I followed. At the back of the shop, in a cramped room that served as an office, was a door that opened to a staircase with abnormally tall steps. Our feet pounded hollowly on the slats, the sound vibrating off the narrow passageway leading to the apartment over the studio. The higher we got, the greater my sense of unease grew.

Stepping out onto the threadbare carpet of the landing, I wondered how I hadn't felt this energy sooner. Everything up here felt… wrong.

Malicious.

Lee hovered before a door painted a cheery sunshine yellow, her hand rubbing the serpentine knob. Her cheeks were hollowed, eyes wide and gaunt as she stared at the flickering light emanating from the crack between the floorboards and the door.

I drew a slow breath, trying not to gag on the putrid tang of sickness that coated my mouth. Fire magic sparked in my chest, reacting to an instinct demanding a fight. At the same time, healing water magic flooded my fingertips.

"Lee." She jerked at my use of her name, her elbow cracking against the wall as the single word wrenched her from her stupor. "Are you alright?"

"I… I will be." She smoothed a hand down her shirt. Smudges of dirt streaked the front from when I'd knocked her to the ground. "If you can help her, I will be." Her smile didn't match her eyes. Then again, it wasn't much of a smile to begin with, more like a curling of the corners of her mouth that would rather go down than up.

"Listen, about Logan. She's—" Lee gulped down the thought and tried again. "She's in a lot of pain. She's my little sister, and I can't… it hurts to see her like this."

I had a funny feeling whatever secret the witch guarded wouldn't remain hidden for long. Secrets had a way of doing that when things went from bad to worse, and if every instinct screaming at me was correct, this was about to hit hurricane-level nasty.

I tugged a chain out of my shirt and clutched the silver-encased vial that blazed white-hot at my touch. It was a habit I'd picked up over the past few weeks when drawing on my inner strength. It helped me to remember what I'd done, how *I*, an untrained God, had locked a creature of incredible power inside this very cage—much like Lee had helped me shut away Kaleal.

"Let's see what we're dealing with." I gripped the knob and shoved the door open. Lee stuck close to my back, expression tight as she closed the door behind us. The witch traced some runes carved into the doorframe before finishing four symbols across the top with short, precise strokes of yet another Sharpie.

As she secured the room, I took stock of what I had to work with. A single, bare lightbulb dangled from a cord strung across the ceiling.

The glow it cast was dim and yellowed. Occasionally, it flickered like the thick, white candles scattered on a few tables. At the far end was a bed. I felt for the vial again as I approached the fey sprawled across the twin mattress.

She lay so still I would have thought her dead if not for the slight movement of her chest. Beneath her, the sheets were wrinkled and crinkly with dried sweat. A duvet snarled around one foot, but hung mostly off the bed, pooling in a mass of faded orange fabric on the floor. I hovered beside her, clamping down on the urge to gag at the rank odors of vomit and stale sweat.

She looked a little like Lee with her oval face and willowy frame, but her hair was also longer, her brows sharper, her limbs frailer. However, those weren't the most telling differences between the sisters.

I glanced at the witch who dropped to a knee beside me, gripping her sister's hand tightly as she wiped a moist cloth across her sweaty brow. Their magics intertwined: Lee's bold and brash while Logan's was soft and hazy, a faint pulse I could barely detect.

"A succubus?" I asked. While it wasn't abnormal for fey of different races to marry and have children, typically their offspring shared the same type of magic.

Lee nodded. "Different fathers."

I tapped my toe against the floor. Still strange, considering their mother had possessed such incredible power, but not as strange as the utter *lack* of magic I felt from the fey. Even if she hadn't fed in some time, her abilities should still be an inferno given her heritage.

I knelt beside Lee and pinched the sleeve of the succubus's shirt. The fabric was stiff and riddled with putrid, brown stains. My heart twisted. She truly was little more than skin and bones. I understood now why Lee had said this was something I needed to see for myself.

Logan was dying.

I went to smooth her sleeve back over the dried sweat dusting her skin, but inhaled sharply and moved the fabric up instead. Veins black as tar and thick with sludge rose in ridges from her body, starting near her delicate elbows and reaching deep into her clothing. She didn't so much as twitch when I tugged the neckline of her shirt down—my gnawing sense of horror expanding when similar lines emerged, nestled neatly around the base of her neck. The veins, dozens of them, pulsed greedily with each pump of her heart.

A coppery tang filled my mouth—my teeth had cut into my bottom lip.

"It's a curse." Lee's grating whisper was a gunshot in the quiet of the room. "A curse unlike any I've ever seen."

I feathered a touch over the throbbing bundle twining at the base of Logan's neck. "Keep talking."

"I know what curses look like." Gone was the sister scared for her family. In her place, the spit-and-steel witch I'd met at the bar. "It's been a while, but I've cast a few myself. They're effective. Especially if you don't want your subject to know what you're up to."

Lee tossed the cloth into a pile by the door and smoothed her thumb over Logan's knuckles. "But curses are rarely this complex. They don't need to be complicated to get the job done—whatever the job may be. I know it's rune magic, but I can't figure out what the combination means. Just like I can't trace the signature back to the source."

"That's something you'd normally be able to do?" I asked.

"Absolutely. I know my magic. I know my runes."

I massaged my shoulder, drudging up what little I knew about witch magic. "Have you tried dismantling the runes? If you can see them, you should be able to scatter them." The strength of her magic and her unique set of abilities definitely would give her an edge.

A muscle in Lee's jaw ticked. "Of course I've tried, I'm not an imbecile." She scrubbed her palms together, her anger not entirely directed at me.

"I can find the magic. I can trace it back to its root form. I can read the runes. And I can pick them apart." She bit off a low growl. "But they keep coming back. The runes won't go away. No matter what I do, they return as strong as ever. I don't understand why."

The witch clenched her jaw so hard I worried she might crack a molar. "I'm more powerful than the people casting this particular net, so this should be cake. But it's like the magic is warped. There's something about it I can't put my finger on."

I rocked back on my heels. "Have you brought in another witch to look? One who might understand the runes better?"

"You don't understand," Lee snarled. "I *am* that witch. I'm the best there is when it comes to rune magic. I know everything there is to know about runes and how they operate. I *created* the ability to combine spells with ink and infuse them into skin. I'm the one who witches come to when they don't know where else to go."

She inhaled sharply through her nose.

"There is no one else."

My temples pounded, reminding me of the very magic she'd worked on me. The rune she'd created and infused with such power to contain that of a God. I bit down on the inside of my cheek.

"What do the runes say?"

"What?"

"You said you've read them. If you dismantled them, you must have understood what they said." I spoke slowly, carefully, like a soldier snipping the wires on a live bomb. "What did they tell you?"

"There are three of them." Her voice had tempered, her brow smoothed. "Witches like the number three. It's singular. It's prime. It's unique because when folded in half one way, the shapes are identical, but that's not the case when folded in half the other way—we witches like things that contradict. It reflects the true nature of the world."

It didn't escape me that she ticked off the three reasons on her fingers.

"Three is an easy number to work with: salt, sand, and blood are common when creating any spellwork, but that's true of nearly anything. Three witches are more powerful than one or two, but four can create chaos." A shadow of a grin graced her lips, and she shook her head.

Despite the impatience wrapping its tendrils tight around my bones, I listened attentively, giving her a moment to process her thoughts. Without her coven for support, I wondered how often she discussed magic freely.

"I'm rambling. I'm sorry." She tugged at her lower lip. "You asked about the runes. Like I said, there are three of them and they're simple, standard ones at that. They represent binding, cleansing, and disruption."

I looked down at Logan, her form still so terribly still. "Together, would those kill someone?"

"No. I mean, not necessarily." Lee caught my eye. "The runes are critical for witch magic to work. So is the power behind them. But intent… that's the sucker." She snapped her fingers. "That and whatever they've changed about the magic they're using here."

"Alright." I squeezed the vial one more time before slipping it back beneath my shirt where it dangled beside a pair of silver rings. "I think I get the picture."

"You think you can help?"

"I think I need to look at this curse for myself."

Chapter 7

I flattened my palm against the succubus's sternum and dragged my trio of magics to the surface of my skin. At first, they recoiled from the command, drawing back from whatever wrongness seeped from her pores, but after some coaxing, the tendrils mixed with Logan's weak powers.

"What are you doing?" Lee asked softly.

"I'm going to see inside her, get into her head. It's difficult to explain, but when I heal someone, it's not like I cast my magic over them and they're fixed." I frowned in concentration, struggling to find the right words as my magic delved deeper. "It's more like I become one with them, a spectator to the disease. That allows me to see what I'm working with and fix it."

"But she's not injured."

I bit back a curse. "Will you trust me?"

"Since you leave me no choice."

"Then let me work."

There was no earthly sensation comparable to slipping into another being's skin. I imagined the atoms of my body vibrating so fast they dissolved, slipped between the atoms of another, and reformed on the other side. I felt no temperature, knew no taste. Only the buzzing of my magic encasing me kept me from breaking apart completely.

When I reformed inside the succubus's mind… I slapped my hands over my ears, bending in two, nearly screaming at the assault on my senses.

First—the wind. It ripped across my skin like millions of razors; its shrieking, single-toned wail would have shattered my bones had they existed in this realm. It was impossible to see and I couldn't focus, not with the way the gusts ripped at me. The thick taste of rot and waste, dense enough to coat the inside of my mouth, saturated every hissed breath I ripped into my lungs.

I forced my way upright, using my magic to turn the wind against itself, and discovered a world flecked with bits of black and white and gray—reminiscent of the static of an old tube television tuned to nothing. I attempted to scatter it, but only sent the particles swirling, a dizzying dance of dust that blew over a barren wasteland.

I squinted through the haze, wondering where the fey might be.

She should be here somewhere.

It was strange—the lack of texture and personality. I wasn't sure how others viewed their minds, but I typically found them to be like homes—riddled with random decorations and thoughts. The fact I couldn't see anything beyond the vast, white nothingness wasn't a good sign.

I shivered, the temperature dipping so low my magic was incapable of battling it back. I needed to move, to find the succubus. But when I attempted to walk, my feet held fast, suctioned to the ground by dense mud the color of the sludge that pulsed in Logan's veins. It twined around my magic, not quite making contact, but somehow, some way, I knew it wanted to.

I dragged in more air, glanced up… and every muscle inside me locked up.

There she was.

The succubus, dangling in midair. The black that was neither ooze nor smoke swirled around her body. It lapped at her skin and nipped at her tattered dress and stringy hair. The parsley-colored fuzz that was her magic fought valiantly against the invasion, but was no use. From here, I could tell that whatever this curse was, it was destroying her magic. Her essence. Her soul.

The curse was eating her alive.

I considered the runes Lee had mentioned, but didn't understand how they came together like this. How something magical could destroy magic itself.

I attempted to scrape away some black stuff coating my jeans, but it held fast, sticky like taffy and equally stretchy. No matter how I tugged and pulled, it only left more gore on my hands while holding fast to my being, rendering me immobile. The curse dampened my abilities as it crept closer, prodding at *my* soul for weaknesses. An opening.

If I waited here any longer…

It might find a way in.

With a muttered curse and a soft apology for the succubus I couldn't protect, I wrenched my magic back along the golden channel that connected my soul to my body.

And left this cursed world behind.

Chapter 8

A tremor spiked up my arm, a lingering remnant of my exhausted shaking, and I clenched the empty coffee cup as if it were the only thing grounding me to this reality. Maybe it was.

Lee had wrapped a fuzzy blanket around my shoulders, but despite the rip-roaring heat of the apartment, my core refused to warm. This was a chill that I wasn't convinced was entirely physical.

Seeing Logan there, suspended…

Her magic leaking from her in soft waves.

I swallowed hard and flinched at the shriek of the teakettle—so reminiscent of that howling screech of the lashing wind—and Lee shot across the kitchen to remove the pot from the burner.

"May I have your cup?" Lee spoke cautiously, her hand extended toward the wide-brimmed mug. My limbs had loosened enough for me to offer the stoneware. The steam blurred her features as she poured what she called a *fortifying concoction* into the vessel. "You're looking a little more like yourself. Not up to kicking my ass yet, but not standing at the precipice of the afterlife either."

The corner of my mouth lifted.

This witch didn't owe me anything. I'd cornered her outside her apartment. I'd made her help me. I'd failed to fix her sister. Yet here she was, trying to make me feel better.

"Logan is six years younger than me," Lee offered, either not sensing my lingering unease or deliberately ignoring it. "And she's more carefree than I'll ever be. She never cared about the differences between our magics. Heck, she loved her father doting on her as much as he did. She loved not being under our mother's thumb like the prodigal child I was made out to be." Lee braced her elbows on the island and leaned against them, gaze slightly unfocused.

A moment later, she snapped back, the memory dissipating like dandelion fluff in the wind. "Logan embraced being a succubus in the truest sense of the word. Not necessarily the soul-sucking part, but everything else that comes with it..."

A rusty laugh creaked from my throat, mingling with her quiet chuckle. "I'm familiar with their antics."

I took a long sip of the tea and cataloged the tastes obscuring the rot that still coated my tongue: spearmint, lemon, something sharp and smoky—maybe black licorice. I sipped again, appreciating the warmth finally coiling around my spine, soothing the ache. I'd never liked licorice much until now.

"Logan's always been the light in my life." Lee set her mug down with a thump and slipped into a chair across from me at the rickety kitchen table. It bounced as she braced a foot on one of its lopsided legs, steadying it in practiced habit. Even now, half an hour after dragging me from her sister's room, the witch wasn't able to meet my eyes. "My mother was the darkness, the demanding presence wanting more and more from me. But my sister... she is the light. She is always so happy, even as a baby. No one can ever make me laugh like she can. So when the curse took hold..."

Lee's shoulders slumped with defeat.

"If you say it's a curse, I believe you." My nail caught in a chip along the rim of the mug. "I don't know what the runes mean, but I can tell you they're draining her magic." My teeth dug grooves into my chapped lips. "Consuming it, destroying it. Destroying her."

I battled back my unease and locked it in a chamber inside of me, a chamber full of things I didn't want to deal with. Back straight and throat clear, I described the shrieking wind, the blinding static, the frigid landscape, the smoky, oily substance that bound her sister in an impenetrable bubble.

Lee sniffed wetly, but her eyes remained clear, calculating. At some point she'd resumed pacing, chin gripped between her thumb and index finger. "I learned curses from my mother, but she never mentioned anything like this. I wonder…"

"Yes?"

"What are the implications?" She braced against the apron sink and stared out the quartet of dusty windowpanes at the empty street. Drizzle dampened the dawn light. "Does this curse only affect my sister? Will it spread? Has it spread already?" Her back stiffened. "I don't like it. There are too many unknowns."

She released the sink and returned to the table, arms clamped tight around her middle, brows furrowed in deep thought. The pink pattern of the laminated floor beneath her feet had faded in a straight line. It was clearly a path she used often.

Her uneasy pacing reminded me of someone else, and my stomach knotted. Ryder was almost always in motion, especially when he felt challenged or frustrated. He'd often march across a room, fingers speared through his dark hair, muttering words in a language too fast for me to interpret, prowling lethally until he figured out a plan.

"Do you think she'll die?"

Lee's quiet question shattered my stained-glass memories, the shards falling around my feet like pretty splinters: useless. I blinked up at her and she repeated the question.

I chose my words carefully. "I don't know. We Gods recently stripped our Hand of his magical abilities and he survived. So have countless others who had their magic removed because of crimes they'd committed. But that was part of a ceremony. I don't know if someone can survive their magic being torn from them by a curse."

My breath caught and I forced the words out, anyway. "I don't know if she'll *want* to survive."

Lee flinched and turned back to the window.

I may have never wanted my magic and all the responsibility that came with it, but if someone took it from me, if someone stripped it from me without me having any say in the matter...

I couldn't imagine what that loss would do to me.

"How long do you think she has?" The witch sounded drained. Resigned. Her fervent hope from earlier doused.

The blanket slipped from my shoulders and pooled around my waist. I didn't miss it. "I don't have the answers you're looking for."

"But you're a God." Her voice was a whip, barbed with nettles and thorns.

"But I wasn't trained as a God." I'd never resented my upbringing, but I loathed the feeling of helplessness that such an admission brought. "I have to learn, same as you."

Lee's mug crashed into the wall and shattered. "That's not good enough."

"I didn't say it was." I stared at the pale green lines streaking down the off-white paint. "I can tell you she's not sick. If she's not sick, all the healing magic in the world can't touch her. What I can tell you is that she's fighting. Her soul is fighting to survive. That's promising."

Lee's eyes screwed shut, and she banged the side of her fist against the counter. I imagined her counting to ten in her head, fighting to regain control over herself before she did something she truly regretted. I didn't blame her for her frustration. Standing here in her home, telling her all the things that I, one of the most supreme of all magical beings, could *not* do for her—I disgusted myself.

Lee's next question shattered the tension like a baseball flying through a window. "Will you help me?"

Could I?

She continued, "I don't know who else to ask."

I drew a ribbon of flame from the burner she'd reignited for a fresh pot of tea and fiddled with it, the warmth melting my thoughts into one steady stream:

I had promised to help Lee in exchange for her aid. However, there were many unknowns. Lee was absolutely right in questioning what this curse meant. If it wasn't directed at only her sister, it might affect me. My magic was the core of magic, after all. And if it latched onto me, the result would be disastrous.

The blue center of my inner flame beckoned, and I spiraled deeper into the warmth of the familiar. Finn would have begged me to think this through carefully, noting the danger of the situation. But Joseph, the God of Air and my ever-practical friend, would probably tell me it was my duty to see this out. My lungs seized when I recalled leaving them behind, abandoning them to the dogs of the Earth Temple and the United Nations.

I'd told Pyra I needed to understand the world in which I lived. I'd sworn to her I needed time to find myself. I'd vowed to use the time to absorb what I learned both from humans and fey.

The flame vaporized between my fingers and I lightly traced the thin band of water wrapped around my wrist, bracketed by a pair of oaths.

Until now, I'd only pursued jobs that required me to stay put for one or two days at most. The less time something required my attention, the more likely I was to help. I wasn't looking to settle down or solve all the problems in one area. I wanted to spread my talents, to expose myself to those who were connected to me. I wanted to feel helpful and to master my magics.

I was also constantly on the run, knowing that a certain incubus with more connections than I could ever fathom, was monitoring my progress, occasionally popping up when least expected. I touched my lips, remembering the heat that sizzled between us every time we connected, the wild thrashing of magic and emotion threatening to set us both ablaze.

I'd been on the run for three months, one eye forward and one eye warily watching my back, when Rory had called with his not-so-simple request. For whatever reason, though I'd had dozens of other favors filling up the memory of my cheap phone, I'd accepted.

And I'd stayed.

I prodded the mark at my temple through the plastic, closing my eyes at the subtle sting. Maybe I was ready for more. Maybe this was a sign, coming here, taking this job, following Lee, finding her sister. Maybe I needed this: a bigger goal, a bigger task, a bigger challenge.

"Yes, I'll help you." My answer was careful, measured. "I already said I would. I will not leave you to deal with this alone."

"Thank you—"

"I wasn't done." I cut Lee off, an unbreakable wall erecting between me and her gratitude. I didn't deserve it. "I'll help you, but like I said, I don't know how to do that yet. That means research and finding out if there's anyone who might have a clue. Someone who has maybe been exposed to something like this before."

I took Lee's spot at the window and braced my hands on the sink, elbows locked as I scanned the world outside the window, mirroring the witch's earlier quiet contemplation. The drizzle had stopped, but a thin layer of clouds lingered. Suddenly, my mouth went dry, my chest pounding as a deep sense of urgency flooded my veins.

"If you can reach out to anyone you might know, that would help. Otherwise—any tips on the nearest fey library?" I turned from the window.

Lee mulled over the question. "Probably Ontario. There are a few in New York, but they aren't anywhere near as big and you might not get anyone to talk as easily."

"Alright." I moved back to the window, incapable of ignoring the knowing fizzle in my chest. I'd waited too long, I sensed it in my bones. I eyed the shadowed corners of the alleyways, the spaces between the cars, the rooftops…

There.

A hunched figure with massive, bat-like wings crouched on the corner of a three-story house. It stood still enough that a passerby could have confused it for a gargoyle, until its head shifted, angling downward as it scanned the street.

Icy heat blasted through me, the intense desire to both flee and be found rendering me senseless. I dropped to the laminated floor when the creature's head lifted, glowing golden eyes zeroing in on Lee's house. Her kitchen window.

"I have to go," I gasped, ignoring the gaping witch as I crawled to my bag. Was it too late? Had Ryder seen me? Was he about to launch through the window? "I've waited too long. I need to go."

"What did you—"

"Too late," I cut her off. "But you should amp up your wards, set up some extra protection spells or something. I'm leaving so I don't put you or your sister in any more danger."

I glanced back at the witch who'd followed me into her studio. "Do you have an alternate way out? Like an alley? Somewhere that I can slip into the shadows and hide?"

"Yeah." She pointed with her Sharpie in a white-knuckled grasp, her confusion potent. "It's through there. The door doesn't have any alarms so you can go right out."

I nodded and started forward, but then reconsidered and glanced back at Lee. Her chin shot up and her eyes narrowed at my fixed attention. "If you need me, Rory can get you my number. You can also use the oath you swore. I'll feel it and will get back to you as soon as I'm able." She nodded sharply.

I turned my back. "Lee?"

"What?"

"I'm glad you're not your mother."

I made my escape.

Chapter 9

The stack of books hit the counter with a dull thud beside the librarian's hand. She raised an elegantly arched brow, first at the pile of dusty paper, then at me. The smile that quirked her lips died as she measured my expression: a mixture of frustration and exhaustion.

"Not there either, dear?" she asked. A muscle in my jaw ticked at the endearment. The woman was barely old enough to be my mother, and, if the yellowed stains on her thumb and forefinger were any sign, she was probably younger than she looked at that. "I'm afraid that's all we have here."

I squeezed the skin between my brows, attempting to drive back the headache pounding dully behind my eyes. "Would you mind checking again?"

"I'm sorry, but I ran another search while you were looking over these texts." She motioned vaguely at the table where I'd camped out for the past nine hours. "Nothing else came up. If there are any other books about curses in this building, there's no record of them."

I sighed. Ontario had two libraries that catered to the fey and both turned out to be huge busts. Nothing I found so much as hinted at a curse, or so much as an *idea* of a curse that could destroy magic. Nothing about black ooze or static or a destructive force capable of turning a once-lively fey into a shell of herself.

I scanned the magazines on a rack behind the librarian, mind sluggish and eyes blurry. Most of the reading material was written in small, sharp print that barely made sense, too.

A fire engine wailed as it passed the doors.

I nudged the books farther across the table. "Thank you for your help, anyway."

Marley—as her nametag proclaimed—shoved a mass of curly, blonde hair behind one ear and tapped the top cover with a viciously long fingernail. She was surprisingly human given her occupation, but one who, I'd discovered, was well read when it came to the fey. She scanned the room, which had emptied in the hour before close, and cleared her throat.

"You seem like such a nice girl—" the tic in my jaw returned "—but I think there's another place to consider."

She beckoned me closer, voice dropping conspiratorially low. "This isn't widely known, but the Castle of Glass may have what you're looking for." She promptly smacked a hand across her mouth as if she'd spoken out of turn and I hadn't the faintest idea why. What was wrong with the Fire Temple? Had Pyra, the spitfire God who headed the establishment, done something unspeakable?

I racked my mental databank, recalling the headlines I'd scanned over the past few weeks, and came up empty.

It wasn't the first time I'd considered calling up my friends—or the first time I'd considered stopping in Geneva or Rome to check up on the vast libraries I would find there. I knew my fellow Gods would be more than willing to help. Joseph was a wizard with books and research, and both Oron, the God of Earth, and Pyra had grown up in temples—unlike the God of Air and me. It was possible any of them might know something I didn't.

But I couldn't bring myself to reach out.

Couldn't bring myself to surrender my independence yet.

Calling up my allies, asking them for help… an ashy texture coated my mouth. It tasted like defeat. I had set out on this journey to figure out myself, to make a name for myself, to solve problems independently. I'd asked for six months away from the responsibilities of managing the massive problem overlooking us all.

No, I wouldn't reach out yet. Maybe if I couldn't find an answer in the next week or so. But if two of the dozens of fey libraries didn't have what I needed, I needed to keep searching.

"—I hear the Dragon of Fire is incredible to see in person. This morning, I heard on the radio that they were glad it finally woke up." My attention piqued with the librarian's excitement. The Dragon was the one Beast I had yet to meet, and I made a note to check in with the Kraken later. Maybe, now that a few days had passed, It wouldn't be so irritated with my decision to lock Kaleal away.

Marley plowed ahead, face alight when she realized she'd reclaimed my attention. "Granted, if there's one monster I'd avoid at all costs, it's that Kraken. I've read it's absolutely ruthless and has only gotten worse while guarding the remains of the Water Temple." The woman's smile faded, and she scraped at a sticky spot on the counter with a fingernail. "Of all the libraries at the four main Temples, I'd heard Water had the most comprehensive. It's too bad it's gone."

My gut hollowed. A low buzzing sounded in my ears. My home. My former home. Lost forever beneath the waves of the North Sea. I'd been there before. Once. It was where I'd met the Kraken and unlocked magic for the first time in two thousand years. I'd witnessed the ruins of the once magnificent castle firsthand. I swallowed heavily, shoving past the pulse of pain.

"Since that's not an option," I said lightly, forcing a smile I didn't feel into my voice, "and the Fire Temple is too far for me to travel, do you have any other ideas?"

Another siren wailed outside and a flicker of red light splashed across the wall behind Marley. Fire magic prickled in my palms.

"I mean, aside from talking to a witch, since they craft curses… not really." Her nails clicked merrily on the counter. "Though elves aren't a bad option either. They're intuitive when it comes to magical manipulation."

A shudder ran down my spine when I remembered my first and last encounter with elves. They'd sided with my second-greatest enemy, attempted to shackle me, had taken my magic for their own, and then nearly killed me with it.

I wasn't a big fan.

But if the witch who knew everything about curses was stumped…

"Do you know where they're based?" I asked.

"Elves are typically nomadic, but I think they have a central compound for training." Marley tapped a few keys on her computer and ran a finger across the grimy screen. "Yes, here it is. In Ireland." She scribbled a note on a pink Post-It note and slapped it on the counter in front of me. The word Cogscraig was underlined twice.

With great reluctance, tucked the note into my pocket. "You've been very helpful."

"Of course, dear. Is there anything else I can—" She smiled, but her expression tightened as she focused on something over my shoulder. I turned to look as another blare of sirens surged down the street and a fey sidled up beside me.

I hadn't heard the door open.

I mentally checked my shields, praying I hadn't slipped because this guy was powerful. More powerful than Lee, and she possessed some of the most potent magic I'd sensed outside of the Gods. What was worse: I couldn't identify his signature. I didn't know what he was, which could make things more interesting if he were territorial about this area.

"I realize it's almost close, but I'm told this library has a rare book

I'm looking for," the fey said, brushing flecks of fluffy snow off his sleeve.

I mulled over his American accent. A *cultured* accent dripping with enough honey to draw a whole hoard of flies.

"Absolutely." Marley beamed and leaned forward, the buttons on her blouse straining against her bosom. "What are you looking for?"

"It's an old book, but has a few different titles." He started rattling off a list and she turned to the computer, lethal nails pounding at the keys. I inhaled deeply, expanding my senses as far as I dared. Something about this fey felt familiar. Something about the haze of his magic or the darkness of his tone. The answer hovered achingly out of reach.

He sighed with frustration and I heard fabric rustle as he folded his arms, sending more snow cascading to the ground where it puddled at his feet. "Alright—how about *Temperamental Magic Through the Ages: A History of the Art of Curses?*"

The librarian's gaze snapped to mine, then to the book topping the stack I'd deposited. What were the odds that someone would show up looking for the exact book I'd finished reading minutes ago? That couldn't be a coincidence.

Silence hovered between us, delicate and strangely beautiful—in an ominous way that, when broken, would result in disastrous consequences.

I wondered if the fey beside me followed the woman's gaze. If he, too, had seen the book. If he wondered about my presence.

Marley's red-painted mouth parted, and I didn't stick around to hear what she said. With a whirl of my jacket, I turned from the counter and snagged my bag without so much as looking at the fey. Intent on getting out as quickly as possible, I darted for the door, mind cranking—keenly aware of the two sets of eyes boring into my back.

If someone else were looking for those materials, then maybe I was onto something. Maybe there was more to this mystery than one fey. My fist clenched around the note in my pocket. Maybe the elves weren't such a bad bet.

I was so focused on making my escape that I nearly tripped over a pair of legs partially blocking the door. A fey had sprawled across a bench, legs extended over the side. He'd thrown one arm across his eyes, the other clutched his stomach as if holding his insides in, and scrawling across his skin—

Shock sucker-punched me right in the face.

Ropy veins stained black crisscrossed the backs of his hands and disappeared into the sleeves of his puffy olive coat.

The incubus was in so much pain he didn't hide his signature. That realization jarred something loose in my head, an answer sliding neatly into place. But before I could swing to look at the fey at the counter, my fire magic blazed hot and wild, roaring up through my chest in a burst I barely suppressed.

After another glance at the fey who I mentally promised to come back for, I shoved through the double set of glass doors and emerged on the sidewalk where chaos reigned. The wind snagged my hood, tearing it back. Through the blowing snow loomed a monstrous tower of flames two blocks ahead.

Windows popped and shattered, raining glass as flames ripped down the sides of one of the city's many massive skyscrapers. Frigid wind snagged stray sparks and coals, sending them flying onto the streets below. Already, flames swirled like a pit of snakes at the base of the behemoth, white-hot tendrils reaching hungrily for other buildings nearby.

Smoke and ash darkened the cloudy sky. Despite being blocks away, it was difficult to breathe. Rather than waste energy cleansing the oxygen, I pulled a stretchy, gray scarf over my mouth and nose and started forward, snow and ice crunching underfoot. My trek across the deserts of Egypt had taught me the value of scarves and bandanas.

Now I never went anywhere without one or two looped around my neck.

The tower groaned and the top of the building exploded, fire shooting from the roof like a vengeful demon emerging from the underworld. People screamed as they ran, following the pointed fingers and shouted calls of the police officers ordering them to safety.

When one officer attempted to block my way past the perimeter, I knocked him aside with a gust of wind, barely hearing his shouts about the danger. The danger here was obvious. My ability to stop it? Not so much. I hurried, the only person moving against a current of bodies. It wasn't long before people cleared a path, driven aside by both the magic I'd unleased and the invisible blocks I'd erected.

The smoke grew denser the closer I got, but nothing could conceal the blaze that seemed to only grow, no matter how much water the firefighters sprayed from an abundance of hoses. The ground grew slick as rivulets of water froze in the icy temperatures.

Dousing this inferno would require magical intervention. I considered my options as I shoved past another helmeted man in a stiff, yellow jacket. Depriving the flames of oxygen was probably the most efficient way to extinguish them, but I risked smothering anyone still trapped inside. A storm might work, but I was more likely to whip up a blizzard rather than a thunderstorm given the current conditions.

Another groan from the tower.

It wouldn't be long before it came down.

When it did—no one standing below was safe.

I was almost on top of it now, heedless of the pounding feet, the blasts of the hoses, the intensity of the suffocating heat. My thoughts remained clear, almost tranquil. What I needed to do would require all my concentration.

"What in the blue flame do you think you're doing?" A woman yelled as I tugged off my fingerless gloves and shoved up my sleeves.

I ignored her and raised my hands over my head slowly, allowing the magic to build. At the apex of the circle, I stopped, my body vibrating with the intensity of what I was asking it to do, my knees bending, my core lowering as I braced for impact.

I closed my eyes. Measured my pulse.

When they opened again—my hands unclenched.

"To me," I whispered.

The world went quiet for one beautiful, crystalline moment. The billowing flames caught mid-ripple, the haze of smoke clearing enough for me to see the crews and the flashing lights and the rush of people. They all seemed completely and utterly still.

Then the fire hit me. Smacking right into my hands, rolling up my arms, roaring into my skin where my hungry magic devoured it, extinguishing it upon impact. Sweat streaked down my face, soaked my clothing, but still I braced, imagining what it looked like from the outside, a violent stream of intense flames tunneling from the tower into a human being.

More and more the fire came, faster and faster, nearly knocking me over, but forward I pressed, one painful step at a time, pulling the flames toward me. Into me. Not a single ember escaping.

Everything inside me hurt, but it was controlled, manageable. I could do this. I could finish the job. I buckled down on the power, embraced the potent heat, my grip unshakable. I burned blue, the vicious core at the center of the hottest of flames.

Through the flickering waves of orange and red and yellow, I could make out the tower, the steam rising from the iron beams and charred remnants of wooden walls. The other buildings, too, yielded their destructive inferno. Smoke and steam trickled upward, for while the flames were gone, the searing heat remained.

Finally, after what felt like hours but was more likely minutes, I drew in the last flame and extinguished it with one lingering thought.

I mopped at my face with a singed sleeve, ruefully noting the way my skin glowed like coals as I cooled, glad I'd learned enough control to salvage my clothing from the flames. Then the thought passed, leaving me with nothing but amazement. This wasn't the most challenging magic I'd used in recent weeks, but it was the most impulsive.

And I'd succeeded.

Warmth that had nothing to do with the fire filled me. Belatedly, I realized I was smiling. Not a smirk or a grin. No, this was a full smile, one that stretched my cheeks and crinkled my eyes.

I felt incredible, not only magically, but as a person, too. I'd helped in a situation where few others could, and I'd done it on instinct.

The wind whipped around more snow, lashing at the hair that had pulled loose from my braid. I turned from the smoking mass of rubble and faced the gaping firefighters, men with helmets dangling from their fingertips and women shielding their eyes against the intensity of light that was me. The awe on their faces, fey and human alike, reverberating within me.

I'd done that.

I'd done something good. Something that mattered.

Beyond them, one being lingered, swathed in darkness and sin. The fey from the library, the powerful one that put me so ill at ease. The incubus who hadn't disguised the red-gold beacons that were his eyes. He brought his hands together, once, then twice. The silent applause somehow thundered through me.

My smile slipped, and I wondered if he'd had something to do with this. If he'd known I was in town and sought to draw me out for reasons I couldn't fathom. I peeled my scarf from my face, uncaring of the bite of the bitter temperatures, tuning out everyone and everything except for him.

I reached out, my Water magic reaching for his, and again, as they coiled together, I felt that strange familiarity. Something about it, about the way he wrapped a supporting arm around the sickly fey from the library and propped him up, made me want to believe that he wasn't responsible for this fire, but that instinct made me more distrustful.

I withdrew my magic, intrigued when he didn't resist. Though, I wasn't sure what reaction I'd expected. As he drew the hood of his coat up over his swath of dark hair, I glanced back at the incubus swaying on his feet.

The same curse draining the life from Logan was slowly killing him, too. Of that, I was sure.

Maybe they knew something that could help.

"Wait," I called to their retreating backs. I darted between firefighters and bystanders with their cell phones held high. "Wait a minute."

Thunder rumbled. Snow fell in thicker bands. The wind whipped it into thick, spiraling waves that briefly obscured the incubi from my vision. I cursed, shoving my way between two women swathed in scarves and hats, chattering as they stared at the destruction left by the fire. More people emerged from the buildings, heedless of the blinding snow, packing the street. I panted as I pushed through them, aiming for the alley beside the library. The one I'd sworn I'd seen the incubi entering. But when I finally cleared the crowd and hovered at the mouth, I found it empty.

I couldn't even sense the other fey's impressive magic, no matter how far I flung my senses.

They were beyond my reach.

Pain lanced my fingers as I punched the wall, then collapsed against it.

They were gone.

Chapter 10

"I need your eyes," said the man beside me.

"Excuse me?" I closed my magazine and turned to him, my head lilting to the side. Five hours into the flight to Ireland and they were the first words my row companion had uttered. It was a silent relationship I'd appreciated as it gave me time to plan.

His eyes rolled behind wire-framed glasses. "That came out wrong. I meant, can I draw your eyes?"

He wanted to what? Did he recognize me? If so, this was by far the strangest approach yet.

I toyed with the fuzzy end of my braid. I'd cleaned the smoke from my clothing, but the stench lingered in my hair. I'd also tried washing with coconut-scented shampoo—because even coconut was preferable to char—to no avail. "I suppose that's a little better."

The man sighed gustily and muttered as he swiped at the iPad in his lap with a slender, black stylus. He jabbed at the screen. "It's what I do. I draw people." He slid the pen across the screen, turning the page brusquely, revealing pages of sketches. A woman sitting on a park bench, one foot pulled up beneath her, head tipped back in laughter. A boy clutching a raggedy bear. A man's hand with a stump where a pinkie should be. A woman's face, worn and weathered with time.

"They're beautiful," I whispered.

"I have an exhibit. I'm collecting new material."

A witch in a purple blazer splashed with white flowers bumped my elbow as she walked to the bathroom. She muttered an apology without looking at me. To the man, I asked, "And you need my eyes?"

"They're sad." He opened a new page, this one white and clean as fresh milk. "Beautifully so."

I leaned my cheek into my palm. Maybe he didn't recognize me. "Normally people comment on the color, not the emotion."

"I have no claim to normalcy." He scratched at the screen impatiently, the outline of two orbs forming. "And these drawings are in black and white. Color is unnecessary."

Not sure how to take that, I settled back in my seat. It was a tad too firm for comfort. The speakers bonged overhead, and our pilot warned about upcoming turbulence.

"So?" the man implored.

"Do you need me to do anything?" His mind intrigued me. Why not indulge him? "Look at you or something?"

"Nope." With quick flicks of the stylus, thick lines formed what I assumed were my irises. "What you were doing earlier was fine."

Ok, then. I flagged down the flight attendant and asked for a glass of water before pulling out the pink Post-It note from Marley. Cogscraig was a blip on the map not far outside of Limerick. The city wasn't necessarily a popular destination area, but thanks to some help from a human friend I'd helped a few weeks back, I'd finagled the correct connecting flights with relatively little hassle. She'd also scored me some deep discounts on tickets, which was good because my wallet felt thin these days.

The guy beside me sighed gustily and erased several lines.

There were still a few hours to go on this particular plane, but I hoped to be on the road early the next morning, even if the last flight landed late. It wasn't like I had time to waste.

I wondered what the elves might know, assuming they weren't too mad at me for leading the charge that had killed four of them in Rome a few weeks ago. In theory, they shouldn't be too caught off guard. The race *was* known for producing mercenaries and assassins. However, they lived longer than most in their career fields because their ability to absorb magic made them infinitely more difficult to kill.

A figure hovered in my periphery. I glanced up at the attendant gripping not one but two glasses of water. He smiled. "I hope you don't mind my presumption. I thought I'd get a jump on your next request."

I shook my head. "Not at all." I lowered the tray from the seat in front of me before taking them from him. "You're astute."

"Considering these two make nine glasses since we took off, the deduction was hardly difficult." Another passenger caught his eye down the aisle and the attendant smiled again. "If you need anything, please ask."

I downed the contents of one cup in two gulps, the liquid temporarily sating the thirst that never seemed to fade. The water in the other glass sloshed with the motion of the plane. It reminded me of another time, another flight. A time when Finn had truly begun lowering his haughty walls, revealing a fey whose compassion ran deep.

When he'd learned of the migraine I'd been suffering and how they'd plagued my youth, he'd figured out that I was bottling up my magic. The kelpie had explained I needed to constantly use my magic or I risked it building up again. If that happened, it might burst out more violently than a mere headache, especially now that I possessed three of four elements.

It was one of his many lessons I'd taken to heart.

"That's the look," the man beside me muttered. "That one right there."

My shoulders stiffened and I tried to ignore him. I'd grown used to constant stares and questions, but I'd learned to shake them off since

I'd ventured out on my own. However, there was something about this level of attention, of *knowing* that I was being watched, that made goosebumps skitter across my arms.

To distract myself, I dipped a finger into the remaining glass of water and reached for the thread connecting me to the Kraken and tugged.

Come out, come out, wherever you are, I called to my Great Beast.

Sometimes It would take a few minutes to answer my summons, but when two minutes stretched into ten, I wondered if something was wrong. Was It still angry with me? Could It have been *that* against my decision that It would cut me out completely?

I checked for the silvery thread that linked us and tugged, calling out with more concern. The line pulled taut, clearly connected to something on the other end. Something that wanted nothing to do with me.

After a few more minutes, I gave up and withdrew from my mind. Fine, if the Beast wanted to act like a child, so be it. It wasn't like I'd needed Its help right now or anything. I'd only craved a bit of conversation.

I sipped at the water.

The nerves cramping my stomach told a different story.

"Do you want to see?" The man beside me offered his device, interrupting my troubled thoughts. "It's rough, but it's done."

Tentatively, I took the tablet. He'd captured the strip of my face from above my eyebrows to the middle of my nose, the same area a mask might cover. He sat at my right, so the rune on my temple wasn't visible to him, but he had sketched the trio of freckles barely visible along my hairline. The centerpiece, though, was hauntingly breathtaking. As promised, my eyes were inked in black and white, the expression in them so filled with despair I gasped.

Was that how I looked to the world?

This sad girl with the sad, lost eyes?

"It's tragic." I rubbed my sternum and returned the device.

"It's beautiful," he countered. "There's always beauty in the broken."

Chapter 11

The Ducati revved twice. I took that as my cue to get off. I hadn't expected to love the short ride outside of Limerick, the vibration of the bike, the chilly wind tearing at my long hair beneath the helmet. But I had. I made a mental note to pick up one of those suckers for myself as soon as I was done saving the world.

I unsnapped the heavy, visored helmet that reminded me of the ones the Order soldiers used to favor, and passed it over. Ian, the guy who'd given me a ride, surprised me by snagging my wrist rather than the plastic he'd insisted I wear.

"Are you sure you're going to be ok here?" He tilted his head at the fortified walls and sweeping gate of what I could only describe as a military compound. "I've heard stories about Cogscraig. And, no offense, but you're a little thing."

I tugged my arm from his grip, touched by the worried lilt in his lyrical voice, the anxiety in his stormy eyes. Compared to the human with his thick neck and bull-like stature, I was small. "I'll be fine."

How fine was an entirely different story.

The motorcycle rumbled again as I checked the straps of my bag, peering up at the spikes that topped the wall and the fey that stood behind them. I'd drudged up Ian at a pub near the airport and paid him fifty bucks and a story to bring me here. I hadn't realized how far out of the way it was or that the compound was as secluded as it appeared to be, with woods on two sides and a lake on the other. The path to the towering gates was unpaved.

"You said you're one of the Gods, right?" Irritation flared. Ian with his leather jacket and scruffy beard wasn't supposed to cling. He was supposed to drop me off and leave. If things went wrong, I didn't want to accidentally take out any innocents. "Like, the real Gods?"

"I'm certainly not one of the fake ones." I stepped toward the gate, eying the bulbous, black cameras scrutinizing my every move. Stone walls stretched for at least a mile on either side, maybe more.

"I heard one of the Gods got into a bit of a fight with the elves at the Order headquarters." He shifted on the leather seat, the motor still rumbling. "That wouldn't have been you, by chance, would it?"

I closed my eyes, recalling the malicious glee in the elf's face before my pixie friend killed her. The six-foot-something fey with icy blonde hair and eyes the exact shade of merlot. The elf who would have happily killed me because Geoffrey had told her to. "I've fought a lot of beings," I hedged.

Ian nodded like it was the answer he'd expected. He twisted the key in the ignition and the black beast between his legs died. "Then I'll wait here. When you come out, I'll get you back to town."

"You don't have to—"

"Unless you can use compulsion or whatever it's called like my succubus of an ex-girlfriend, there's nothing you'll be able to do or say to convince me to leave a girl alone with a bunch of fey who probably hate her guts." He settled back on the bike and fiddled with a bag by his knee. To my amusement, he removed a battered paperback romance novel. "I have a sister your age. I'd bloody my knuckles on a man who abandoned her in the middle of nowhere."

I stared at him, both amazed and amused at his stubbornness. "This may take a while."

He opened the book and shoved the bookmark in his pocket.

CHAPTER 11

The gates to Cogscraig swung wide as I approached, and two fey clutching crossbows appeared in the wide opening, faces concealed in the shade. The elves had arrows notched in place, their fingers resting on the triggers. I had no doubt they'd use them, too, if their matching scowls indicated anything.

I tensed. *Promedis ad*—pixie slang for *'at your ready'*—passed through my thoughts.

"You're not welcome here, God of Water," the one on the left called. Yeah, I was definitely picking up on putrid waves of hostility. "You best turn back around and return whence you came."

Whence. Did people seriously still talk like that?

I brought my hands up, palms flat. "I need some information, that's it. Once I get it, I'll be on my merry way." I stopped a few yards from the archway of the gate.

The one who hadn't spoken lifted her bow and propped the butt against her shoulder. Her fingers twitched and the safety audibly clicked off. "I wouldn't come any closer if I were you," she called. "One more step and I won't hesitate to cut you down."

I eyed the bolt. It looked heavy. Maybe armor-piercing. "There's this curse—"

"We don't want to hear your worthless lies." The elf who'd first addressed me raised his crossbow, mirroring his comrade's stance. "Leave before you aren't able."

My hackles rose and a jolt of electricity shocked across my skin. "You refuse to hear me out about a curse that could annihilate an entire race of fey? A curse that could conceivably spread to your people, too?" My voice rose, carrying over the compound walls. "You're seriously that obtuse?"

Twin twangs sounded. I flung one bold away with a crackle of lightning and snagged the other in midair. I swallowed hard, adrenaline pounding in my veins, as I stared down the silvery shaft of the arrow that would have planted between my eyes. My arm didn't so much as tremble as I lowered the bolt, metal dribbling from my fingers as it melted. The other bolt was buried in a tree to my left, half its shaft imbedded in the thick trunk.

The guards had already dropped new arrows into place, fingers at the ready.

"You wanna play? I can do this all day," I challenged.

"Let her through."

I dropped what remained of the arrow and squinted past the trigger-happy elves at a tall figure who'd emerged behind them. The owner of the rough voice added, "Let's hear the illustrious *God* out."

My molars scraped together as I strode forward, guard raised and magic at the ready. If there was anything I hated more than being shot at, it was being openly mocked.

Behind the stone walls, I found what truly was an old-fashioned military compound. On one side stretched long rows of barracks, their exteriors as simple as they were uniform. A blacksmith with a massive hammer pounded away at a forge at the other end of the facility and scents of roasting meats drifted from a kitchen drifted from somewhere beyond.

A dozen kids in a corral with several round targets perched on the lower rungs of a fence, longbows dangling from sun-kissed fingers. Despite the bite of winter in the air, they wore breeches and soft white shirts. A cluster of elves wearing pads and clutching wooden swords stood beside them, expressions as closed as the children were wide-eyed. A dozen more elves in sleek uniforms of silver and royal blue bracketed a fey with short, red hair and a deep scar that started at her temple and crossed her face diagonally, tapering off over her cheekbone. Her right sleeve hung limply from an empty socket, and she braced her left hand on a short sword at her hip.

Like the elves who'd assisted the Order, my Iridescence picked up on a distinct void of magic coming from the group, like a black hole—white and deep and void.

"I'm Lennox," the elf drawled. "Lennox McAvoy. I'm in charge of this establishment, as much as anyone can be. I'd say I'm impressed you'd have the audacity to show up here, Water God, but I've heard of your recklessness. Appearing at the gates of the one place where you're universally hated, where you've been ordered to be shot on sight, sounds exactly like something you'd do."

I shifted on my feet, a dozen comebacks flashing through my mind. "Good to know I've become so predictable."

Her half-smile kicked up a notch. "I'll reward you for your boldness, however. If you'd like to speak with or any of our people, you must first win a fight."

I hooked my thumbs in my pockets, scanning the crowd as a murmur went up. A few fey grinned and my stomach dipped.

Lennox continued, "I'm aware of your abilities, but this won't be like any match you've ever been in before. This is a fight without magic, a fight of pure skill, a fight against one of our best. A fight that, should you lose, ends in your death."

A few cheers went up as the fey bunched tightly together, eyes bright with bloodlust. Overhead, the sun glimmered merrily, its yellowed rays doing little to warm my skin. I kept my face blank. I wasn't afraid of fighting. Nor was I afraid of dying. But still my nerves jangled.

"And if I win?" I asked.

The elf quirked a brow. "If something that unlikely were to occur, then you would determine the outcome. Death or otherwise. Do you think you can handle that?" Lennox asked, thumb circling the hilt of her sword. "Or will you take the only chance you'll get to leave with your tail tucked between your legs like the dog you are?"

The elves roared with laughter.

I barely resisted blasting them with the wildfire roaring in my veins.

Good, let them underestimate me. Let them mock me. I wouldn't run. I needed answers, and I seriously doubted I'd stumble across any rogue elves on my own.

"Tell me what I have to do."

Promedis ad, indeed.

Chapter 12

I tested the edge of the sword they'd given me. I'd barely applied pressure and blood dripped down my thumb. I sucked it off. Given their desire to see my blood staining the ground, dull blades wouldn't have surprised me. Anything to make my demise slower and more painful.

My personal dagger, the replacement I'd picked up for the blue-bladed weapon I'd given to Pyra as ransom, was strapped to the outside of my thigh. I rarely needed it, preferring the weightlessness of my icy weapons instead.

Across the corral, Lennox spoke with a stick of an elf wearing a Yankees ball cap. Strawberry blond hair curled around the edges. I squinted, tugging on my scarf, unsure if they were talking or arguing. Her shoulders were rigid, but he slouched against the fence, arms slung around the top rung. His face brightened as he fired off some retort and Lennox relented, motioning at the circle with resignation. With a whoop, he hopped the fence and slipped his jacket from his shoulders, tossing it beside mine draped on a post, heedless of the chill in the air.

I sheathed my sword as he approached. The elf moved like wind, streamlined and confident. I'd thought him tall from far away, but up close he topped out at close to seven feet. His eyes twinkled as he extended his hand. "I'm Lachlan, and I'll have the joy of attempting to extract your heart from your ribcage today."

I eyed his hand as if he'd offered a coiled rattlesnake. With extreme reluctance, I took it, thick calluses scratchy against my palm. He nearly wrenched my arm out of its socket with the exuberance of his handshake.

"Lennox wanted to cut pieces from you herself, but I convinced her it would be much more fun to watch." Lachlan firmed his grip when I tried to pull away. "I've never fought a God before, but I've heard the stories. Will you promise to make this battle as fan-freaking-tastic as I'm hoping you will? It might be the highlight of my day."

"Only the highlight of your day?" I asked dryly. "Here I was hoping to at least make your week."

He turned his hat so the bill shaded the back of his neck. "You're that impressive?"

"Are you normally this excitable?"

If his grin stretched any wider, the corners of his mouth would touch his earlobes. "What's the point of living if you don't love every second of it?"

"I wouldn't underestimate him." Lennox jumped the fence, and the crowd cheered. "He's one of our most skilled fighters. You'll have your work cut out for you, Water God."

I tugged again on my hand. Lachlan chuckled. "Good to know," I said.

Lennox's eyes danced first across the elemental brands stacked on top of one another on my shoulder, then the variety of oaths banding my skin, before flicking wine-colored eyes up at me. My mouth went dry at the hatred glittering in their depths. What had I ever done to her?

She reached into her back pocket and emerged with a bracelet of pounded metal. Bells clanged a warning in my mind. I recognized that cuff, and I wanted nothing to do with it.

"Know what this is?" she asked. "It's a special band only elves can create because we are the only fey to not have magic yet know how to use *all* magic."

Lennox was oversimplifying. Elves had magic, but it was peculiar. They could only mimic magic used against them, stealing bits of it for their own use. Weak elves could only wield another fey's magic for a few minutes, but stronger elves could possess it for hours or days.

"This handy little device is powerful enough to trap magic, all magic, including a *God's* magic, right beneath the wielder's skin." Lennox opened the band and tapped it against her palm. "As long as it is on your wrist, you won't be able to tap into any of those elemental skills you hold so dear."

As she approached, I realized Lachlan had deliberately latched on to my hand. They'd effectively trapped me here. I hadn't pulled away earlier, and to struggle now would be a sign of weakness. I had no choice but to relent.

"If you intend to go through with this fight, you must wear this cuff, Water God. When we say no magic is allowed, we mean it." The elf lowered the cuff to my skin but didn't close it. I felt it lapping at my energy, binding my magic to its strange, silky surface. "Oh, and don't get any ideas about removing it yourself. Only elves can do that."

I wanted to scream, to shout, to do anything to get out of this mess. I didn't want my magic bound. I didn't trust these elves as far as I could spit. But I hadn't come this far to back away now, to run from a direct challenge. I needed answers—*Lee* needed answers—and I wouldn't let a little magic, or lack thereof, get in my way.

"I want you to swear something first," I gritted out.

"Oh?" Lennox eyed my oaths with distaste. "We don't swear oaths."

"Not an oath. A promise." I stared her hard in the eyes, forcing her to see how deeply I meant every word. "A promise on your soul, a promise from your people, a promise on your *honor,* that you will take this off me when I win."

When. Not if.

The phrasing wasn't lost on her, and a glimmer of what might have been respect flickered across her face before she closed the cuff around my arm. "I swear."

Lachlan dropped my arm, and I nearly staggered, stunned by the waves of what I could only describe as nothingness coursing through me. I'd anticipated not using my magic, I'd expected it to feel strange not having it dancing at my fingertips. But this—the debilitating energy that seemed to suck at my very soul, locking down vital pieces of my being—this was on another level entirely. I drew in a deep, calming breath and stepped away from the elves, trying to shake the uneasiness from my limbs.

For the first time in a long time, I felt weak.

Lachlan's gaze roved across my face. I knew I was pale, sweaty, my anxiety riding high, but I drew my sword. "When do we do this?" The sooner I got the cuff off, the better.

"You may begin once I leave the arena," Lennox said. "Unless you'd rather take on both of us at once."

Any other day I would have risen to the bait, but if I were going up against their best, I couldn't risk an iota of recklessness. This fight would already require all the skill I'd ever learned from Rose and then some. I refused to dishonor her by adding to my plate.

Lachlan flexed his jaw, brow lowered in concentration, face steely, then drew his sword. Its width was easily twice mine. As we tapped weapons, the darkness I'd glimpsed in his expression melted away, leaving youthful exuberance behind. "Ready?"

"To cut you down to a reasonable size?" I kept Lennox in my periphery. "Any day."

He moved back three steps and spun his weapon. "Don't go easy on me now."

"Never." I charged, my blade smashing against his with all the power I could muster. His eyes went wide as his sword buckled but held. I wasted no time withdrawing, my weapon snaking toward his side. He laughed as he blocked again, fluidly countering my speed.

Losing my magic may have rattled me, but Rose had repeatedly drilled me in sparring before I'd figured out the extent of my Water magic, before I'd tapped into my Fire. I was not someone to be underestimated.

I drove Lachlan back, my weapon a blur as I charged. He was quick, but I was quicker. I had to use that, had to find an opening and fast. He had height and weight against me, and I was willing to bet he had greater stamina, too. My pulse was already quickening. I had to end this before it truly started if I stood any chance at survival.

Metal screeched on metal as he caught the angle of my sword just right and whipped it up, bringing our bodies together as he hooked his cross guard around my blade, locking it in. I cursed viciously as I yanked on the weapon. It refused to give so much as an inch.

"You're good," the elf growled, bearing down on me. "But can you handle when the tables are turned?"

He shoved me back and kicked out, catching me in the gut. I fell to the ground, lungs seizing. I thanked the stars I'd held onto my sword, because I barely got it up in time to block the downward arc of his. The weapon skittered off, deflected. I rolled out of the way, gulping in air.

I had to get up, had to stand. I was as good as dead on the ground.

With a grunt of pain, I scrambled to my feet, immediately going on the defensive. Lachlan had drawn the second sword strapped to his back and handled both weapons at once with ease. I tried to regroup as I danced backward, but the elf never let me get farther than the reach of his blade. I grunted and a bolt of panic shot through me when my back came up against the slats of the corral.

The elf grinned brutally as the tip of his blade dug into my arm, opening a long wound. Blood trickled into my hand. "You're wearing down, Water God. Sure you don't want to cede?"

Resolve ignited deep in my gut, flaring hot with a burst of anger. "Never."

I thrust my sword down and away, dropping the weapon while simultaneously leaping back to grab the upper slat of the coral. I used my momentum to launch myself up and *over* the elf. Shock flickered across his face as I curled over his head and landed in a crouch, my leg sweeping out and knocking his from beneath him. One of his swords went flying, landing somewhere in the crowd, which unleashed a roar of approval.

I caught his ribs with a second kick that made him groan. He countered with a thrust of the sword he still held tight. I didn't flip back fast enough. The tip sliced through my shirt, grazing my collarbone.

Lachlan braced a hand on his knee and stood with a grunt, his smirk playful, and he winked at me. Winked. "Someone's been hanging out with pixies."

The crowd released a sharp hiss, the sound eerily similar to a rattlesnake, and goosebumps dotted my arms as I raised them in front of me, middle fingers circled with my thumbs—a pixie sign for *'come at me.'* I brushed sweat from my chin with my shoulder and hitched up a corner of my mouth. "Afraid?"

"Never," he parroted my own word back at me and flung his sword into the dirt. What? He'd had the steel and the reach. Who gave up an advantage like that? "This got a heck of a lot more interesting."

He charged, fist swinging for my head. I rocked back and snuck a punch up through his guard, catching his cheek with a glancing blow. His elbow lashed out and snapped into my ribcage. I gasped at the bruising impact and it was his turn to knock my legs out from under me with a brutal kick to my thigh.

It should have wiped me out, but I rolled like Rose had taught me to, tucking deep and hitting the ground in a way that allowed me to pivot and pop right back up. I slapped a hand against my thigh, reaching for my dagger, but my fingers scrabbled over the jeans.

"What—" I glanced down, but a glimmer of silver in my opponent's hand brought my attention right back up.

"Looking for something?" He twirled the dagger in the air, a triumphant smirk splitting his face. The crowd unleashed a cheer that rattled the rocks under my feet. "My, my, does this look familiar?"

When had he—

My stomach sank as my lips drew back in a snarl, remembering the way he'd brushed against me when he had me pinned against the corral. He must have swiped it then.

"I'll give you one more chance to give up." He blocked my path, penning me in the center of the arena, anticipating my plan to use the walls to my advantage. "But only one more. After that, I can't guarantee what happens to you."

I scanned the surrounding faces helplessly, finding not a single friendly one. Lennox was positively smug, her thumb hooked in her pocket, arm stiff and straight as she watched her fighter gloat. I wasn't going to beat him with my fists. I doubted he'd let me close enough to use my legs. And he'd cut off my escape route. But then…

Behind him, a few feet away near one post. A flash of metal, hot in the sun. The sword I'd flung away earlier.

I brought my eyes back up to his, careful to keep an edge of desperation in them. He didn't appear to have noticed my distraction.

"You would let me go?" My voice trembled. Not with fear like I'm sure the elves heard, but with excitement. "I back down now and you'll let me leave?"

White teeth flashed and Lachlan risked a glance to the side, at his leader, who shook her head slowly, cardinal lips pursed with amusement. "Not in one piece."

I bounced on the balls of my feet as I made a few quick estimations, channeling the spirt of Rose. She'd taught me that pixies were most lethal when pinned down.

I was no different.

I tossed my ragged braid behind my head and allowed some cockiness back into my face. Lachlan shifted uneasily, his brows pulling together. He twirled my dagger in a circle, but he'd lost some of his swagger.

"I guess I must reciprocate." I launched at him, dust flying as my shoes caught in the dirt. He reacted, widening his stance as he extended the weapon, intending to impale me upon the point. I reached out, the tip of the blade splitting the skin on the back of my hands, and grabbed his wrists, knocked the knife aside. I used his arms to direct his momentum and slid between his legs while also reaching for the sword. The elf wheezed when his back hit the dirt and I popped right up, spinning on him with the weapon in my grip.

I barely heard his protest as I dropped on him, straddling his chest and pinning his arms down with my thighs. The point of the blade pressed against his jugular. Blood trickled down my arms as I held position, both of us knowing there was no shaking me loose. Not without him slicing his own neck wide open.

"Do you cede?"

The elf's lips twitched, a buttery smile spreading across his face. No rage. No anger. No frustration. Only acceptance and a whole heaping of respect. I seriously didn't understand this guy.

The blade nicked his skin as he swallowed. "Best of three?"

Chapter 13

I rubbed at my wrist around the metal cuff, not sure why the elves hadn't removed it yet. I'd won fair and square. Lennox glared at me from across the table, her index finger tapping its surface as she battled with her disbelief.

Lachlan stood behind her, slouched against the doorframe as he picked at his nails with a needle-thin knife. Every so often he'd whisper something to another dour-faced elf standing beside him, and her lips would twitch. He'd been the one to dress my wounds after the battle. I figured it was punishment for failing to remove my head from my shoulders.

He'd also returned my dagger and thanked me for not holding back. The guy was a complete mystery.

"What exactly is it you'd like to know?" Lennox asked venomously.

I hooked a fingernail under the cuff and tugged again before offering a condensed version of how I'd arrived. Lennox sat still as stone but for her single tapping finger. Sometimes I wondered if she were listening, her lack of empathy so apparent. Outside, three tones sounded from a gong-like bell and a couple dozen feet pattered past the doorway.

"I can tell the curse is destroying magic, but I don't know how to stop it," I finished.

"And what are you asking of us?" Lennox shared a look with a male elf who sat in a chair beside the desk, arms folded across his broad chest. "The fate of the daemoni are of little consequence to our kind."

"Daemoni?" It was a term I couldn't place.

Lennox traced the raised edge of her scar. "Incubi. Succubi. Their kind."

"Oh." I was unaware of the history the two fey races shared, but clearly it was an ugly one if the level of vehemence that filled her voice told me anything. "I heard elves are among the most creative of the fey, able to manipulate nearly all magic in ways never considered. Because of your abilities, I'd hoped you might have some insight about breaking the curse."

Lachlan grimaced. He'd put his knife away.

"I see." Lennox planted her hand beside a stack of documents written in Elvish and stood. "Did you learn that before or after you slaughtered my sister?"

I closed my eyes against a swell of dismay and disbelief, remembering the elf Geoffrey seemed to favor, the one who led the others. Of course, that elf had been her sister. I'd thought I'd recognized something in her face. Definitely in the eyes.

I chose my words carefully. "I wouldn't call that a slaughter. We were at war with the Order, and they chose their side. They nearly killed me before—"

"You called in some pixie freaks to cut down my people without thought or regard for the role they may have played in the grand scheme of everything." I flinched when Lennox's fist crashed into the desk, her lips twisting as she leaned in close. "My sister was working to gain intelligence about the Order's operations. She was close to uncovering some of their deepest atrocities. You interrupted months of hard work that came at substantial cost. Had you waited—"

"If I had waited any longer, valuable allies of mine would have died," I snapped. My mind was a mess. This underground operation Lennox spoke of was news to me. I'd never disguised my hatred of Geoffrey and his plans. Why no one had reached out to me or my friends was beyond comprehension.

"I don't care about whatever scheme you cooked up." I snagged Lennox's shirt, pulling her so close barely an inch separated our faces. A muscle in her cheek jumped. "Geoffrey should have been removed long before the other Gods and I got to him. As far as I'm concerned, the temples fell two decades ago. It was believed that two Gods—*that I*—were killed in the attacks. You had two *decades* to make your move, two decades to wipe Geoffrey and the Order out. You waited too long."

I shoved Lennox away when movement flickered in my periphery. Before the female bodyguard made contact, dagger in hand, I caught her arm and twisted it behind her back in a move I knew hurt and drove her to her knees. "Drop it," I hissed, twisting harder. "Drop it now."

She whimpered and the weapon clattered to the floor. I kicked it away, held her fast for another moment to prove my point, and released her. Lennox regarded the scene with a blank expression that I knew promised punishment for the elf at my feet. Lachlan snagged the brim of his hat, obscuring half his face.

"I had a lot of hard decisions to make very quickly," I continued as if nothing had happened. "I don't care that those decisions *disrupted* your work. I don't care that you *had plans* to take down the Order. *I don't care.*"

I rounded on the elf again, barely refraining from touching her this time. Inside, I was a firestorm. Had I possession of my magic, this entire building would be burning down around us. How dare she accuse me of this, after everything I'd been through, to have yet another leader criticize me for action that should have been taken when I was still an infant...

I'd had enough.

"Geoffrey tried to kill me more than a half dozen times." My heart seized. I remembered those he *had* killed. The ones who hadn't escaped. "And not once, *not once,* did you or any other fey reach out and fill me in on plans to wipe him out." I planted my hand on the back of a chair to disguise my shaking. "I don't regret the decisions I made, not for a single second. Your sister got between me and my enemy. She got involved in a war. In war, people die. I'm sorry she's dead. I'm sorry I played a role in that, but she made her choices."

The silence that filled the room after my shouting seemed equally loud.

Lennox eyed me and straightened her shirt. She first scanned the faces of her subordinates, then picked up a folder from her desk and tucked it into her elbow. "I'll have nothing to do with the daemoni, and my people will have nothing to do with saving so much as one member of their race."

Outside I was shaking. Inside I was screaming. I wanted to think that had I held my tongue, she would have said something different about my plea. However, deep inside I felt that it had already been a lost cause. Lennox had never intended to help me.

The elvish leader sniffed. "And we'll have nothing to do with the Gods either. That's my final decision. The elves will never stand beside you. If you or any of the others ever show your faces around here, you will die. And it will be painful," she promised. "You may take your leave."

My head swam, and my ears buzzed. "What about this?" I asked, extending the cuff.

"What about it?"

The buzzing stopped. "You swore to remove it if I won. You swore on your honor."

The elf tilted her head. "What honor? You had none when you commanded others to kill my people. The world is better off with the most reckless of the Gods rendered powerless."

My vision went white. I couldn't breathe. The pain roaring through me was too much to bear. Lightning crashed inside me, trapped with nowhere to go. She was going to die for this. For putting the weight of her mistakes on my shoulders. For stealing my magic. For rendering me useless.

With a scream, I tore my dagger from its sheath and lunged forward, uncaring that I was validating her claims of recklessness. I would have plunged it through her spine at the base of her neck had a pair of arms not caught me around the waist, wrenching me back.

"Give it back," I shrieked. "Give it back, you bastards."

I clawed at whoever held me, my fingernails digging bloody grooves in their skin. They swore savagely before grabbing my arm. Another elf moved to my front. I kicked out, catching him in the gut. He grunted but still grabbed my writhing legs and held them tight.

"You swore." I screamed at what little I could see of Lennox's retreating back. "You swore to me, you traitor."

"Shut up," Lachlan hissed in my ear. He was the one who'd stopped me from stabbing her in the back. "You're only making this worse."

What did he not understand when I said I didn't care? I squirmed harder. As she lifted a hand in parting, I yelled, "I'll remember this Lennox McAvoy. I'll remember the day you lost all respect in the eyes of the fey. I swear on my crest I'll make you and every one of your people pay."

Lachlan attempted to close his hand over my mouth, but I bit his palm and the tang of copper coated my teeth. He snarled and nearly dropped me as he wrenched his arm away. "Freaking wildcat."

"Dump her outside," the other guy holding me said. "Get her through the gates and be done."

As I registered the words, the fight left me. Lennox was gone. I couldn't see her, and she would not change her mind. Lachlan tensed at my back, and I could all but hear the thoughts swirling around his head.

"You can let me down." It killed me to say the words, destroyed me to give up like this. "I'm done."

"I don't think so," the male bodyguard said and jerked on my legs, leaving Lachlan no choice but to either follow or dump my upper half on the ground to be dragged. "Like I trust a word coming from your treacherous mouth."

The words should have incensed me. Should have shocked me into action. But I'd gone numb, tucked away in the recesses of my mind. Lennox had stripped me of my magic, my fight, and my hope. I didn't know how I was going to help Lee, how I was going to get my magic back, how I was going to find the strength to so much as stand.

I felt Lachlan watching me, saw the questions swirling in his lavender gaze, but I didn't engage him. Didn't want to. They were literally carrying me through the town like a trussed up turkey, and I accepted it, my pride left shredded back in Lennox's office. I barely noticed the lack of commotion, the silent stares of those who'd been so vocal not an hour before, when they'd called for my blood to soak the earth.

I had nothing left.

The elf holding my feet abruptly dropped them when we passed the outer gate, but Lachlan helped steady me on shaky legs before releasing me. The shadows had yet to retreat from his expression and he gripped his elbow, shoulders hunched, the posture oddly childlike. "Are you going to be ok?"

I pondered the question. Behind him, a crowd had gathered, their silence piercing some of the eerie numbness encasing me. "I haven't been ok for some time. But I'll survive. I have to."

He pinched the tip of his pointed ear and nodded, stepped back.

"Ready to go?" Ian asked. I turned and found him perched on the

Ducati, its engine purring. I hopped on the back, not saying a word, and twined my arms around his stomach before burying my head in his back as he roared down the road, back to the city.

I hoped he wouldn't notice the streaks of salty water down the back of his leather jacket later.

Chapter 14

I did not divulge what transpired at Cogscraig to Ian, though stars love him, he was the definition of persistence when it came to details. I did, however, ask him to drop me off at whichever pub was nearest to the edge of town. I had no intention of staying within the city limits for long.

"Would you mind changing that to the BBC?" I asked my server, pointing at the television propped in the corner of the room.

The girl who seemed to be about my age glanced at the previously recorded football match playing on the screen and flicked a brassy lock. "Whatever floats your boat." The look she gave me indicated what floated my boat was definitely not within the norm. "As long as this place stays dead, my manager won't care."

As she flounced off to scrounge up a remote from behind the bar, I hunkered lower at my table, fiddling with the cuff. The band fit my wrist perfectly: not tight enough to cut off the blood supply, nor loose enough to fit over the bones of my hand. Interesting divots dotted the metal, and someone had polished it to a gleam.

If it weren't filled with an iron core of evil, I might not mind it.

The TV channel changed and a woman anchor with a bottle-green top and corkscrew curls interviewed a man with salt-and-pepper hair about a recession in Australia. The closed captions scrolling at the bottom of the screen showed that it wasn't the only country struggling economically because of heightening nuclear tensions.

Keeping one eye on the screen, I pulled my phone from my pocket and clicked past most of the newer messages. I needed to get a new number soon. Too many people were figuring out how to contact me. I tapped open a message in the middle of the mass and held the phone up to my ear.

It rang twice before the line clicked open. "Lee?"

"It's never a good sign when a God calls you and not the other way around."

"Maybe I need something from you."

"I'm swearing off religion."

I couldn't hold back a chuckle. "Touché."

"What do you want?" Something clattered in the background and I imagined the witch shutting herself in the office at the back of the shop. "It's the middle of the afternoon. I'm a little caught up here."

"How's Logan?" My stomach twisted.

Lee's voice softened. "She's about the same. I know you said you didn't do anything, but ever since you visited, she's been fairly stable."

One of the knots loosened. "That's a good sign."

"You figure out how to break the curse?"

I closed my eyes against the headache throbbing at the base of my neck. "No. Not yet."

"Then I guess we got nothing else to say to each other."

The line went dead.

Well, huh.

I'd hoped she might know how to get the stupid cuff off, but I wasn't about to call her back.

I closed the phone and snagged the glass of dark soda the waitress had left near the edge of the table. I'd already checked my dwindling supply of cash and probably shouldn't have come here considering how little I had left to my name, but I'd hoped the caffeine would give me the jolt I needed to figure out my next steps.

A graphic wiped across the television and footage of a scrawny girl and masked boy appeared. I sat up straight, my glass forgotten, soaking in the image of Pyra and Oron leaving the U.N. Headquarters.

Pyra walked stiffly, cradling a stack of legal texts, keenly aware of the cameras fixed on her. It was strange to see the God of Fire so clearly out of her element since she always moved like lightning tracked her steps, but despite the stiffness, she held herself straight and proud.

With a defiant glance at the reporters, she popped a cigarette in the corner of her black-painted mouth. Her bob of fire-engine-red hair rustled in the breeze as she lit it with a flick of her taped fingers. The material was a special product produced only by her temple that created enough friction for the God to start fires at will by snapping

Pyra shielded her mouth as she muttered to the God of Earth. He had to lean down about a foot and a half to hear her. Oron appeared the same as always, including that perplexing black mask pulled over his head, obscuring his face and neck. He moved with the fluidity of an assassin, his white uniform of the Earth Temple flowing gracefully around him, unconcerned by the attention.

He took a book from Pyra's stack and shoved it under one armpit as they stepped before the shouting reporters. Pyra answered their questions, keeping her answers brief.

No, the world's leaders were no closer to striking a nuclear deal.

No, they didn't know when they might reach an agreement.

Yes, as the world's teenage saviors, they were still heavily involved in negotiations.

And no—Pyra's eyes flared tauntingly—they didn't know where their leader was.

The First of Four. The one who'd gotten them into this mess.

The God of Water.

Me.

My skin felt stretched too thin. Frustration pounded a tempo hot and fast inside me. Same questions. Same answers. Different day. Only this time, my friends were unaware that their illustrious head was out of magic and nearly out of ideas.

I flipped open the phone again, but this time I clicked to my contacts and highlighted one name. It was really a letter: P. P for Pyra. The one God who'd guessed my game and attempted to stop me from leaving. The one God who'd promised to give me time to figure my life out as long as I returned. I hadn't known the spitfire for long, but she'd kept her promises to the letter.

I toyed with the pendant at the end of my necklace as I circled the call button. The chain had caught on the back of the helmet and I'd forgotten to shove the vial back under my shirt. Without magic, I was basically useless. This was a problem bigger than myself, bigger than the curse. This was a problem that I'd need backup…

My grip on the pendant tightened. What was I thinking? And how could I have not thought of this sooner? I slowly uncurled my hand, revealing the silver-encased vial nearly as long as the width of my hand.

I *had* backup. Kind of.

I gulped down my drink, my core warming despite the icy liquid, and carefully set one of my precious bills on the table. A minute later I was out of the dim light of the pub and in the dark of the street, another long shadow among shadows.

I kept to the ditch along the side of the road out of town, dodging broken bottles and crushed cans, while keeping an eye out for headlights. My breath fogged in front of my face and I drew my scarf over my nose. I didn't need the additional warmth, the fire magic locked in my skin kept me warm, but it reminded me of my childhood. Of holding my mother's gloved hand on long December walks, bundled in a bright pink coat, our noses and cheeks rosy from winter's bite. It had been years since I'd given winter much thought. In my early elementary years, my father sent me to an athletic boarding school on the East Coast where I spent most of my days in a pool, on a plane, or planted in a dorm room. I'd rarely ventured outside.

Dead grass crunched beneath my boots, and I hunched my shoulders. The silvery moon cast twisted shadows across the ground. The wooded area that circled the edge of Limerick was about a five-minute walk from here. That gave me time to think.

My vial was far more than a piece of jewelry. It held the soul of the last remaining djinn on earth—who also happened to be one of the oldest living fey. I'd trapped him inside the vessel in a last-ditch effort to both stop him from killing me and free the nero he'd enslaved for hundreds of years.

Overall, it was a win-win...

For everyone, except for Phenex.

Or was it Xenith?

I kicked a softball-sized rock into the dry, whispery weeds and checked my hood. It remained in place, obscuring my face and hair. I'd used the second name, the djinn's true name, to trap him inside the vial, but it didn't feel right on my tongue—somehow slimy, like okra.

Whatever he preferred to be called, I knew he was beyond angry. The way he saw it, he'd already served his penance, answering the wishes of morons for thousands of years while he earned his freedom. Granted, once he'd gained said freedom, he'd devoured his siblings and enslaved an entire fey race. So, while he definitely deserved what was coming, that didn't mean he was pleased about it.

It was a big reason why I hadn't let him out yet. I didn't know how to deal with him. It wasn't like I could set him loose again. There was no telling what he would do in retribution, and I still didn't know how to fight against that kind of power. He was virtually unstoppable, practically immortal with his profound gifts.

But they were gifts I needed to employ now. Today.

I glanced back at the long, vacant road before veering to the left. I dipped under the boughs of a tree as I searched for the stream I'd spotted on the ride with Ian. I might not have a way to tap into my water magic anymore, but I still felt most at ease when I was around the stuff. I'd need it to fortify my nerves if I had any chance of getting through this.

In the woods, insects whirred, and I caught the soft, indiscernible chatter of wood nymphs whistling through the bushes. Twig-like fingers reached for my jeans and boots, and I sifted through my bag until I came up with a chocolate candy bar. I unwrapped it and left it on a chunk of rock as payment for traveling through their territory. Hopefully, it would be enough.

Another twenty minutes and a few false starts later, I finally found the slow trickle ebbing through the dirt and crunchy, dead leaves. I followed it as it expanded, its speed increasing as it neared a clearing. There I stopped. The moon shimmered overhead, its reflection broken, like the choppy waves at sea among the dusting of clouds. It would have to do.

I slung my bag on the ground and toyed with the vial. I was fairly certain that as the djinn's master he couldn't hurt me, but I wasn't sure if that would stop him from trying… especially once he figured out I didn't have magic, which he would probably sniff out the moment he emerged.

I gnawed my lip and held the vial up by the chain so it twisted before me. The silver shimmered like the surface of the water under the moonlight. How did one summon a djinn? I scuffed a foot on the ground, cleared my throat, and cupped the pendant in my palms. "Uh. Phenex? Are you there? Could you come out?"

Nothing.

While the vial typically ran warm, I couldn't detect any of its other temperature fluctuations. Sometimes the silver would burn hot enough to burn my skin. Other times it ran icy cold. I chalked it up to the djinn's emotions. But now I felt nothing. No response.

I brushed the end of my braid over my nose. Phenex was a stubborn, secretive creature. He wasn't one to be lulled by soft voices and simple words. No, he needed a stronger touch. I dropped my hair, gathered my strength, and in a loud voice I commanded, "Djinn Xenith, your master summons your presence."

The silver brightened and the glass twitched, but still… nothing.

No djinn.

I prodded the vial. "Now."

The vessel trembled and the silvery branches that encased the container shifted, reaching for the corked cap, and pried it off. A stream of black smoke slipped out and ghosted across the ground. The shadows at the base of an evergreen morphed into something resembling a human.

I gritted my teeth as I stared at the djinn who stood with his head tipped back, face angled toward the moon. Even without my magic, I could sense his power. It radiated from him: compelling and lethal.

It surprised me how much I'd forgotten of his appearance. Phenex's features were remarkably nondescript—neither beautiful nor ugly, tall nor short, wide nor thin. He'd pulled his dark hair back so it hung in a sleek tail that stopped just past his shoulder blades. The djinn inhaled deeply, savoring his first moments free from captivity.

"Hey there, Phenex." I couldn't bring myself to address him by that *other* name. It felt far too formal, despite our rocky history. "Long time, no see."

His shoulders stiffened beneath his heavy, lapis lazuli cloak. Slowly, so incredibly slowly, he turned on his heel. I swallowed hard at the barely restrained fury that deepened the lines around his mouth and drew his dark brows together in a vee.

The djinn's lips puckered. "You."

So much meaning was conveyed in that one tiny word.

"You."

I shrugged flippantly. "Me."

He moved so quickly he blurred. It took everything I had to keep my cocky grin in place. He stopped inches from me and swayed slightly, peering down his nose. I could feel his body heat. The djinn snatched the vial and squeezed it so hard his knuckles blanched. A low growl slipped out, and he wrapped his hand around my throat.

"If I could, I would rip your carotid artery out and hold it until you ran out of blood, if only for the pleasure of feeling your life leave your body." His lips pulled back from his teeth and he leaned in closer, our noses brushing. His fingers squeezed but didn't choke. I raised up on my toes, ignoring the prickles of goosebumps on the back of my neck.

"No. That would be too quick for what you deserve, little God." His breath washed over my face. It smelled faintly of rosemary. "First, I'd drain the very magic from your being, *then* slice you open, two-inch slits at a time, and slowly bleed you dry. I'd want you to know what was coming to you, know the nightmare that you created for yourself. It's the least you deserve."

"That's quite the imagination you have there." I held his gaze. "Had some extra time on your hands to time to think, have you?"

Phenex's golden eyes blazed, but he allowed me to remove his hand, one finger at a time. I resisted the urge to rub my throat. "But I think you're capable of more. Where's the disemboweling? Shoving my arm in a hornet's nest? How about using fire ants? Or acid?" I shoved my hands in my pockets and rocked back on my heels. "Maybe a vicious iron machine with chains sewn to my ribs to rip them apart when a timer runs out? Now those are creative ideas." I shrugged. "I'll give you tonight to think on it."

For four whole seconds, he didn't react. Then his eyes narrowed imperceptibly. "I'll bet your soul tastes sweet, like honeycomb."

"You would know." Djinn had a nasty habit of stealing the souls of their masters after they used up their three wishes. "Too bad I hold the keys to your existence… for now."

"Where's the ancient one?" he asked, changing the subject. I narrowly held back my victory dance. "I'm tired of talking to you. You aren't worth the words, anyway."

My lips thinned. "Locked her away, too."

Phenex jerked back, his hand rising to his sternum. I couldn't have surprised him more had I offered to free him. Then he laughed. Loud, dark laughter that shook the ground. He clutched his stomach, whooping in air, and brushed away tears gathering along his eyelids.

"You locked away an Original God." He ran a hand over the top of his head. "You, a wisp of a girl, took one of the most powerful beings to ever live and locked her in her room like a naughty child." He chuckled again. "You have no idea the wrath you face when she gets out."

"She's not getting out."

"Oh, she'll get out." Phenex picked up an oak leaf and rolled the stem between his fingers, absorbed in the fluttering edges. "Secrets like her never stay hidden. Kind of like you and that lovely new bracelet you've picked up. Try it on for the fun of it, hmm?"

Damn. Of course he'd noticed. "Let's say I made a bad bet."

"Elves are always bad bets." The leaf, brittle and brown from the changing seasons, fluttered to the ground. Phenex surveyed me with interest again. "What were you doing with elves?"

"That's why I've summoned you today."

"You mean to tell me this *isn't* a courtesy call?" The djinn smacked his chest with an open palm, eyes rounding comically. "There goes that rumor I heard about you being one of those nice and cuddly Gods."

Heat flooded my face, and he grinned sharply, knowing he was getting to me.

"I'm having an issue with a curse."

"Aside from my cursed existence, I assume."

"Yes." I dragged out the word, eyeing him. What was his deal? He was far too jovial. "You see, I need you to get rid of one for me."

Phenex lazily crossed his arms, but I caught the hint of danger that crossed his face. It reminded me of nature videos I used to watch, the one of an adder coiling to strike. "Get rid of a curse? For you?"

"That's how the whole wishing thing works, right?" My gut tumbled; had I missed something? "As long as I'm not asking you to kill someone outright or for unlimited power, you have to grant whatever I wish for. So, I wish for—"

"No."

I blinked rapidly. "No?"

"N. O. Two letters." He flicked up two fingers. "Fairly obvious meaning. Dogs understand the word." Phenex moved back in my personal space again, hovering over me like the grim demigod of death I imagined him to be. "Though, you do fall below dogs on the spectrum of intelligence."

"What do you mean, no? You have to—"

"Ah ah ah." He curled his fingers inward to examine his nails. "I exercise my veto authority."

"Djinn can veto wishes?"

"When you're as powerful as I am, you do."

"Can I at least ask you—"

"No."

My heart was pounding again. Sweat streaked my palms. "What about the cuff? I wish for you—"

"No." His mouth curled in the most sinister smile I'd seen from him yet. "Don't you understand, Water God? I have zero intention of granting any of your wishes. My soul is already damned. At least I get a kick out of watching you live in misery, too."

Like quicksilver, he snatched the vial from around my neck, flipped the top, and vanished into its depths, leaving me alone. And confused.

Chapter 15

I tried three more times to get the stupid djinn out of the vial.

Apologies. Praise. Threats. I refused to debase myself to outright begging. However, no matter what I said or how fervently I scrubbed the surface of his vessel, Phenex staunchly refused to come out.

I stifled a shriek of outrage and jammed the vial back beneath my shirt for safekeeping. Djinn should come with handbooks. I never would have guessed they could refuse to grant a wish—as long as it didn't fall into one of two realms: direct slaughter and ultimate power. The fact that Phenex not only could refuse to help, but had done so gleefully…

I tore a chunk of jagged bark off a pine tree and tossed it to the ground.

My brain felt a little fuzzy, my eyes bleary. The exhaustion I'd fended off all day was finally catching up. I briefly considered placing the call I'd wanted to earlier, but it seemed like too extreme a decision to make on this little sleep. Instead, I glanced at the clock on my phone and figured that if I crashed now and got up at dawn, I'd be able to nap for two or three hours. Enough to recharge.

I paced the clearing, scouring the trees. Normally, I had no issue sleeping outside, but my distinct lack of usable magic made safety a little trickier. I wouldn't be able to erect my normal safeguards, but I also didn't have enough money to spring for a room anywhere, not even a dirt-cheap one. Aside from that, it would take me an hour to get back into town. An hour that cut into my precious little sleep schedule.

A giggle sounded from the leafy branches at my left—probably one of the wood nymphs I'd paid off earlier.

Wait. The wood nymphs.

An idea flared. I opened my bag and rummaged around the meager contents before emerging with an apple with only one significant bruise and three granola bars. My head bobbed as I weighed my options, then balanced the apple on the trunk of a fallen tree covered in soft, springy moss.

"Nymphs of the woods, I require your assistance." Nymphs had a tendency of twisting words for their own devices, so I struggled to come up with the right words in my plea for help. "I, Zara Ramone, find myself uniquely defenseless and utterly alone. In exchange for your watchful eyes, I leave this offering from the last of my food stores. Should you deem it worthy, I ask you to protect me through the first bloody rays of dawn."

The forest had gone quiet. Not so much as a chitter of insects in the dead grass. I squeezed my eyes shut, counted to three, and when I opened them, the apple was gone. A heavy sigh rolled through me. They'd accepted. Thank the stars.

I hooked an arm around a branch of a tall deciduous tree and levered myself up, methodically climbing higher until I found a thick branch that extended into the branches of another tree, one that still stubbornly kept its brown leaves and lacked branches low to the ground. For one dizzying moment, I launched myself from one tree to the next, desperately wishing I had my Air magic to assist me, and grunted when I smacked into the trunk. Safe.

A little more maneuvering and shifting, and I finally found a bough hefty enough to support my weight and straddled it, my back against the bark. As I exhaled slowly, I realized the insects had started up again. A soft breeze touched my cheeks, and I burrowed a little deeper into my jacket. The nymphs had given an all-clear. A smile touched my lips as I removed my sheath from my thigh and balanced it on my lap, one hand on the leather and the other on the grip of the weapon.

I refused to put my entire security in the hands of a foreign fey, no matter how the rules of the fey realm worked. And with that final, not so comforting thought, I fell into a fitful doze.

- - -

Tinkling giggles and murmurs that sounded like bone-dry leaves rattling in the wind pulled me from my slumber. As I scrubbed dried drool from the corner of my mouth, two thoughts hit me:

There was way too much light for it to be dawn.

My dagger was missing.

I jerked upright and nearly fell. The murmuring stopped as I looked around wildly. No, it was definitely mid-morning. Maybe closer to noon, if the yellow glimmer through the foliage overhead was any indication. My request to the nymphs had only extended to dawn, and it appeared they'd taken their payment for the precious additional hours my laxness had cost me.

I groaned and rubbed my temples. The headache was gone. So was the bleariness. Many of my aches and pains had also diminished, but I couldn't help but curse myself. Without that knife, I had no defenses.

I was out of options. I had no choice now. I had to call in reinforcements.

But when I dipped my hand, the one with the cursed cuff that felt far too cold to be normal, into the pocket of my jacket...

I found nothing.

"Are you freaking kidding me right now?" I shouted at no one. My fury was a hot and wild thing. I knew I wouldn't get anywhere screaming at the devilish creatures notorious for tricking stray travelers, but I felt so incredibly alone. It was a foolish feeling. I'd been alone for months. Months. But right now, in this moment, I was an island.

I was also going to lose my mind if I couldn't figure out a fix and quick.

Still cursing, I pawed through my stuff. The nymphs had left my clothing alone. I still had Phenex's vial, my rings, and the empty wallet in my back pocket. The three granola bars remained untouched, not that I was hungry, but beyond that things were looking grim.

"You've gotten through worse," I told myself, needing to hear the words out loud. Anything other than the quiet chill of the woods. "If you can survive not only Geoffrey but Kaleal, too, this is cake."

As I talked, I yanked the band from my braid and unraveled the shredded mess. The familiar motions of creating the French braid helped soothe me, driving back the panic brewing in my belly.

Calm again, I threw my bag around my shoulders and, after squinting through the thick canopy dappled with sunshine and brown, swung to a lower branch. My descent was slow, but the focus it required quelled my unease. When it came to the final drop to the ground, a longer drop than I was comfortable with, I was myself again.

The hair on the back of my neck prickled as I brushed off my knees. Warily, I scanned the clearing, crouching slightly, bracing for attack. Anything.

"Stars above," I whispered before slapping my hand over my mouth.

Whatever I'd expected to find, it wasn't this.

The elf at the edge of the clearing was impossible to miss.

For starters, someone had stripped him down, leaving him stranded in a pair of plaid boxers and a strip of white fabric taped over his mouth. Scars of all shapes and sizes decorated his muscular arms, which were folded and bound across his well-defined pecs, partially obscuring a trio of jagged scars. The scars continued up his torso and legs where a rope looped around one ankle, suspending him upside down from a tree. Loose, strawberry blond hair feathered across a tumble of leaves and grass as he twirled in a slow circle.

When he finally spun to face me full-on, one rough eyebrow lifted… or rather fell depending on how you looked at it. His eyes twinkled with wry humor.

"What are you doing here, Lachlan?" I asked, unable to disguise my amusement in my voice. When he only grunted in response, shoulders wiggling, I recognized the ridiculousness of my question and flushed. "Er. Right. You're a little caught up there, aren't you?"

Something that might have been a chuckle worked through the thick gag.

He must have come looking for me, though I couldn't imagine why. Lennox had made it extraordinarily clear the elves never wanted to see my face again. The nymphs must have caught him approaching while I slept and bound him, leaving him behind to show they'd upheld their end of the agreement. Granted, they might have wrapped him up tighter than a chuck roast for their own amusement. Nymphs were peculiar creatures like that.

I smoothed my braid and stepped into the sunlight, squinting at the shock of brightness. The nymphs had left a bundle of clothing in the middle of the clearing, Lachlan's Yankees cap perched right on top. Beside it the bundle lay a double recurved longbow with wood so dark and polished it gleamed. No arrows, though. The nymphs must have squirreled those away.

For a moment, I considered leaving the fey in his miserable predicament. He kind of deserved it for trying to sneak up on me while I slept. But another part of me, a more *rational* part of me, wanted to know why he'd come. I crossed the clearing before I could overthink it.

The wind rustled some leaves as I knelt beside him. The scratches I'd left on his neck still looked raw, and a pang resonated through my chest. I dismissed them and worked the gag out of his mouth, taking care to not touch his skin. It wasn't like I had magic anyway, but maybe he could pick up the residue of it through osmosis. I couldn't be too careful around elves.

"About time you woke up," he said, voice rusty.

I sat back on my heels.

"For a woman who's at her most vulnerable," he glanced meaningfully at my wrist, "you sure sleep like a bear."

"A bear?"

"Hibernation?" He squinted one eye as if trying to discern my intelligence or apparent lack thereof. "Now how about you get me down? I lost all feeling in my foot about two hours ago and I don't think I'm supposed to have this much blood in my brain."

I propped my chin in one hand. "Why would I do that?"

The parallels of this conversation to the one I'd had with Phenex weren't lost on me.

"Because you're a decent sort." He grinned the grin of a five-year-old wanting one more cookie before bedtime, a grin that scrunched up his entire face and crinkled the skin around his eyes.

"Sure." I snorted. "Allow me to rephrase: why would I help someone complicit in an agreement meant to trick me?"

He hummed low in his throat. "Because you've learned magic is overrated?"

"Not this kind of magic."

"Guess I'll have to take your word on that." His smile, impossibly, widened. "Unless you'd be willing to share some with me. That would be legit."

I scratched my neck, eyes rolling up to the barren branches overhead as I dug deep for patience.

"I can help you get it back."

Exactly what I'd wanted to hear. "You can?"

"Only if you promise to fight me for real this time. Magic and all."

"Let me get this straight." I made a show of looking up his body where the rope still wrapped tight around his foot. "You're the one who needs *me* to get you down, but somehow *I'm* the one who owes you… for unlocking *my* magic… after, I assume, I get you down from there?"

"Yep."

"You're crazy."

His laughter shook me. "I'm not denying it."

I braced my hands on my knees and stood. "Yeah. I've been there, rode the ride, bought the shirt. I don't do crazy anymore. If you can't help me, then you're useless to me. I'll figure out another plan that doesn't involve cutting weird fey down from trees."

I didn't have another plan, nor did I think I would come up with one soon, but he didn't need to know that. All he needed to see was my retreating back and realize that he was all alone out here with a bunch of tiny, wicked nymphs for company.

"Hey now, don't get your panties in a twist. Wait one minute."

"I don't think you're in any state to be commenting on my underwear." But I turned around anyway.

Lachlan tilted his head to the side, which must have taken some effort considering how stiff he probably was from hanging upside down most of the night. "You don't have to fight me. Get me down and I'll remove the cuff."

"Can't you unlock it now?"

"Nah, the key's in my clothes." I zeroed in on the unguarded bundle. He chuckled again. "By all means, sort through them. Try using the key yourself. You might melt it, though, because it doesn't like being handled by non-elves."

I froze before I pinched the black shirt on top. "Only you can touch it?"

"I mean. You can touch it, but you can't use it."

I removed the shirt and, sure enough, there was a key—barely the length of the first digit of my pointer finger and flashy gold. Hard to believe something so small could trap something so immense. "How do I know this isn't a ploy? That you won't trick me again?"

"Hold on a hot second." He must have twitched because he was spinning again, a little faster than before. Indignation washed across his face. "For starters, I didn't trick you. I did my job. I fought you. As far as I was concerned, it was a fair trade. The same as we've done with others needing help.

"Second, I'm not my mother. Her resentments run deep, but I don't agree—"

I nearly toppled over. "Lennox is your mother?" But they seemed so different.

His hands twisted under the ropes. I imagined he used them a lot when he talked. He seemed like a guy who favored visual expression. "Unfortunately, yes. I love her dearly, but how I came from someone as uptight and arrogant as she is, is beyond me."

No. I didn't think I'd ever understand Lachlan. Not in a million years.

Not that I wanted to, I reminded myself. He was a means to an end.

"Anyway, she was wrong. She should have kept her promise. That's why I stole the key and ran to find you." The way his gaze slanted away from me told me he was lying or, at the very least, concealing something. "See. I'm the pleasant sort, too."

"Uh huh." It physically hurt to not pick up the key. I wanted to. I'd heard his assurances. But I didn't want to risk vaporizing it. "To make sure we're square: I get you down and you remove my shackle. Right?"

"That's right." He nodded soberly, tone grim. "I swear on my name, my home, my honor."

I let it slide that the elves apparently thought they didn't have honor.

"Alright." I eyed the bow, wishing the nymphs had dropped an arrow in their haste to get away. Or that I still had my dagger. "How do you propose I get you down?"

"Do I have to do all the thinking here?"

"I still have both my legs on the ground," I chided. "I can leave at any point."

He rolled his eyes. "Use my bow."

"With what arrows?"

"It makes its own."

"Oh." Why didn't I trust that glint in his eye? "What's the catch?"

"I mean, it's cursed."

My nails curled into my palms. More curses.

He continued, "But it's not so bad."

"I'm not touching it," I said. Nope. Not going anywhere near it. "You can find your own way—"

"TruthTeller isn't malicious." Lachlan's free leg swung lazily. "But she's true to her name. She'll produce as many arrows as you want, and those arrows will fly true and hit their target every time. But each arrow comes with a truth."

"A truth?" I glanced down at the smooth, molded wood. That didn't sound so bad.

"Yep. A truth about yourself. A truth about the world. Sometimes, a truth about what's to come. Hard to say what she'll send your way." He smirked.

I chewed my lip. That sounded like a pretty incredible offer. "What's the downside?"

"You have to be willing to accept what she tells you." He grimaced as he tried to flex his bound leg with little success. "Whatever she tells you is the truth. The whole truth. Not everyone can handle that kind of stark reality."

I frowned. "What do you mean?"

"We all tell ourselves lies. People tell us lies. People we don't know spread lies about things that don't apply to us." His head tilted again. "Those lies change and shape the world. Sometimes they make us feel comfortable, in control. Other times they are necessary evils to get through a difficult time or situation. Facing those lies… that's a whole other reality. A reality that has driven some mad."

Maybe that explained some of his peculiarities. I circled the bow as if it were a wild animal, my arms crossed across my chest. I couldn't help but be intrigued by the weapon, by the challenge it presented. What truths might it tell me? What truths might I not be willing to face?

"Go ahead. Try her out." The elf's voice was weirdly alluring. Maybe he was drawing me into the craziness that was his universe. If so, it was definitely working. "You know you want to."

The bow was already in my hand, my fingers on the string. It felt awkward in my grip. I'd only wielded a longbow at one practice session that had gone so poorly that, when Rose had gotten over her peals of laughter, she had declared me inept. I also didn't have the right gloves to handle this weapon, but his were too big for my hands.

However, when I got my magic back, my raw fingers would be healed. And Lachlan said it always fired true. A bit of momentary pain seemed worth it to me.

"Draw it back and focus on what you want to hit," the elf instructed. "When you have your shot set, you'll feel the magic tingle a little. That's the arrow. Let it fly and be prepared for the—"

I released the string before he finished his thought.

I should have let him finish.

The truth transformed into a very real, very visceral thing. It kicked like a horse, crashing into my chest right above the heart, knocking me to the ground. The bow uttered two sentences, a few simple words tinged in silver and gold, a toneless voice that sounded in my head with such absolute surety I knew Lachlan hadn't lied to me:

Geoffrey saw the error in his ways. He would not have been your enemy had you not forced him to take up the mantle.

Lights popped behind my eyelids and I dropped the weapon as I choked, rolling to my side as I clutched at my chest, forcing the bile back down. My head spun, the world tilting out of focus as my mind raced. Everything in me screamed, railed against those words, against the starkly-stated truth.

That—he hadn't wanted me dead? When Geoffrey had reached out to me through the bond when I'd first gained my magic? He'd spoken the truth when he wanted me to come to him so we could discuss my intentions?

It had to be. The bow only spoke in truths.

But—it said he wasn't my enemy. Not that he hadn't wanted me dead.

Pain blossomed as I dug my fingers into my skull.

What did it mean then?

I'd created the monster that so relentlessly pursued me?

"You're holding up better than most I've seen on their first time." Lachlan's stray comment sliced through my muddied thoughts as they swirled. "Not that I ever doubted you. The truth hurts, even for a God, but you haven't run off screaming, so there's that."

"Yippee freaking doo." I drew in a deep breath, savoring the crisp, clean quality to the air, feeling it wash over and through me as if cleansing my sins. Lachlan had unraveled himself from the ropes in the time that I'd floundered in my head and was finishing buttoning up his shirt. "How can you stand it? Does it ever run out of truths?"

"Will people ever stop telling lies?" His lavender eyes were somber as he straightened his collar. His hat was already firmly in place, brim carefully arched. He'd tucked a tan trench coat in the crook of his arm. "I've had TruthTeller for more than a century. I've had to face a lot of truths in that time."

It wasn't an answer.

But I wasn't sure I wanted to hear it, anyway.

I pushed myself upright without taking his hand. "I think I'll leave her with you if it's all the same."

"You're not the first to say that." The elf shrugged on his coat.

Yeah, I doubted many were willing to pay the price of wielding that kind of knowledge. Not if my first hit was any sign. I rubbed at a spot on my chest that wasn't exactly sore in reality, but still hurt mentally. Then again...

"The truth can be a dangerous thing," I said. "Can't that knowledge be used maliciously?"

Lachlan tipped his chin, like I'd finally understood a key point. "Can't all knowledge be used maliciously?"

"Would you stop answering my questions with questions?"

His eyes narrowed with mirth and I held up my arm before he could speak. "Don't. I already know what you're going to say. How about you be useful and get this cuff off?"

"Of course. Give it here." He motioned and when I made it clear I didn't want him touching my skin, he snorted and grabbed my jacket. His fingers were cool through the weight of the fabric, and the elf was careful to draw it back, only exposing the metal as he rotated my arm. "The tricky part is finding the—there it is." He slipped the key into a small hole in the cuff and turned. The hunk of metal promptly fell off and landed in the grass with a soft thud.

Nothing happened at first, but I could feel it like the buzz of electricity signaling an approaching storm, like a backdraft before an explosion, like an incoming tsunami sucking the ocean back from the shores, using its offering to feed its mighty power. Pulling and pulling and pulling....

And crashing down upon me. I gasped dramatically, heart in my throat, my knees buckling again under the weight of it all.

Air. Fire. Water. Immersing me in sensation, clamoring for attention, demanding I use them, abuse them.

Magic as vital to me as oxygen.

Magic I hoped I'd never take for granted ever again.

"Twin curses." I forced the magic to heel, drawing it deeper into me where it scrambled riotously, my entire body tingling as it reconnected to my bones and blood and soul. It wanted to burn and drown and soar, and I went lightheaded from the sensation. "I'm so glad you're back."

"You always talk to your magic like that?"

"I used to," I replied to Lachlan. "Then I realized I was talking to a manipulative psycho."

He chuckled, eyes dancing. He thought I was kidding. I wasn't. "Feel better?"

"Yes. Much." Funny how we were talking about truths and that was a lie. I wasn't sure how I felt at all. Better wasn't the word for it, though. "Thank you."

"Anytime." He shook out his leg, the one the elves had bound, probably still getting feeling back in his limbs. "What's the plan now, boss?"

"The plan is that I go one way and you go another."

He flipped his hat back around and I frowned. "While technically that's a plan, there are definitely better options."

"You're not coming with me."

"Yes, I am."

"Is this why you were following me?" For the fourth time today, I cursed the fact he was an elf. If I could lock him in a cage of air, I wouldn't be having this conversation, but I knew he'd use that magic to break free and then do stars know what.

"Yes."

"Why?"

"Because you're badass."

I blinked. That one hit me right between the eyes. "Pardon?"

"You're awesome. You fight bad guys and have this incredible magic. Now you're out helping everybody while *also* trying to save the world." He splayed his fingers, wonderment etched on his face. I'd never met someone who embraced their emotion so freely before. I found it highly disconcerting. "And I want in."

I so did not need this. "No."

"Come on." He dropped to his knees, hands folded together, and shuffled across the grass. "I promise to be quiet."

"I don't think you understand what that word means. This is a one-woman show." I circled my face with my hand. "I don't work well with others."

Lachlan rocked back on his heels, picked up TruthTeller, and methodically unstrung the weapon. "That's ok. I don't work well with others, either. Guess we'll have to figure this out together."

I would have laughed at the absurdity of this conversation if it wasn't so serious. "Give me one reason I'd let you come with me."

"Because you want to figure out how to stop a curse that could destroy magic." He smoothed his hand over the wood and I stared when it went limp. Seriously. One second the bow was a bow and the next it was... flat and flexible as a belt. He rolled it up. "And I know something that will help you understand it."

How did I get myself into these kinds of situations? "Bury the lead much?"

"Always. What I know is something you're definitely going to want to hear."

I still couldn't get over what had happened with his weapon. "I'm going to need more than that."

He tucked TruthTeller into his coat. "Let me come with you."

"Not until I know that you know something."

He huffed. "Who made you so distrusting?" I slanted him a look. "Fine. I know of a fey who was exhibiting signs of everything you described: black veins, comatose state, sweating, and fever. This fey's… friends thought they were going to die… but then they were cured."

He could have told me the world rotated clockwise and I wouldn't have been more surprised. "A daemoni?"

Lachlan stood, shaking his finger in my face. "Let me come with you."

"Fine. You can come with me." I had no choice. Not if this gave me a lead. I'd figure out how to get rid of him later. "Now where's this fey and how did you find out about this?"

"Ask the nymphs. They were talking about her while you slept."

Chapter 16

I was never leaving a city without at least a dozen granola bars in my bag ever again.

"These are crap," was the first thing Lachlan said when I pulled out my last source of food for the foreseeable future. He tapped the nutrition label on the back of one. "Where are the nuts? The protein? Fruit? Granola bars aren't complete without at least two kinds of dried fruit. These are sugar blended with sugar and covered in more sugar."

I tore the bars from his hand, unwrapped them, and set them on the same mossy log where I'd put the apple yesterday. "You're pretty judgmental for someone who didn't bring any food. At all."

"I was in a hurry." He lay back in the grass, uncaring of its stiffness, feet rocking back and forth as he gazed up at the lacey white clouds overhead. "But trust me, as soon as I find a decent grocery store, I'm showing you a good time."

"I'd appreciate it if you refrain from ever using that phrase in reference to me ever again." I backed away from the log and settled on a patch of earth about fifteen feet from the fey. I still felt a little faint from the rush of magic flooding my veins, but it was abating. Kind of.

"If you think the nymphs are going to want your sad excuses for food, you are sadly—oh." Lachlan rocked up on his elbows. A slight figure dropped from the branches of a pine tree and landed in a crouch beside the food. I'd never seen a wood nymph in person before, only heard them chittering in the background, but there was no doubt what this was.

Her frame was slender, her dark brown joints spindly and heavily angled. Dark hair strung with leaves and downy feathers dangled past her shoulders and moist, black eyes not dissimilar to those of goats, blinked rapidly as she surveyed first us, then the food.

"Hello there." I leaned back on my hands. "I was wondering if you would extend your assistance with something." Though tricksters at heart, nymphs didn't steal offerings. They only took food or clothing in exchange for something else.

She rose on her haunches, stretching legs that angled backward—like a deer. Overhead, a second set of eyes watched us from the inner depths of a pine tree, no doubt measuring us for threats.

"I don't want to injure or capture you. Neither does my companion." Lachlan shrugged and fell back on the grass. "This morning he heard your people discussing a curse that had affected one of your own. That individual got very sick and, if he heard correctly, thankfully recovered. You see, that sounds very similar to a curse that's slowly destroying a friend of mine, and she isn't getting better. Would it be possible for me to meet your friend to see what might have aided her in her recovery?"

The nymph cocked her head and purred. I couldn't tell if it was a warning purr or a thinking purr. Her friend chirped, but I wasn't any closer to understanding their language. Gods came equipped with a unique gift that allowed them to both hear and speak in all languages, but sometimes it took a minute to kick in.

I exchanged a glance with Lachlan. "That's the last of my food and among the last of my supplies. It's not an offering I make lightly, but it is one I make out of necessity. I want to stop this curse from spreading to more fey if I can."

The nymph splayed her twigs of fingers in a coaxing manner, chirped at her companion, then snatched up the bars. She turned her back to us and scampered off, using her extra-long arms to help her run.

"I think she accepts." Lachlan sprang to his feet at the same time I did. "Let's go before she changes her mind."

- - -

The nymph led us to a hovel of sorts. The trees stretched so tall they seemed to brush the clouds. Their roots, some pulled from the ground, formed archways through which we walked. The leaves wove together densely, remarkably green and alive despite the time of year, making it difficult to see the dappled sunlight through their veins. The temperature dropped a few degrees, and I was, once again, thankful for both my fire magic and the worn, beaten jacket shielding my skin.

Every so often, I'd catch the blink of eyes: some midnight and some milky, but for the most part the other wood nymphs remained hidden. My skin itched. No birds called. No insects whirred past my head. The nymphs also didn't chatter like I'd grown used to, as if afraid to shatter the silence with anything louder than a whisper. The only sound came from the crunching of leaves and dried branches beneath our boots. I'd shushed Lachlan at least twice when he'd pointed out similar observations—loudly.

The nymph who'd accepted my offer stopped at the base of a thick clump of roots, thrust one thorny arm at the darkness beneath, then dove inside. I rolled my shoulders. I wasn't the biggest fan of small, dark spaces.

"Seeing as you're the big, bad God and all, how about you go first?" Lachlan muttered in my ear. "I'll grab the rear in case anything scary pops up."

"Last in, first out?"

"I meant if something pops up from behind." He executed a karate chop. "Someone's gotta have your back."

"Right," I said dryly. "And you'll scare them off with your ferocity."

A pair of the long, needle-like knives I'd noticed him fiddling with back at Cogscraig threaded through the spaces in his fingers. "And these."

I examined the points of the weapons, impressed with his sleight of hand. "Might want to put those away before you take an eye out."

"That's kind of the point." He cackled softly at his pun, but tucked them back into his sleeves, regardless. I made a mental note to watch out for those needles—and maybe get some of my own.

We had to crouch to fit into the burrow that only got smaller as it narrowed to a tight room woven among the tangle of roots protruding directly beneath one of these unnaturally tall trees. In the middle of the room, crouched around a spread of green and yellow leaves, were three nymphs. I recognized *our* nymph—as I'd taken to calling her—because she crunched loudly on a granola bar.

The other two sat back on their haunches, berries red as lipstick kisses in hand as they chewed. One boasted a head of white hair that resembled dandelion fluff. The other was so scrawny a moderate breeze might blow her away should she venture outside.

"Greetings." I sat cross-legged on the ground right inside the entrance. "My name is Zara Ramone and my companion"—*temporary* companion, I amended in my head—"is Lachlan McAvoy. We seek answers to a curse that, until now, we only knew to be plaguing the daemoni community."

My nymph chirped and the three fey blinked at the same time.

Creepy.

I took it as a go-ahead to continue.

"I heard that one of your own was also affected recently by a curse that blackened their veins and they nearly died. As the First of Four, I'm hoping I might examine that fey to understand what allowed her to recover." I scratched the oath farthest down on my wrist, one spun with a moon and stars. "I promise to be delicate and to not waste your time. I'm hoping that I might be able to help a friend before it's too late."

The nymphs drew closer, their murmuring too soft for me to make out distinct syllables.

Lachlan cleared his throat from where he sat beside me. He was so tall the top of his cap brushed the ceiling. Bits of dirt speckled it, but he didn't seem to mind as he watched the nymphs curiously.

The murmuring, so much like the rustling of leaves and the whispers of bushes, cut off. I chewed my lip. The nymph so painfully thin it almost hurt to look at her tentatively moved toward me. Her frame shook so hard her joints rattled.

"You don't have to do this if you don't want to," I said, my palms flattening perpendicular to the ground. "If you aren't one-hundred percent certain it's ok for me to examine you or your magic, then I won't. I will search elsewhere for the information I need."

The rattling stopped, and she appeared to inhale deeply, before sliding two feet closer. She wasn't close enough to touch yet, but she was definitely gathering her bravery around her like a cloak. Cracked, brown lips parted, and she finally spoke words I could understand, though the cadence was jilted.

"It is. Ok. I am. Stiff. Is all." She slid a few more inches closer, arms and legs splayed wide to help balance. "I was. Lost. In the black. And white. For so long."

There wasn't enough oxygen in the tiny room. I swallowed hard, fighting past a wave of nausea. Black and white. She must be talking about the static. The static combined with the black veins and comatose state sounded exactly like the curse eating Logan.

The nymph crouched, back legs crooked wide with her arms braced between them, the image she presented Zen. "Your. Kindness has. Reached our ears. Blessed God of. Water." She gripped my hand, her fingers barely long enough to wrap around my index finger. The sense of awe that filled me at her trust was baffling. She didn't know me, had never met me, but what she had heard was enough for her to believe in my good intentions. "It would be. An honor. To help."

Her magic, the wispy, spindly magic that fit her to a tee, caressed mine, inviting me in. It was comforting, like a misty embrace, and I didn't have to sink very far since she offered herself so easily.

I waded through the energy, marveling at the scents of wet moss and dried pine needles that mingled pleasantly. Whatever static had consumed her was gone, but I couldn't tell if it had taken some of her magic with it. I parted the swaying branches of a willow tree shot with the greens and golds that formed the core of her magic, and I found what I was looking for.

The broken remnants of three runes were seared into the side of its trunk. Chills showered down my spine and across my legs as I stared at the black, crooked slashes. I couldn't have read them without knowing what they already said, but it was definitely them: Binding, cleansing, disruption.

I scrunched my eyes shut as I brushed the first of the runes, just a corner, wondering if it would suck me into another realm. When nothing happened, I opened one careful eye and traced the lines of black. Still nothing. It was as if the rune had been cleansed before the owner broke it, shattering all signs of its former magical signature.

I did the same with the other two runes with similar results.

Finally finished, I followed the yellow-gold trail that marked my soul back to my body. The connection severed when I emerged on the other side. The nymph had curled up in my lap and purred softly as I stroked the back of her neck. I didn't remember how we'd gotten into such a position, but she glanced up at me, liquid eyes wide and honest.

"Were your efforts. Fruitful?"

"No, I'm afraid not. I can see the curse. It's clearly the same thing that's affecting my friend, but yours is broken. Did you do something that would do that?"

Lachlan tilted his head and ran his knuckles over his lips, lavender eyes boring into me as if scouring my soul. It was a dark look, a deep one, and I felt a little uncomfortable.

"We gave her. Mashed peas and water. That is all," said the nymph with the shock of white hair. "We don't. Experience sickness. Treatment is foreign."

The nymph rose from my lap and settled back on her haunches. "I wish we could be. More help."

The nymph who'd brought us to the hovel chirped from somewhere at the back of the room and emerged from another tunnel, lugging something silver that looked suspiciously like...

"My dagger!" I exclaimed. Behind her was another nymph dragging my phone. A third clutched a bandolier of knives. I reached out for my weapon, eager to strap it back into place. "What do we owe you?"

Nymphs were always about equal exchange.

The nymph I'd examined sampled a raspberry from the pile on the leaves. "No exchange. It is enough. That you always. Consider. Those who remain. Out of sight."

As I puzzled over her words, Lachlan reached past me and snagged the bandolier, crowing with delight. "I'd wondered if these were gone for good. They used to belong to my dad, you know, forged in an old elvish technique that has been lost through the generations. These puppies here can—"

"Thank you," I interjected, flabbergasted with my companion. "For your courtesy and your understanding. I'm glad you're feeling better now."

The fey gave no real outside reaction, though I swore her heavily wrinkled face softened. "My granddaughter. Will lead. You back to the road. You need not. Fear getting lost. Under her supervision." The last sentence was spoken as a warning, and the little fey who'd taken my granola bars ducked her head quickly. "Best wishes. God Zara."

There was nothing left to do but head back outside.

I'll admit, there was nothing like that first breath of fresh air after leaving a cramped, dark space. Lachlan seemed to mirror the sentiment as he swiped the dirt off his hat.

"Well, that was something else." He loped ahead and turned to face me while walking backward. "Can't say I thought I'd ever see a village of nymphs. Granted, I doubt we'll ever be able to find it on our own again."

"It's fascinating," I said, glancing back at the hovel that had disappeared among the trees. "How all the different fey live and interact. How they've returned to their lives and adapted to the world two thousand years after getting their magic back. I mean, many choose to still live among humans, but then you see things like that. It's..."

"Breathtaking."

"Exactly."

The trees grew farther apart the more we moved away from the home of the nymphs. The green of the trees and bushes soon faded, the mysterious magic that gave the hovel spring-like life disappearing. Winter became more evident once again in the deadened branches that we shoved through, and my breath clouded before my face.

Our guide was careful to stay within view as she hopped over rocks and skirted logs. Sometimes, though, she would lead us to a fallen tree that was impossible to scale, so we'd have to go around, and I inwardly cursed her quirky nature. No doubt she was getting an untold amount of joy from watching us struggle.

"Where to next, boss?" Lachlan asked after a while. Sweat had gathered along my forehead and my panting had quickened from all the exercise. There had to be a faster, more efficient way to travel. "What's the plan?"

"What makes you think I have a plan?"

"Because you're the kind of person who's always thinking three steps ahead."

Ironically, I nearly tripped over the root of a tree buried under a pile of dead leaves. "You don't know me."

"But I've known people like you." The elf shoved the arms of his jacket up to his elbows. "I'm the exact opposite of your kind. It's why we get along so swimmingly."

"Care to elaborate?" If I concentrated hard enough, I could see the paved, two-lane highway up ahead. I was sure mirages weren't a thing in the middle of the woods. Even woods that belonged to nymphs. Pretty sure.

"Think about it. If you have another 'planner,'" his fingers hooked in air quotes, "with you, then you're constantly butting heads because they have one idea of how the next three steps should go and you have another. However, if you have someone like me," he pressed a hand to his chest dramatically, "who is spontaneous and wild, then all I can do is work with what you've got going on and add to it."

Huh. That made a fair bit of sense. We pushed through the last tangle of trees and I threw out my arms and spun in a slow circle, head tilted back to stare at the blue, blue sky. Seeing so much of it all at once, and not through the reaching, scraping branches of hundreds of trees, felt like a blessing.

When I turned to thank the nymph, she'd already vanished into the thicket.

"So?" Lachlan smacked some dirt off the hem of his coat and tapped his heels against the asphalt to knock away the dried leaves clinging to the soles. "Where are we off to next?"

"I need to find another fey library," I admitted when I'd finally caught my wind. "There was something strange about those runes. I'd like to do some more research."

I watched the elf. Maybe now he'd realize most of what I did about wasn't glitz and adventure. Maybe he'd take his leave; all the better since he was still close to home.

Instead, to my dismay, he took my idea in stride, nodding thoughtfully as he drew his coat closed over the knives draped across his chest. "Seems reasonable enough."

Well, if I couldn't shake him yet, I might as well use him. "You wouldn't know where any fey libraries might be, do you? Big ones?"

Lachlan's quicksilver grin flashed wide. "Look at you, already asking me for help. What did I say? A fabulous team in the making." Why did I feel like he was patting me on the head like a puppy? "And, as a matter of fact, I *do* know where one is. A big one. The biggest."

He threw his arms wide and rotated them in a circle as if that gave me any indication to the scope of what he was talking about.

"Care to share where?"

"Sure, boss." The elf moved so he towered head and shoulders over me, then squeezed my biceps. I wrinkled my nose and wiggled out of his grip. It only made sense he was the touchy-feely sort. "How about we get to South Africa first and then you follow my lead?"

It wasn't a question. I bristled. "Why's that?"

"Because I think you're still fixing to leave me in your dust." He flashed another grin and spun on his heels. As he walked along the road, uncaring of my disdained glare, he whistled a jaunty Irish tune that matched the beat of his steps.

This might prove trickier than I'd figured.

Chapter 17

A flaming arrow whizzed by my head.

"I'm never listening to you again," I shouted at the elf, wheezing.

He popped up one shoulder, twisted mid-stride, and fired two arrows without so much as a flinch from TruthTeller's recoil. A whinnying scream went up behind me, but I didn't dare look as the elf whipped back around and sprinted harder to match my pace.

"We found the library, didn't we?"

"Yeah." I winced at the blast of a shotgun, then redoubled my efforts. My lungs screamed, my legs ached, but still, I ran, harder and faster than I'd ever run before. I was a swimmer. Swimmer. All this running was way out of my element. "But you neglected to mention it was smack in the middle of centaur territory."

A wild whoop went up, one that was quickly picked up by the two dozen other centaurs thundering behind us, hooves kicking up the red dust of the plain. While not desert territory, few trees dared grow under the relentless rays of the sun. I cursed and skidded to a stop, then threw out an arm, launching a sweep of air that knocked a few fey right off their legs. Most, however, remained upright, weapons clutched in their hands, bare chests gleaming with sweat as they released another unified howl.

I cursed again and ran to catch up with the elf, wishing there were more hills or valleys. Maybe a stack of boulders to duck behind. Anything but this vast expanse of dirt and tall, brown grass.

Lachlan glanced over his shoulder, seemingly unconcerned considering two more flaming arrows had volleyed over his head. "How was I supposed to know the centaurs had reclaimed this territory? They've wanted nothing to do with the plains for the past thousand years."

"I'm still blaming you for this," I hollered, wincing when an arrow nicked the side of my calf.

His grin was all teeth. "I'd expect nothing less, boss."

"How far to Durban?" I gasped.

"A few miles still." Lachlan stopped and fired three more shots. Three more fey buckled, forelegs streaming blood. He wasn't aiming to kill, merely to incapacitate. I'd made it clear I didn't want any more death on my hands, but these warriors weren't making it easy. "You know, this wouldn't be a problem if you'd set their village on fire as I suggested. You could also try carving a river to sweep them away. Anything."

He caught up to me and snagged my wrist, tugging me along faster behind him, TruthTeller still clutched in his other hand. "Hurry now. Wouldn't want to see your gorgeous face on a spit roast."

"I told you. Starting a fire in this drought could have disastrous consequences." I nearly tripped, my legs barely keeping up with the pace set by the elf. He jerked me to the right as a bullet zipped past my cheek. "And there's nowhere near enough water in the area to make a river."

My throat ached from all the shouting.

Lachlan veered a hard left, and I wondered, not for the first time, if he knew where we were going. "That's lame. You should figure out a way to overcome those limitations."

I snorted and nearly choked. "Sure. Let me break the parameters set by the universe."

"It's ok." He changed his grip, lacing his fingers between mine. I frowned. "You need to think more creatively. It's a handicap I can help you overcome."

Something about the horizon ahead didn't look right. I couldn't figure out what, not with all my attention spent on staying upright and not getting shot.

"At least you still have Air," he yelled.

"Why do you say that?"

"Because that's the only way we're surviving this." That crazed gleam was back in his eyes, the one I knew better than to trust. The one that made me wonder how many screws were loose in that head of his. "Hope you can fly."

I jerked, my heated body trembling with a sudden chill. "I can't fly."

"Why not?"

"I don't know how to." It was the truth. I'd only been able to fly once, and that was immediately after gaining my abilities over the element. Every time I'd attempted to soar since then ended with me flat on my face or worse. "Seriously, I can't do that."

"You're afraid." Lachlan kept his gaze fixed ahead. I stared at the part of his neck shaded by the fraying edge of his cap. "That's the fear talking."

"No, I honestly can't—" I broke off when I figured out what was so wrong with the sky. We were veering toward the edge of a cliff. A very tall cliff, if the ground below was any indication. In a few seconds, we'd be vaulting over the edge. "Are you insane?"

"We've already gone over this," he laugh-shouted, keeping his hand clenched around mine. "Now let go, boss."

We were coming up too fast. I couldn't slow down. Not in time.

"Let go."

A few more steps.

"Let go!"

Together, we jumped into nothing. For a moment, I felt that weightlessness. That impossibility of floating, as if gravity had temporarily loosened its hold on me and me alone. Then it wrapped taut like a chain and we were falling. Someone was laughing.

"Hit me," the laughing man yelled. I opened my eyes, my heart nearly kicking out of my ribs as we plummeted, the red rocks below approaching faster and faster. Lachlan tugged my arm, which he miraculously hadn't released. His face glowed with pure, radiant joy. "Trust your magic, boss."

His insanity must have been infectious.

Because I did.

Like ripping a Band-Aid from a wound, I yanked away my control and screamed when it caught me, caught the elf, and lifted us.

I clawed at the air, a desperate dog-paddle that I almost immediately abandoned when I understood my magic would not let me fall. It had me. It wasn't going to hurt me.

I was flying.

My chest swelled painfully, adrenaline crashing through me, and I, too, started laughing.

Lachlan whooped as he released me and veered off, nimbly taking control of the magic for himself. When I'd released my abilities, some of it must have smacked him, like an attack, and he'd absorbed it.

"You did it," he shrieked when he finally stopped barrel-rolling toward the setting sun. "I knew you could."

I didn't bother to respond. Instead, I tucked my head and somersaulted through the wind, thrilled with my own abilities, wondering why I hadn't trusted myself sooner.

But deep down, I knew why.

I knew exactly why.

Chapter 18

"Care to share what's up with the mark on your face?" Lachlan asked casually. Too casually.

I'd caught him staring at the tattooed rune on more than one occasion. We stood outside the Water Temple in Durban on the southeast side of South Africa, straightening our clothing. We'd finally landed and, for as much as he claimed he hadn't been here before, Lachlan had known exactly where to go.

At a cursory glance, it looked more like a swanky hotel than a temple with its wide overhang and doublewide doors with sparkling windows, but that went to show what I knew about temples. My parents had never taken me to mass as a child because they were too busy shielding me from the Order which, to be fair, was out to kill me.

Or... *had* been out to kill me.

I recalled the truth spoken by a certain bow that shall-not-be-named and quickly shoved it back into a compartment in the back of my head where I stored other things to 'deal with later.'

"Only if you explain how you were able to pick up flying so quickly." I moved out of the path of a blue-skinned fey intent on reaching the swinging front doors and winced when pain radiated through my leg. "That was impressive, how you knew exactly what to do yet had never done it before."

Lachlan pulled off his cap, ran a hand through his sweat-dampened locks, and jammed it back on. "I can't accept much praise. It's what we're taught to do. Get creative. Since our magic comes with obvious limitations, we're taught as children to adapt to whatever we get." His gaze tracked down my body and settled on my leg. "Are you sure you only got grazed by an arrow? Your leg is still bleeding. Shouldn't you have healed by now?"

Now that the adrenaline was fading, my leg had developed a rather sharp ache. I tugged on the hem of my jeans and choked when I discovered the bullet hole piercing the side of my calf. They'd shot me. The centaurs had freaking shot me.

"I think it's time to get you some help." Lachlan bent at the knees and looped an arm under mine in support. "Luckily, we came to a Water Temple, huh?"

I felt too lightheaded to roll my eyes at his bad joke. We hobbled awkwardly through the front door of the temple, me hopping on one leg as the elf bent practically in two to accommodate the extreme differences in our heights. The teenage fey with shockingly purple hair manning the front desk glanced up and her mouth fell open.

Now, her reaction could have been attributed to several things: elves, in their roles as mercenaries, rarely appeared in public unless they were on security detail or about to make a kill. I was also trailing a stream of sticky, gold-tinted blood across the floor. And, of course, I happened to be the God for which this temple existed.

"Oh my Gods, it's you."

Naturally, she honed in on the latter of the three options.

"Oh my Gods, the God of Water just walked in. She walked into *our* temple. Our temple." It felt weird being referred to in the third person to my face, but considering her shock, I let it slide. The fey's hands slid away from her now, very pale cheeks, and she blinked rapidly as she scanned the foyer. It was a very nice foyer filled with comfortable seating, a few well-placed plants, lots of light. However, I was bleeding rather heavily, and the bullet was probably still inside me… which was why I hadn't healed. That thought made me queasy, because despite everything I'd been through, a foreign object was lodged inside my body.

"Hi, yes. It's me." I smacked the front desk louder than I'd intended, and sucked in sharply as Lachlan rumbled with silent laughter. To my horror, the girl's eyes brimmed with tears. Big, fat tears. "Listen. I promise, another time, I'd love to sit and chat. But I kind of need a little help right now."

"You," she choked back a sob, "you, Zara Ramone. *The* God of Water. An actual God. You want to talk to *me*." The tears officially overfilled their wells and streamed down her face in long, shiny rivers. "This may be the best day of my entire life, my entire *existence*."

Considering she looked all of fifteen years old, that wasn't as dramatic as she made it sound.

"Are you gonna be ok?" Lachlan asked, hitching me up a little higher. She fanned her face rapidly, and I worried that she might faint. She was far too pale. "You kinda look like you're going to puke."

"I—I—I think so." She fanned her face again.

I snapped my fingers to get her to focus and shifted in a way that allowed Lachlan to absorb more of my weight. The pain was lancing up my leg, and it had become difficult to not think about. I bit back a groan.

"Is there anyone I can talk to? A supervisor maybe?" I asked. Her big, blue eyes were remarkably clear as she blinked at me incomprehensively. My frustration mounted. "See, I've been shot. You can tell by the blood pooling around my shoe."

It wasn't that bad, but if we waited much longer, there was a serious risk that that might happen.

Lachlan shook his head softly when the girl stared blankly at me some more. "Can you be a dear and call someone? Anyone?"

The fey turned to him and hypnotically reached for the phone. She punched the button at the top of the console harder than necessary and choked into the receiver. "Sir, the God of Water is in the lobby. She'd like to speak to you."

The phone hit the cradle with a crack.

"Do you mind if we—" Lachlan hooked his free thumb over his shoulder—"take a seat over there? For a minute? My companion here isn't exactly the lightest—" He wheezed when my elbow slammed into his ribs. "I mean to say, she is *lighter* than a feather and I'm worried she'll float away if she doesn't sit down."

The girl-fey was beyond words, and I wondered if this was what it was like for Hollywood celebrities meeting superfans. The elf took her silence as a go-ahead and was in the middle of maneuvering me around to hop back to the plump, floral-patterned recliners framing the front window when an exasperated voice sounded.

"Zoe, we have talked about this before. I don't care what material you like to read, your fantasies have no place at work. Oh—do you need assistance?"

I assumed that second bit was directed at me and the elf.

Lachlan chucked again, his reaction reminding me so much of Ryder that I was tempted to smack him again, and swiveled us back to the front. The woman supervising poor Zoe took one look at my face, my eyes, my hair—and dropped her clipboard in her haste to bow. If I were standing on my own, I would have shuffled to hide my discomfort.

"Please don't do that," I squeaked. "I don't know what to do with bowing. I appreciate it and all, but I'm just a girl. From America. Who would rather go incognito most days. Could you please, uh, stop? Yeah?" The woman straightened. "Thanks."

"I apologize profusely for not seeing to your needs immediately, Ms. Ramone. Zoe here is new and a bit scattered sometimes." That was one word for it. "What may we help you with today?"

I motioned vaguely at my leg and the shimmering trail of blood, wondering if it was somehow only visible to me. "You wouldn't happen to have a doctor on-site, would you?"

The supervisor glanced at the floor, brushed Zoe aside, and snagged the phone. A few button pushes and a softly relayed message later and a harried-looking fey with glasses propped on a nose that would make a bulldog proud darted into the lobby. He shoved his spectacles up and examined first my leg, then me.

"Come with me," he murmured brusquely.

Lachlan had officially given up on trying to help me along, and, when it became clear a gurney wasn't about to appear, he hoisted me up in his arms and followed the doctor. "See, I told you we make a good team."

"Don't worry, it's only my pride that's wounded," I managed. He held me remarkably firm despite our fast clip down the hallway. The doctor's long, white coat flapped around another corner and Lachlan picked up his pace.

"Like magic, pride is overrated," he said. "A sense of humor, that's much more useful."

"I think you have more than enough of that for the both of us."

The doctor held open a swinging, steel-plated door. Lachlan strode through, examined the office, and promptly dumped me on the examination bed in the center of the room.

"Ow," I complained, edging back on the crinkly white paper. "A little respect would be nice. Remember, I'm a God here."

"Trust me, I got that message loud and clear back at reception." The elf dropped into a chair with a tear in the vinyl seat cushion and crossed one leg over his knee. "Shall I moon over you, too? Attempt a dramatic faint? I've been practicing."

As I glared, the doctor moved to my side and gently moved my leg so he could get a better look at the injury.

"My, my. You did manage to get shot, didn't you?" His icy fingers released my limb, and he ambled his portly figure over to one of the many white cabinets lining the room. When he reemerged, he dropped some lethal-looking tweezers and a rather sinister needle on a tray. "No worries, though. Once we get the bullet out, you'll be right as rain."

I recoiled when he maneuvered the needle to my leg. "What's that?"

"Oh. Morphine. This is somewhat stronger than the normal stuff, which is necessary considering your magic will probably destroy it as quickly as it can. I only need a minute, so we have time." He pushed his glasses up again, and he moved to a better angle. I wondered what kind of fey he was. His signature was muddled. "Fortunately, it's not in there deep. And given who you are," his second chin wobbled, "your magic should take care of the rest in a matter of seconds."

"Don't worry, boss, I got my eye on this guy. If he tries anything funny, he'll have to figure out how to remove a knife from his spine."

The doctor sniffed and turned to the elf who was, of all things, running one of the blades we'd recovered from the nymphs over a white whetstone.

No. I would never understand what made this elf tick.

"Right then." The doctor raised thick, white eyebrows. "Ready? Lean back."

I did as he asked and lifted my eyes to the ceiling. "Let's get this over wi—" I clenched my teeth when the needle pierced my skin. A minute later and the pain had numbed enough for the doctor to jab his tweezers inside my leg. Not that I was looking. I could handle a lot of things. Most of them in the heat of battle. This came nowhere close to that.

"Say, doc, what's your name?" I asked over the soft sound of steel grinding against stone.

"Sayad. Sayad Muorari." His spectacles slipped down his nose again.

"I've worked here for the past… oh… maybe seventy years or so."

"Really?" I recalled the size of the building, the carefully cut lawn, the pristine windows that sparkled as if they'd been cleaned that morning. "This place seems a bit large, considering the Gods—and magic—fell out of favor."

It was true. Most Water Temple subsidiaries I'd come across were small and old or huge and so new the scent of paint still clung to the walls.

"Ah, there you are." I assumed Dr. Muorari was talking to the bullet because next there came a slight sucking sound and then the clink of metal on metal. The relief was almost instantaneous and my magic swept toward the injury, healing abilities already at play. The doctor answered my question next. "That will happen when you cater to the largest community of selkies in the world."

The word sounded funny. I rolled it around a few times in my head as I recalled what type of fey that was. I knew they were primarily water-based—oh yes. People of the sea who shed their seal skins so they could walk—albeit painfully—on the earth. Considering his size, I wondered how large he was in animal-form.

"Would you like to see it?"

"You have it here with you?" I gaped. Selkies typically took great care hiding their second skins. Considering it was their most vital organ, it only made sense.

The doctor barked out a rather seal-like laugh. "The bullet, dear. The reason you're in my office?" He gripped my calf and twisted it a few different ways. The morphine had already worn off. "Your wound appears to have healed nicely. Hope you don't mind the scar." He pointed to a pucker the size of an M&M. "That should fade in a few years."

I pulled my leg up on the crinkly paper and traced the circle. "I'd rather not see the bullet. Thanks." Though part of me wondered if he would keep it, maybe frame it to put in the lobby with a placard: 'Water God successfully saved from potentially lethal leg injury here.'

Stranger things had happened.

The doctor set the bullet aside as I rolled down the hem of my jeans and fingered the hole torn in the material. It had grown stiff with dried blood. Good thing they were dark-washed, but still, I'd need to come up with the funds to replace them from somewhere.

"If you don't mind my asking, Ms. Ramone, but what brings you to Durban? Or was it solely medical care you sought?" Dr. Muorari settled back on his padded stool, eyes wide behind his lenses.

I hesitated but figured that since I had a doctor right here, I might as well see if he knew anything. "I'm on a mission to help a friend before a curse kills her sister. For the most part, it looks like any other illness: fever, exhaustion, lack of appetite." I thought of Logan and the incubus from the library. The one I wished I could track down, but had no way of doing so. I hadn't felt that other fey's magic anywhere else I'd gone. "The curse, though, has one unique sign. It creates a black sludge that flows through her veins. It's—"

"Black veins?" the doctor interrupted.

My heart jumped. "Ring a bell?"

"Yes." He hastily stood. "We have an incubus here right now, in fact. Sounds very similar to what you describe. Our resident witch also found evidence of a curse, but hasn't made heads of tales of how to stop it."

"Can I see him?" I'd already hopped off the table, glad my leg could support my weight again. Lachlan stood at my elbow, my bag slung around his shoulder, expression somber.

"Right this way."

Chapter 19

It was definitely the same curse.

I could tell that much without delving into his magic. The poor fey wasn't as far along as Logan, but I could already feel the effects on his magic.

"Bless the blue flame," Lachlan breathed, referencing the eternal fire burning at the entrance of the underworld occasionally credited with miraculous situations. He traced an x across his forehead as if to ward away evil. I felt his gaze fall on me next. "This is what you're trying to stop?"

"Unfortunately, yes." My fingers shook as I wiped a damp washcloth across the fey's forehead. He was burning up, his dark skin feverish through the cloth. He'd already sweated through the new clothing Dr. Muorari told me the nurses had changed him into an hour earlier. I nearly gagged on the cloying scent of sickness radiating from his pores.

His body was losing a fight it was never designed to win.

"He arrived at our doorstep seven days ago," said the doctor at my elbow. His sharp gaze scanned me, missing nothing, "fatigued and feverish. At first, we thought the sun and dehydration had gotten to him. But two days later, he hadn't improved. Then his veins turned black, and we knew we weren't dealing with a run-of-the-mill illness."

I nodded mutely. A week from relatively healthy to incapacitated. A week. Sympathy clenched like a knot in my gut as I brushed damp hair back from the fey's forehead. Even after seeing that affected incubus in Ontario, I'd hoped this curse wasn't spreading quickly. I sucked my lower lip between my teeth and bit down, hopes dashed.

Sensing the shift in my mood, Lachlan held out an arm and escorted the doctor to the door. "Thank you for your help, but your God needs a moment. Alone."

The door closed behind him, and I dropped my head into my hands, massaging my temples. "Thanks. I needed a minute to process all this."

"*I* needed a minute to process this," Lachlan countered. "I heard what you said back home, but I didn't imagine it was like this. This is truly awful."

"I thought your kind weren't fans of daemoni." I wetted the cloth using the tiny sink beside the bed and mopped up the fey's sweat again. I wasn't sure what else I could do.

"I'm not a big fan of generalizations." He paused. "Or stereotypes. Our kinds have their differences, yes, I'll give you that much. But no one deserves this." It was strange seeing him somber, his light eyes more translucent than normal in the dim light of the room. "Would you mind walking me through what happened with your friend? Why you can't do whatever weirdness with your magic and fix him?"

I weighed my options. Did I trust Lachlan? No. But he had proven sticky as a burr and offered flashes of cleverness I'd originally glossed over. He was also observant and, most importantly, he *cared*. I could respect that.

Keeping that in mind, I laid out my experience with Logan. I spoke slowly, methodically, saying the words out loud, as much for Lachlan's benefit as they were for my own. I measured each sentence, weighing its worth. The more I spoke, the more the puzzle spread out before me, and I wondered why I hadn't attempted to rationalize and brainstorm like this earlier.

Probably because I'd been alone.

That truth shamed me.

I recalled the fuzziness of the static, the shriek of the wind, the unyielding scent of decay, the swirling black mass eating the succubus alive, slowly wrenching her beautiful magic from her soul rope by stringy rope. It made me sick thinking about it.

"She's still alive?" Lachlan asked when I finished.

"As far as I know. I talked with her sister a few days ago." I brushed the brand on my shoulder. "She would have contacted me if anything had changed."

Because that would have meant I'd failed. I couldn't imagine the fury Lee would unleash if that came to pass.

Lachlan's chair creaked as he leaned back. "It's a shame you can't cut off the curse's connection to the magic. If it had nothing to latch on to... it would go away."

My fingers clenched in my hair, and I slowly raised my head from my hand. An idea formed, spinning, weaving into shape. "That's it."

The elf cocked his head when I dropped to my knees beside the bed, re-energized, my magic a boiling, roiling mass as it braced for whatever was about to happen, whatever threat I was about to face. "What's *it*?"

The idea was still half-formed, but the more I thought about it, the longer I allowed it to percolate, the clearer it became. "I've been thinking about this all wrong. I thought I needed to go after the source, but what if I can separate the source from the victim?"

"Isn't that what I said?" Lachlan moved to my elbow. "Care to explain what's going on?"

"I should have thought about this sooner." Lost in my own thoughts, I dragged the sheet back from the incubus's chest and splayed my hand flat across his sternum, ignoring the silky feel of veins pulsing beneath my skin. "Lachlan, you're a genius."

"As glad as I am to hear you finally admit my intellectual prowess, I need you to be clearer." He tugged my elbow back, fingers gentle but firm. "I have a feeling you're about to do something totally reckless. And, while I'm in one-hundred percent support of that, I'd like to know what's going on in your head."

I smoothed the frizz in my hair, forcing myself to breathe. Inhale. Exhale. Repeat. The familiar mantra helped me shove some of the crazy aside. "When I tried to heal Logan, I didn't have time to attack the virus. I was just getting an understanding of what I was up against. I convinced myself that because I couldn't help her then, I wouldn't be able to help at all. Not without knowing what I was up against."

Bubbles of adrenaline fizzled in my belly. "But I don't *need* to know what I'm up against. I need to isolate the curse, like you suggested. While it prodded my magic, it didn't go after it. It stayed focused on hers. I think I can use that to help this incubus. I might be able to use my magic to contain his magic and cut the curse away."

The elf ran a hand over his mouth. "You think you can do that?"

"I think it's worth a shot."

"Then what are you waiting for?" His eyes glimmered. "Let go, boss."

I didn't hesitate. I couldn't afford to wait. I didn't want to risk talking myself out of this half-baked plan. I pressed my hands to the incubus's chest and shoved myself into him.

For a moment, there was black. Dense, fathomless black that sucked at my soul as I tumbled from my body. Before the fear could mount, before panic could lap at my heels, a glimmer of golden thread trailed through the nothingness and attached itself to my foot. My soul's connection to my body. A bond so pivotal that if severed, I might never find my way back.

From the darkness a second thread appeared. This one silver and thinner than the gold wire—fishing line to knitting wool. That thread, too, trailed from my foot and extended back into the black.

I'd barely processed the strangeness of it all when I crashed into the ground that formed the incubus's mind. Last time, the impact stunned me into shocked silence. This time, though, I was prepared and more than ready to fight.

The shriek of the wind barely had a chance to howl before it went silent.

What was sound but vibrations through the air?

Flames flared around my feet—it appeared I didn't need my lighter where fire didn't technically exist—chasing away the speckled black and white static. The fire burned a path forward through the mist, a path bracketed by flames flickering twice as high as my head.

It sensed what I could not.

The curse.

The dark, swirling mass at the end of the road and the shimmering, white runes carved in stone at the dead end.

I didn't know where the incubus was, where he'd tucked his soul away, but it had to be here somewhere. My best bet was the curse had sucked him into its depths like it had with Logan.

As I marched down the path, careful to keep my eyes forward, my grasp on my magic fluctuated. Sometimes it was Air that flickered. Other times my Fire strained. Each time it happened, I buckled down, trusting my magic to guide me to the curse and for those twin trails to return me safely home.

I had this. I could stop this. I *would* stop this.

When I reached the end of the road, I hung back from touching the runes, taking stock of what I was up against. The curse itself was chaos. More horrible than I remembered it. A tornado of shadow and oil, spinning tall as it cradled the soul of the incubus at the top. Every so often, a piece of the tornado would split away, a slender arm that reached for the fey's magic and sliced off a chunk. The incubus flinched at each snip, every nip.

"Enough."

I felt the curse notice me, its writhing body flickering as if it were a living, breathing thing. Maybe it was.

"It's time for you to go." I set my stance, feet shoulder-width apart, arms lax at my side. Fire wrapped in a semi-circle around me, Air encircled me, and Water hummed beneath my skin. "I'm more than happy to show you out."

It didn't wait, the swirling, crashing magic smashed against mine with the might of a speeding freight train. My panes of Air cracked and buckled, shoving me a closer to the roaring flames at my back, but they held.

"Is that all you got?" I screamed at the runes at the base of the curse, runes that reminded me of markings that used to glow like white lightning on the forehead of my most hated foe. I gritted my teeth, doubling my resolve. "You think you can take me down that easily?"

Black magic drew away from the incubus, dropping him to the ground as it approached me, prowling like a roaring, swirling panther. It swatted at the flames, clawed at the ribbons of air that lashed at its hide, but to no avail. I kept one eye on the soul of the fey, and only once I was sure the curse had abandoned him, deserting his magic for a much mightier feast, did I strike.

Blue ribbons of cleansing Water snapped out, arcing high overhead, swirling around and around. Faster and faster. "Go."

The curse reared, realizing too late my intentions. Thousands of blue threads cut off its path back to the fey, instead driving it closer to the runes. The curse couldn't push past the raw ability that Water had to heal, not without getting sucked inside, so it retreated. I redoubled my effort, pushing and looping and ensnaring the black mass in a ball. Around and around it went until a sphere formed.

My back ached, my head pounded. But I wasn't done, yet.

Slowly, painstakingly, I drew a ring of flames around a sphere of blue. I imagined the curse shrieking with pain as I forced it back, forced it into a tighter, smaller ball. Water and Fire were both capable of cleansing. If I couldn't heal something, sometimes the best thing to do was burn it out.

My skin felt raw, my throat dry, but I gritted my teeth and buckled down against the pain. Two-thirds of the way there.

Already sensing what I required of it, fine wisps of Air slipped around the twin spheres of pulsing light, locking the magic up tight. I clenched my fingers, squeezing my magic tighter around the curse.

Suffocating it.

Binding it.

Smaller and smaller, the ball folded in on itself. I'd known it. Deep down, I'd known it. The curse was tied to the daemoni magic. It didn't know what to do when faced with mine. It had nowhere to go. And soon—soon it would be nothing at all.

Across from me, beyond the mass of magic that shimmered brighter than the surface of the sun, a silhouette rose from the ground. It raised first one arm, then the other.

Triumph took flight inside me. The incubus was still alive and very much free.

I pressed down again, muscles straining, every ion of my soul shrieking with pain, and, with one final thought, I crushed the curse in a burst of white light that left afterimages flickering behind my lids.

I couldn't feel the curse any more.

Exhausted and drained beyond belief, I released my hold on my magic and allowed it to fill me once more. It throbbed, a beating pulse of success humming in my veins. We'd done it. We'd cut the curse from its source.

And it had died.

I pressed my index and middle finger to the top of my hairline and dragged them down to my brows. I didn't understand why. I didn't know what it meant or where I might have learned it, but it felt right. The gesture seemed necessary.

With that final thought, I turned on my heel and followed those twin strands of gold and silver back into the black abyss that marked the realm where lost souls lingered. Followed them back to my body where the gold thread glimmered—and the silver thread that connected to Lachlan shone.

Of course.

He had some of my Air magic in him.

We were connected until that magic faded.

When I opened my eyes, I found myself draped over the body of the incubus. While still sticky with sweat, he no longer reeked of death and rot, no longer burned with a foreign fever.

Lachlan leaned close, his hand between my shoulder blades. "Welcome back."

I grinned up at the relief on his face. I probably looked delirious or drunk or both. Beyond the incubus hovered the doctor, his fingers trembling along his hairline, much like mine had earlier. My mouth went dry. Instead of dragging them down his forehead like I'd done, he instead brought his fingers to his lips, eyes lowering in reverence.

What was happening here?

A powerful hand stroked firm lines down my back and I leaned into the touch, willingly allowing the elf to ease the tension coursing through me.

"He's looking much better," Lachlan rumbled. "His veins aren't black anymore. Whatever you did, boss, it worked."

"I think he'll be ok," I whispered, too confused and relieved to process much more in that moment. "He's back in this fight."

"And I think it's time to get you a bed."

"Hmm?" I had a feeling it was going to hurt when I finally recuperated my magic, but for now, it was nice to fall back in the haze that was slumber. "Make sure the doctor doesn't do anything weird to me."

"Does this mean you trust me?" Lachlan's arm hooked behind my back.

"Not in the least." I squinted up into his lavender gaze. "But we do make a good team, don't we?"

Chapter 20

Juice dribbled down my chin and I bit back a groan as I sank my teeth into the flesh of the apple again, cleaning it to the core. It had been at least a week since I'd eaten this well. Lachlan had won me over with his homemade granola bar concoctions—complete with something he called flax seed and a mixture of dried or strangely petrified fruit I'd learned to accept without comment—but there was no replacement for fresh fruit.

As if picking up on my inner musings, Lachlan snagged a pair of bananas from a bowl in the center of our table and dropped them on my plate without looking up from his book. I eyed him carefully, wondering what seemed different about him. Since when did he have a Houston Astros hat?

"You need the protein," the elf said.

I considered putting the food back to annoy him, but shrugged and peeled one of the yellow fruits from the base. I'd slept for two days straight after forcing the curse from the incubus. Two very long days that Lachlan told me were quite eventful… for those among the living.

For starters, the incubus opened his eyes about ten hours after my head hit the pillow. He started drinking broth two hours after that. Lachlan relayed that had worked the nurses and doctors at the temple into a frenzy.

I stopped shoving chunks of banana in my mouth and glanced

around Lachlan's shoulder at the large reception desk where Zoe was hard at work—pretending like she wasn't watching me from the corner of her eye. It was unnerving being around so many people who worshiped the ground I walked upon. I'd only agreed to come down and eat in the main area because Dr. Muorari convinced me it would be good for people to see me doing normal things—especially at one of my affiliated temples.

To his credit, while I was the subject of many stares, few approached.

I scrubbed at my eyes, wondering if there was time for another nap.

"Don't you dare think about it." Lachlan turned a page in his book. Something about the history of dragon hunting. "If anyone deserves their beauty rest, it's me."

"Whatever weird mental connection you seem to have formed with me… ends now." I jabbed my napkin, careful to keep my voice low. Humans and fey alike filled every table of the abundant dining room, and I was acutely aware that all eyes—and ears—were on me. "It's weird and creepy, and I need to have my secrets."

"Oh, you have your secrets," the elf muttered. He closed his book. The temple had provided us with new clothing, and he'd opted for a long-sleeve marigold shirt that brought out his eyes and fuchsia skinny jeans—which looked good on no one. "And I can't read your mind. Let's get that much straight. But you try living among the same few dozen people for about a hundred years and tell me you don't learn every nuance of every facial feature in the world."

"You weren't even looking at me."

"Maybe I have a third eye."

"Whatever you do, keep its location to yourself," I mumbled. Why wasn't there bacon? I swore I'd ordered bacon when we'd sat down. And eggs. What kind of breakfast didn't feature bacon or eggs? Our server had also mysteriously vanished.

"Speaking of secrets—you owe me a story about that rune on your face." Lachlan propped his chin on the back of his knuckles. "I told you a story. You owe me."

"Yeah. Cuz that's going to happen in a room full of *overly attentive patrons*." I raised my voice for the last few words. The clatter of forks hitting plates and glasses clinking quickly followed. I was about to say more when my phone buzzed at my elbow. I snatched it up to scan the screen.

"Did your friend finally get back to you?" Lachlan had confiscated my phone until I'd fully woken up. The first fey I'd texted was Lee an hour ago.

"Yep."

"And is our next destination N—" he grinned gainfully and winked at a fey with straight hair the same shade of silver of mine— "wherever she is located?"

He'd been pulling these little stunts all morning, almost dropping little hints to our awed onlookers, only to pull back at the last minute. My eyelid twitched. We needed to get out of here.

"Looks that way." I clicked off the phone and shoved it into my pocket. "She's wondering why we aren't on a plane already."

Seeing as the incubus was recovering, I was eager to help Logan and put her sister's mind at ease. I ran my teeth over my thumbnail. What I was doing wasn't a solution to the curse by a long-shot, but it bought me time while I figured out the greater problem.

"So we're leaving? You don't want to stick around? Bask in the glory of your stardom?"

I couldn't get a read on his tone. Lachlan, though a carefree sort, didn't strike me as someone who craved the spotlight. If he was telling the truth, and he assured me he *always* told the truth, then he was only hanging out with me because of the danger I seemingly entrenched myself in on a daily basis.

And the thrill of my magic.

Not that he'd be getting another jolt of it anytime soon. He was strong, so strong that he'd maintained his hold over Air for about a day. A day, he later informed me, he would have spent much differently had he not been standing watch over my unconscious form.

"It's a good thing you packed our stuff already." I scrubbed my hands down the front of my stiff, dark-washed jeans that I badly needed to break in. Unlike the elf, I'd opted for attire that allowed me to fade into the crowd. "I'll make some calls on the way to the airport. See what deals on flights we can score. The temple gave us some of the offerings, but we can't blow it all at once."

Leaving now also came with the added bonus of leaving before one of my *friends* caught up with me. There was no way they hadn't heard about this latest stop.

"I still don't understand why you don't confront whoever it is you're running from." Lachlan motioned to the waiter who'd finally reappeared. Oh good, maybe there was still time for bacon. "It's not like you lack the ability, or raw power, to tell them to shove off and have them seriously consider ignoring you."

I nearly choked on my orange juice. Yeah. Try telling that to Ryder. He was the last being on earth who would accept me telling him to shove off. Ryder was more likely to pin me against a wall, hoist me up, and kiss me so senseless I couldn't remember what words were, than listen to me tell him I neither needed nor wanted him.

Lachlan's eyes flicked over my shoulder and he casually set his mug on my empty plate, brushing both to the side. "We've got company, boss."

Company that most definitely wasn't our human server.

I squared my shoulders, sensing the signatures of those approaching.

"Ms. Ramone, I'm pleased to see you've made a full recovery." I turned to look up at Zadid, the head priest of this particular temple, as he stepped up to our table, hands carefully folded behind his back.

"What you accomplished, the aid you rendered, is nothing short of miraculous."

I couldn't pinpoint exactly what I didn't like about Zadid, though he looked a bit like Geoffrey with his shaved head and dark eyes, but I didn't. My response was colder than it should have been because of it. "How is Modi, anyway? I haven't had a chance to check in on him."

"He's well." Zadid tipped his head in thanks. I imagined it wouldn't have been good business having someone die in a temple known for healing. "He's eating again. Nothing solid, but some yogurt and mashed banana. His magic is also returning. More slowly than I think he'd prefer, but what can you do?"

I bridged my hands on the table. "That's good. I'd like to be kept abreast of his recovery. It will help me in my search for an actual solution for the curse."

Zadid's face darkened. "Of course. His recovery is why I'm stopping to see you today, and not for the obvious reasons."

"Something else we can help with?" Lachlan asked. I wanted to kick him. The last thing I wanted was to be tied to this place for a minute longer than I had to be.

"I doubt there's a shortage of situations for which your assistance is required," Zadid said, his tone steady. Maybe that's why I didn't like him. I preferred my beings more emotive. "And while I'm sure we could put you to work, a more pressing request passed across my desk this morning."

He produced a letter from the wide folds of his sleeves, one stamped with an actual wax seal. I didn't know those existed anymore. Lachlan's brow lifted as I smoothed the bold slashes of cursive that composed the letterhead. I glanced up at the sprite. "I don't understand."

Zadid folded his hands, head gleaming under the lights. "Word of what you accomplished here has reached certain… circles. I have the honor of informing you the Prince of Sin himself has requested your assistance resolving similar matters closer to his home."

Lachlan rubbed his palms together, a wicked smile touching his lips. That couldn't spell anything good.

"Should I know who that is?" I asked.

"Prince Ridley Caron, ruler of the incubi and succubi, would like to see you immediately."

Chapter 21

The metal spire rose high overhead, spearing the heavens. It was both a steely statement and a gaudy representation of reality. I rolled my eyes at the couple snapping selfies in front of the replica of the Eiffel Tower before loosening the scarves around my neck and rushing to catch up with the sweep of Lachlan's new, *maroon* trench coat.

He passed me a bright purple, thirty-two-ounce bottle of water, which I greedily sucked down. "Thanks."

"Dehydrated?" he asked. "And don't lie to me."

I rubbed the beanie Lachlan had plopped on my head, proclaiming it an adequate disguise at the airport. "My throat is still dry, and we'll need to pick up a gallon or two of moisturizer. Otherwise, I don't feel much stranger than normal."

The elf nodded, accepting my words as truth. And they were. Las Vegas, at least the flashy Strip part of it, anyway, was nothing like the desert. I was well aware of the differences because a few months ago I'd suffered immensely while trekking across Egypt to find the God of Earth.

My pace slowed as I watched the sea of faces, not sure what I was looking for. Some were gleeful, others glum, and there weren't as many fey here as I'd expected. Certainly not as many as I'd encountered in the magical hotspot of New Orleans.

We had stopped in The Big Easy before continuing on to the West Coast—and I'd billed this *Mr. Caron* for the flights. He thought he could demand my time? He could pay for it. I owed it to myself and to Lee to help her sister before I wined and dined with some high-roller.

After delving deep into Logan's mind and suffocating the curse that was killing her, I'd rested for another two days. Only when I was positive the succubus was on the road to recovery did I give Lachlan the go-ahead to leave the city. Not that he was complaining. He'd pestered me so badly I'd blasted him with Fire magic to shut him up, and he spent the better part of twenty-four hours mastering the ability.

I blinked, realizing I'd stopped and was staring at my reflection in the white glare of a window featuring touristy items. I so rarely stopped to look at myself anymore. After Geneva, after *Rome,* I'd doubted the kind of person I was meant to be. I wasn't sure if I liked her. But now I could meet my own gaze without flinching, without my eyes dancing across every other surface before finally meeting their double.

This girl looking back at me wasn't the same girl who'd fallen off a trawler in the middle of the North Sea. She wasn't the same one who'd blown up a helicopter and flooded a city block to save her friends. Not the same one who'd literally created a lake from nothing to destroy any army. Not the one who'd buckled down deep and found something hidden inside herself that gave her power over one of the most mythical beings on earth.

Physically, I had changed, too. My face was narrower, my jawline firmer, my eyes harder with the realities they'd faced. I'd regained some of the muscle mass I'd lost in the months since ending my swimming career rather abruptly, and I'd picked up a plethora of scars.

The changes were also apparent in my confidence and in the

compassion I relayed in my actions. I was realizing my mission, living it. I had a better grasp on the world and what was both demanded of me and what I demanded from it.

I was starting to understand the woman I was meant to be. She was not the headstrong teenager shoved into the shoes of a reluctant superhero.

"I never took you for a sequin girl, but if you really want that shirt that says 'I heart LV' in red *and* pink, I'll steal it for you," Lachlan drawled. I attempted to throw an elbow into his solar plexus, but he dodged and dipped so his lips hovered close to my ear. "Or maybe something with feathers is more your drift."

"Can you be serious for once?" I grumbled.

"Pretty sure you are packing more than enough seriousness for the both of us." The elf popped his collar in such a way that, when combined with the cowboy hat he'd snatched from a mannequin at the airport, made him look utterly ridiculous. "I'd prefer you keep my share while you're at it."

I shouldered my way back onto the crowded sidewalk. "If one of us didn't focus, then we'd be in the middle of Berlin right now, talking the police out of arresting you for your kleptomania."

"I prefer to call it temporary borrowing." He snatched a pink snapback dangling from a girl's backpack and traded it for his cowboy hat, which he promptly dropped on a bench. "And I'd rather do that than call myself Narcissus any day."

"What are you talking about?"

"Are you not the God who stopped to admire her reflection for five solid minutes?" Lachlan flashed a sunny grin at a teen with hair clips of daisies strewn throughout her updo. "It's ok. Don't worry about it. I'm glad you're picking up new habits. Face it, boss, I'm rubbing off on you in all the best ways."

"Add that to the list of things I never want you to say to me ever again."

The elf chuckled and threw his arm around my shoulders, drawing me out of the path of a scowling, bearded man large enough to heft a forklift without breaking a sweat. Despite the long flight and the grit of pollution and dirt lingering in the air, Lachlan still managed to smell cool and refreshing: like falling rain laced with a tang of lime.

"See how I saved your life? Prevented you from becoming a pancake on the ground?" he asked. "This is *me* being part of the *team*. And *you* never have to worry about reciprocating. Unlike most of my people," he gestured at my arms, "I don't fixate on balancing my sheet of favors."

Up ahead, I glimpsed the jets of water I'd been searching for. A mixture of eagerness and foreboding blended unpleasantly in my gut. "Do you think we'll find more cursed daemoni here?"

"If I were a betting fey, and rest assured, I most definitely am, I'm dropping all my money on red—Yes." Lachlan squeezed my shoulder before handing over another bottle of water. "I expect we'll find many of them, in fact."

"You gamble?" Why did that catch me by surprise?

He took a swig from a third bottle—which definitely did not smell like water—and threw his arms in the air. "Adrenaline junkie, remember? Doesn't matter what it is: petty theft, gambling, *cliff diving*." He shot me a meaningful look, at which I shook my head. "I'm all in. Life is about the journey, not the end."

"You should get that screen-printed on one of your hats." The full fountain was coming into view. It called to me like a baseball field to a pitcher. "Are you ever going to tell me what was up with you when you heard the prince wanted to see me?"

After his initial gleeful reaction, the elf's mood had slipped into something more pensive. He'd refused to talk about it, but I figured I'd give it one more shot before tumbling into the lion's den.

"Another story for another time," he murmured. "Unless you're willing to tell me more about this Ryder bloke who's got you hopping from continent to continent."

I'd accidentally let the incubus's name slip on the airplane, and Lachlan, naturally, fixated on it like he did all things related to my personal life. I sealed my lips and drew us to a stop beside the railing keeping the crowds back from the fountains, ignoring the bright lights of the hotel behind it. I was loath to admit it, but I missed Ryder. I actually missed him. Much more than I'd thought I would. Part of me had hoped leaving him behind would stifle the strange craving I felt for him, curtail the way I was drawn to him.

But it hadn't.

And it wasn't only him.

I missed Finn's quiet moodiness and Joseph's bookish humor. I could use a dose of Rose's cocky attitude and Pyra's strange collection of apt quotes from dead philosophers. I even missed the mystery that was Oron and his veiled upbringing. They were my friends, people I counted on. And someday soon I'd be able to face them again.

"Maybe another time," I parroted.

"That's what I thought."

I turned to watch the display and crossed my arms on top of the railing, propping my chin on my gloved knuckles, enjoying the feel of the mist coating my skin.

Was it deliberate? The prince calling us to The Bellagio? Of all the casinos and all the hotels on the Strip, he called us to the one with an obvious water feature out front?

I glanced at my phone. We had a few minutes to wait.

The sound of the crowds faded, and I settled in, quietly content watching the arcs of spray.

- - -

I barely glimpsed flashing lights, a jangle of cheers and electronic beeps, before an incubus dressed straight from *Men in Black* with hair dark as nightmares stopped Lachlan and me as we crossed the threshold of the casino. He didn't touch us or unleash his magic. His mere presence was enough to stop us mid-stride.

"Welcome to the Bellagio, Ms. Ramone. You may call me Rogue. I'm Mr. Caron's personal assistant." The incubus dipped his head, the rest of him remaining stoically immovable. He didn't acknowledge the elf, and it was impossible to see his eyes beyond the extreme tint on his rounded Carreras. My palms prickled. Something about him felt familiar. "Mr. Caron sends his regards."

I scanned the rows upon rows of machines, the tables around which humans and fey alike congregated, smiles sharp and eyes bright as they handled an array of cards and dice and tiny balls. "If now isn't a good time, we can always come back," I said. I was basically broke, but maybe if I traded a favor, I could try my hand at one of those tables. My old best friend Kaz and I used to play poker to pass the time on our swim tour.

"That won't be necessary, Ma'am." Rogue shifted, his wide shoulders blocking my view of the casino floor. I frowned. "Mr. Caron has arranged a room for you while he wraps up his business."

I weighed the sound of the fey's voice, measured the vibrations in it. He wasn't lying, but he wasn't telling the whole truth either. I offered a tight smile and folded my hands. "By all means."

"If you'd follow me." With a sharp nod, two more incubi stepped behind us, effectively boxing us in as Rogue escorted us around the edge of the room to a row of elevator doors, specifically one guarded by a pair of dudes in slick suits and matching shades. It was that elevator that Rogue approached. Its doors rolled open without the incubus pushing a button or waving his hand.

Lachlan hummed a soft tune I vaguely recognized as we stepped inside the small, mirrored room. The doors closed at the backs of the other two guards. I scratched my arm through my jacket. I didn't like the feeling of being herded.

"How did you do that?" I asked once the elevator lifted, the movement seamless.

"It's keyed to magical signatures." Rogue braced his hands on the flat rail circling the cage, his legs crossed at the ankles.

"How does that work?" Lachlan pressed his thumb to the gleaming glass, then a few more fingers, and, with a cheeky grin, he smudged the prints. The muted light radiating from behind the glass panels softened the expression. "Signatures aren't exactly like fingerprints. In many cases, they're similar, differing only in types of fey, maybe a little about strength, but not by much."

I drummed my fingers on my sleeve, right over an oath with a nautical compass on the point of my elbow, remembering the wand the troll had presented back at Iridescence. I thought it was capable of more than what Lachlan described. I also knew Finn's magic felt different from Ryder's, and Ryder's magic had always felt different from the magic of other daemoni I'd encountered. There had to be more differences between magics than simply type.

"That may be true for lesser fey." Rogue's tone was heavy with implication. I bristled in defense of my… friend. "However, that's hardly a universal truth, Mr. McAvoy."

How did he know Lachlan? I hadn't mentioned my companion when I'd responded to the message demanding my presence. Few knew I had a companion these days. I'd gone solo for months. Maybe someone at the hotel had blabbed? I was dealing with royalty, I supposed.

"Magical signatures are exactly like fingerprints, dental records, and snowflakes. Both easily acquired and measured." The incubus lifted his chin, appearing to look down his nose at the elf. "Though I suppose technology has never been a strong suit of the elves, considering you keep yourselves rooted in the history of magic rather than progressing with it."

"There is a certain value to history, don't you think?" Lachlan smeared more fingerprints across the wall before propping his shoulder against it, uncaring of the silent guards at his back. "Without understanding the past, however will you decide how to venture forward?"

Rogue ran his thumb over the curves of his nails. "There's a difference between knowing the past and being consumed by it."

Tension practically snapped between the two fey, and I stepped between them before whatever was happening reached its apex. "Were you able to use our signatures to identify us so quickly on the main floor?"

Rogue wet his lips with the tip of his tongue and raised his shades, revealing eyes the exact color of a blood orange: dark red along the rim, lightening to yellow-orange in the middle. Their shape, and the predatory gleam in their depths, tugged at me. Why did he seem so familiar? Should I know him from somewhere?

"Ms. Ramone, I can assure you that even with that flimsy excuse for a hat, you're by far one of the most recognizable beings on the planet. None of that has anything to do with your signature."

I sucked my lower lip into my mouth. I hadn't expected the warmth of his comment to hit me, to trickle down my spine like honey. Rogue smelled like nutmeg and coffee, and found myself leaning closer to the mysterious fey, head lilting to the side as I snatched at the elusive piece of information preventing me from understanding what drew me to him.

Before I made a total fool of myself, the elevator slid to a stop and the doors opened. Rogue lowered his glasses with a knowing grin, and his arm brushed my shoulder as he followed the two guards out into the hall. Lachlan snagged my elbow and gave it a shake as he drew me against his side. "Head in the game, boss. Don't let his umbra affect you."

I didn't know what that meant, but I didn't dare ask as we followed the incubi down a hallway lined with frosted glass windows. I assumed we were on an administrative floor, though I couldn't hear anything behind the closed doors.

Rogue stopped at the end of the hall and opened a door, ushering me through first. "Please make yourselves comfortable. Should you require anything, please ask Bryce or Lux, here. They'll know how to get a hold of me."

I stepped into the room and turned around, fingers hooked in the straps of my bag. "Hey, Rogue, one more question." He regarded me silently, carefully. "Are you leaving them here to keep us from leaving… or to protect us from something?"

A slow, sinuous smirk slid across his lips. "Yes."

And he closed the door.

"What do you think he meant by that?" I tossed my bag into one of the dozen chairs ringing a long, glass table.

"Which bit?" Lachlan dropped into swiveling seat beside my stuff and propped his grimy boots on the sparkling surface of the table. Flecks of dirt and grass sprinkled down. "He would have been better off with a name like Cryptic."

"All of it." I huffed and circled the room. The incubus had escorted us to a corner office with two walls of windows overlooking the hubbub below. I ripped off my beanie and tossed it behind me as I stared down at the chaos. Beyond the tall buildings and spinning array of lights, the glimmer of sand stretched far into the horizon.

"What was that?" I spun to face the elf who had unearthed a granola bar from the depths of his coat. I recognized it as my least favorite kind with raisins and coconut. "You and him. What was that?"

Lachlan shoved half the bar into his mouth and chewed. "Not everything is your business."

"No. Something was going on between you two. What am I missing here?"

"Knock it off, Zara," Lachlan snapped. I jerked back, gripping the back of the chair I stood behind. It was the first time he'd ever lashed out at me, the first time he'd used my actual *name*, and one of the few times I'd caught a glimmer of something very dark behind his jovial façade. "You don't need to know everything all the time."

Tension hummed between us. If he still had a sliver of my fire, I imagined he would have erected a roaring wall of flame between us. I scanned the other two walls of clouded glass, wondering if we were being watched inside this aquarium. Wondering who might be trying to hear inside this room despite my soundproof barriers of Air.

I pulled out the chair and slipped into it, perched at the edge of the seat. I sensed the delicacy of whatever tenuous thread existed between us. My response here might give me the out I so desperately thought I'd wanted, but I found myself saddened by the idea of breaking our bond.

"Listen." I smoothed a thumb down the soft skin on the underside of my forearm, mentally counting the black oaths emblazoned upon it. "The rune on my face, it's not nothing. It's also not something I got on a whim or to rebel. I got it for protection."

"For yourself?"

"For the world."

The elf picked up the granola bar he'd dropped to the table and took a small bite.

"An ancient God lives inside my head. The first God of Water, one of the Originals." Why were these words so easy to say? Why had I feared them so much until now? "She's very powerful and extremely manipulative. Lately, she's become too much for me to handle on my own. As my abilities grow, her control over me expands, too. So, I found a witch who could help me lock her away."

I tapped the table with a tattered nail. "I worry that if she isn't contained, she'll overcome me, and I don't know what she intends to do once she gets my magic."

I dropped my head to the table, simultaneously relieved and exhausted. I could only imagine what the elf was thinking; how insane I sounded. Two souls living in one body. How often could something like that possibly come up in conversation?

I opened eyes I hadn't remembered closing when a weight dropped in front of my nose. A granola bar. One with prunes and orange zest and a sprinkling of raw honey. My stomach growled. My favorite. The knot that had formed in my chest relaxed. I eyed the fey and then his gift.

"You should eat."

I straightened. Seriously? That was it? "That's all you have to say?"

"Seems straightforward enough." Lachlan kicked back in his chair again, boots tapping a beat on the lip of the table. "You had a problem. You solved it. From what I know of you, I'd expect nothing less."

I tore off a piece of the bar and popped it in my mouth, savoring the citrus on my tongue. "But you don't have questions? No exclamations of how impossible it all sounds?"

He flipped his hat backward. The pink clashed horribly with his hair. "Boss, after two thousand years, magic is back. The Order was annihilated. We could all die from a nuclear blast tomorrow. You truly think living with a second soul inside of you is the craziest thing to happen in the past year?" Lachlan wagged his finger. "Gods are weird. They've always been weird. They do things the rest of us can only dream of doing. You arguing with an ancient soul of another ancient God is par for the course."

I didn't know what to think. Couldn't remember how to chew. It was fortunate breathing was automatic, or else I may have ceased doing that, too.

He didn't care.

My biggest secret in the world and Lachlan acted like... it was merely another fact.

Who was this guy?

"How long do you think this prince will keep us waiting?" Lachlan removed his needles from his coat sleeves and held them up to the light.

Just like that, I could move again, think again. I chewed some more. If he could act like everything was cool, if the end of the world wasn't potentially drawing down around us, then I could, too.

"Are we betting here?" I asked.

"We are in a casino, aren't we?"

"Alright." I turned out my pockets, rooting through the pieces of gum and loose change. "Ten cents has it over half an hour."

Lachlan whistled through his teeth and pushed his hands in his own pockets. He, too, produced a dime. "You're on."

And so we waited.

Chapter 22

To my quiet fury, I won our bet.

My rage simmered for a good hour as I paced from my chair to the bank of windows and back again. I'd asked to use the restroom earlier, but an opportunity to explore never presented itself when the burlier of our guards insisted on escorting me down the hall.

The bathroom matched the rest of the floor with its clean lines and frosted glass. My boots squeaked over the white tiles as I approached the mirror and pretended to freshen up. No trash in the receptacle or soap scum in the sink. The vents didn't hum as they moved air through the ducts. Everything was ridiculously spotless and orderly right down to the pine needle reed diffuser perched on a corner of the vanity.

When it became clear I wouldn't find anything of interest, I exited. The guard walked me back to the conference room.

Another freaking conference room.

I snorted and Lachlan opened one bleary eye. Shortly after losing his inadvisable bet, he'd pushed five chairs together and fell asleep on them like an awkward cot. Though, before he'd passed out completely, he'd warned me against blasting out any windows or setting any fires. His faith in my emotional control was incredible.

"What?" he asked.

"Well. It's a conference room."

He pressed the backs of his hands to his eyes and blew out a long breath, a sound I now recognized as one he reserved for handling my most precarious of rants. "And?"

"And you have no idea how long I've evaded being trapped in one of these again."

He dropped his head back on his pillowed arms. "I care... why?"

I hopped up on the table beside him, dangling my boots near his nose. "I don't like conference rooms. So much time spent in one place, so little productivity achieved. It's almost like they're designed..." I trailed off, rubbing at a sudden ache in my chest. Was that music? I jerked my eyes to the windows, then the door.

"Boss?"

I slid off the table jerkily, eyes closed and ears alert, trying to recapture the mournful violin I'd sworn I'd heard. A dark vibration swelled within me, massaging sore muscles and heating my chilled skin. I leaned into the sensation, dismissing the prickles in my palms and shushing the concern babbling in the back of my mind. The scent of dried lavender tickled my nose and I moaned, my magic wafting out of me, strands slipping through the cracks in the windows and under the door in response to my unasked question.

Another low rumble, the bass tone thumping in my chest, matched the pounding of my heart. I was wrong. It was more than one violin; it was an entire symphony.

My spine arched as the sensual pulse of the beat branched through me, caressing me. It eased the ache that had buried itself deep, twining around my spine. The colorful threads of my magic responded to the touch. Fire purred as it brushed against the soft, smoky folds of this other magical source. It reacted elusively, first teasing the fiery mass of red, then sashaying through the blue of my Water before mingling with the lightness of Air.

CHAPTER 22

The scent of lavender strengthened as I stumbled toward the door, not sure where my legs were leading me, but needing to go, *needing* to find the source of this wonderful bliss.

I heard my name, like the last echo in an empty chamber, but before I could search for the source of the sound, another vibration gripped me, shivered up each limb, and pinned me down. I was vaguely aware of my physical body collapsing, tumbling to the ground.

Inside, I felt so good. I'd never felt so… *alive.*

I shivered at another quiet caress. My neck arched as I caved to it, needing more. Whatever it wanted, however I could get it, I'd do it.

That's it, little God. Tell me your secrets, the magic seemed to whisper.

I knew this place, this dark spot in my mind. Just like I recognized the red metal door with a dented center and melted frame ringed with runes.

What's this... the other magic murmured.

No. We shouldn't be here.

We definitely shouldn't be leaning against the wall, rubbing at the marker in the upper left corner, smearing it across the side. From behind the door someone screamed, a sound so filled with fury I stumbled back.

The vibrations that had felt so wonderful before now crashed against me like the dark waves of the ocean amid a storm. Another touch, one meant to caress, felt like a slap, and flames roared up, blistering my veins as it fought against this foreign power that I now realized had lulled me in and sucked me under.

The lavender turned to ash on my tongue as I reclaimed control, a tidal wave at my back and a trio of tornados at my front as I forced the other magic back. The broken hallway of my mind, the door that carefully concealed an ancient, horrible power, melted away.

I'd never felt so violated.

Whoever was behind this was would *pay.*

"Zara—" It was Lachlan. Lachlan who'd called out to me. Lachlan who'd caught me when I fell.

Lachlan who I shoved away now as I scrambled upright, my skin smoking as acid rain dripped from the ceiling. I shielded him from its burn.

"Enough." I wrenched the door open and unleashed a whirlwind so powerful it launched our guards down the hallway where they smashed through a wall. I moved like light, maybe morphed into a beam myself, because in a blink I stood over them, hands at their throats, squeezing as they writhed while I ripped away their oxygen.

"Tell me what is going on here," I screamed. Glass windows splintered as the hallway shook. From behind closed doors, porcelain shattered and water sprayed as I relinquished control of my abilities. The flood at my feet sucked at my skin, letting me know it was here, it was close, and like the fire roaring through the overhead tiles, it was angry.

One incubus choked, his face purpling as he gagged. My fist hardened. "I want answers." He shook his head, gagging. Too bad. "If you don't have them, then I don't need you."

Without waiting for more, I flung him to the ground, pinning him beneath the steadily rising water with one foot before turning to his companion. The incubus was clawing at his neck, skin riddled with broken capillaries as his purple tongue flailed wildly. He twisted in my grip, trying to get free, but it was no good.

I was beyond caring.

For him, I had a special kind of pain. A horror that would make him pray for the underworld.

His eyes popped wide as I reached *inside* him and pressed *down*, his organs straining, bones bowing as I—

"You've proven your point, Ms. Ramone." I stilled. The man beneath me sucked in a breath so shrill it was nearly a scream. "If you'd please, release my man."

Slowly, oh so painfully slowly, I lifted my head. My braid slipped over my shoulder, limp from the rain that I halted with a razor slash of my hand. Standing at the end of the hallway were two shadows of men in dark suits wearing darker expressions. "Rogue."

The incubus bowed in recognition, his acknowledgment somehow mocking. "Ma'am. Release him, would you please?"

I barely heard him. The guard in my grasp screamed as my grip tightened around his arm, bending it back at an angle that promised to break it. I fixed my attention on the figure that stood beside Rogue. The being who stood a head taller than the crafty incubus, the one I realized was the source of that infuriating magic.

Rogue was right.

Signatures were exactly like fingerprints, and his were smudged all over my body.

It was *his* magic that had ripped away my defenses. *His* magic that had violated my personal space, my very mind. *He* who had ripped away my very being and nearly succeeded in wrenching secrets from my all-too-willing lips.

At my back, I sensed Lachlan raise TruthTeller. I glanced over my shoulder as he aimed, face steely. He nodded first at me, then at the creatures down the hall.

With a snarl, I tore my magic from the guard, ruthlessly crushing the guilt that bloomed at the sight of black blood on his lips, and dropped him. His head cracked on the floor. Rogue winced. At least he was still breathing. The floodwaters receded, exposing the other fey, who sucked in a horrible gasp of air and coughed violently as he hacked up the water he'd inhaled.

I rose to my full height, one fist wrapped in fire, the other encased in sparkling ice, and addressed the fey whose face I couldn't make out. The one built like a puma and pulled the shadows around him like old friends.

"I take it you're Ridley. The Prince of Sin. The one who called me all the way out here only to *screw* with me." Lightning flickered from my fingertips, filling the air with the tang of ozone.

I'd known Ryder had secrets.

I'd known there were things daemoni could do that I had no idea about.

But never in my life, even with Kaleal privy to my every thought, never had I felt so immensely violated.

I marched down the hall, overhead lights bursting, raining down glass as I passed beneath them, trusting Lachlan to have my back. The incubi held their ground. Rogue's eyes narrowed, but I refused to look at him, my attention only for the man he served. The man whose face I still couldn't see. Why wouldn't he show himself?

"You're the bastard who snuck into my head, invaded my thoughts, nearly stripped me senseless. That doesn't make you powerful. That makes you a—"

"But you broke free, didn't you?" The fey's low, shy voice broke through my rage in a way yelling and fighting never would have.

"What?"

"You realized what was happening and you forced me out." The incubus inclined his head so it caught the light cast by one remaining bulb, revealing a long face, a slender nose, and chilled amber eyes. "Not only did you force me out, but you rallied in spectacular fashion. Your magic returned to your control as if you'd never lost it."

"No wonder fey hate your kind." I spat at his feet. "That kind of violation? For a test? You're despicable."

Rogue stepped between me and the prince. My mind spun as I glanced between the two, noting the similarities of their features, their matching dark hair, their unnerving beauty—profound even for creatures of their kind.

"I don't think you understand the magnitude of the feat you pulled off, Ms. Ramone," Rogue said. "Magical abilities aside, few have the mental fortitude to push an incubus of my brother's talents out of their minds. In fact, I've only ever seen one creature outside of immediate family pull it off. This was nothing personal, merely a test of your—"

I swore a grenade detonated inside my brain, turning everything inside to a dripping, bloody massacre of thoughts and brain matter. "Are you high? Nothing personal?" My skin crawled. I was practically shrieking, my throat raw as Lachlan loomed behind me, a shadow ready to reap retribution.

Rogue's lips pinched. "I didn't—"

"Nothing personal? Do you realize…" I ran out of words, the carnage of my emotions rendering me speechless. I remembered the secret I'd nearly spilled to complete strangers. If the prince had managed to turn the lock, to kick that door in…

I wasn't sure if I would still be me.

I felt myself falling. But I wasn't. I definitely wasn't.

My feet were beneath me but… smoke. Smoke was everywhere, surrounding me.

A figure stepped from the swirls of gray, hard hands bracing my shoulders, forcing my head up and back. Rogue. Concern and something that looked like pained loathing creased his face. I tugged against him, but he held me fast.

"I'm sorry," Rogue said. Two words that dunked my burning body into a pool of frigid water. "I apologize for being so cavalier with your emotions, for allowing my brother to delve as far as he did. I'm sorry for the pain I've caused. I wanted to test you, to see how far I could push you. I selfishly wanted to see what mettle you were made of, to test your caliber of power, to see your true worth."

I shoved him back, hissing as if he'd stung me. His hands flipped up, and he made a show of stepping back.

Part of me wondered if he was bewitching me, turning those orange-gold eyes on me to calm me down, to let him in. However, I couldn't sense any magic at work. Nothing except his desire for my understanding.

"I will never forgive you," I said, looking past the incubus to the prince, who lowered his gaze, wondering why Rogue was doing all the talking. Something wasn't adding up. "I don't understand why you felt that violating my mind was necessary, or in what world anything like that would be alright. But at least I know..." I swallowed hard and motioned for Lachlan to lower his weapon, which he did with a grumble. "At least I know now what you are capable of—so I never make the mistake of lowering my guard again."

Both fey nodded grimly and Rogue stepped forward again, but I held up a hand, frost tinging my fingertips. To him I said, "And you. Who are you? What aren't you telling me?"

The fey flashed a quicksilver smile.

A smile that reminded me so much of another it made me dizzy.

My gut clenched tight. The sense of familiarity I'd felt before spreading, the door opening. No. There was no way. Not—

"I'm Ridley Rogue Caron, the true Prince of Sin, the leader of the daemoni." The grin spread. "And I believe you're very close with the youngest of my siblings—Ryder."

Chapter 23

I splashed my face with cool water, avoiding my eyes in the oval mirror. I wasn't a fan of these sinks, the ones that looked like bowls placed on the table. At the very least, the bowls should serve a better purpose, maybe be detachable. Otherwise, what was the point?

The spray weakened, and I reached out to the Kraken, frustrated with Its lack of response. Nothing. Not a tentacle, not a suction cup, not a sarcastic comment. Nothing. What was going on? Why wasn't It speaking to me?

I wanted to know what It thought about the attack.

Had I overreacted? I didn't think so.

With swift fingers, I laced my hair back in its standard braid and opened the door to the bathroom that opened out into the rest of the suite. The suite that Ridley had escorted Lachlan and me to under the guise of goodwill and the promise of answers.

My need for answers drove me to follow, even though my mind railed against the idea.

When my eyes caught the incubus's across the room as he leaned a hip against the marble kitchen countertop, I hoped answers were all he would try to whet our appetites with. I was loath to forgive the prince for what he'd ordered his brother to do to me anytime soon.

Speaking of the brother, my gaze tracked across the room and its delicate furnishings until I found the cluster of shadows in the corner of the room, smoke dancing at his feet. Ridley had introduced him as Rim on the way upstairs. The fey hadn't spoken since I'd snapped at him in the hall.

My throat worked as I blinked back my emotions and came to stand beside Lachlan. The elf gripped my shoulder, hard, and it cheered me to see TruthTeller propped against a gold settee nearby. I'd strapped my dagger to my thigh in case I needed it in a pinch.

Lachlan released my shoulder and dipped to grab a glass from an end table. "Drink this. It'll help with the shock."

I dipped my middle finger into the liquid. Water with a hint of fresh lemon and mint. No poison. No alcohol. No elements I didn't recognize. I downed it in three quick gulps, uncomfortably aware of the prince's attention. "Thanks."

Beyond asking us to follow him to the penthouse, Rogue—no, *Ridley*—had said little since revealing Ryder was his brother. Looking at him now, especially having sampled the familiarity of his magic, I was still kicking myself for not noticing the familial resemblance sooner. The prince was shorter than both his brothers, standing about as tall as me, but possessed their body type: lean yet not thin, with toned muscles of iron.

It wasn't only the physical characteristics. It was how Ridley held himself, the confidence he wore like a second skin, the quiet control that radiated from him, the powerful punch of magic that tickled my nose and made me feel like sneezing.

He was like Ryder.

Or maybe Ryder was like him.

I should have guessed the incubus who toyed with my heart was royalty. The cockiness he wore like a mantle now spoke volumes.

Ridley rounded the island, and I turned to follow his trajectory as he crossed the room, like a flower following the sun's arc across the sky.

He popped the button on his suit jacket and sank into an armchair with deep, royal purple cushions, waving for me to do the same. The settee pressing against the back of my knees was long enough for both me and Lachlan, but I ignored his offer.

The prince dragged a hand through his hair—again, much like his brother. "You're looking a little less pale, Ms. Ramone."

"Why did you pretend to be someone you're not?"

Ridley arched a brow. "Call me curious. I've heard of you, of what you've accomplished—hard to not be aware these days—but I wanted to see for myself how you acted around those who could be considered... below your stature."

"I don't appreciate liars."

"A sentiment we share." He casually swirled a tumbler of amber liquid in his lap. "Would you please sit? You both look terribly uncomfortable."

I said "I'm good" at the same time Lachlan chipped in "don't mind if I do."

The elf winked at me and dropped onto the black cushions, his boots finding the coffee table. TruthTeller lay flat across his lap as he draped an arm over the back of the furniture. At some point he'd flipped his hat forward. Feeling awkward, I lowered beside him and perched on the armrest.

"You don't like liars," I said. "Yet you misled us downstairs."

"Misled is a good word for it." It was difficult to pin down his tone. It matched my spine in its rigidity. "Because, if you think back, not once did I lie to you. Yes, my middle name is Rogue. It's the name I prefer in certain circles. I was *not* ready to see you yet. And I don't have a personal assistant, so," a corner of his lips kicked up, "I supposed you could say I'm my own personal assistant."

I mentally flicked through our limited conversation and bit back a curse. He was right. Though he hadn't told the whole truth, he hadn't lied. I tried a different peg. "Ryder didn't mention he was related to royalty."

"That's hardly surprising. We haven't exactly seen eye-to-eye for some time." Ridley sipped his brandy and crossed his leg, ankle over his thigh. "He's become a bit of a dark horse around here. Ryder lives by his own rules, walks his own path, and avoids this city like the plague. He doesn't claim the Caron name any longer, and we're all the better for it."

The swaying of his raised foot suggested otherwise.

I tugged on the scarf around my neck. I desperately wanted to ask more about Ryder, about their strained relationship, but Lachlan nudged me with his elbow. His glance told me to get to the point.

"Why are we here?" I bit out. Ridley's magic swirled chaotically about him. I'd noticed even down on the casino floor that he did little to rein it in, exactly like that fey back in—my jaw clenched. Just like that fey back in Ontario. I mentally berated myself, realizing that if I hadn't been so distracted earlier, I would have put two and two together long before now.

"You invite me to your home. You bait me in your offices. You send your brother to attack me in a hallway." I gritted my teeth. "What do you want and how does it relate to the curse?"

"I need your help."

"You mean your trip to the library in Ontario wasn't productive?"

"I wondered if you had pieced that together, yet."

I shifted, fighting to keep my patience. "What happened to that incubus? The one you were with?" I recalled the fey's gaunt face, the way he clutched his hand to his chest as he wheezed helplessly.

The shadow in the corner of the room shifted, and Rim's magic slammed up against the barriers I'd erected. The incubus scowled as Ridley waved him off. I'd clearly hit a sore spot.

"We lost Merek a few days ago," the prince said. The air vibrated with his sorrow. "Among those in my court, he was my strongest ally. He was also Rim's oldest friend."

My stomach churned. I remembered how I'd felt when Kaz died, when the Order had ripped her away from me. When I'd found her cold body. "Words can't express how sorry I am to hear that. It's painful, losing someone you love."

Rim drew back, ceasing slamming his powers against my own, eyes glowing gold as they found mine. His scowl deepened and he pressed a knuckle to his teeth. I angled my head in response, allowing him to read the truth on my face.

Ridley observed our silent conversation. "His loss brings me to the crux of this all. We need your help, Ms. Ramone. Without it, thousands of daemoni like Merek may die."

My inner fight wilted. It had been awful enough knowing the curse had already affected a handful. I'd hoped for the best, and the best slipped through my fingers like sand.

"Thousands?" My voice creaked with the word.

Ridley twisted his long fingers in his lap. "Yes. It is an unfortunate reality that I, as the head of our fey kingdom, have been forced to face head-on. After finding you in Ontario, after hearing about your feat in South Africa, after interviewing dozens of people about your strength of character—" I scratched my chin, wondering who exactly he'd dragged into his offices— "I felt confident in my assumption that you would want to know."

I tapped a quick tempo on my thigh. "I am." I licked my lips, roping my thoughts together. At my side, Lachlan rolled TruthTeller into a ball. Given what Ridley had just revealed, we weren't going anywhere. "What have you learned?"

Ridley's shoulders relaxed a touch. "That incubus, the one you helped save, he's the only fey I know of to emerge from the curse alive *and* retain his magic."

So he hadn't heard about Logan. For now, recognizing Lee's propensity for privacy, I decided to keep that information to myself and see where this headed. I brought my scarf to my lips as Ridley rose and strode to the kitchen. Moments later, ice clinked in a glass.

"It's killing them." I hadn't confirmed that yet, though I'd guessed as much when I'd found Logan struggling against the mass of black chaos. Her magic was too deeply ingrained, too much a part of who she was. Losing it would have the direst of consequences.

"I've already lost more than a dozen. A few survived but not many."

My heart skipped in my chest, its beat uneven. On one hand, it was fortunate there were survivors. However, there still remained a number of far bigger issues at hand: how many daemoni would be affected? What percentage of them would survive without my aid? Was this curse capable of spreading to other races?

And, most important of all, who was responsible for it?

As if sensing my inner turmoil, Rim shifted where he stood, back in the corner of the room. His lamp-like gaze had dimmed since our earlier standoff, and he swiped at some scruffy locks dangling in his eyes. What role did he play in all of this? What could he contribute to the cause? Or was he merely muscle for his older brother?

Ridley leaned across the glass coffee table separating us and offered a glass of water, a curl of lemon zest on the corner. I appreciated that he'd given me a moment to process my thoughts uninterrupted. I took the cup but didn't drink from it, and he took his seat once again.

"How many fey are you monitoring right now?" I asked.

The prince's eyes darted across my face. "We're currently treating two dozen others in various stages of progression in a remote location. While they are receiving the best care my family has to offer, a few don't have much time left." His throat tightened. "The number of those affected by the curse has doubled in one week, and I'm getting word it may double again."

I ran a hand down my arm, mentally counting the vibrations emanating from the oaths, remembering the trials I'd faced before earning those promises and how I'd overcome them. This was it. This right here was my chance. If I stood any hope of solving the riddle of this curse, of the mystery it presented, it would most likely be with the head of the daemoni clan at my side—if only for the fact that it was his race facing potential magical extinction.

The stakes for him, both as a leader and a magical being, were at their highest.

At my side, Lachlan raised his eyebrows, lavender eyes sympathetic. For now, I could count on him to stay by my side.

I also had a personal stake in all this.

Ryder was an incubus. A powerful incubus from, as I now knew, a powerful bloodline. While I might still be figuring out how I felt about him, about his broodiness and obsessiveness, and, at times, possessiveness… I didn't want to lose him.

I didn't want to lose any more of the daemoni.

"I'll do my best to help." Phenex's vial thrummed against my skin, and I dropped another of my carefully held cards. "I've replicated what I did in Durban once. I'm confident I can do it again."

Ridley raised his glass to his lips and drank deeply, no doubt his mind racing with what I'd revealed.

I continued, "But I warn you, it's an incredibly slow process and it isn't a long-term fix. We still need to find the root of this curse and shut it down, or else… I'm not sure what will happen."

"On that, you and I are in agreement." The prince straightened his lapel and stood, his royal aura snapping back into place. I mirrored his movement, but when he reached across the table, I drew back from the handshake.

"I have one caveat." My gaze flitted to the wide windows and the darkening skies beyond them. A storm was rolling in.

"Ryder can't know I'm here." From the corner of my eye, Lachlan rubbed his hands together gleefully. Ridley didn't so much as blink. "You won't tell him. Your family won't tell him. No one tells him. Not a word, not a whisper." Despite my misgivings, I offered Ridley my hand. "If someone breaks that pact, if he shows up, I will be gone so fast you'll wonder if you found me in the first place."

Smoke twined around my hand, stroked my wrist, and my flames rose to meet him.

The prince nodded. "You've got yourself a deal."

Chapter 24

"You are welcome to stay here for the rest of the evening." Ridley opened the door to the first room, revealing a king-size bed with immaculate white sheets and plump pillows. Sunshine danced across the long dresser upon which sat a television screen so thin it made paper look fat. A bedroom on the other side of the suite was arranged similarly. "However, I understand if you'd prefer to find alternative accommodations."

I was inclined to leave, but I needed to be careful with the money from the temple, and Lachlan filched most of what he needed. Also, as much as I didn't want to admit it, I needed to get some actual sleep tonight. I doubted I'd be able to do that on the streets of Vegas.

"This will work," I said, my mouth dry.

"Perfect." Ridley crossed to the living room window that overlooked the Strip. I'd never been in a penthouse before, and figured I'd probably never experience the luxury on my own terms, but I could easily see why people paid top dollar for places like these. "Tomorrow I'll show you the hospital where we're keeping those affected by the curse. It's near my estate. You're welcome to stay there while you work."

Ridley's eyes ghosted over Lachlan and settled on me as he placed two keycards on the counter. "Of course, my offer applies to my cousin here, too."

His cousin? Was he talking about Lachlan? The elf snorted and picked at his cuticles.

"Wouldn't want to put you out of your own home, mate," my friend said, gnawing a hangnail. "And don't bother keeping your judgmental ways in check, I much prefer the bitterness of honesty to the sweetness of lies. Not like we've ever met before, anyway."

"I know enough." The prince gave me one last nod and strode through the door held open by Rim. The bigger incubus brushed some lint off his jacket, as if the gesture could somehow brush us away, and vaporized in a cloud of smoke.

I blinked, wondering if Ryder could do that.

"Slippery creatures aren't they," Lachlan called, his head stuck in the refrigerator as he rummaged through the contents. "Can't live with them. Definitely could live without them."

I slammed the front door and twisted the lock. "Cousin?"

"What was that?" His voice sounded muffled. "Did you know this place comes with not one but three kinds of pickles—"

I jerked him out of the fridge by the back of his shirt and pushed him against the stainless steel, my finger spearing his chest. "You knew exactly who he was? From the beginning? And you allowed him to carry on like—"

"Watch it." The elf's eyes went flinty and his abs flexed. "You don't know what you're talking about."

I rose on my toes, steam radiating from my skin. "How about you clear it up? Because I could bake you into a crisp right now for that stunt you pulled."

His hand closed around my finger as he lowered his face to mine, our noses almost brushing. "Were you fuming too hard to hear me say that I'd never met him before?"

"And photographs were invented yesterday?"

"Listen once and listen well because I won't say this again." Lachlan's lip curled. "I don't appreciate baseless accusations about my character. I've been nothing but honest with you, and this is how you reward me? By turning on me the moment an attack is volleyed?"

Something twinged in my chest, but I held firm. "One of those fey raped my mind. If you knew anything about this—"

"I don't, ok?" The elf slammed a hand on the counter. The sympathy softening his face dampened the aggressiveness of the motion. "There is a history between the elves and the daemoni. A long and bloody history. But it's also that. History. I wasn't even born when all that went down."

I stepped back and he darted away, an animal freed from its cage. I dragged my hands down my face, my anger draining as something new curdled in my gut. He was right. To my knowledge, the elf had been honest with me, and I hadn't known him long enough to accuse him of hiding secrets. Of course he had secrets. Everyone did.

"Does this have anything to do with the comments your mother made in Cogscraig?" I asked finally. "And what you decided not to tell me a few hours ago?"

Across the room, Lachlan's eyelids lowered to half-mast. "It's entirely possible a thread connects the three events."

I glanced at the digital clock on the wall. Aside from a few granola bars, neither of us had eaten for the better part of the day. Add that to the emotional turmoil I was still struggling to process, and it didn't surprise me that we were at each other's throats.

"If I cook up something for dinner, would you tell me about that history?"

The elf rubbed his chin. "Bartering now?"

"You're not the first being to tell me I get in my own way because of my temper." I opened a black cabinet door and rifled through the contents. Mostly canned goods. High-end canned goods, but still canned goods. I wondered if this was standard fare. "Figured it was time to try a new tack."

"I'll bite."

I emerged with a glass jar of spaghetti sauce. "Can you eat this?"

The elf was careful to not touch me as he took the container. His lips moved silently as he ran through the list of ingredients. "Fortunately, I'm not vegan or we would be in a pickle." He twisted the cap and the seal broke with a pop. He sniffed the contents before passing the jar back to me. "Speaking of pickles, hand me the one with dill. I need to snack while I talk."

Relief rolled through me like the tide coming in. He wasn't hiding in his room, avoiding me for the rest of the night. He certainly wasn't leaving. Lachlan was going to talk to me. We might be ok.

I handed the elf the container he requested and crouched to rummage through more cabinets beside the oven, blindly searching for a saucepan. Considering I'd wanted to get rid of him from the get-go, it surprised me how attached I'd gotten to the elf.

Lachlan smacked his lips and hummed thoughtfully as I shifted things out of the way. It appeared the penthouse came stocked with every appliance known to mankind, but pots and pans were in short supply. How peculiar.

"I'm finding it hard to believe you're related to the Caron family," I said. My fingers closed around the rubber handles of two stacked saucepans. Bingo. "Your abilities are so different."

Lachlan waited for me to stand. "Are they, though? I absorb the abilities of others, sucking in their magic and wielding it for my own purposes. Don't daemoni operate the same way? Don't they absorb the magic of others to fuel their own?"

I flipped on the faucet at my back and directed a stream of water into the larger of the pots. "But their magic looks nothing like the magic they steal. They deal in shadows and allure. That's not like anything you can do."

Lachlan licked vinegar off his fingers. "I didn't say we were the same, only that we operated the same." He dipped back into the twelve-ounce jar and fished for another spear. "There are big differences. I have to be attacked directly or freely given the magic, but that magic fades with time. Daemoni simply absorb magic from the world around them, typically through lust, love, or sex. Direct contact, though, often comes at the cost of a soul, so I suppose obtaining magic has a downside for both of us."

Lachlan popped a pickle into his mouth and considered me lazily. "However, I have a feeling an incubus could absorb your magic directly with none of those prerequisites if it came down to it. Gods are the root of all magic."

I flushed, remembering the burn of my body when a certain incubus pulled me close, his tongue tracing mine, drawing my powers from me like I was his favorite soft drink. It had been our first kiss and one I couldn't get out of my head.

To hide my reddening cheeks, I dumped the tomato sauce into the second pan. It smelled a bit too sweet for my liking, but I'd eaten worse. The pots clanged against the spider burners, which I manually lit. "So you're related. Then why the bad blood?"

The elf capped the jar—which had three tiny pickles left swimming in a sea of juice—and removed his needles from his sleeves. He toyed with them when he was nervous or particularly thoughtful.

"There's a belief among our people, one that says the daemoni are dark and the elves embody light," he murmured. A vice clamped around my insides, and I turned to rifle through the cupboards for dried pasta. I had a feeling I knew where this was going.

The elf continued, "Long story short, one prince got jealous of another prince and started a war over it a few thousand years ago. About four hundred years ago, one of my ancestors tired of the whole deal and tried to end it. She gathered a small contingency of talented elves, snuck into the daemoni palace, and slaughtered most of the royal family in their beds."

Water splashed as I dumped an entire pound of pasta into the pot. My hands trembled, and I folded them carefully before turning to face him.

"The children?" I whispered.

The elf batted the jar between his hands, avoiding my eyes. "Even the children. Only one survived by hiding in the walls, escaping notice."

"The Caron line." It wasn't a guess. I turned back to the stove and stirred the food. A few more minutes and everything would be ready. Dinner of champions.

"Right." His tone grew distant and my shoulders hunched, realizing that while Lachlan was physically in this room with me, his mind was lost somewhere else.

This was the darkness I'd sensed earlier.

The part of his soul he forced down deep.

"The elves got their revenge, but the fey community condemned them for it. For what they did, my ancestors were ridiculed, criticized, chased out of the country," he spat. "They were cowards, fighting without honor. We lost our homes, our territory. We've been ostracized to the point where most of my kind prefer to live like humans rather than learn about their magic. Those of us who accept the gauntlet thrown at our feet have few places to go. We serve as personal guards or mercenaries. Alone—forever."

I flipped off the burners with a thought, abandoning the meal and going to my friend whose knuckles had gone white around his knives.

"I had nothing to do with what happened… but I could kill my family for what they did. I thought getting magic back would be cool, but it's nothing but a curse. Now, I look out for me. Because I am all I have."

Lachlan went quiet. I reached for him and set aside his knives. Then I turned his body on the high stool, swiveling him so I could wrap my arms around him. Against my ear, his heart hammered, and slowly his arms closed tight. His chin rested on top of my head. I stroked his back.

It was all I had to offer.

Some wounds my Water magic couldn't touch.

That took something more powerful than any element.

"You're not a bad person, Lach." I didn't know where the nickname came from, but it felt right. "You're a little strange and more than a little intense sometimes, but you're not bad."

I pulled away and brushed his jaw, imploring him to look at me.

"I don't know how any of this will end," I said. He raised his head, eyes riddled with shadows as they met mine. We both knew I wasn't talking about the fight between the ancient fey races. "I don't know if I will survive what's to come. But if I do, you'll always find a place in my home… wherever that may be."

He reached for me, lacing our hands together like he always did when he tested my limits, seeking something I hadn't known I could give him. Though he didn't say anything, I knew he'd heard me. And that was enough.

Chapter 25

A night of restless sleep did little to ease the frustration coiling through me. It probably had something to do with the bed being too soft and the pillows too fluffy. I'd ended up using my spare shirt as a pillow as I curled up on the carpeted floor.

Despite the purple bruises beneath my eyes and my dragging limbs, I couldn't help but throw my head back with laughter when the large, black SUV rolled up beside me and the elf as we stood curbside the next morning.

"Cliché much?" I asked of the incubus who stepped from the backseat while sliding on a pair of sunglasses. The heavily tinted windows made it impossible to see if anyone else was inside. I pointed at the tires so large they stuck out from the wheel wells. "This is ridiculous. I feel like you're about to slap some tape over my mouth and throw me in the trunk as your driver speeds off."

"Rest assured, Ms. Ramone, I learned a valuable lesson about personal space yesterday," Ridley drawled. "I suppose it's fair to warn you, machine guns are installed beneath the hood."

He stepped back with a slight bow, and motioned Lach and me into the ostentatious excuse for a vehicle. I took a seat in the far back and ran my hands over the supple, white leather. I wondered what it was like, having this kind of luxury available at a moment's notice. Not one day in and I could already see how addicting it might be. Lachlan grumbled but ended up folding his large frame in beside me, where he quickly got lost in messing with the sound system.

"And I suppose the rims turn into propellers?" I asked our host as he settled into his seat. As much as I enjoyed the perks of this gig, I wasn't thrilled to be anywhere near him. However, I couldn't let those poor fey down because of a grudge—no matter how well warranted. "Is the mafia after you or something?"

"Or something." The prince waved a pair of fingers across the partition separating us from the driver. The SUV rolled forward as the window slid closed. "It pays to be over-prepared."

I tapped my lip, thinking of all the heartache I could have saved myself had I been better prepared for what was come. "I suppose you have a point."

Lachlan looked up from the controls where he had been flicking the seat warmers on and off. "Where are we going, anyway?"

Things had shifted between us since last night—something subtle but definitive.

Ridley offered me a manilla envelope, and I wished he would remove his glasses. I preferred seeing people's eyes. It helped me understand what they were thinking. I popped the clasp and shook it so some pages fell into my hand.

"Our hospital is on the outskirts of town." Ridley leaned across the seat and snagged a thermos of what smelled like vanilla latte from a cupholder. Today, he wore jeans and a blue sport coat over an orange button-up shirt. "I've provided copies of the charts of every patient we've treated. Though..." he turned toward the window, "*treating* might be too kind a word. We're mostly keeping them comfortable for as long as we can."

On the outside, he seemed completely put together, not a hair out of place or speck of lint to be seen. But I recognized the lines etched across his forehead and the rigid set of his mouth. How long would it be before similar lines folded into my own skin? Some days I felt a million years older than seventeen.

I fanned through the paperwork without seeing it. I already knew what the problem was, and I doubted medical records would prove any more illuminating than anything else I'd researched. But I'd give it a shot.

"I'll see what I can do," I said, the words sounding lame to my ears.

"Thank you." Ridley took a long drink from his mug. "Any help you can provide will be welcome. My sister runs Cura—our name for our makeshift hospital—and is thrilled you agreed to help. This curse has run her ragged." He paused, amended, "*All* of us ragged."

He had a sister? How many Caron siblings were there? I swallowed back the question, figuring I didn't need to understand the family dynamics at play. Instead, with my thumbnail, I underlined a sentence written by a careful hand. The script was clear and precise. "She's a doctor? That's cool."

The more I learned about the fey universe, the more fascinated I became. Very little was as it seemed. Every story I remembered reading as a child, and most reactions from the fey I'd encountered, made the daemoni out to be sex fiends or prostitutes—creatures that embraced the sinners and transformed the saints.

In some ways they embraced their proclivities. The Caron family owned at least one casino—and probably more if I wasn't kidding myself—and resided in Sin City itself. I'd also met Ryder in a club he owned, one of many under his entrepreneurial umbrella. But yet, they still seemed so… normal. If that word truly applied to anyone.

"Every member of our family claims multiple professions," Ridley said, ignorant of my thoughts. The hard set of his mouth relaxed. I wondered what the prince would look like if he smiled. For real. Not one of the smirks of which he, like his brother, was so fond. "We were forced to adapt to human standards amid the magical drought, same as all fey. While I appreciate all we've accomplished in the past two thousand years, it's far more entertaining with magic."

"Oh?" Outside, a barren, dry desert rolled by. I swallowed, mentally checking my magical reserves, the reach of my abilities. Lach pulled a familiar purple water bottle from his pack and handed it over, reading me perfectly. "Where do your talents lie?"

"Aside from running the family business?" Ridley watched me chug the water and hand the empty bottle back to my friend. "Consider me a career politician of sorts."

Lachlan rolled his eyes. "Sounds fascinating." Though I was glad he'd joined me, I knew he'd rather be jumping out of an airplane at ten-thousand feet right now.

"Of sorts?" I prompted.

"There's more to politics than being the face of a campaign." Ridley drummed his fingers on his thigh. "Besides, the most successful politicians rarely claim one office."

"You game the system," I deadpanned. "Playing both sides from the shadows, manipulating the world around your fingers."

The incubus spread his arms, expression angelic. "Assume what you like."

The SUV slowed and rolled to a stop. Our host popped open the door. "We're here."

For all the beauty of its name, Cura was a large, solitary warehouse rising several stories into the sky. From the outside, it was utterly unspectacular: four walls, three rows of uniform windows, two garage doors on rollers, and a parking lot with enough spaces for maybe a half dozen cars. I shielded my eyes as I stepped from the dark of the vehicle, scanning the desert. There wasn't much else out here besides dirt and some plants.

"The nearest highway is over forty miles away." Ridley moved beside me. "We own everything you see and then some. We like to maintain our… seclusion."

"Secrecy," I countered.

"I never claimed to be transparent."

"I have as much at stake here as you do. I'm not about to blab to the world what's going on here unless you're torturing people." I frowned, then accepted the bottle of water he handed over. I broke the seal and drained it in a matter of seconds, much to the incubus's thinly veiled amusement. "You aren't torturing people here, right?"

"Not at this particular location, Water God." My eyes narrowed and the corner of his mouth ticked up marginally. I knew he was dangerous. I'd experienced that much first hand. And while I didn't think I'd ever get past that, part of me wanted to like him, like I was weirdly fond of Phenex. At the end of the day, we were all-powerful fey playing powerful games. I was as dangerous as they.

Ridley turned back to the hospital, hands tucked in his pockets. "Are we enemies, Ms. Ramone?"

I traced the oaths circling my wrists. "I wouldn't consider us allies."

"And?"

"And I haven't forgotten what you asked your brother to do to me less than twenty-four hours ago."

"Nor should you." He watched his driver lift the hood of the SUV for Lachlan, who immediately started fiddling with something. Probably the machine gun. "You should always remember a threat. Better advice: face everything that comes at you as a threat." Despite the glare of the sun, he removed his shades. "It's not a pleasant way of viewing the world, nor a particularly easy way to live, but it will help you survive it."

"The threat?"

"The world."

I wondered again about his actions at the casino. Ridley was strange, bipolar almost—running hot, then cold, hostile to compassionate. But beneath it all, he held firm to his control, locking it under a thick layer of steel and ice. Were his actions meant to be a lesson? I wasn't sure how to feel about that.

"Am I a threat to you?" I asked.

"Always."

A weird sort of pride bubbled up inside me. "I wasn't expecting you to be so direct."

"Oh?"

"It seems tactless, letting an enemy have that kind of knowledge," I explained. "Some politician you are."

Ridley laughed, the sound rich and creamy. "I recognize the kind of person I'm dealing with and I adapt to them. You, my dear, prefer direct conversation above all else." He slid his glasses back on. "Besides, I never called you my enemy. Only a threat."

I didn't want to like him. I wanted to hate him. I wanted him to let me do my job and then let me go, forget about me entirely. But I found myself drawn to him anyway, a metaphorical moth drawn to the flame, wanting to peel back his personality and see how deep those layers went.

"You and the elf are very close," the prince observed. I jerked at the sudden change in conversation. He faced me now, drawing my attention from Lachlan, who scowled at his grease-streaked hands.

Despite what he'd said earlier about learning his lesson, Ridley crowded me, the toes of our shoes practically touching. "And you've been together, alone, for more than a little while now, a relationship that most I've talked to can't seem to figure out." His tone went viper soft. "You put the pieces of the puzzle together, Water God, and you tell me what picture forms."

Where was he going with this and where was this coming from? "How is this any of your business?" I snapped.

"Everything is my business."

"Then I'd say those you talk to have a very misogynistic way of looking at the world." My temper crackled, freezing over. I leaned in, close enough to feel his body heat. "If you think you know me so well, then why don't you spit out what you mean to say, *Prince*?"

His irises swirled a lethal combination of black and orange. Static shot between us as his magic reared up, clashing with mine in a battle of wills. "I don't like how you're messing with my brother."

I sneered. Say what? "I'm going to need a little more here. Are you talking about the brother with whom you're so close he's never mentioned you? Or perhaps the brother you sent to assault me yesterday?" My heart thrashed in my chest; my body vibrated with rage. "Or is there another brother I should know about?"

"Your lack of respect—"

"You know nothing of who or what I respect." I snagged the collar of his shirt and dragged him against me. Sand swirled in the air, the ether writhing with my temper that finally flared with fire and his twisting web of smoke and mystery. "And you have as little say in *Ryder's* life as you do in mine."

Ridley's skin thinned, revealing a hint of the onyx monster he and most of his kind kept locked away—the second form I knew boasted horns and wings like a creature straight out of a horror novel. I wrapped my hand around his throat, uncaring of the sweat beading on his forehead or the way his nails dug into my shoulders as I shoved against him with my magic.

My voice softened, lethal as any blade, these words meant only for the prince. "But know this: I am not disloyal. I do not cheat. And those I love, I love with everything I have."

I thought of my parents, of Kaz, of Finn.

I loved them that way, with every atom of my being.

I loved them so much that it hurt. It gnawed at me, ripped at me, knowing three of them were gone and one... one I was afraid to face for fear of the disappointment I'd see on his face.

A pair of amber eyes flashed behind lids I didn't remember closing, and my heart burned in an entirely different way, a way that squeezed my lungs until I couldn't breathe from want.

I opened my eyes and stared unblinking into Ridley's own. "Your brother and I are not together. We are not dating. And some days, I'm not sure if there's more to our relationship than his possessiveness and my need to belong somewhere, with someone who accepts me."

I took a deep, shuddering breath, and with it, came the cooling sense of calm. The temperature inside me no longer fluctuated between tundra-chill and lava-hot.

"That's ok because we have time. And we both understand that." I swallowed. "But if you think, for one moment, that Ryder would be upset that one of my close friends is of a race that yours despises over a war hundreds of years old, then you don't know your brother at all. He would never. Never." My teeth bared as I spat the word. "Be that shallow."

I pushed the Prince of Sin back, knocking away his grip with an invisible whip, uncaring of the eyes fixed on both of us in a mixture of shock and awe.

Ridley's held only respect.

I wondered, again, if I'd somehow passed another of his tricky tests.

"Well, isn't this a wonderful turn of events?" I turned at the sultry, slow voice of the succubus who'd stepped up behind me. "Someone dressing *you* down for a change, brother. How long has it been? Three hundred years? Four?"

Now that I was expecting members of the Caron family to pop up like rabbits, I easily saw the resemblance between the new fey and Ridley. Like the rest of them, she was darkly beautiful with scarlet red lips and daffodil eyes peeking above thick, black frames. A long, white lab coat with rubies embroidered along the edges framed her limber body. Like Rim, she towered over the eldest brother.

She bobbled a clipboard in her arms and extended her hand. "I'm Rue."

I took it, noting her blunted, blood-red nails. "Zara."

Rue. Ridley. Ryder. Rim.

Their parents had embraced the letter 'R,' hadn't they?

"You match your picture." Rue flipped her clipboard around and, sure enough, a picture of my face was printed in the upper right corner of the top page. Her smile behind the thick sheaf of paper turned sheepish. "I can remember any name, but I'm not great with faces. But, when I found out you were coming, I figured I'd give it the ol' college try." She swung her arm with gusto, then seemed to remember something and inclined her body slightly, her bow respectful. "Though I must admit, I've heard a lot about you, too."

I needed to ask Lachlan about all the bowing. It seemed to be happening more frequently.

"Some of it good, I hope," I said. Ridley had moved past us and now held open a door to the hospital. As the succubus chattered about the things she'd heard, I entered the building, a shaky breath rattling past my lips. Past the entryway, beds covered in sheets so white they looked like piles of snow filled the main floor. I brushed past the prince and moved to the center aisle.

Lachlan pulled up beside me. "That's a lot of beds. Fifty or sixty at least."

"Fortunately, Ridley says only about two dozen are filled," I murmured, rifling through the pages the prince had given me in the SUV. It didn't feel very fortunate at all, though. Two dozen was still too many. Too many fey who might lose their magic if their bodies didn't succumb to fighting the curse first. Two dozen fey, some of whom I noticed were so caught in the curse's spell they couldn't raise their heads to see the new arrivals. From the edge of the room, I could see the black vines of their veins clinging to their necks and spiraling down their arms.

"He wasn't kidding about being prepared, huh?" Lachlan mused. "But it paints a bit of a grim picture, don't you agree?"

I felt Ridley's stare burning a hole in my back. I had a feeling if he was being honest with me, he fully expected most of these beds to fill with fey over the coming days and weeks.

It was enough to make my knees wobble.

"What are you doing?" Lachlan asked.

Without realizing it, I'd lifted my hand, my middle and index finger pressing against my hairline, and drew down to my brows. The same sign I'd made when I'd locked away the curse in the incubus. The same sign I'd never before used elsewhere in my life.

"I don't know," I whispered. I didn't stop to think about it. Instead, I walked to the nearest bed and crouched beside the incubus laying there. My heart fractured a little more. He was older—in human years he looked to be about seventy. His veins were fat against the frail skin of his arms, the black sludge in them vivid. A wisp of white hair curled at his temples, limp and soaked in sweat. Someone had recently changed the sheets because they were only slightly damp, but he seemed so frail, so breakable, so… translucent.

I glanced at the paperwork on the table beside his bed. "Hey there, Francis. My name is Zara." I took his hand, his skin thin and papery beneath my touch. "You don't know me yet and that's ok. You don't need to know me. You just need to know that I'm here now, and I'm going to do what I can to make you feel better. I need you to hang in there for me, though. Can you do that?" A sliver of yellow-green irises peered at me from behind heavy lids. He blinked once and I smiled reassuringly. "Good. Now grit your teeth and hang tight. I'll be right back."

I rose and moved to the next bed, dragging a short, rolling stool behind me. I sat and greeted the young succubus lying there. She was slightly more alert but equally incapable of speaking. I made a point of grasping her hand, of stroking her brittle, black locks, and moved on.

Lach joined me by the fourth patient and clung to my side as I moved down the row. I barely felt the careful glances from the healers, the scrutiny of the daemoni royalty, and quietly thanked the nurses who left a stool ready and waiting at the next bed on my way around the room. At the end of the last row, I massaged my temples, trying to quell my nausea.

"What do you think?" Rue hovered at the foot of the bed, pen poised over her clipboard.

What a loaded question.

"I think… this is worse than I imagined." I accepted the granola bar the elf thrust into my hand and took a bite, chewing but not tasting the cranberry-cherry medley. "I'll have to move patient by patient, severing the curse's ties one by one. It's a slow process, and takes me a few days to recover in-between, but that's probably our best option. Unfortunately, that doesn't solve the bigger issue of breaking the curse. We'll play it by ear, I guess."

"That's what I'd hoped you would say," Ridley said. He stood not far from his sister. His face clouded as he looked out over the sea of beds. "I'm sorry you had to see this, that you weren't introduced to our people during a more favorable time, but…"

I cut him off. "If there's anything I've discovered, it's that my role is far more complicated than fate makes it seem." I took a bigger bite of the bar, feeling my energy returning. Lachlan was many things, but he was truly a master when it came to keeping me fed. "I don't see a reason to wait. I'll finish eating this, drink some water, and get to work."

The relief radiating from the two royals was potent. Ridley snapped his fingers, calling over one of the half dozen attendants floating between the beds, drying damp foreheads and stringing IV bags of saline.

As I crammed the last of the granola in my mouth, Lachlan pulled me aside. "Are you sure you can do this? Not that I'm not encouraging you to take any risks, but… helping Logan was even more taxing on you than that incubus. I know you won't admit it, but are you sure this is something you want to do?"

I tugged the bottle from his hand. "I can't do nothing. Not when I can do something."

He eyed me, then shrugged, apparently having appeased his conscience. Now it was full steam ahead. "Which of your magics will I sample today?"

There was some level of security that came with tethering myself to the elf. I didn't know if he could help in a pinch, but it was comforting knowing he stood on the other side. "Let's try Water this time, it might give us some luck since it helps with healing."

He trailed his fingers through his hair, expression thoughtful. "Too bad we went with Fire in New Orleans. Water would have been much cooler to have with the Gulf right there."

I cuffed his arm and drained the water bottle before settling down beside Francis. "Now remember, like we discussed with Logan, if you feel like I'm in any danger, try tugging on the connection we share and see if you can pull me out."

He flipped his hat backwards, indicating he was game, and his bicep flexed beneath my touch. The elf's pupils dilated when I zapped him with a prickle of icy magic. His quicksilver grin flashed, and he snagged his own water bottle and opened it. A bubble of liquid rose from the opening and twisted a few times. "I *so* can't wait to see what I can do with this later."

"Focus."

"Sure thing, boss."

An incubus in a dark suit and flashy sapphire tie stepped into the room, holding out a cellphone. "Mr. Caron, sir? Call for you. Sounds urgent."

The prince grunted, looking torn, but crossed the floor, arms folded, expression thunderous.

"Alright." I addressed Rue and lifted the incubus's arm, measuring his thready pulse. "I'll start with Francis here, who's the farthest along according to the charts I've seen. We'll see how things go from there." I rolled up my sleeves and glanced over the patient's file.

Why was I stalling?

Inhale. Exhale. Inhale again.

"Alright Francis, I know you're made of tough stuff. Let's get you some relief." I pressed my hand to the thin skin beneath his throat and started channeling my magic into him—at the same time a voice screamed for me to stop.

But it was too late.

I'd already fallen.

Chapter 26

The lack of static and fierce vibrations tipped me off first. As much as I'd hated the television screen fuzz and wailing winds, their absence meant something had changed. Something that probably wasn't very good.

Dark, sticky ooze clung to my boots as I trudged forward, squinting at a faint, pulsing light in the distance. While not flecked with static, a dense, soupy haze lingered. Within minutes, my shirt clung to me like plastic wrap, damp from the not-humidity.

I was so focused on moving forward I nearly tripped over Francis's body, covered in sludge and muck as it was. I knelt, brushing what I could away from his eyes, nose, and mouth. He was weak, so incredibly weak, but when my fingertips glowed blue, ready to blast the world with my magic, he gripped my wrist with surprising strength.

"Leave me," he croaked.

I shook my head. "If I can help, I will."

"There's nothing you can do. I know it, you don't. But you will." I had to put my ear basically on his mouth to hear him. "This… it's like nothing I've ever felt before. Like a monster gnawing at my bones, sipping at my blood."

Sweat and gore covered every inch of my body, but I sat down anyway, leaning closer, trying to not miss anything. The incubus's eyes weren't open anymore. His fingers hung limply in mine. "It's relentless. And they're angry, Gods they're so angry. I don't..."

"They?" I shook his shoulders, his head lolling. "Don't what? What else? Who is angry? Can you describe them?"

"... three..."

He released a small, choking gasp. Tensed. And I felt his soul release its grip from the husk that remained of his broken body. The incubus dissolved in my arms, the gray dust that was his soul flecking the dark ground.

I hovered there, suspended in my shock, then plunged my arms deep into the sludge, clawing and slashing at the putty, spraying blobs and chunks of whatever the curse was composed of everywhere. Warm wetness trickled down my cheeks. Tears. I was crying.

The fervor of my strikes slowed until my arms dangled uselessly, coated in mud as more shudders coursed through me. I felt wrung dry, twisted like a dishtowel from my toenails to the roots of my hair. Francis was gone. I'd been too late to save him.

The weight of my grief shocked me.

I hadn't known him. I'd barely known his name. But I'd literally held him in my arms when he breathed his last, when his magic fled his body.

His magic.

I blinked, realizing the shuddering wasn't coming from me. It came from all around. The dark, depressing realm reeking of stale and filth was shaking. In the distance, an ominous something cracked, worse than a tree splitting in a storm or lightning smacking the desert, crystalizing the sand.

Horror clenched my core in a vice.

I needed to go.

With the incubus gone, his mind was collapsing, the curse disintegrating, its task complete.

Maybe I could follow it—the idea blazed bright, but when I tried to stand, tried to reach out, tried to do something, anything, I couldn't. I couldn't move. The slime held me tight, banding my legs and hands to the ground. I reached for my flames to lash out at the ooze, to sear it away from me, but came up empty. All of them. All three of my magics gone. Stolen by whatever this awful *thing* was.

I tipped my head back to scream, wondering where Lachlan was.

If he even knew anything was wrong.

The prickle started in my chest, spiraling deeper and deeper until it hit the gore and exploded. Waves engulfed me and I let them drag me under. The water pounded, swirling and sucking, and soon I was lost, the darkness reminiscent of ocean depths erasing the black and bloodied world around me. All that remained of the once-beautiful mind of a cursed fey.

I landed painfully, my knees jarring as I smacked into the tile. I panted, scouring the blinding white light as I clawed at my shirt, my jacket, groped at my hair and face, noting the lack of stickiness at the frantic touch. I needed to know I was, in fact, real and whole and astoundingly alive.

My breathing stabilized as my vision cleared. It wasn't until I scented the medicinal, sterile quality all hospitals seemed to have, that I believed I was back. That I was whole. That my magic was still with me.

A hand squeezed my shoulder, the same spot Lachlan always touched whether in support or in play. Sure enough, I blinked past the sheen of tears limning my eyes and found him kneeling beside me, hovering protectively. He extended his hand, fingers spread, and I grabbed it, squeezing that I was ok.

His nose touched my hair as he sighed in relief.

On my other side stood Ridley, arms crossed and body strung tight. Sunglasses shielded his eyes, but a muscle ticked along his jaw as his chin dipped. His shadow of a brother emerged behind him, expression impassive as he perched on a cabinet of supplies, bouncing a ball of black nothingness against the wall. I wasn't sure where Rue had gone, but knew she must still be close.

"You good, boss?"

I sucked air in through my nose. "I don't know."

I went to drag my hands across my face out of habit and barely suppressed a whimper. Smudges of black tar stained both. I scrubbed at the stains with the pads of my fingers, but still they lingered, embedded in the grooves of my skin and the beds of my nails. I longed to burn them away, went to reach for my flames, but hesitated when the warmth touched my face.

"What's wrong?" Lachlan pulled me to my feet, lavender eyes flicking from my raised hands to my face. "You look… haunted."

"Do you see—" I swallowed, turning my hands over and finding more of the same blackness.

"See what?" Ridley this time, his face set in stone.

"Never mind." I lowered my trembling arms. They couldn't see… whatever it was. Maybe it was an afterimage of the curse. Or maybe part of the incubus still clung to me, even after death.

The incubus.

I nearly tripped over Lachlan's lanky legs as I darted for the bed, leaning in to check Francis's pulse despite knowing what I would find. "He's dead."

"Yes." Lachlan sounded distant, like a badly tuned radio. "He passed not long after you went under. When you didn't come out immediately, I had to drag you out. I guess that connection thing we share is as strong as you thought."

"He's dead." My eyes burned, but the tears had already dried, spent in the wasteland of what remained of Francis's soul. The grief, the yawning, gaping grief that had consumed me in his mind threatened to pull me under now. It would be so easy to tumble back into that abyss, to surrender to the sadness and stress.

Unable to stand it any longer, I turned my back on the incubus's body. "I was holding him and he died."

The prince cleared his throat and ignored the wild look Lachlan shot his way. "What else do you remember, Ms. Ramone?"

"I remember you shouting for me to stop. But… that's it."

"So you don't remember why I wanted you to stop? What I'd learned in that call I took?"

"Obviously not," I gritted. My skin felt too tight, my lungs too big. I was about to split open. My chest pulsed painfully, the sickly gross sensation spreading inside me, much like the ooze I'd abandoned minutes ago. I dreaded the words about to pass my lips. "What happened?"

"That call was from an associate of mine from South Africa. That incubus you helped? The one that drew me to call you here in the first place?" The void that had cracked open inside of me spread, crackling along the edges. I didn't want Ridley to finish his thought.

"He died," the prince said. I flinched at the bite in those words, my arms drawing around myself tightly. "I was told he was fine one minute and the next he was screaming bloody murder, clawing at his skin… and then he slumped over. He was gone the next moment."

I couldn't look Ridley in the face, afraid of the truths I might find there.

I felt lost. A speck of dust floating in the air. Two fey I'd thought I could help had died. One of them I'd promised the worst was over. The other crumbled to nothing as I screamed for him to hold on. But Logan—how was Logan? I ripped my phone from my pocket, fingers whirring over the buttons as I shot off a text. My heart squeezed and my foot tapped the floor until the device pinged. A breath shuddered from my lips. "Logan is alive. She's still with us. Weak, but with us."

What did that mean? Was she next? Were succubi immune to…

whatever had happened just now? My body swiveled, the need to pace overwhelming me, but Lachlan blocked my path in one direction and Ridley the other.

"Logan is… the other fey you helped, I assume?" the prince asked. His blood-orange eyes glimmered. "Any other details about her condition?"

I scanned the face of the phone. I considered firing off another text, but instead lifted the device to my ear. It rang once before the witch picked up.

"Something's gone wrong, huh?" Lee observed huskily.

"Two incubi I helped in the same way as your sister are dead."

A pause. "Logan is stronger than how you left her. She's eating solid foods and keeps fiddling with her magic, but nothing else has changed."

I bit my lip and closed my eyes, counting to five as I absorbed the blow of the good news. "If that changes—"

"Fix this, Water God. I will not bury my sister."

The line went dead.

I waited a beat, bobbling the phone in my stained and blackened fingers, and tucked it away. Rue returned as I relayed everything Lee had told me.

"Well, that gives us a starting point—" Rue started to say, but I wasn't having any of it. I stared down at Francis's body, at his broken veins and translucent skin. A fey I could have helped if I were stronger. Or more knowledgeable. Or—

"I failed." The words were a gunshot in the dark of night. I jerked to Ridley, needing to see him acknowledge what he wasn't saying, despite the news about Logan. "I failed. You know it. I know it. The dead most definitely know it." The prince winced, but I saw it, that flicker of confirmation. I'd wanted it, needed it, but still, *feeling* it was like razors slicing across my skin.

"Zara, I'm sorry." Ridley's soft voice slashed me to bits. "I tried to stop you, but I was too late. We'll figure it out. Knowing that one of them is still recovering… that's good. It—"

"I don't have any answers for you. I'm…" My mouth worked, but no sound came out. "I'm no closer to figuring this out than I was when I saw Logan lying on that bed." I shuddered, unable to continue.

My head roared, my body trembled. I couldn't hold this in. It was too much. The grief, the pain, the despair. The black staining my hands. "I'm so sorry, but I can't be in here right now."

In true Zara fashion, I turned heel and sprinted out the exit. Mist brushed my skin when I shoved my way through the heavy door, but it thickened to a drizzle as I strode out into the mess. The world knew what I knew, what I wanted to say but couldn't find the words for. I dropped to my knees beside the SUV, the drizzle increasing to pounding rain that stung like needles.

No thunder.

No lightning.

Grief wasn't always a loud affair.

Sometimes it struck quietly but viciously.

As the rain fell, drenching the desert in tears, I raised my hands, the inky blots stark against the gray-white clouds. They didn't fade, didn't smear.

A truth that refused to wipe away.

Chapter 27

When the words blurred on the page, I called it a day.

I tore a piece of wax paper that had encased a sandwich made with natural peanut butter from Lachlan and stuck it inside the book before closing it. It was one of dozens surrounding the suede couch on which I lounged. One of dozens of books pulled from the massive shelves on each of the library's four walls that yielded little to no new information about the curse.

Ridley had shown me the library a few days ago during a tour of his mansion, which, as promised, was situated about a mile from the hospital. This room reminded me of Belle's library from that movie with the Beast, only less dusty.

The lamp at my elbow flickered, and I glanced at the door where wispy feathers of smoke slipped through the crack beneath and solidified into the shape of the incubus himself.

"You know doors typically come equipped with these things called handles, right?" I shifted the book to the top of a stack at my elbow. The black markings on my fingers had, thankfully, faded, so I figured they must have been some sort of residual imprint in my mind. "They're these little levers that you turn to either push or pull to get to the other side?"

"I'm familiar with the concept." Ridley hooked his thumbs in his pockets and crossed the mosaic floor. It was a work of art: glass pieces the colors of emerald, sapphire, milky-white, and onyx worked into the depiction of a serpent swallowing the moon. "Those handles, as you call them, have the downside of not working when the lock is engaged."

I eyed the door with a frown. Lachlan must have locked it when he left earlier, after a vague mention of riding motocross or learning to fly a single-engine plane. He did not see the entertainment in pouring over books all day—not that I blamed him. "What can I do for you, Prince?"

Ridley pulled aside a long, velvet drape and peered through the window that stood taller than he did. I frowned at the brightness of the sunlight highlighting his features, and groped around the side table for my phone to check the time.

"When was the last time you left this room?" he asked.

I finally unearthed the device only to find it dead and tossed it back among my collection of used coffee mugs. "That depends. What time is it?" My jaw popped with a heady yawn.

"After ten in the morning." He tied back the drapes with a flourish. That explained why it was so bright outside.

"Ten o'clock on..."

"Pardon?"

"What day is it?"

"Stars, Ms. Ramone. You can't be serious."

But I could be, and I very much was. While Ridley had set aside rooms for Lachlan and me, and they were beautiful rooms with monster-sized beds and carpets so plush I nearly sank to my knees, I'd chosen this room as my particular cave. It was where I'd stayed for, what I realized was three days, after that disastrous first encounter at Cura.

I'd briefly brainstormed with Ridley that evening. We agreed the curse must linger within those who survived and attacked the magic that remained. Ridley also felt that those behind the curse had learned of my involvement and must have tweaked their spell so it could detect and assault my magic, too. Now, I spent my time dedicated to finding out more: whether more was breaking the curse or tracking down the perpetrators in this wide, wide world.

"I finally figured out how to read this book that was giving you trouble." I tapped the text I'd set aside when he'd walked in, then stretched, the bones in my neck popping. "There might be a way for us to track the magic, but the details are vaguer than I'd like."

"That's promising, and I'd like to hear more, but not in this room." Irritation flared as Ridley faced me square on. He didn't approach either physically or magically, but I got the sense he was caging me in. "You need to get out of here for a bit. A change in scenery may give you some perspective."

I considered arguing, but figured he might have a point and followed him to the door, straightening my clothing as best I could. It could probably stand a good washing. Ridley seemed to agree because he cocked one brow as he eyed me. Today, he looked positively princely, with his cashmere sweater, tailored slacks, and polished wingtips.

"Your wardrobe is fully stocked." He held open the door and followed me into the hall. "And you could use a bath or six."

"Are you saying I smell?"

"No, you reek."

Smoky tendrils wafted off his shoulders, and I bit my tongue as we marched down the hallway. The entire way, he muttered to himself. As we started down a large, spiral staircase, I thought I heard a snatch of, "Ryder would kill me if he saw this," before increasing his pace.

The incubus's shoes were silent in the foyer, which was as open and sparsely decorated as the rest of the house. I couldn't help but notice the windows, so many windows, that lined the front and sides of the house. Despite evidence to the contrary, I'd always kept a mental image of daemoni being creatures of the night.

The prince guided me into a kitchen that was a lot of white on white with some stainless-steel appliances to break up the monotony. As I slipped onto a padded stool, I speared my fingers through my hair, barely repressing a shudder at the grease I found. Maybe Ridley was right to pull me from the library.

Rue turned from yet another window overlooking the desert, a cup of what smelled like coffee in hand. She paused mid-stir, lips pursing as she took in first her brother and then her guest. "So you are alive after all, Water God."

"Zara," I corrected. While I didn't mind Ridley using a more formal title, mostly because I still didn't like him very much, it bothered me not hearing my given name. "Just Zara."

The doctor hummed softly in something that was neither agreement nor disagreement and leaned against the quartz countertop, hair shifting over her shoulder as she brought her mug to her lips. The counters were flawlessly clean, not so much as a crumb marring the surface. It made me twitch. I promptly pressed a thumbprint to one speckled bit. There. An imperfection.

I glanced up when the prince started opening cabinet doors, rattling pans and plates with a vengeance.

"So, tell me, what's got my brother all worked up?" Rue took another small sip. "Did that elf of yours say something? Or is it because you're trying out roadkill cosplay?"

A skillet clanged when Ridley dropped it on the stove. "Seriously, Rue?" he huffed.

"What? This is the first time I've seen you in the kitchen, let alone using it. Of course I'm going to ask questions."

"First off, not what I was talking about." He jerked open the fridge and rummaged around. "And second, if I've never been in here before, then how do I know where everything is?"

"I didn't say you were stupid."

I missed Ridley's retort over another jaw-breaking yawn of mine. I'd never seen this droll side of the Caron sister. Granted, I'd only talked to her that one brief time, and already I liked her better than her other two local brothers. Her attire was more formal today: ruby silk top, gray slacks, white lab coat, and the same thick, black frames. She dressed the part of a polished CEO. I admired it.

My mouth watered at the salty scent of sizzling bacon and I gripped the counter to keep from rushing the stove. I couldn't remember the last time I'd had bacon. And eggs? I could die happy.

"Where is that friend of yours, anyway?" Rue twirled her cup. "It's strange to see you without him, and he's too large to hide in the shadows."

"I don't think Lachlan would want to hide in the shadows, anyway. He's much happier being in the middle of everything, and he's not shy about making that clear, too." My chuckle sounded rusty to my ears. "I'm not sure where he is right now, but he must be doing something more thrilling than watching me read books all day."

"So, he left you to work so he could have fun?"

I shook my head at Ridley's terse assessment, and accepted the glass of water he slid across the counter. "No. I wouldn't say that. Research and reading aren't his forte. He's a doer more than a thinker, believes if you attack something hard enough or fast enough that you'll overcome it."

"Sounds like a volatile way of living." Rogue sprinkled a handful of peppers over the pan.

"Maybe. But that doesn't mean he's wrong for living that way." I wasn't about to cop to my own recklessness before these two, but I had to admit that I used to operate a lot like Lachlan did. I pushed my empty glass back across the counter. "He owns up to who he is. I don't begrudge him that because he's had my back for the past few weeks. He listens to my ideas, but is also willing to step in and make a decision when it counts. His willingness to throw himself into whatever's happening has saved our lives on more than one occasion." I thought about our encounter with the centaurs in South Africa.

"We complement one another. He forces me to confront my weaknesses, and I restrain him when he's getting to be too insane." I rubbed my palms over my thighs. "It works for us."

Ridley dumped his creation onto a plate and passed it to me along with a fresh glass of water. My stomach practically jumped at the enormous pile of eggs and mushrooms and peppers and *bacon.* I fell on the food as if I'd never seen it before.

The incubus exchanged a look with his sister. "If you don't slow down, you'll choke."

"You don't understand." I moaned when I crunched into a crispy strip of meat. Its salty, sweet, smoky taste was something I'd desperately missed. "I can't remember the last time my meals didn't include some kind of grain. And meat? Forget about it."

"More of the elf's influence?" Rue asked.

I froze with my fork midway to my mouth, but she sounded more curious than critical, so I shrugged. "Sure. He's vegetarian and I forget to eat often. Put those together and it makes sense. Besides, we were on the move a lot. Granola bars and fruits are easy to transport."

"Oh, to be young and free again," Rue sighed. I eyed her, wondering how old she was exactly. The succubus tucked her hair behind her ear. "On that note, I need to get to Cura. One of our healers texted me about two new patients coming in today." She snatched a crossbody purse off a hook on the wall and threw it on. "*Zara,* it was lovely seeing you today. I hope to see both of you later."

She shot Ridley a glance full of hidden meaning before flouncing out the door. I shoveled another forkful of egg in my mouth before I could ask about it. It wasn't my business, anyway. Just like this wasn't my home and, sometimes, this life didn't feel like my own.

Ridley busied himself with gathering up various bowls and the skillet. I finished my meal in silence, though the food that had tasted delicious on my tongue settled like a rock in my gut. Having Rue in the room had eased the tension that lingered between the Prince of Sin and me. Now that it was the two of us alone in this massive house… I swore I heard the library calling my name, urging me to fall back into its comforting, pulpy depths.

"I know you think I'm a bastard." I paused mid-chew, glancing around the kitchen to ensure it was, indeed, Ridley who had said that. I swallowed hard, wondering if the sentence was a trap.

The incubus plunged his hands into the soapy water. "Normally, I'd be fine with that. It comes with the job and I don't particularly care what anyone outside my family thinks of me." His hands stilled in the water as he thought over what he'd said. "Scratch that. Sometimes I don't even care what they think."

Two bites of food remained on my plate, but I'd given up on them entirely. "You don't need to explain yourself to me."

His head dipped in agreement, and he placed a neatly rinsed plate in the dish drain. It was bizarre, seeing the prince wash his own dishes. Like watching a dog play piano or something. Weirdly unexpected. "I realize that. But I want you to understand where I'm coming from. As my sister pointed out, only about a dozen beings on this planet understand the situation I'm in on a daily basis. You—and your fellow Gods—are among them."

I swirled the water in my newly refilled glass, but didn't drink from it. I appreciated his directness, but this entire conversation felt like something out of a dream. "I can work with you even if I don't like you."

Blood-orange eyes heavy with amusement captured mine, before shifting back to the sink. He'd already finished about half the dishes.

"A few days ago, you said Ryder had never mentioned us, that you knew nothing of our family. Was that the truth?"

"I have no reason to lie to you."

He weighed Rue's mug, heavy with soapy froth, in both hands. "I kicked him out."

I'd suspected as much, having pieced together the hints Ryder had dropped and added them to Ridley's abrasive personality, but it was still a shock hearing the truth dropped out there like that. Or what he said to be the truth, anyway.

"Ryder is the youngest of my siblings—there are seven of us, in case you're counting." Ridley plunged the mug into the water and massaged it with a yellow sponge. "He also suffered immensely from the youngest sibling syndrome. He was spoiled and selfish, spending money as if he could pluck it like leaves from a tree."

I set down my glass and realized I'd leaned forward unconsciously.

"That's not to say he wasn't kind. He was. He was a smart kid, quick on the uptake and funny in a way that none of us understood." Ridley dried his hands on a lacey towel. "But as he grew into his status as the youngest prince of a mighty fey household, he changed. Those parts of him that made him such a wonderful person to be around got buried. He also only found time for those he thought were worth it, typically people he could get something out of."

"Where were your parents in all of this?" I couldn't help from asking. "Couldn't they have stepped in and helped? Or did they encourage his behavior?"

The room darkened marginally, my magic spiking as his pressed against me. It faded so quickly I wondered if I'd imagined it. "Ryder never knew our parents. They were murdered not long after he was born."

A sickly mass wiggled in my gut, greasy tentacles spinning my stomach into knots. I couldn't help but remember Lachlan's confession, the story he'd told about the massacre of the daemoni royal family. But hadn't only one child survived? Ridley confessed to having six siblings, three of whom I'd met.

I looked up from my hands clenched tightly on the counter, bracing against the hardness in his gaze. He continued, "I was there that night, when it happened. Still a boy by our culture's standards. I escaped. Fortunately, my other siblings were away at our retreat in the mountains."

I wanted to vomit. "I'm sorry. I didn't—"

"There's no way you could have known." He pulled the stopper in the sink and stared at the swirling, soapy water. "Stars know it's been hundreds of years. But perhaps you can better understand my reluctance when it comes to your friend."

"But you gave him a room in your house." My hand pressed against my chest as if keeping my ribs together, stopping my insides from spilling out. "You didn't hesitate."

Ridley shook his head. "I may never be ok with what I witnessed that night. However, I also realize your friend wasn't alive when the raid happened. Like you said earlier, I might not like him, but I will tolerate him. Though I did, I admit, succumb to my inner feelings when we first met."

My view of Ridley had taken a hard turn. I had no doubt he was leaving out details, even now I felt like he was avoiding something vital to the story, but I sympathized with him, compared myself to him. I'd spared Geoffrey's life, despite, at the time, believing he had ordered the attack that killed my parents.

But now I saw things differently.

He was not your enemy until you forced him to take up the mantle.

I wondered exactly when Geoffrey had changed his tune. I'd recognized the horror in his eyes when he'd spotted me escaping the inferno that had been my childhood home. At the time, I'd mistaken it for hate. I wondered what else I'd mistaken regarding the former head of the Order. I needed to look over more of those documents we'd recovered after the battle when I made it back to Rome.

"If I may continue." Ridley's stiff, overly formal request drew me back, and I realized I'd accidentally finished my water for lack of anything better to do. "As the head of our clan, it fell on me to deal with Ryder. His antics were causing problems for our family, for our race. There were relations I was trying to retain at the time and things weren't going well."

Ryder sounded like every petulant teenager since the dawn of time.

"I'd given him any number of warnings, offered him a variety of outs. Nothing stuck. It was bearable until a scandal about two hundred years ago." Ridley leaned against the counter. "A young witch died at a party he hosted. The details of what happened exactly are still unclear, no one in attendance was particularly sober, but as the host, responsibility fell on his shoulders."

My eyes burned as I thought about that poor girl, about Ryder. About how horrible that must have been... for everyone. Ridley fisted the damp towel, eyes glazed.

"They held a trial, and ultimately he was found not guilty for what had gone down. The evidence wasn't there. However, it *was* determined Ryder had cultivated and created a system that supported the bad behavior that ended up resulting, albeit loosely, to that girl's death." The prince released the fabric and popped his knuckles. It sounded like kernels in the microwave. "They determined the best course of action was to temporarily disown him from the Caron name, deeming him too risky to keep connected to the royal household, until he could learn restraint."

Ridley met my eyes, the turbulence I'd glimpsed earlier quelled. "I could have vetoed their decision. Ryder begged me to not carry through with his punishment. But I sided with the court; I told him he would never be worth anything. And I meant it."

I shuddered. For Ryder to hear that from his brother who'd practically raised him... I could only imagine how horrible I would have felt.

"He left without packing a bag, dropped his last name and any association he had with it, and started a new life." A slight smile touched the incubus's lips. "A life where he's proven me wrong on every count."

The stool creaked as I leaned back, stretching muscles that had gone to sleep as I sat there. The prince was right. I did think he was a bastard. Based on what he'd done to me and what he'd done to his brother—and probably countless other human and fey—he was calculated and crafty. However, I also recognized his motives weren't purely evil or cynical, either.

He played the long game, and, for him to still be alive now, in the position he held, he played it well. As was evidenced by the turnaround with Ryder.

I wondered what exactly it was Ridley had wanted to gain from me that day in the Bellagio, what information he'd hoped to learn, or the lesson he'd wanted to impart. He'd told me it was a matter of wariness and not trusting the world. But was that all?

"You alright there, Ms. Ramone?" he asked.

I stood, face pinched with thought. I held out my hand, drawing forth my magic and lacing it around me at the same time. "Please, call me Zara."

Chapter 28

Shoes hammered on the hardwood floors outside the kitchen and I eyed the doorway, holding back a chuckle when Lachlan appeared around the corner, a wide grin splitting his face. He finished tugging a Red Sox cap over his damp hair and hooked an arm around my neck. The elf pressed his nose to my braid and inhaled.

"Oh good, you showered today."

I swung an elbow out, but he danced away before it landed.

I may have adapted to being a morning person, but it defied all reason that Lach didn't care what time of day it was—he could wake up in seconds, chipper as a squirrel.

He shoved two oranges in his trench coat pockets. In the two days since I'd told Ridley about Lachlan's eating habits, I'd noticed more fruit around the house. The elf spoke around the end of the banana he'd bitten off. "And you're trying on some of those clothes Rue picked up for you." Large hands gripped my shoulders, spinning me on the stool. His light eyes swung down my length, stopping at the blue gray, knee-high boots I'd pulled over my jeans. "Those look too pretty to kick ass. I expect you to recover your old pair when we get back."

I drained my cup of coffee. I drank so much of the stuff lately, it practically ran through my veins. "You're coming with?" I hadn't expected that.

He guided me off the chair. "Miss seeing the daemoni court in action? Without being on trial for anything myself? For shame."

"The prince was cool with you coming?" Maybe I should have grabbed a thermos because this scenario wasn't computing.

"Who do you think invited me?" We clattered down the stone staircase that led to a long, sloping, circle drive out front where an SUV and a succubus with hand-drawn eyebrows waited. "That dude is a kitten when you get to know him."

Ridley? A kitten?

"I think I need more of an—"

"No time, we're running late as it is." Lach shoved me into the vehicle and nimbly jumped in behind me. The succubus closed the door before misting into smoke and slipping into the driver's seat. The elf asked, "You have everything you need?"

"I wasn't aware I needed anything," I grumbled.

The elf scratched his head through his cap and settled back as the desert passed by. I squeezed my phone in my pocket. I'd checked in with Lee earlier and everything was good, but I couldn't help the tightness in my chest that never quite went away.

"What have you been up to?" I asked.

"A little of this and that. Drag racing, cliff jumping, gambling." He winked and passed over the pouch that used to contain my herbal supplement. I first noted its weight, then squeezed it and peered inside. My lips parted at the sheer volume of crumpled bills. "Nothing as exciting as stopping a city from flooding or extinguishing a forest fire, but I had energy to burn."

"Sounds like you've been having fun." When the elf made no effort to retrieve the cash, I shoved the bag into my pocket. Rue may have replaced my wardrobe, but I'd kept my pine-green jacket. I preferred its heft, the canvas material, the way it swallowed me whole, turning me into another face in the crowd.

"Say the word and I'll add you to my reservation for diving with sharks this afternoon." Lach's toes tapped on the floor of the vehicle, his excessive energy seeking an outlet. "Or I can cancel if you're ready to finally split from this place."

"I can't do that." And I didn't want to. This wasn't about Logan anymore. This was about an entire race of fey. Fey who didn't deserve what was happening to them. Fey that included Ryder, Ridley, and their family. If any of them contracted this curse, and there was something I could have done to prevent it, I didn't think I'd ever be able to look myself in the face again.

"I'm invested here, Lach. The daemoni need me, *Ridley* needs me." Why I said that, I wasn't sure, but I moved on. "If I left, what would that say about me? What kind of God doesn't care for her people? What kind of God jumps ship because the going gets tough?"

Lachlan tapped my hand, which was squeezing the life from the vial around my neck. Another time, another struggle, another desperate situation. "I figured that was the case, boss. But I think you needed to hear yourself say it, too."

I mulled over those words as we lapsed into silence, each looking out our own window. I was glad the elf had glued himself to me like he had. For months, I'd been alone, something I freely and willingly embraced, but I hadn't realized I'd grown *lonely* during that time. And there was a difference. Lachlan had filled that void and then some, his optimistic attitude and acute observations countering my personality perfectly.

The SUV eventually rolled to a stop, and I blinked out at the fountain. "The Bellagio?"

"You know it. The Caron home base and center of their activities: illegal, political, or otherwise." Lachlan threw open the door without waiting for our driver and hauled me out. He and I were going to have words about this whole touchy-feely thing he had going on today. "Now hurry up."

Lach pushed me along as I dragged my hood up over my hair. It was probably too late for the gesture to matter, but it made me feel better. At the entrance, a security guard in a spiffy, blue plaid suit waited, shades fixed on the bridge of his nose. A white cord scrolled from his ear. He muttered into his lapel, and, with a flick of his wrist, gestured for Lachlan and me to follow him to a familiar set of elevators.

Instead of going up, we went down.

Down, down, down.

The farther down we dropped, the greater my anticipation grew. There was still so much I had to learn about the fey. To see the daemoni court in action wasn't something I'd ever expected to be a part of.

The elevator stopped as Lach added the swoosh of a grin to his smudged smiley face on the mirrored wall. We stepped out with our guard, who leveled a look at me, a look difficult to decipher behind his standard-issue shades. "While you are permitted to watch from the proceedings chamber, I've been instructed to take you to one of our booths instead. Is that suitable?"

At my blank expression, Lach piped up. "Go big or go home, my man."

"Very good. Should you change your mind at any point, I'll be waiting outside." The incubus unlocked a bottle-green door and opened it to reveal a dark room. "This chamber is sound-proofed from the inside and the glass is two-way. As long as the walls remain intact—" I frowned. Why did I get the feeling that comment was directed at me?—"you will hear and see everything, but won't be seen or heard yourself. Again, should you require my assistance, knock twice on the door. Thank you again for visiting, Water God."

He shut us inside with a slight bow.

"This is going to be *good*," Lach said. His excitement mirrored my own.

As he collapsed into a chair with a cushion of feathers, I went to the window, wishing I had a photographic memory so I could remember every little detail later. Our room was on the second level, overlooking an expansive chamber packed with dozens—maybe hundreds—of fey kneeling on jewel-toned cushions. They all faced a line of seven high-backed chairs. Each was handcrafted with a different wood and engraved with swirling patterns I couldn't yet interpret.

In the center, sprawled in a throne of hickory, was Ridley. He'd donned yet another slick suit, though he'd lost the sunglasses. He propped his cheek on his knuckles, eyes hooded. With similar expressions on either side of him, sat Rue and Rim.

An incubus with a gold button pinned at his lapel emerged from the shadows behind the thrones, hands clasped, and muttered something to Ridley who tipped his chin in acknowledgment. As the fey stepped back, he waved a hand and long golden curtains that lined the wall across from and, I assumed, beneath us, drew back. I gasped. The action revealed dozens more fey tucked away inside rooms, also kneeling in subjugation as they waited patiently for whatever was about to happen.

Ridley levered himself up using the curved arm of the chair. "Good afternoon and thank you all for being here today. Your attendance, as always, is appreciated. I realize many of you have come from far and wide, and it's a delight to see so many faces, both fresh and familiar."

He paused, linking his hands behind his back. I swore his eyes darted toward the glass behind which I was concealed.

"For four hundred years, I've held my position as Prince of our great nation. For four hundred years I've listened to your questions, concerns, and complaints. I've maintained our long-standing tradition, where, regardless of magical ability or the lack thereof, wealth or poverty, strength and weakness, we've gathered once every three months as we are today, to hear you out." His head tilted as he scanned the room. "We are not a people of one, we are a people of all, and I, along with the rest of the Caron family, will continue to do all we can within our power to help serve you."

Rue and Rim inclined their heads.

"Let's begin." The Prince of Sin took his seat, spine straight as he perched on the edge of the chair. A succubus in a gold dress stepped away from the wall, a clipboard held before her, and started rattling off a series of names.

"Lach." I sensed the elf turn to me because I was incapable of looking away from the assembly. "What exactly does Ridley do?"

The elf drummed his fingers on his thigh. "Oh, a number of things, I suppose. He's the head of Caron Enterprises, managing a significant number of properties primarily tied to wealth or sex in some fashion, in recognition of where their people excel based on their primal talents."

A fey in a tight blue top and skirt that skimmed the top of her thighs slipped to the front of the room.

"He also operates as a head of state." In the reflection of the glass, Lachlan dipped into one pocket, then another, searching for something. "He manages one of the five ancient fey kingdoms, holding meetings, discussing contracts, obligations, negotiations, and such. The fey world isn't necessarily separate from the human world, and we are a major component of human politics, but we do hold our own courts."

Below, the fey held her hands stiffly at her sides.

"And today, like he does every quarter, he's hearing directly from his people, offering his wealth and guidance to those who follow him."

The female fey spoke, her voice sweeter than the pink bubblegum I'd loved as a child. The kind that turned thick as tar after two chomps. "My prince, my mother lost her job because of a lingering illness and my father passed away some time ago. I'm the eldest of my four siblings, and I've had difficulties finding employment. Are there any openings where I may find work?"

Ridley smiled faintly. "I'm sure we can figure something out. I'll have you speak with Elise." A succubus with generous curves stepped from the alcove behind the chairs. "She will secure you a position that works with your talents."

The fey dropped into a curtsey, head bowed with relief. "You're most kind, dear prince."

The fey in gold called out another name, and from the crowd stepped a balding, heavyset incubus with drooping jowls. He asked for help with a new business venture, and Ridley responded by calling forward an incubus armed with a sheaf of green-toned paperwork.

I pressed against the glass, fascinated with the proceedings as more fey were called to the front of the room. Most asked for help with various requests along a similar vein, but others aired grievances—things from human intervention to concerns about magical application.

Ridley gave each speaker his full attention and responded thoughtfully. For answers he didn't know, he would defer to Rue, Rim, or a variety of the fey poised behind him. Not once did he sound impatient or bored, despite probably having heard similar requests thousands of times over again. Instead, he expressed genuine concern about the needs of his people. Hours passed as I stood there, palm against the glass, watching the head of the daemoni nation handle his subjects.

He cared. He truly cared.

"It's incredible," I said.

"He wanted you to see this," Lachlan said. I glanced back at my friend. He balanced his whetstone on his lap, but no weapons were in sight. "When you're done saving the world and all that jazz, this will be part of what awaits you. These past few months, you've been taking part in the process without knowing it."

My lips parted. It was true. I hadn't held a formal gathering like this, but I had been meeting with fey and humans in their communities, doing what I could to help. To listen.

A tingle ran down my spine.

"There's something I've been wondering." I watched my reflection in the glass. "Ridley is a prince."

"Yes."

"And his siblings are princes and princesses."

"Stands to reason."

"Then who are the king and queen?"

I turned back when the elf didn't reply, ignoring the way my insides twisted like taffy. Lach's eyes were hooded, his expression tight, his lips pursed. He tugged on one of his long fingers and picked up the whetstone. "Do you really need me to answer that?"

My head buzzed and butterflies exploded in my chest, only to be swamped by the oozing sense of dread. The heavy weight that came with all power hooked its claws deeper into me. I worried my lip and turned back to the window, struggling to see past the glow of my eyes.

On some level, I'd known what I was, the power that came with it. The responsibility. I'd certainly used that position to my advantage in many circumstances, using my status as a God as both a weapon and a shield.

"It's a pleasure to meet you, Majesty."

It was one of the first things Ryder had ever said to me.

I lowered my forehead to the cool glass, staring blankly down at the congregation.

Majesty. Queen. He'd used the phrase a few times, but I'd always thought he was being flippant. Another layer to his flirtation. I'd never once considered it to be a title. A truth. A reality of which I was ignorant.

It explained the bowing, the gestures, the words of deference, the wide eyes and darting looks. While part of me acknowledged nothing changed, that whether it was God or Queen—both were merely words in the English language—this actuality rang home far louder than I'd expected.

"Are you ok?" Lachlan rose to stand beside me at the window.

I fingered the interlocking loops of my braid. I'd offered the elf in a place by my side, for stars sake. I knew that the Water Temple was my home, where I belonged, but I'd never looked far enough into my future to realize what that might look like. To imagine that it would look like this, the fey court and its proud royal family at the helm.

I cleared my throat roughly. "I'm ok. A little shaken, but alright."

"Before you get too caught up in your head, you should know a title is only a title. They're letters dressed up in fancy finery, then propped up on pedestals above other words." His eyes reflected the fey kneeling on the cushions below us. "There will always be those who see you for only that purpose, like everyone down there. The way they see it, you are someone with the power to do something for them.

"That's why I wanted to follow you. Your magic intrigues me. It will probably always intrigue me." He drew a deep breath, then turned us so we faced each other, our shoulders resting against the glass. "Plus, there's the adventure to it all. Getting close to a God? Without dying? Following her path? Only the most daring of fey would attempt such a feat. Who am I to turn down that challenge?"

It stung, hearing him talk about our relationship like this. Like something casual and disposable. I fiddled with the zipper pull at the base of my jacket. Lach was here now, but he wouldn't always be. I felt foolish now, thinking we'd grown closer as friends. Perhaps my emotions were one-sided.

At least I could appreciate the elf's honesty.

"Talk to me, boss."

I couldn't hold it back, not since the question ate through me like acid. "Is that all I am to you? Something to play with until you get bored and abandon me like a broken toy?"

The elf huffed and tugged on my arm, but I jerked from his hold. His face contorted. "You've got it all wrong. That didn't come out the way I meant it. You… you are a challenge, Zara. And I will always appreciate a challenge. Yes, I tracked you down because I wanted to sample your magic. And, yes, I still want to know what craziness will happen in your world next."

His head rocked back, and he waved his arms a few times, gathering the words to him. "But I also like you as a person. Believe me when I say I am here now only because of that." The elf squeezed his hands like he wanted to shake me. "All you've done for four days is sit in a library and read. I could have left at any point and I'm still here. Is that enough evidence for you?"

I snorted out a laugh and shuffled on my feet, weirdly bashful. The warmth of his words chased away the chill of responsibility. I risked a glance up, appreciating his tiny, self-satisfied smirk.

"You are brave and talented and witty… and you're kind. You have all this magic and all this power and, Gods, the influence you wield is incredible, but you don't seem to realize it." He chuckled dryly, looking out across the congregation. A woman in pink stood at the front, hands outstretched as she pleaded her case. "No, that's not right. You know it, but you don't seem to mind it or worry about it. You also don't use it the way many would expect you to."

The elf tucked some hair behind my ear, and my heart somehow both bled and healed at the same time. "You honestly care about people, boss. You might not show it well, but you are compassionate. I like that. It's why I want to help you, because at the end of this all, I know the world is going to be a better place because of it."

He clicked his tongue and pointed at the Carons below. "Even if you keep terrible company."

I couldn't take anymore. In a rare move, I threw my arms around his middle, hugging the elf as if it were the last hug anyone would give on earth. "Thank you," I whispered, not really knowing what I was thanking him for. "Thank you."

"Told you we'd make a good team." He nudged me back and crossed to the door. "Ready to go?"

"Yeah, I think—"

"What about the curse?" A shout from the hall ripped through me like hurricane-force winds, and I snapped back to the glass as a short incubus with slicked-back hair and a strong nose rose before the royal assembly. "What are you doing about the curse? You're sitting up there like simpering fools, listening to all these rudimentary complaints, when there's a real possibility our race could be wiped out. What do you have to say about that, *prince?*" He spat the word like a slur. "What are you doing to protect our people? Because from here, it looks like a whole lot of nothing."

My heart hammered painfully fast. I pressed my hand against my brands where the pain of the accusation lingered. Darkness settled around Ridley. The small smile he'd sported all day vanished. His once welcoming demeanor became cold and direct. The Prince of Sin rose and stalked toward the edge of the dais. The subject recognized the movement for what it was, but, to his credit, he held fast, eyes narrowed and lips curled.

Gunmetal smoke swirled around them.

"While the curse afflicting our kind is very real, the rumors of genocide are overblown." Ridley's voice boomed like thunder. "Unfortunately, I don't have a fix for the situation, but I am, by no means, ignoring the problem. My sister treats the wounded daily. My brother absorbs their pain."

That's what Rim did? As with pleasure, incubi could take pain?

Ridley moved down a step, head held high, addressing those hiding their whispers behind their hands. "We have lost a few. And dozens of others face the loss of their magic at the very least, or death at the worst. Even one cursed succubus or incubus is too much, and I feel your pain as keenly as I feel my own."

Darkness fanned around him, that strange magic daemoni possessed adding a layer of danger to the prince's words, reinforcing the bite of agony he didn't conceal from his voice. "I have called upon the very best for help. Some of the world's greatest magical minds are looking into the situation. I don't have answers for you yet, but I will. Or I'll die trying."

Goosebumps scuttled down my arms, the hairs standing on end.

"What you're doing isn't enough." The incubus wouldn't give up, yellowed eyes aflame. "You say you have the best magical minds on the job? But what about the Gods? Why haven't you called on them? Isn't this their job? To fix crises? What is this if not a crisis?"

A rumbling of conversation; heads nodded in agreement.

"What if I told you a God was working on it? That one is working on it at this very moment?" Ridley asked. My teeth screeched as I ground them together. "What would you say then?"

"I'd say since you don't have a fix, we're all as good as dead."

I didn't wait to hear Ridley's response.

I didn't wait to hear any more of that conversation.

I blocked out all sound, all feeling. Blocked out my doubts and my failures. I kicked down the door with a sharp, direct blast of wind.

"Get me to the casino floor," I snapped at the startled security guy who'd led us down here.

Lachlan followed on my heels. "What's your plan?"

"I want to forget." My hands fisted in my pocket. My phone buzzed, but I flipped it off, too disgusted with what had happened, disgusted at myself, to care about whoever was calling. My blood simmered at a point right below boiling. If anyone were to touch me, they'd get burned. “For one night, I don’t want to think about who I am or what I’m supposed to be doing.”

Chapter 29

Lachlan fumbled with the lock. "How was I supposed to know you can't get drunk?"

I leaned against the outer wall of the Caron mansion and fiddled with my braid. He couldn't have known my magic burned the alcohol from my system the moment it made it past my lips. I wasn't sure if it was Fire or Water, but whatever it was, I wished it had an off switch.

Too bad we hadn't stumbled upon any of the blue-green lightning in a bottle Ryder had poured for me at the club when I'd met him. *Eliriah,* nectar of the Gods he'd called it, was one of the few things that worked on beings of my power. I missed it and the incubus who'd smiled so wickedly at me over shots of the stuff, more fiercely than ever before.

Despite the setback, Lachlan and I had wandered up and down the Strip, burning through a considerable chunk of Lach's recent winnings at poker tables, slot machines, and other games. He hadn't cared about the money, and I allowed myself to escape in a world I'd never experienced before. At three a.m., we'd called it a night. The elf could barely stay upright, and I wanted nothing more than to collapse into a bed. Or a couch. Or the floor if it looked comfy enough.

"Why does this place even have locks? Don't the Carons turn to smoke? And who would be dumb enough to steal from the Prince of

Sin, anyway?" Lach cursed. I batted him aside and turned the handle, pushing the door open to the elf's astonishment. Ridley must have given him the spindly key as a joke.

"Remind me to kick the prince's ass in the morning," Lachlan slurred. "And would you warm up for a second?" He referenced the ice forming on the walls. In my exhaustion, my control had slipped. "The frostiness is doing nothing for your complexion."

Now that we were back in the mansion, the events from earlier had come rushing back. My anger and frustration reclaimed their mantles. Thoughts of sleep scattered like dandelion fluff in the wind. The lack of progress made me cranky, and I resolved to call in reinforcements in the morning. Doing nothing, like I was now, was helping no one. The daemoni deserved better.

As Lachlan stumbled over to a white leather couch with gold embellishments, I headed for the gilded staircase. I wanted to get some more reading in. That book had seemed promising yesterday. As I crossed the foyer, movement snagged my attention. I squinted into a sitting room off to one side and changed course, shoving my hands in my pockets, not sure what I was looking to get out of this conversation, but primed for… something.

"You look about as fantastic as I feel," Ridley drawled, pulling the wispy haze of his shadows back into his substantial form again. He took a swig of the clear liquid that smelled like peppermint. "I'm glad you came out today."

I stopped in the doorway. "This looks cozy."

The incubus slumped in a chair with small, white cushions upon which were embroidered flowers the color of fresh blood. A spindly table that appeared barely strong enough to hold up the vase of white lilies on its surface was beside him, its surface scored with water marks. A baby grand piano took up residence in the corner beside a wide bay window overlooking what I knew to be meticulously maintained gardens. A few portraits of people I didn't recognize were framed in silver along the walls.

Ridley coughed. "This was Rush's doing." Ice in his glass clinked as he waved it around his head. "This entire house was my brother's design. He appreciated the finer things. China plates, gold inlays, furniture, instruments crafted by the hands of legends. Of all my siblings, he was the one who cared about that kind of stuff. I let him have his way with the mansion."

Was.

Past tense.

Ridley snagged a bottle at his feet and sloshed more into his glass.

"When did he die?" I wasn't sure what made me brave enough to ask. It could have been the early hour or Lachlan's words or Ridley's cavalier attitude itself.

The incubus's eyes flared orange and his lips curled. "You sure you want to go down that road?"

"I think you've already started down that path yourself." My shoulder hit the doorstop.

"Right you are." He set the glass down without drinking. "Rush passed away a few decades ago. Plane crash. The wreckage burned so badly, there was nothing of his body left to recover." The incubus stood and moved to me, looming with that ugly smirk on his face. "You know there were seven of us, but did you know you've met all who remain?"

My breath escaped me in a whoosh.

Three of his siblings—three of *Ryder's* siblings—were dead.

"What about children? I mean, you've been around for hundreds of years. Surely you've..."

He traced a soft finger down the side of my face, edging closer. I wondered why I didn't pull away. "Rush died with his fiancée and their two children. Ransom and Rey were brutally slaughtered in a war a few hundred years ago, well before they'd considered the matter. Rim has never cared for close companionship, and Rue refuses to let herself hope."

That phrasing sounded strange. I tugged the ends of my sleeves over my hands. "And you?"

His expression turned wistful. The moonlight streaming through the window caught his dark hair, turning it blue in the night. "Incubi and succubi find love a difficult and complicated matter. You're aware of how our magic works, how we breathe in passion and desire, how we whittle away at the souls and magic of other fey, turning their lives and abilities into fuel we can use." Ridley crossed his arms over his chest. "As you can imagine, that makes it difficult to find a companion outside of our own kind."

My breathing went shallow. I examined his face, finding nuances I'd never noticed before. Like the thin, white scar running along the side of his nose and the slight dip in his chin, like a smudge in a drawing.

"Not that there's anything wrong with that, but it limits the gene pool a bit, so our kind are encouraged to branch out, to find what we call our krav legara." Ridley leaned closer, a black swirl in his irises. I'd never realized how clean he smelled, like oranges with a hint of nutmeg. "Roughly translated, it's our soul's counterpart. One of the few non-daemoni from whom we can drink freely, without fear of harming."

My pulse thudded in my ears.

A memory tugged at the edge of my vision, tantalizingly out of reach. I remembered the earth shaking, a glimmer of gold, the sense that I'd never be the same. The memory flitted out of reach and I fell back into Ridley's eyes, found myself leaning into him, too.

"It's tricky," he said. "Those special creatures are incredibly difficult to find, and when we do, there are often obstacles in the way. Current relationships. Racial boundaries. Physical limitations. Age. Time."

He sighed gustily. "To find someone capable of overcoming all that and more, it takes more than skill or luck. It takes fate." The prince's eyes danced wickedly.

"It's a love that's pure and enviable. To find someone who matches our power, our strength, our magnetism. The allure of being what we are." His lips curled and our bodies brushed. "There's a legend that says daemoni will only know true happiness when they find that being—it's that elusive."

He'd snared me, pinned me like a butterfly to a piece of paper. It was as if he were pulling me closer without touching me at all. My hands came up, flat on his chest, but I didn't push away. Nor did I pull him in. I swallowed, breathing in more of his clean scent. "How will you know when you find that person?"

Ridley brushed the underside of my chin. The darkness of his magic swirled between us, warm and wispy. "Rush described it as a click." He tapped the center of my chest, right above my heart. "Right there. A click like all the pieces of his soul he'd never known were broken—mended. A click that told him something dangerously precious was within reach and he needed to handle it carefully. Ichika was that for him and so much more."

I felt like I was wandering through fog, thick and velvety. Ridley's hand moved up the slope of my jaw, over my cheek, and tangled in my hair, brushing the edge of the knot I'd woven on a whim this morning. A design I'd mastered months ago because it fascinated me, touched me.

It was a gift from Ryder.

A gift I never wanted to lose, though I couldn't explain why.

Ridley hummed low in his throat, his chest vibrating beneath my hands as he turned my head to the side, tracing the bumps of the knot, the tight twists, the hair worked over and under in a complex series of maneuvers that had made my arms ache. The way the incubus traced it, the way he held me close, was reverent, attentive. I leaned into that touch, my neck extending, leaving myself open and at his mercy, recalling the complexity intertwined within the four-leaf clover, wondering why it felt like I'd seen it somewhere.

Why it felt so familiar.

Ridley's throat clicked when he swallowed. "I see."

"What?" I grabbed his arm, jerking him down to eye level to see him better. "What do you see? What does the symbol mean?"

His eyes were soft, the wicked spell he'd woven around us disintegrating into dust motes. "You should have told me—"

"What's going on here?"

I went to stone, a sculpture carved of ice despite the steaming, searing heat of my blood. My vision tunneled, Ridley's face all I could see as my brain bobbled and seized. The distinct sensation of vertigo smashed into me, and the prince threw his arms around me to keep me from falling on knees that no longer existed.

I knew that voice.

I drew in a deep breath, dragging the air in through my nose, luxuriating in the smoke and cinnamon I used to dream of at night. When I was alone. When I admitted to myself I may have made a mistake leaving everyone behind.

Electricity sparked through me, my magics awakening first.

Then my heart kicked into gear, thrashing wildly against my ribs. I blinked, my vision clearing, and I turned in Ridley's hold, barely feeling it anymore. Because there he was, the moonlight illuminating every beautiful feature of his face, tangling with the smoke emanating from his shoulders. Ryder, the boy I craved like I craved security, like *home*.

He stood tall, his lean figure rangy in dark jeans and a black shirt. He'd tucked his wings away and his chest heaved as if he'd arrived at a dead sprint. Pale, drawn face. Dark hair, tinted emerald and ragged from the wind. Feverish, golden eyes that blazed hot when his gaze met mine, then flicked past my shoulder to... his brother. He frowned, small crinkles spider-webbing around his eyes.

Oh stars.

How this must look.

"It's not—" Ridley squeezed me, and the wind expelled from my lungs. I tugged against the prince, surprised when his grip solidified and I whirled back to my captor, ice dancing at my fingertips. I opened my mouth to tell him off, to say something, anything that would explain this... and the prince winked.

He leaned in, brushed the underside of my chin with a knuckle, his voice soft as butterfly wings. "It's for his own good," he said.

And his lips crashed against mine.

Chapter 30

Kissing Ridley was nothing like kissing his brother.

Ryder was a bolt of lightning: raw and splintered and beautifully dangerous. When we came together, it was waves thrashing against the side of the cliff, the freefall from the heavens without a parachute. Thrilling. Exhilarating.

Alive.

My hands came up as Ridley deepened our kiss and I sank into it, the memory of Ryder's touch vanishing as the prince's cool lips caressed mine. He was a hidden river weaving through the mountains, a sip of iced tea on a hot summer day, a night on the beach under the glow of the moon. He tasted like the peppermint he drank, sharp and refreshing. He pulled at my magic, drawing it to him lazily. As our magics melded, I recognized a hint of something bitter, like how I imagined dandelion greens would taste. It was unlike everything else about him, but when I reached for it again, it was gone, as if it had never been, and the mint overcame me once again.

I allowed it to pull me under and pressed closer. Ridley groaned softly, pulling me tighter, our magics mixing in a sensual dance. For one eerily perfect moment…

I was lost.

Then Ridley nudged me back, his forehead pressed softly against mine as he brought my fingers to his mouth, his breathing uneven, eyes screwed shut as his lips moved in silent prayer. My emotions, my magic, my being had short-circuited.

Why, why, why.

Why me, why now? Why kiss me at all?

Why did he feel so good?

I nudged him, blind to everything but his face, the intensity of his concentration, and he opened his eyes, shimmering pools of orange-tinted sunshine. His mouth quirked in a sad grin.

Somewhat wistful.

"Hope that helped," he whispered against my fingers.

Three words strung together... that didn't make a lick of sense.

I squinted at him, frowning, head light and mind cloudy, but Ridley gazed past me, face brightening, grin spreading as he drew away. Another set of hands, not his, circled my waist, pulling me flush against a hard chest.

"You bastard," Ryder spat, his tone as harsh as his hold on me was gentle. One large hand splayed across my belly. "What are you playing at, Ridley?"

"Oh, so you *do* know my name. You haven't written in so long, brother dear." The prince drew back, sliding into a sinuous crouch, one arm extended. "Aren't you going to show me how much you missed me?" His fingers twitched come hither.

Ryder pressed a hot kiss to my ear, a stream of his native language rolling off his tongue as his hands seared over my body, igniting the heat once again. Then he was gone. I swayed there, silent and confused, only able to watch as Ryder threw himself at Ridley who vaporized in a burst of smoke. Ryder cursed viciously and followed suit, slipping into a misty, shapeless form I'd never seen him use before. The swirling black and gray masses tangled, thrashing, and disappeared through the wall.

Something heavy crashed in the adjacent room as fist met flesh in a punch.

"That all you got?" Ridley harassed. "Are you sure you want to hold back? All these decades later, and you're going easy on me now?" He cackled, and, at the sound of wood splintering, I went to go to the incubi, only to find my limbs as limp as the rest of me. "I seem to remember you hitting harder when I kicked you out."

I felt like I should be doing something to break them up. To stop this. I was, at least, part of the reason they were at each other's throats. But I couldn't bring myself to... bother. I folded my hands in front of me, waiting for this mystifying calm to fade.

"And you're still the same asshole you were back then." Ryder's tone was frigid, and he grunted as something heavy crashed into a wall, causing the floor to vibrate. "Arrogant. Self-centered. Taking and taking and taking."

Everything went ominously quiet. I dragged myself around the corner, using the doorframe to prop myself up. This angle allowed me to see most of the main level. Ridley had drawn magic from me, a lot of magic. That, combined with the one-two emotional punch of his unexpected kiss and Ryder showing up out of nowhere, had my insides feeling all kinds of watery.

A large ball of smoke tumbled from the room, an occasional limb flashing into sight in the chaos as the brothers sparred. They fully materialized on the staircase, mouths spread in crude grins as they panted. Ryder held the high ground, but Ridley didn't let him keep it for long as he lashed out with a series of punches to the gut that Ryder almost entirely blocked.

"And never giving." Ridley continued their conversation lazily as he hopped playfully to the marble floor of the foyer. A purple bruise spread across one cheekbone and a long scratch ran down his neck, but he remained unaffected by pain as he bounced on the balls of his feet. "Come on, little brother, tell me more. I don't see you for two hundred years, and when I finally do, I'm locking lips with your girl. Surely you're more pissed off than that."

A chill trembled in my chest. Was that all he thought of our kiss? Locking lips? It had felt like much more to me. I stared down at my palms. Both Ryder and Ridley had said their kiss would strip away part of my soul, but then—

I reached down deep, finding myself whole and unbroken.

My magic rebuilding so quickly it was as if it had never been gone.

Did that mean...

Ryder roared and barreled down the stairs. He vaporized at the base, then reappeared in front of Ridley and roundhouse kicked him through the front door and into the yard. "It's like I never knew you."

"What exactly did I miss here?" Lachlan appeared at my side, hat in his hands as he scrubbed at bleary, bloodshot eyes. He wasn't slurring anymore, which I took as a good sign. "I assume the dark horse has returned home."

A body flew through the splintered front doors and hit the ground in a burst of white dust. The impact cracked the very floor at my feet. I found myself caught between staying here, the security of my wall, and monitoring the fight or intervening.

Intervening seemed like so much work.

My shoulders twitched. I felt suspended, locked between two opposing realms: one of crystal clear clarity and another of wonderful, nullifying fog.

The incubi tumbled back outside, and I decided I was doing fine staying on the periphery.

"Ryder showed up and Ridley kissed me." The words felt surreal, and I touched my lips as if to confirm they'd formed the syllables. The elf shoved his hat back over his tousled hair but said nothing. He tugged a pear from his pocket and snagged my hand, drawing me outside to the covered porch area for a better view. "The next thing I know, they're fighting and..." I waved at the driveway where a winged creature swooped low, nearly impossible to see in the dark.

"You cheater," Ridley hollered, laughing again before being drilled into the ground. If he was laughing, was there any real danger? The part of me that had come to understand Ridley and his motives suspected the prince had a solid grip on this situation.

Though I still couldn't understand why he'd kissed me.

My braid flopped as I shook my head. Was I dreaming?

"I see." Lach took a bite of his pear and offered a second to me.

"Ryder is pissed and Ridley has gone crazy." I rubbed at an itch on my shoulder, surprised to find it bare beside my black tank top. When had I removed my jacket?

"So, to make sure I'm getting this straight. You've kissed both of them."

"Uh huh."

"And neither of them turned you into a shell of yourself? Because, I assume, that any kiss with either of them is toe-curling to the n'teenth power... which would be enough to drain even a powerful fey of part of their soul."

I turned from the battle, my arms banding across my chest as I spun within myself again. "Yes."

He whistled. "Well, I'll be. Just when I thought you couldn't get more peculiar, it turns out you're a krav legara for not one but *two* fey princes."

For a phrase I'd never heard before, people sure were throwing it out there a lot today.

Lachlan whistled again, sank his teeth into the pear, but drew back with a furrow between his brows. "Don't tell me you're hot for the Prince of Sin." He wrinkled his nose then smiled at my befuddled headshake. "Good. Though I wouldn't blame you if you were. He's good for you."

The elf finished chewing as if my entire world weren't crumbling to pieces. This was so confusing and so messed up—on several levels. Me? The equivalent of the mythical soul mate for both Ryder and Ridley? In what universe did that make sense?

Metal screeched and I glanced up in time to see a crumpled ball that used to be Ridley's armored SUV slam into the prince himself. He somehow caught the thing, drove his arm into the ground to keep from sliding, and then reared back to chuck it at his brother with a manic curse.

"Why do I feel so weird?" I was starting to feel more like myself, though still completely uninterested in dealing with this throw-down.

"You feel weird? Is that why you're staying out of it?" Lachlan tossed the core of his pear out into the yard. "It makes sense since normally you'd be in the thick of things spinning up fire dragons or weaving webs of darkness or some otherworldliness you seem to favor."

He dropped onto the porch swing as something exploded in the distance. The resulting mushroom cloud of red and orange was reflected in his eyes. "How weird do you feel?"

"Stupidly calm." I sat beside him. The itch was getting worse, and I scratched harder, digging my nails into the skin. "Like, Ridley and I were having this wonderful moment. It was dark, and he kept telling me all these things about his family and the daemoni culture and it felt... I don't know. It felt right. Like we were supposed to be there." A thought hit me and I sat up straight. "You don't think it was that pheromone thing? Like Rim used on me at the Bellagio?"

Lachlan braced a hand on my shoulder. "Chill out, boss. He couldn't use his umbra on you if he tried. That pull? It was probably that bond you share kicking in. Plus... sounds like the moment was rife for a hot make-out session."

I dropped my head into my hands. "Could you be serious for once?"

Fists smacked skin, and Ridley cursed loudly. Then came another crash and a second SUV rocked on its wheels, a large dent in the driver's side door. I assumed the prince had hit it, but by the time the dust cleared, he was already gone. Magic leaped to my fingertips when I heard Ryder scream, and I longed for my lighter. I was finally starting to feel like myself again.

"I'm always serious," Lachlan responded dryly. His eyes followed my nails. "Should your brands be glowing?"

I ignored him, caught up in the trio of magics quarreling for release inside of me. A sharp snap splintered the air and Ryder screamed again. "Hold that thought," I snarled, a plan forming in my head. "I have some teenagers to pull apart."

Lachlan saluted me with two fingers along the bridge of his cap as I jumped over the railing of the porch, ready to do some real damage, when a blast of green light knocked me off my feet. My head smacked the ground and prickles of white exploded behind my eyelids as something like claws ripped through my side. I heard someone shout my name as I screamed, squinting through fading emerald light at the silhouette hovering a few yards away.

"I think you have a bigger problem to deal with first," Lee said.

Chapter 31

I pressed a hand to my side and felt wetness as I rolled to my knees. Gravel nipped at my bones, helping shake some lingering dizziness. "Lee? What are you doing here?"

"You lied," she spat. "Logan's dead and you vanished off the face of the earth."

I reached for my shoulder, transfixed in the blue light playing over my bloodied fingers. "When did she die?" I rasped.

"Yesterday morning."

My jaw locked and I squeezed my eyes shut, pressing the heels of my hands to the sockets despite the gore. The pain at the Bellagio. The phone vibrating in my pocket. In my anger, I'd switched it off and had completely forgotten to turn it back on. It explained the itching of my Water brand, the light it cast now. It was calling to me, warning me. I'd made her swear on her oath, the one shimmering bright on her neck, and I'd ignored her pleas for help.

"Lee, I—"

"I don't want to hear it." Emerald light flared from her fingertips, casting long shadows from her cheekbones, causing her eyes to glitter hauntingly in their sockets. Her jeans were slung low, her top cut high, revealing the sharp jut of her hipbones and the concave quality to her stomach. She was gaunt, a wisp of the fiery witch who'd so bravely told me off all those weeks ago, all her time and energy poured into saving her sister—no matter the cost to herself.

"You told me you would help." Lee's voice was a shard of shattered glass. "You promised to find out what was happening. You said you fixed her and then..." Her chest rattled with the force of her gasps; her barely contained sobs. "You weren't there when she started screaming; when she ripped at her own skin from the pain of her magic being pulled from her, inch by horrible inch. And you weren't there when she died in my arms."

Lee's eyes were dry and hard as marbles as her hands fisted at her side. "You failed her, Water God. And you failed me. I'm here for retribution—to rebalance the scales against your sins."

I rocked so my weight rested on my toes. Water prickled in my fingertips, a familiar ally. "I don't want to fight you—"

A thunderclap rippled across the heavens, green light flashing as a panther slipped from a rend torn between our world and another, further evidence of Lee's abilities. The beast turned glowing red eyes on her master before launching herself at me with a snarl, claws bared. I raised my arm, ready for round two with the witch's familiar when a heavy body thudded to the ground, leathery wings drawn tight against his back. The cat squealed as Ryder backhanded her with a fist like stone. She crashed into the side of the mansion in a plume of white haze, mewled once, and went limp.

"Yeah, I don't think so."

I'd never heard this voice from him before. One silky as the nightmares that nibbled at my subconscious, yet rough as stubble flecking his jaw. Ryder popped his knuckles as he dropped his second form, horns slipping back beneath his wave of hair, wings smoothing away, skin lightening to its normal olive. Shit-kicker boots crunched over the gravel before he hoisted me upright. He tipped my jaw up, eyes swirling with barely restrained fury, brushed at the dried blood beneath my eye, and gripped at my skull, right over the unraveling knot in my hair.

His lips brushed my ear. "You stay right there, glowstick. I've got a small mess to clean up." The incubus drew back, eyes half-lidded. He brushed my chin again. "And then I'm coming for you."

Fireworks erupted in my core, popping and sizzling—wondering what *that* entailed. He glanced over my shoulder, popped his chin up, and allowed another set of hands to draw me from his cocoon of warmth and smoke. He flashed a cocky, white grin that slipped from his face as he cracked his neck, turning back to Lee who'd risen from her crouch over her familiar.

"I don't know who you are, but I know you've been tailing me. And now it doesn't particularly matter who you are because you attacked my girl when her back was turned." He gestured lazily with his hand. "You're about to become a smear on my boots."

With a soft murmur, Lachlan drew me back to the front stoop where Ridley lounged in human form, watching the proceedings with interest, hands shoved in the pockets of his slacks.

"My fight isn't with you, incubus." Lee reached into her jacket and withdrew a black Sharpie. "Step aside now. You don't have to get hurt."

Ryder roared with laughter that cut off abruptly. "As if you could hurt me."

A hand of earth burst from beneath him and snatched him up, pinning his arms and legs before snapping back, trying to pull him into the hard desert ground. I blinked and he vaporized, a ghost of smoke fanning wide, then drawing tight as he solidified once more. Ryder dodged the fingers of a second grasping hand and scored the earth with a bolt of something that could only be described as black lightning. The ground shook beneath my feet.

Lee jerked as if burned, but kept her Sharpie pressed to her skin where she tied off another rune. "You daemoni. So predictable. But what will you do when your smoke doesn't stand a chance?"

A loud roar crashed around us, forcing Lachlan and me to throw our arms over our ears. Vicious wind gusting faster than the strongest hurricane ripped past me—she'd formed a funnel, a vacuum that pulled Ryder in. He faded into mist but only succeeded in being sucked into the mass faster. The wind swirled, tightening in a maneuver I'd used before, forming a barrier of gravity and air itself.

The howling cut off. The smoke that was Ryder thrashed about in his confines for one quiet second. Two.

The barrier exploded.

He'd hardened the wisps into millions of tiny spikes and thrust them outward so painfully quick I'd only spotted it when he withdrew into his normal form. Before he touched the ground, a dozen darts blasted his way, cast by the witch's quick hand. He snorted and walked *into* the hailstorm, moving effortlessly as the weapons bounced off his hardened skin.

"I'll never understand what daemoni can do," Lachlan muttered beside me. "But it's freaking cool as all get-up." I nodded silently, arms slung around my knees as I physically restrained myself from jumping up to help. I got the feeling this was something Ryder needed to do alone.

"Why won't you fight me?" Lee shrieked, retreating as the incubus advanced. "This is nothing. You've seen nothing."

"You're not a War Witch. You reek of power, but this isn't your forte. I thought I was being nice, allowing you to get some hits in," he drawled. "But if you're asking for it..."

Ridley chuckled darkly and every hair on my body went rigid.

Thunder rumbled as colors swirled around him, darting and dipping and thrashing as he pulled them in tight, wrapping them in shadow. Not once did he stop his slow and steady approach. Lee's eyes darted from one side to the other, face ashen as the Sharpie tumbled from her fingers. The colors blurred together, forming a shape within its swirling midst.

An ugly, awful shape.

One with tusks and too many legs and a mouth that sucked and gulped at the oxygen. I wanted to look away, wanted to pull away, wanted it to stop as it morphed again—this time twisting into a creature covered in eyeballs and slime. I'd only caught a glimpse before it merged back into the mass that had swallowed the witch, a dark haze of black lightning that engulfed half of the yard.

For one moment, all was quiet.

Then Lee screamed, the sound shrill as a circular saw slicing through a sheet of metal. A sound I knew would accompany my dreams for decades to come. A sound that had me jumping to my feet and sprinting across the yard as Ridley called to my back:

"Are you ready to meet the nightmare hounds, too?"

I didn't know what a nightmare hound was or if I was ready to, in fact, come face-to-face with such a creature. But Lee sounded like she was being murdered, and she didn't deserve that. She may have asked for Ryder's worst, but her sister had just died. The pain she felt was a knife through the gut that I understood.

The cloud of blurred pictures blew away the moment I barreled into the perimeter.

Ryder held Lee in a chokehold, the muscles in his arm bulging as he pinned her head back against his chest. It wasn't necessary. She'd gone limp with horror.

He snagged her wrist and bent it back at an angle. "Had enough? Or shall I snap this, too?"

She gulped wetly, sputtering as she blinked back the ugliness he'd shown her. Her dark skin was ashen, the whites of her eyes bloody and damp with tears.

"Ryder, stop." The words zipped from me like a bullet from a chamber. "That's enough."

He raised his head from her shoulder, a viper rearing back before striking. To my relief, his eyes weren't swirling anymore, though the amber was brighter than it should have been, hot with bloodlust. "She hurt you."

"She did." I raised my hands placatingly. "But she doesn't deserve this. She's in enough pain already. Let her go. Please."

He traced her neck with a nail honed to a knife's edge. "Only for you, Zara."

Chills scattered through me at the sound of my name on his lips, dark and full of meaning I couldn't think about right now.

He released Lee who crumbled to the ground, trembling uncontrollably. I shot him a look, but he lifted a brow, his meaning clear: He wasn't going anywhere as long as she was present. With a scoff, I dropped to her level.

"Lee."

She didn't respond.

"Will she be ok?" I asked Ryder.

"Probably." He shrugged. Like he cared. He'd only stopped for my sake; I had no doubt had I waited a minute longer, he would have snapped her wrists if not her neck. "Give her a few minutes to allow the nightmare to wash away."

Again, I contemplated exactly what a nightmare hound was as I waited for her to meet my gaze. After a few minutes, she finally stirred, as if rising from a deep slumber, and it relieved me to see more of *her* in her expression again—clutching tight to her fury.

I jumped in. "Lee, I'm so sorry. I'm sorry for not getting your sister the help she needed. I'm sorry I don't have any answers for you. I'm sorry I wasn't able to keep my promise.

"I can't say I know exactly the pain you're experiencing, but I know how it burns." My palm pressed against the center of my ribcage hard enough to bruise, a futile attempt to keep my heart from thudding through the walls of my chest. "I know how the pain starts right here and branches outward, a million tiny teeth and claws scratching and shredding everything you have left, gnawing away at your sanity one iota at a time."

Lee's arms roped across her chest as she listened. I dragged in a ragged breath, not seeing the witch anymore, but instead the grim set of my father's face, feeling my mother's warm embrace. Hearing Kaz's abrasive, snorting laughter.

"Some days, it's all you can do to open your eyes, to drag in that next breath, to *stand*." My own knees felt wobbly, and I blinked down at my hands. "The people I've lost were ripped from me. Violently. Taken from me by those who had no right to do so, those who didn't know me, didn't know my motives, didn't know my pain. They wanted to hurt me. And they did."

I clenched my fists, still seeing the impression of the black blood staining the webbing of my skin.

"I've never lost anyone because I put faith in someone else to keep them safe. I don't know what that feels like, how gutting that must be." My jaw clenched, and I moved forward, noticing the damp track marks across her cheeks, the glimmering droplets quavering on her chin. "I know what it is to want revenge. To want to grab hold of it with all you are and *do* something about it. I know that isn't a feeling that fades… unless you face it."

I slid my dagger from its sheath at my thigh.

"Glowstick, what are you doing?"

I flipped the weapon around, so the edge bit into my palm, offering it to her.

"Enough," Ryder growled, but he hesitated when I caught his eye, shook my head. I needed to do this. Had to do this. For the both of us.

He cursed.

I continued, "I swore an oath. I swore to help. I didn't say I could save her, but I said I would try. In your eyes, I haven't." I looked through the opening in my arms. "So if you feel the only way you can fill that gaping hole in your chest, to mend your soul, is to kill me—I won't refuse you that."

Ryder made a sound dangerously close to a whimper, but held himself back.

"It's your choice, Lee." The dagger shook in my palm as she ran a finger down the grip, our eyes still connected, unflinching. "You make the decisions that shape your world. Make your call and stand by it. It's all you have when this is all over."

I kept my eyes on her face as she picked up the knife and hefted it, the lights from the mansion reflecting off the silver. She paused, lips pursed, throat working as she stared at it. I didn't so much as blink as she lowered the blade, the point leveled at my throat.

I nearly shuddered with relief when she slid the dagger home in its sheath.

"Damn you," Lee whispered. "Damn you for being so… so…"

"Human?"

"I was going to say, un-God-like, but that works, too." My hand tangled in one of hers and she wrenched me to my feet, dragging me against her. She pounded my back twice with an iron fist. "You robbed me of my sense and my revenge."

"You needed to decide." As I pulled back, the edge of her collar shifted, revealing something that froze my core. Something I hoped had been a trick of the eye. I jerked the neckline of her V-neck across the top of her shoulder.

"Zara, what the—"

A slow, sickly horror filled me.

Beneath her skin ran thick, pulsing veins of black.

Chapter 32

The chill of the water was a shock on my heated skin.

A good kind of shock.

One that had me scooping another palmful from the faucet and splashing it on my face again. I closed my eyes and tipped my head toward the overhead light. Dozens of thin, red, spidery lines decorated the backs of my eyelids. They reminded me of the black veins weaving over Lee's chest and shoulders.

I dunked my entire face under the stream.

Oh Kraken, if you can hear me, now would be a fabulous time to speak up.

Radio silence.

Why have you abandoned me, I pleaded with the Great Beast. *Why now? Why at all?*

Still nothing. I didn't know where to turn for answers, so I shoved it to the back of my mind. Another problem to deal with another day.

I cut the flow of water and patted dry with a towel. After our latest dismal revelation, Ridley had escorted me to the bathroom to quote "clear up the gore and stuff" and led Lee to one of the many upstairs rooms to get some much-needed sleep.

I felt the opposite of tired. I was revved. I was angry. I was hopped up on adrenaline.

And despite everything that had happened tonight, despite knowing what I needed to deal with in the morning, anxiety thrummed through my veins. After months apart, months of thinking and second-guessing, and the past few days where I'd truly come face-to-face with how I felt…

Ryder was here.

I twisted my fingers together and a shiver tremored down my spine. The same tremor I'd felt whenever he was near, whenever he was closing in. I wondered if it had anything to do with us being… whatever krav legara were to each other.

I wasn't sure how to process that information yet. Not only was Ryder someone who fate had apparently shoved in my path… but his brother was, too—if Lachlan was to be believed. His brother, who I still kind of resented for how he'd treated me—both when we'd met and when Ryder had showed up unannounced.

I'd never given much thought to who I might end up with one day, or to relationships at all for that matter. Between school and competitive swimming, there were hardly enough hours in the day to pursue my dream, let alone waste daydreaming about boys and all the complications that came with them. I'd listened to enough gossip from my teammates to know relationships came with drama that didn't interest me.

I shook out my shoulders and let the thoughts flow off me. Another problem for another day, right? Like I'd told Ridley: We had time. I didn't need nor want to make any serious decisions regarding my romantic future anytime soon. Though that wasn't to say I couldn't have a little fun in the meantime. I swept my hair into a loose braid, snapped off the light, and opened the door. My pulse jumped.

"Ryder."

The incubus leaned against a wall in the darkened hallway, arms crossed, one boot balanced on the other. Somewhere along the way, he'd smoothed his blue-tinted hair and wiped the dirt off his hands.

He'd propped his shoulder against the wall, but I recognized the tension that rippled through his hard muscles, the strain that tugged up one corner of his mouth, the fixed set of his warm, golden eyes.

I sucked my bottom lip between my teeth, an action that drew those beautiful eyes downward, his expression heating. My blood warmed in response, and I drew up on my toes, hip resting against the doorjamb as I stared at his lips, his deepening smile, the dimple that appeared amid his stubble.

Stubble I'd never seen before, even in the heart of the desert.

I wondered how it would feel under my hands.

His head tilted and his gaze returned to mine, his irises molten, the desire in them raw enough that a fist clenched in my chest, my heart thundering its answer. Slowly, Ryder straightened his rangy, six-and-a-half-foot height. He prowled closer, measuring my response.

My shallow breaths.

My heated skin.

The pulse pounding in my neck.

One step. Two. Three. He was nearly against me, the fronts of our bodies brushing, and the wonderful aroma of cinnamon and smoke filled my lungs. A scent that both calmed and thrilled. A scent of happiness, of belonging, of *home*.

A scent I'd never take for granted again.

Unbidden, my hands lifted, and I traced the edges of his open jacket, the only contact I allowed myself, my breath shuddering with forced restraint. These moments felt delicate as the dust of freshly fallen snow. One wrong breath, one errant movement, and the beauty would disintegrate.

And I wanted to absorb as much of that beauty as I could before I couldn't any longer.

Ryder's throat bobbed. He reached out to cup my cheek, his fingertips trembling, betraying his calm demeanor. His warm breath feathered across my face as he dipped closer, the distance between us shrinking.

"There's my glowstick."

My insides liquified at the sound of that name, *his* nickname for me. I pushed up on the tips of my toes, leaning into him, his arm banding around the small of my back. My hand cupped the back of his, encouraging him onward, and a soft hum left my throat. Ryder's pupils dilated. His thumb swept higher, his fingers spanning wider, his touch rougher as he mapped the planes of my face against his callouses.

"Did you mean it?" I asked, my voice deep with need. "What you said before?"

"And what, exactly, did I say before?" His chest rumbled against mine.

My tongue darted out, wetting my lip. His thumb chased it. My eyelids dropped, but I forced them back up, back to him. "You called me your girl." Heat flushed my cheeks, caught between desire and rare embarrassment.

Ryder's eyes flickered with light, and amusement touched his lips as his arms bracketed me, bringing our bodies flush together. I bit my lip again to hold back a moan as he nudged my face higher, his lips scant inches from my own. "You've always been my girl. But I wanted you to figure that out in your own time."

Then his lips were on mine, hard and demanding and everything, absolutely everything, I needed. For one brilliant moment, my mind went blank, a sea of black against an inky sky, before the wildfire that was *him* swept through, scorching my insides. He drew away only long enough to hoist me up when my knees threatened to buckle, wrapping my legs around his waist instead, and his mouth slanted down again. Bursts of light more colors than I had words for exploded behind my eyelids and I moaned, tugging at his hair, pulling him closer, trying to climb on top of him, fit *inside* of him.

My back crashed into the wall, and his mouth was on my neck, teeth nipping sharply at my pulse before soothing the burn with gentle sweeps of his tongue. When he turned his face, the stubble I'd marveled over earlier scraped against my skin in the most sensual of ways. The effect was like tossing gasoline on a bonfire, and I clenched tighter around him, mind numb, barely able to think. Only enjoy.

Our magic twined together, molding and accepting—his smoke tangling with my flame, his wings skimming the surface of my watery depths, his nightmares caressing the soft beckons of the air.

I dragged his head back by his hair, caught a flash of wicked yellow eyes, and pressed my lips to his jugular. His body shuddered at the vulnerability of the position, but he held me tight, growling as I ran my tongue down his throat before kissing each collarbone. One of them was dented in the middle, as if it had broken and healed awkwardly. I paid close attention to the break while marveling at how perfectly our bodies fit together, like lost pieces of a puzzle reunited.

"I can't take it anymore," he gasped when I tugged on the collar of his shirt. He brought my face back up to his and our lips fused together once more, slower this time as we savored the taste, the feel of one another.

His hand curled around the back of my neck, adjusting the angle of my neck as our tongues tangled and something… rippled between us. He drew my magic from me in slow, languid sips. And somehow, someway, I felt his filling me in return, the curls of blackness familiar in a way I might never understand.

He groaned against my mouth, body straining against mine in a desperate need for more.

"Zara."

My nails dragged grooves in his shirt as my blood caught fire.

"Don't you ever."

Ryder peppered kisses on the sensitive skin beneath my ears.

"Ever."

A hurricane crashed in my chest, a tornado spinning me higher and higher.

"Leave me like that."

Our noses brushed, golden eyes searing into mine.

"Again."

I pulled back, lips parted, but not sure what words were about to spill out.

"Uh, guys." Lachlan's easy drawl was the equivalent of a winter snowstorm slamming into a volcano. We turned to the elf. Ryder growled low in his throat when I attempted to unwrap my legs from around his waist. "Maybe the middle of the hallway isn't the best place for..." Lach flourished with a hand. "This."

I tried to speak, but again, no words came out.

Ryder did not share my issues. "How about you find somewhere else to be, *elf*?"

I almost groaned, my stomach bottoming out when Lach twisted his ball cap around. A sneaky grin snaked across his lips. "You mean—right by *her* side." He moved closer, chest puffing. It occurred to me now that Lach was taller than my... I gnawed my lip. What exactly were Ryder and I? Were we boyfriend and girlfriend? Did I want that?

I shook my head when he finished his thought: "You know, the place you haven't been... at all."

With a wiggle of his eyebrows, Lach tugged on a strand of hair that had pulled loose from my braid and darted behind Ryder, who had gone still against me. I caught the elf's half-apologetic smirk before he vanished down the hallway. I couldn't get a good read on the incubus's face. Not at the angle at which he held me. With a groan, he peeled me off and lowered me back to the ground.

"He's right." Ryder stepped back, then flashed me a heated grin. "As infuriating as it is, he's right. We shouldn't do this in the middle of the hall."

I couldn't agree more. As much as I wanted his lips on me again, part of me was glad Lach had interrupted. Too much was happening too quickly. "We probably should talk."

The incubus groaned and snagged my hand, following my lead down the hall. "All the worst conversations start with those four words."

I jabbed his side playfully. "Aren't you the least bit curious about what I've been up to?"

"Oh, I have a fairly clear picture of where you've been and what you've been doing," he said. I halted outside my door, turning under his arm as he lowered his face to mine again, our foreheads touching. "Should I start with the treaty with the tretorraqs in Scotland? Or maybe those wildfires along the West Coast. Or perhaps your first miracle that was helping that blind woman see again."

I opened my mouth. Closed it again. "That wasn't a miracle. She had inflammation that was pressing against her—" Ryder pressed a finger to my lips.

"You've hardly kept a low profile." His hand circled my lower back. "The only bit we haven't been able to figure out, yet, is what you've been up to this past week. I'm hoping that's what you want to discuss."

He glanced at the door and amusement flashed across his face. His laugh was light—no sign of the man who'd sent literal nightmares after a witch anywhere to be found. "Is this your room?"

"Yeah." I dragged out the syllable as he opened the door to the room I'd slept in all of once. He moved to the center, hands on his hips, and scanned it, bemused. I moved inside, too, raising and lowering myself on my toes, observing his careful sweep of the king-size bed. The royal blue comforter with gold tassels at the corners. The tapestries hanging on the walls. The backpack spilling its guts across the dresser.

Ryder snorted and crossed to the bed. "He thinks he's so clever."

"Who does?" Belatedly, I remembered this room didn't have many seating options. I followed him to the bed and settled near the head where I promptly pulled a pillow into my lap.

"Ridley," Ryder replied. "This used to be my room."

I scanned the space again. It seemed so... barren. I tugged at a loose thread.

"It looked nothing like this, of course. Art covered the walls, the floor towered with so much junk you had to practically wade through it." He jabbed his thumb at the closet. "That walk-in is the size of a bedroom itself, and it didn't have enough space for all my shoes, let alone my suits."

I smiled. "I assume you've since learned to live modestly?" I occurred to me now I'd never seen how he lived. I didn't even know *where* he lived. He was a billionaire. He probably had many houses in his portfolio.

There came that laugh again, the one that tickled my insides. "Not in the least. But I learned to spread it out a bit. Having a mansion to yourself gives you that ability."

I tucked that nugget away in the file I kept about him inside my head. I tugged my boots off and dropped them on the floor with twin thumps, sifting through my thoughts.

"Ryder?" He scooted closer on the comforter, giving me his full attention. "You seem more okay with everything than I expected."

His hand shot out so fast I didn't see it, only felt him tuck my hand—the one not unraveling the pillow row by row—into his. "Thought I was going to give you a hard time for skipping out on all of us in the middle of the night, did you?"

"A little."

"If I'd found you during the first week, sure." His thumb traced a circle in my palm. "But your letter was clear. I know what it's like to need space." His smile faded a bit. "All I've done in the time since is make sure you stayed as safe as could be. Well. Me, Finn, and Pyra."

"Pyra?"

He shook his head. "That girl thinks you're the... how did she put it... 'the most badass chick she's never wanted to kill.'" I fought against an earsplitting grin and failed. "You can do no wrong in her eyes."

"That sounds like her."

We both went silent, eyes wandering as we picked over our thoughts. There was so much to say, but finding the right thing was as elusive as holding the moonlight streaming through the window.

"How did you end up with my brother?" Ryder's grip on mine hardened. "I know I have no room to talk since we were never together, but... what happened back there? When I walked in?" His skin turned icy. "I shouldn't ask, but it's killing me not knowing."

I tugged my hand away and cradled it on the pillow, unable to look him in the face. I wasn't sure what to say, how to answer him. Now, an hour later, it all felt like a dream. And what was it Ridley had whispered when Ryder had barged in?

Hope that helped.

I stopped plucking at the string.

Had he known Ryder was coming? Had he been manipulating my relationship with Ryder the entire time? Forcing me to recognize how I felt about his younger brother? Or had Ridley hoped to sway my emotions toward himself? And for what purpose?

My stomach tangled in knots. Both of them made me feel so good in such very different ways, and I didn't know how to process the complexity of it all: bliss, lust, anticipation—guilt. Each emotion adding another sticky string to a web of tangled thoughts that only grew more muddled the harder I thought about them.

"I don't know what to tell you," I finally confessed. I felt like I owed him a better answer than that, but I didn't have one. "I know one minute I was mad at the world, and the next I felt this incredible pull toward him." I dug my nails into the back of my scalp. "I like him. I don't know why, I don't particularly want to, but I do. That's not to say I want to be *with* him, but in that moment, something felt..." I buried my face in the pillow. "It felt right."

Ryder went silent for so long I feared he wouldn't respond. I couldn't bring myself to pull the pillow away, preferring the soft darkness to the hard truth I would find in his face. After a few long minutes passed, he smoothed my hair, then lightly tugged on it to raise me up.

"Zara." It was weird hearing my given name from him. So serious. It matched his haggard expression, his somber eyes, the understanding in them. "When you... kissed..." He sucked on his teeth in distaste. "Did he take any part of your soul?"

This reminded me so much of an incredibly similar conversation we'd had months ago, sitting cross-legged in a gritty, gross parking lot. Another kiss. Another similar question.

"He took magic, but that's all," I replied honestly. Chasing Kaleal through the hollows of my mind all these months had made me incredibly aware of myself and the grasp I retained on that. I knew, in the base of my being, I would know if part of my soul were stripped away.

I knew neither of these incubi would be the one to rip that from me.

Ryder folded his leg up against his chest, fingers tapping a rhythm on his shin. His bright gaze danced across the wall, and I couldn't stand the silence any longer. I hadn't wanted our reunion to be like this.

"Lachlan told me about krav legara," I blurted out. Ryder swung back to face me, his eyebrows winging up. "He says that's what we are. Well. You and me and me and him. I don't know what to believe, but that's what he says. And I think that's what you're thinking."

Ryder dragged his hands through his hair. "What a mess," he muttered, squeezing the bridge of his nose. "My own freaking brother. Isn't that just perfect?"

My insides buzzed, panic fluttering like millions of wings in my chest. "It doesn't mean anything—"

"Zara." He cut me off again, visibly gathered himself, and smiled at me with so much warmth the awful sensation of beetles skittering across my skin subsided."It's ok. I understand. I don't *want* to." He cracked his neck, facial muscles tightening and relaxing as he nodded to himself. It looked so painful, this inner battle he waged, and I was helpless but to watch him fight through on his own.

"But I do understand." He squeezed his fingers, reached for my hand, and loosely clasped it. His thumb stroked the back of it. "And yes, it means something, even if you don't want it to. I'd hoped to give you space to figure out how you felt about me—about *whoever*—on your own. I didn't tell you about the title because I didn't want to add any pressure to the weight you're shouldering already."

Ryder scooted closer, dropping my hand to wrap his around my thigh instead. "Obviously, that didn't go as planned." He chuckled softly. "And now it's more complex than it should be. But glowstick—" I jerked at the endearment, pleased to hear it from him once again—"you don't need to overthink this. You don't have to think about it right now if you don't want to.

"And don't—" he pointed a finger first at me, then the door, "don't let my brother tell you otherwise. If there's anything I've learned from that guy, it's that he's figured out all the angles. I hate him for it, but I respect him for it, too. Don't get sucked in."

I dragged the pillow back into my lap, giddy with relief. Everything I'd hoped—no, *needed*—to hear had come out of his mouth. And Ryder spoke earnestly. I could tell it killed him inside to admit Ridley also meant something to me in the fated course of history. I wondered if he would take it up with his brother at a later date, but for now he was backing off and giving me space.

"He noticed I'd braided that design of yours into my hair," I said bashfully. The incubus spread his arms, palms toward me in invitation to continue. "His reaction was odd, but he definitely noticed."

Ryder's quicksilver grin flashed. He leaned in, his hands finding my hair. "You wove my design? You did that?"

"If I answer, will you finally tell me what it means?"

"Absolutely." His eyes glowed. My skin heated.

"Yes." I wiggled my shoulders and glanced away. "Once or maybe twice."

He dipped, pulling me in again, his lips brushed against mine—something so soft I wasn't sure it *was* a kiss. He ran a big hand over my back and for a few moments, we sat like that, breath mingling as I waited for him to answer me.

"It's my sigil, a bastardization of the family crest." He pointed at a yellow tapestry hanging on the wall. One with a complicated knot in the middle of a diamond of swords. "When I figured out what you meant to me, I wanted to show it off."

A touch of red tinged his cheeks as my mouth dropped open.

"Don't tell me this is like the quarterback giving his letterman jacket to his girlfriend."

He scoffed and coughed into his hand. "Like I'd ever be so cliché."

I jumped to my feet, hands braced on his knees as I grinned into his face. "That's exactly what this is. Don't try to hide it."

He rolled his eyes. "I liked how it looked. That's all."

"Fine." I dropped back to the bed, my feet tucked beneath me. "I'll let this slide for tonight. But I'm not letting this go forever."

He scooted up and fluffed the pillows before falling against them, sprawled out beside me. For now, it appeared we'd successfully navigated yet another precarious ledge in our complicated relationship.

The incubus dragged me deeper into the bed, but left his hand splayed across my back, his fingers weaving designs that I quickly recognized as said sigil.

"Now, why don't you tell me what brought you to my brother in the first place," Ryder said. "Of all the places I expected you to appear, this was among the last on my list."

My humor faded as reality dug its skeletal fingers into my skin once more. I rolled against him, allowing him to pull me closer, breathing in his scent. I told him about Logan, about the fey in South Africa, about the summons to Las Vegas, every detail about the curse—and then some.

He listened gamely, his chest tensing at some of the more difficult details I had to spit out—like the shortened lifespan and how it seemed to only affect his race. But he kept his hands on my sleeves, rubbing my arms, encouraging me to continue.

When I finished, we lay in silence.

"What do you think we need to do next?" he asked.

We. We felt good.

"We do something I should have done a long time ago."

He kissed the backs of my knuckles. "What's that?"

"We call in the other Gods."

Chapter 33

I stared at the phone as if it were a live grenade with its pin pulled. It was pathetic how much I dreaded making this call. Ryder had convinced me to get some sleep before calling up our friends, arguing I needed time to process everything.

Now, six hours of restless slumber later, I wasn't sure if his assessment was correct. The sight of Lee's curse still shook me, I still refused to think about Ridley and that kiss, and I was trying so hard to not think about what Ryder had told me it had evolved into a looming obsession.

"If you don't call him in the next five seconds, I'm doing it for you," Ryder said. Twenty minutes ago, he had dragged a hard, leather chair with tall arms across the library and planted it beside my recliner. The spines of the thousands of books seemed to glare at me as the seconds ticked by.

"Fine." I snapped my phone open, scrolled through the meager list of contacts, and pushed the button with the little green phone on it before I could overthink this anymore.

The line rang once. Twice. The cheap plastic grew slick in my sweaty palms. A third time. The line opened, a bite of a breath before the person on the other end growled, "Listen, whoever you are, I don't know how you got this number, but you can forget it now because—"

"Finn." I dragged my nails down the thighs of my jeans, staring down at my boots braced against the floor as if glued there. "It's me."

For a breath, I heard nothing. My insides twisted and writhed like the Kraken's tentacles. Half of me felt relief hearing my appointed guardian's voice for the first time in months, and the other half truly was frightened he might want nothing to do with me anymore.

I shouldn't have fretted, because the kelpie's tone switched from annoyance to coyness. "Well, well, well. Look who came crawling back to the little people. Didn't I tell you not to forget about us when you got all big and famous?"

I slumped, my hand shaking as it pressed the phone harder against my ear. I laughed. Ryder shook his head in an 'I-told-you-so' sort of way and took a sip of some green tea he'd swiped from the kitchen earlier. "I don't recall having any conversation of the sort."

"That's your selective memory kicking in." Finn sounded out of breath, as if he were running. "But I can't believe you called. I didn't know you had this number. Are you ok? Where are you? Did Ryder find you? Is he with you now?"

He fired off the questions like arrows. Before I could pick one to answer first, I heard Finn open and close a door and call out to someone, "You won't believe who I'm talking to right now." Then he switched his attention back to me, his voice booming with excitement. "Wait. Don't answer anything I asked. We need to see you or we'll never believe it's actually you. Flip to video."

We?

"My phone was made, like, ten years ago," I explained. "Even the quality of the calls I *can* make sounds tinny."

"That sounds like an excuse—"

"I got it," Ryder said loud enough to be heard on the other line. A whisper of smoke touched my cheek and he dropped behind me, carefully situating me in his lap. He propped his chin on my shoulder as he swung his super high-tech phone in front of us. The device at my ear went dead and the one in front of me flashed as the camera kicked to life. For a few seconds, I looked at the image of me and Ryder sitting there—his arms wrapped around me like a koala bear—before our image shifted to the bottom right corner as a new video feed appeared.

I pressed my hand to my lips in a vain attempt to hold back the torrent of emotions that swept through me. Finn sat on what I assumed was a desk, the camera held high as he peered up at it, a beautiful smile touching his pierced lips. Seated in a chair behind him, hands folded on the blotter, face tilted so the sun streaming through a window created a glare on his thick glasses, was Joseph. He seemed older, thinner. His dark hair longer. The God of Air appeared more puzzled than pleased.

"It's about time you stopped running," Joseph said as Finn beamed.

My heart felt full to bursting. This reception was nothing like I'd expected. Anger? Frustration? Definitely on the docket. Certainly not the joy radiating from my guardian's face. These were my friends, my people. People who'd stood by me when there was no reason to, other than they wanted to.

How could I have forgotten that?

"Congratulations, Finn. You've broken her," Ryder teased, tone dry. He pulled me back against him so he could bring the phone closer. "Now quit with the crazy smiling. You look like a maniac. Pretend Rose stopped in with more paperwork for you to file."

I wondered what the incubus was talking about, how the pixie played an apparently negative role in Finn's life, what I'd missed. Our little group had grown cozier in my absence. Something inside me panged, realizing I could have been a part of that had I chosen to be.

Finn carded his fingers through his hair, skewing it sideways. Two new piercings now joined the ball above his eyebrow. "Nice try, but even that damned pixie can't distract me right now. I knew you were the only one she'd allow close enough, Ryder. Where are you guys, anyway?"

"Vegas," I finally managed, blinking out of my stupor and joining the conversation. "I've been here about a week."

"That explains the lack of phenomena," Joseph said. He leaned forward, the angle of the sun shifting. I could finally see his deep, brown eyes behind the lenses. "The pile of reports on my desk monitoring your activities has been strangely vacant lately."

They *had* been tracking me. Judiciously, by the sound of it. I wasn't sure why, but that felt good, knowing they'd been looking out for me. They did care. They always had.

"What are you doing there?" Joseph asked.

"No." Finn pulled the camera down so his face filled the screen. "Before you answer that, I have to ask about the rune on your face." He reached up and tapped the screen. I'd pulled my hair back earlier and had unconsciously shifted so the black mark was clearly visible. "What did you say it was again, Joe?"

"Protection and constraint."

Clouds settled over the kelpie's face as his green eyes narrowed. "Yes. What's the story there?"

Ryder hadn't asked about the mark. He must have seen it, there was no way he could have missed it, but I hadn't thought about it because the rune was just that to me now—a rune. But based on how he squeezed my ribs a little tighter, how he peered to look at the mark himself, I knew he was as intrigued as Finn.

I ran my hand across my mouth and nose. I'd told Lach my truths and the world hadn't imploded. Lee knew and nothing bad had happened to her. My friends deserved to know. Finn and Ryder had been with me from the beginning—Kaleal had nearly killed the kelpie herself in the early days. And Joseph, well, he loved a mystery as much as Sherlock.

"You know that person you saw in Kansas City, the one with the,"

I swallowed hard, "purple eyes? The one who you knew wasn't me even though she was inside of me?"

Ryder's arm stiffened, the tips of his fingers darkening with black smudges. A tinge of fear touched Finn's face as he nodded, clearly wondering where I was going with this.

"She's gotten powerful. Every time I've picked up a new element, she's grown stronger. She can control me, take over my body when she wants, even use my magic to some extent." I stared down at my hands, which I folded and unfolded in my lap, over and over again. "She's gotten so powerful I worried if she took control of me again, she might not let me go. So, I found a witch skilled in rune magic to help me lock her away. That's what the rune is: protection for me and constraint for her."

"How long has this been going on?" Ryder rumbled. Against my back, the muscles of his chest had pulled taut. This was the anger I'd expected, the barely veiled frustration at the secrets I'd kept.

"It never stopped," I admitted, ashamed.

"Why didn't you say anything?" the incubus demanded.

Instead of answering, I focused on Finn's face in the screen, the ashen quality of his skin beneath his tan. Joseph moved into the frame again, perched beside him on the desk, a vee between his brows.

My fingers fisted in my lap. "I couldn't. She wouldn't let me. She did something that prevented me from saying anything. I wanted to. I tried to. Finn—I almost did in Egypt. But it's like my throat locked up and I couldn't breathe until I stopped thinking about it."

"Do you know who this entity is?" Joseph asked.

Despite knowing she was locked in that room inside my head, a tingle of fear coursed through me, wondering if she were listening to this. If she could hear everything I was saying. If she'd somehow find a way out if I spoke her name. I turned in Ryder's arms, needing to say this to him for some reason.

"She's Kaleal. The Original God of Water."

Ryder's golden eyes swirled with darkness. A muscle feathered in his jaw.

"I think she's been flitting between reincarnations of the Water line, searching for something. I believe she's found whatever that is in me." I turned to the screen. "Given what she's done, what she's said, how she's said it, I have no reason to doubt her claims."

Finn looked like he might vomit, but Joseph tipped his head back, thoughtful. "I've wondered if the Original Gods ever truly died, or if they were forced into a strange slumber. I've never felt anything that might have been Lyre"—the Original God of Air—"inside of myself like you're describing, but it's definitely a fascinating concept." Joseph's hair spilled over his shoulder. "You say she's dangerous?"

"Very." I squeezed Ryder's leg. "She's cunning, too. I know she wants us to succeed in our mission to save the world, but she's a mess of contradictions. I can tell she hates me as much as she respects me, and, for now, we appear to be connected because she's saved my life on more than one occasion."

I choked on a breath, remembering the faintness I'd felt back in the tower in Rome, the explosion that had flung me out into the air from fifty stories up. How Kaleal had given me the encouragement I'd needed to survive. "But I think she also wants me dead when I'm no longer useful."

Joseph scratched a small cut on his cheek. "Fascinating."

"Oh yes, fascinating," Ryder drawled sarcastically. Then he lashed out: "Fascinating that a being who should be dead by how many thousands of years may or may not destroy Zara at any point in time. Fascinating that you've been dealing with this all by yourself." He directed that last comment to me with a shake. "And none of us were the wiser. Fascinating."

"Turn it down a notch, Ryder," Finn interjected, though he appeared to be on the incubus's side. "Has she gotten out? Is that why you've called?"

"No." That was all the transition I needed. My personal problems aside, we were facing a very real and very serious problem that demanded our immediate attention. I dove into the conversation about the curse I'd already told Ryder. Finn and Joseph listened attentively, and I felt Ryder forcing himself to calm down, though I seriously doubted he'd forgotten what I'd revealed.

When I finished, Joseph was staring at the ceiling and Finn's eyebrows had vanished under the shag of his bangs.

"I've never heard of anything like this before," the God of Air admitted. My heart tumbled to the base of my belly. I'd kind of hoped with his wide array of knowledge that he would have presented a miraculous a fix. "But I'm intrigued. I believe the key is finding the fey who are behind the curse, but doing that may take some time."

"I might be able to help with that," Finn murmured. "I did some reconnaissance during my time in the military. There may be a few contacts I can reach out to."

Joseph glanced at him and asked about transportation, but I barely heard it. They were sitting closer together than I'd realized, and, as they bounced ideas off one another, I noticed they had an uncanny way of understanding what the other was about to say almost before they said it. They'd grown much closer in the time I'd been gone.

I wondered if Finn had finally confessed to the God of Air how he felt about him. Feelings he'd barely admitted to me after I'd caught him staring at Joseph on more than one occasion.

"Alright, we'll be on the next plane out." I blinked at the screen at Joseph's abrupt words. He tapped his lip. "We're flying from Rome, so it will take some time, but I think we'll have a higher probability of success if we're all together. Plus, when we finally get a lead, we can handle it as a team without waiting for the others to arrive."

I hadn't expected this.

Hadn't expected Finn and Joseph to drop everything they were doing to help rebuild the Order and come to my assistance.

"Guys, I can't thank you enough—"

"None of that, now." Finn swatted at the screen, the chains on his pants jangling merrily as he stood. "When an entire race is facing extermination, and a member of that race happens to be a member of our team who refuses to go away—" he apparently still refused to admit Ryder was his friend—"then we're there. I wish you'd contacted us sooner, but what's done is done."

"See you soon," Joseph said with a tight smile. Something about it seemed off, but before I could figure it out, the call ended.

Ryder dropped the phone in my lap and tugged me against him again, this time with both arms. The heat of his body warmed my soul, and I relaxed against him, reveling in the easiness of the shared moment.

He pressed his lips to a spot on my neck, right beneath my ear. "You have good people in your life."

"I know. I should have remembered that sooner."

"Yeah," he hummed softly, "but it's easy to forget sometimes. We'll get this thing figured out. Don't you worry."

I gnawed on my lip as I leaned against him, my eyes roving across the many, many rows of books. Though the anxiousness lingered, it felt manageable. With these guys in my corner, maybe we could stop this thing before it was too late.

Chapter 34

"Ryder, don't touch that." I smacked his hand away from the tank.

He scoffed and crouched beside the glass, peering at the fuzzy brown mass inside. It reared back, spindly front legs raised and crooked, pinchers bared as its many eyes glinted. A shudder worked down my spine at the intelligence I perceived in that awful gaze.

"I've never seen a tarantula the size of my head before," the incubus murmured, rubbing his chin. I snagged his shoulder and yanked him back before he could touch the glass. "What? It looks friendly."

"It looks like it wants to eat you."

He glanced up, boyish delight written all over his face. "Don't tell me you're afraid of the itty bitty spider."

I bristled, a retort on my lips, when a flash of movement snagged my attention. The creature in question darted forward, spindly legs crashing against the glass beside Ryder's ear, pinchers extended menacingly as it reached for him. The incubus cocked his head and pressed his palm against the glass, aggravating the spider further.

A chuckle rattled my ribs. "I think it took offense."

As the incubus worked the tarantula into a frenzy, I folded my arms, squinting through the harsh light beating through the many windows at the leafy green plants scattered around us. "Would you be serious and help me search for Ridley already?"

Ryder waggled his fingers at the monster, and I swore it hissed as the incubus rose to his full height. "I told you. The greenhouse was my last idea. If you couldn't sense him in the rest of that ridiculous mansion, Ridley's not here." He dragged his hand through his hair, ruffling the glittering gold tints in the locks. One of these days I'd ask how he got his hair to do that, how he changed the highlights on a whim. Today was not that day.

"Then where could he be?" I pinched the wide plane of a banana leaf and kicked lightly at the stone bench beside it. On it, carved from a block of wood, perched a tiny owl with giant eyes that seemed to watch everything. "His driver didn't take him to the Bellagio. Everyone else besides Lee is at Cura and says they haven't seen him. And he's not here. Where could he be?"

Ryder flicked his fingers across the surface of the koi pond that wound through the room. "I don't know. I'd like to think he's off pouting somewhere, realizing he missed his chance—" he shot me a smile that was only half-joking—"but truly, anything could have called him away. He's got a kingdom to manage. He's a busy guy."

True. But considering everything going on at Cura… and in his own house… I wondered what could possibly take greater precedence. Despite my inner vow to deal with the whole krav legara thing alone, I'd hoped to talk to the prince about the secrets he'd so casually overturned in my life, sending it into a bit of a spiral.

I'd heard Ryder out. Now I wanted to know Ridley's thoughts, too.

And he was frustratingly out of reach.

"Did you want to keep searching for him?" Ryder asked. I gave him credit for his patience. Nothing about this was easy or simple, and I knew his insides had to feel as tumultuous as my own, but he handled it all with surprising grace. "Or did you want to head to the hospital? I know you promised my sister you'd stop by to help."

I tapped the silvered surface of a sundial and my pocket hummed.

A glance at the phone and I shrugged. "If he's not here, he's not here. I might as well make myself useful somehow."

The hospital needed help. The nurses had been working around the clock, and Rue had ordered them to bedrest for the next twenty-four hours before they passed out on their feet. Ryder had made a few calls this morning and was waiting for more staff to arrive. In the meantime, I'd promised to assist since I was getting nowhere with research.

Joseph and Finn were also delayed, their search for a flight out of Rome made more complicated by a bad batch of severe weather. While they waited it out and looked for alternate flights, the God of Air had promised to search for answers on his own. His catalogue of books far surpassed my own.

Ryder hooked his arm through mine and wove our fingers together. I tipped my head up, some of the tightness in my chest easing at his easy expression.

"Shall we find your driver? Or would you rather fly?" he asked.

- - -

The spicy scent of cinnamon alerted me to Ryder's presence, and I leaned into his hand when he caressed my back, though I didn't look up from the succubus lying before me, her skin chilled to the touch.

"How is she doing?" the incubus asked, snagging the stool at my side. He picked up the clipboard beside the bed and flipped through the pages. "You checked on her when we arrived seven hours ago, and now you're back. You look worried."

I groaned and rubbed a kink out of my neck. "Seven hours? Has it been that long?" From changing IVs to administering medication to swapping stories with some older daemoni, I'd barely had a moment to eat, let alone linger over my own troubles. It had been a nice reprieve.

"Yes," Ryder said. "Now what were you discussing with the elf about her condition?"

"That *elf* has a name, you know. It wouldn't kill you to use it." While not necessarily unfriendly toward Lachlan, Ryder didn't seem to know what to do with him and monitored the elf with narrowed eyes. I sensed a storm brewing, but there wasn't much I could do about it. I'd let them hash it out in their own time.

I sighed and smoothed the plush, purple blanket draped over the succubus. "I was considering reaching into her and helping her. Maybe I could try tracking the curse again."

I reached for her wrist and brushed the thready pulse of the fey who didn't look a day older than forty, no matter what her chart said. Her dark skin was waxy, her breathing shallow, and my heart ached for her. "But Lachlan talked me out of it. There are too many risks, too many unknowns. Besides that…" I rubbed my tired eyes.

"Besides that…" Ryder prompted. He was a quick study, but he was still confused about what exactly I did when I delved into a fey.

"Ridley and I think those casting the curse learned to detect my magic. I'm only making it worse." I picked up a cup of coffee at my elbow and nearly spat out an icy mouthful. I needed something sweet. The bitterness too carefully mirrored my mood.

Wait. Bitterness. I licked my lips, a memory tugging at the fringes of my mind.

"But before that, *Lachlan* could help?" Ryder traced the length of the fishtail braid he'd teased my hair into this morning. While he'd said nothing, I knew he'd gone out of his way to avoid weaving his sigil into it. I was still deciding how I felt about that.

"Yes," I said. "He was."

The fey in question stirred on the cot behind us, each inhale accompanied by a soft whistle as he slept. If Ryder hovered, Lachlan was static cling at my side, pushing himself to help as many of the daemoni as he could. I wasn't sure exactly what thrilled him about the work since it was mundane stuff, but maybe he merely wanted to help. Like me.

"And before you ask, no, there isn't anyone else I know who could have helped like he did. Not even you." I waited for Ryder to meet my eyes. "He mirrors my magic. He knows exactly what I'm doing and how I'm doing it. Lachlan grounds me to this world. Without him holding tight to that rope—it's feasible I might not make it back."

The coffee didn't sound so bad anymore, and I gulped down a few mouthfuls.

"I respect you and I respect what you can do, but our abilities are too different, Ryder."

He shoved a hand through his hair and shifted so his legs splayed. "I know. I wish there was more I could do, though." He snapped his fingers. "There's so much at my fingertips, so much power and so many people, and knowing there's nothing any of that can do… it hurts."

I released a small breath. Ryder was hurting as much as the rest of us. It was hard to remember that since he'd only just arrived, but these were his people, too. He was a prince of the Caron household, and his people were dying under his watch.

"You're doing plenty," I said firmly. "Every little thing you do, every person you assist, every note you take. It all contributes to the bigger picture. The problem is we have all the pieces, but we don't know what image we're supposed to be creating."

Lachlan jerked on his cot, and I shook his arm.

"I wish you two would get along," I said, glancing meaningfully between Ryder and the elf. "It would make my life easier if you'd stop hissing at each other like cats."

"I don't like how carefree he is with you."

"That's who he is. And he's as good for me as you and Finn and any of the others are." I shook the elf a little harder, trying to snap him out of the nightmare I knew was brewing behind his brow.

Ryder's boot tapped the floor. "You two are close."

His words too closely mirrored Ridley's accusations from when we'd first met, and I snapped, my arms flying out, hands gesturing wildly. "What do you want me to say? I didn't ask him to follow me around the world. I didn't ask him to help save my life, to teach me about my magic. I tried to get him to leave, but he wouldn't. And, you know, when you have someone who turns out to be as useful as he is following you everywhere you go, it becomes damn easy to accept he's there."

I scanned the room, pausing briefly on Rue who bent over a patient checking his pulse. "And now he's basically my best friend. Nothing more, nothing less. It's going to stay that way."

Ryder waited a beat before his stoic expression cracked. He yanked me into his arms and hugged my tense body against him, chuckling when I pushed back, waiting for me to relax. When I did, the incubus nuzzled my neck. "Good. I have enough competition as it is."

"How, exactly, did I end up in the middle of this lover's quarrel?" Like déjà vu, we both turned to Lachlan, who'd opened one bloodshot eye and regarded us resentfully. "Seriously, couldn't you do this anywhere else? Anywhere else that doesn't involve *me*?"

Laughter bubbled like champagne in my stomach, and I threw an elbow into Ryder's side when he opened his mouth to fire off a retort.

"Oh nonsense, leave them be." A succubus with hair three shades lighter than maroon and a deeply-lined face had propped herself on her side, leaning heavily on one black-veined elbow. "It was getting good, too, young man. Then you had to go and interrupt."

Lachlan snorted and rolled upright. He snagged his newly acquired Raiders baseball cap and snapped it on. "Whatever."

The succubus tsked and motioned toward Ryder, who grinned

like he'd learned the sun shone solely for him. "Please, continue. Don't mind me or Norton over there." She waved at the incubus who lay in the bed beside her, who hastily closed his eyes. "Who is this competition? What will our lovely Water God say? It's so perfectly, splendidly romantic."

I buried my head in my hands, shaking it back and forth. I wasn't sure if there was a color hotter than stop sign red, but if there was, it permanently stained my skin. The middle of the hospital most definitely wasn't the time or place for this particular conversation.

"Nah." Ryder saved me from answering, and smoothed a hand over my head. I love-hated how that small motion made me want to purr. "She needs time to think it over. I mean, she'll pick me, but she deserves a chance to think she made that call herself."

I jerked up with a glare at the ready in time to see him wink at the older fey who was positively beaming, hands clasped at her chest.

Lachlan stuck his finger in his mouth and gagged. "Save me now."

"Since you volunteered, you can help me with something," I said brightly. The elf's face fell. "There's a chance Ridley is back at the mansion and I need to talk to him. Why don't you go check?"

"Haven't I helped you enough?" he grumbled, though he slipped off the cot and toed on his boots, anyway. "First getting you your magic back. Then saving your life. Now hospital work and running errands? Oh, how the mighty have fallen."

"Be honest with yourself." I slapped a clipboard against his chest and he stumbled, knees catching the bed. "Was your status that important to begin with?"

Lachlan's laughter boomed, causing heads to turn our way. "This is why we make a good team, boss. You never hesitate to put me in my place." He tore the clipboard from my hands and scanned the page. "I'll also order these supplies Rue needs since I'm in such a *helpful* mood."

"One sec." I snagged the back of Lachlan's coat before he made it too far. "Ryder."

The incubus's bemusement dropped away. His eyes flashed a warning I pretended not to see. "Didn't you say some of your workers were showing up later today? You should probably head back with him. Make sure they arrive safely."

Ryder's hands came up. "Well—"

"Oh, goodie. I always wanted an errand buddy." Lachlan clapped his hands and went to sling his arm around Ryder's neck, but the incubus exploded in a wispy black mass before he made contact.

"Well then. Game on." The elf flipped his hat so the brim shaded the back of his neck. He winked at me, well aware of my antics. "You may be smoke, incubus, but I bet I can still beat your leathery hide back to the mansion."

Paperwork fluttered as Lach tore down the aisle and slammed through the door, shocked stares following in his wake.

"We'll be talking about this later." Ryder's voice ghosted out of nowhere, whispering right into my ear. When I swiveled to seek him out, he was gone. I couldn't even sense his magic. I shook my head, grinning to myself as I snagged a tray of medicine and walked away. I hoped they found some way to coexist. Both Lach and Ryder were too important to me to not get along.

The light to the storage room was on and I stopped short when I found none other than the Prince of Sin himself poking through the bottles of medication. He already held two containers in his big hands. I must have made a sound, a squeak, something, because his shoulders tensed and he swiveled to find me, back bowed and eyes jumpy.

"Zara, good to see you."

"Where have you been?" I dropped the tray on a shelf with a clatter and went to him, only to pull myself back. What was I doing? "I've been looking for you all day."

Ridley grinned with one side of his mouth, but it didn't hold the intrigue I'd grown used to. "I figured you wanted to set me on fire for that kiss. I prefer to keep my skin unblemished for as long as feasibly possible."

At the mention of my magic, flames sprang to my fingertips and my temper flared. "No. You don't get to make light of this." I stomped across the small room, stopping when only a few inches separated us. I ignored the pull I felt toward him, the eerie need to close that last step, and instead raised my voice, looking up into his face. "You don't get to drop a bomb like that on my life and then vanish. You have no right to spill all those secrets and leave me to pick them up on my own."

"You were hardly alone—" he said, but I was having none of it. I jammed a finger into his chest, rattling the pills in the bottle he held. His sunset eyes narrowed.

"Don't you dare try to diminish the role you play in all of this." Wind whipped at my hair, a layer of frost forming on my skin. "I'm not only fated to be with Ryder. I'm fated to be with you, too. So don't think for one second that you aren't—"

My breath left me in a whoosh, the crackling flames of my fury doused. "What are you doing with iodine?"

Iodine was one of the few drugs we'd found that seemed to temper the worst of the symptoms suffered by the cursed. Why? None of us knew. Rue told me one of the healers had doled it out on accident, and, fortunately, it was a happy accident.

Ridley's blank mask snapped into place. "I'm taking them to Rue. She asked for more a few minutes ago."

Spidery fingers of dread tapped the base of my spine. I glanced at the bottles of iodine on the tray I'd dropped. "That's funny, because I was putting some back… at Rue's instruction."

Wispy tendrils of dark magic wafted from his shoulders and I seized his shirt, locking a barrier of air around us. "What aren't you telling me?"

He firmed his lips, his arm curling around his chest.

Chilled fingers of dread stretched the length of my spine, alarm pulsing through me. The thought I'd had earlier. The bitterness. I'd tasted it when my magic had mingled with his, finally remembering why it seemed so similar. It was the cloying, angry stench that seemed to accompany the ooze I'd waded in three times now.

With a swipe of razor-blade wind, buttons popped as I ripped open his shirt down to his heart.

I stumbled backward, hands cupping my mouth as I doubled over in horror.

I was going to be sick.

The prince darted around me and slammed the door shut. He collapsed against it, chest heaving, hand wrapped around the knob to keep anyone from turning it. "You shouldn't have done that."

"How long?" I croaked. "When did this show up?"

He hesitated. "Not very long."

"Before or after Ryder arrived?"

"After."

I choked down another wave of nausea. My magic. My magic had done it again. Acting as some strange accelerant for the curse. It had been building inside Ridley, sure. But to see it here, now, like this…

I rose jerkily, swiping at the tears leaking from the corners of my eyes. The wry humor I'd embraced with Lachlan a few minutes ago was gone. In its place—fear, guilt, concern.

"That's why you vanished."

Ridley eyed me as if I were some kind of wild animal, one he wasn't sure would hide or attack with all its claws and teeth. "It was part of why I made myself scarce. Listen—"

"You have maybe a month," I interrupted, shoving the heels of my hands into my eyes. "But probably less if it's already spread that quickly. Oh Gods, Ridley. This can't be happening."

Everything in me was numb. Not just numb—but void.

I didn't particularly *like* Ridley, but I respected him. I understood his motives, who he was as a leader, and I found him someone entirely worth following.

And that was setting aside the possibilities fate had created between us.

On top of that, I knew his brother, and I liked his sister. Even with Ryder's feelings twisted up the way they were, I knew discovering his brother now joined the list of the cursed would devastate him.

Ridley pulled the pieces of his shirt together, obscuring the evidence. The light in his blood-orange eyes dimmed. He stared down at the floor, then back up at me, resignation set hard in every line of his body. "Yes, that is the timeline."

He spoke so stiffly. Formally.

He'd already come to grips with a reality I was only beginning the horror of digesting.

Vaguely, I realized I was shaking, trembling so hard I could barely stand. I needed... something. And he looked like he needed that something as much as I did. I launched myself at the prince, arms squeezing between his body and the door, pushing myself up against him, offering as much of whatever comfort I could give. He didn't hesitate to haul me against him. His cheek came down on the top of my head and I felt him shudder.

He'd been dealing with this all day, telling no one.

How much pain he must have felt.

To absorb the reality he was dying. Alone.

I squeezed him tighter, inhaling his chilled scent, wondering if the force of my being could somehow hold him together, keep him from breaking. Because he was. He was trying to hold it back, hold the shudders back. But failing.

"There's more," he said. He ran a hand down the length of my back, calming himself. "Something you need to know, something that scares me like nothing else in this world does."

Oh Gods. I drew away, but kept my hand firmly planted over his heart. "What is it?"

"Caron magic is tied to our people. It begins and ends with us. As the head of our people, that means it begins and ends with me." Claws stained with blood raked across my insides. I knew where this was going. "If this virus destroys my magic, if it destroys me... I can't speak for what will happen to my race."

Rue. Rim. The wrinkled old succubus. The fey who'd devoted their energy to helping. The bodyguards who played blackjack when they thought I wasn't looking.

Ryder.

My chest seized.

They could all...

Die.

I blinked hollowly, my tears all dried up.

"Then we have to beat this thing," I heard myself saying. "We have no choice."

Chapter 35

I lost track of events after that.

I remembered telling Ridley he needed to talk to his family. I'd refused to keep his secret.

I remembered the slow, silent walk to the mansion.

I remembered the tears that tracked down Rue's face, the black eminence that expanded from Rim. The roar of frustration from Ryder when he transitioned to his second skin and launched himself into the skies.

I remembered Lee grabbing my hand and asking if I could hear her.

After that, the memories came in blips.

Some I knew were real, like throwing myself against Lachlan's unbreakable grip when I attempted to return to Cura. Or the books with blood-stained edges from where I'd cut myself while flipping through them too quickly. Or when I shoved a bowl of broth across the counter at Ryder, telling him he had to eat or he would pass out.

Other memories I wasn't so sure about. Like the clawed hands that hooked around my throat and choked the air from my lungs as I thrashed on my back. Or the billowing red clouds flickering with tongues of orange lightning that rolled across a field littered with bleached bones and fat clusters of flies.

The iron door that once stood so tall and straight and pristine...

Now dented midway down as if damaged by a well-placed kick and rusting at the hinges.

- - -

"Do you think you'll be able to figure this out?" Ryder asked.

It was the question I'd tried so hard to not ask myself. The question everyone had avoided asking me over the past two days—as far as I knew.

It was also the question I was least-prepared to answer.

I fell back into the mud, uncaring of the grime working into every fiber of my clothing, and focused on the sensation of the rain pattering against my skin. I squeezed Ryder's hand, but didn't answer.

I couldn't.

Except for when Ryder had first learned about his brother's condition, we'd been virtually inseparable. But the desire to be together, to absorb each other's presences, wasn't one-sided any longer. The time I'd thought I'd had to think had exponentially diminished. The future, as I saw it, had morphed into one starless void. I clung to him as much as Ryder clung to me. It wasn't healthy. But everyone in that household was grieving in their own special way.

"You will." Ryder's voice was firm. "I know you will. But Zara—"

I mentally blocked him out after that, knowing where he was going. He wanted to talk about the connection I had with his brother, about the bond, about the opening fate had presented to me. Ryder wanted me to talk about that, talk about how I felt. What it was doing to me—knowing someone I was meant to be with was in such a predicament.

I didn't want to hear it. I didn't want to think about it. I admired Ridley for far more than some fated link between us, and that was what had driven me outside today. I wanted to think about the lessons he'd taught me during our short time together.

That held much more value to me in this moment.

Much more than a romantic notion of some futuristic relationship.

Ridley was the only other being I'd ever met who shouldered relatively the same weight I did as the head of a group of people seeking direction.

He was the only fey to show me the world as it could be led—fairly and evenly.

He'd shown me the value in lying, but doubled the value I put in the truth. He'd shown me how to listen to others, how to lead a group of people who didn't agree with one another. He'd demonstrated compassion and selflessness—and guilt.

It wasn't just Ridley I felt numb about. It was an entire race. It was the life of someone I cared about deeply—and could care about more if given the time. It was about the future of all magic.

As if the bombshell of Ridley's condition weren't bad enough, learning the destruction of his magic would mean the destruction of all magic down the line had a singular dampening effect on everyone. It was humbling in the most awful of ways. Apparently, he couldn't hand over the title of prince, either. It was a bit of a 'till death' sort of job. And even if he could, he'd be handing power to another incubus or succubus who was as at much a risk as anyone of being cursed.

Slab of titanium, meet hard place.

I licked the rain off my lips and raised the hand not clenched in Ryder's cool grip, staring up at the gray sky through the starfish of my fingers. Why was it I could do this so easily, that I could spin up tornadoes of fire, turn any room dark with a thought, but I couldn't stop one stupid curse?

"Hey boss, would you at least *consider* turning off the waterworks?" Lach's strawberry blond head appeared between my middle and index fingers. The elf had no reason to stay here. I wasn't working any crazy feats, I wasn't battling any monsters, slaying any demons—that he could see. But still he stuck around, by my side, standing over me. In the rain. His hand rested on the pommel of a sword he'd swiped from a suit of armor in an upstairs hallway.

"They issued a flash flood warning about two hours ago," he continued. "There's speculation the Strip may wash away if this torrential downpour keeps up."

I snorted.

The forecasters had never seen a storm like this and were trying their best to keep up. I wasn't bringing in moisture from afar. I only allowed the ground to get so saturated before the liquid evaporated and went right back up, feeding the clouds. It was a perfect, self-feeding, never-ending cycle of a seemingly endless downpour.

"The Strip will be fine," I murmured.

"I'm glad at least one of us is certain about that." The elf unbuckled his sword belt and dropped to the mud beside us, resting the weapon across his thighs. Ryder stared ahead dispassionately. He no longer voiced opposition to the elf's presence. He seemed to understand now, especially after Lach goaded me out of the hole of my room with a fight of Fire, that the elf wasn't going anywhere.

He truly claimed a unique spot in my life.

"Where's Lee?" I asked.

Lachlan rubbed his nose. "Upstairs. She insisted she could help with Ridley to give Rue time to help at Cura. Lee says her curse isn't spreading anywhere near as quickly as the daemoni, and the last thing she wants to do is stay in bed all day. It's a good thing she's helping, too. The number of cases tripled overnight. This thing—it's getting worse."

My jaw clenched and I swore I heard a molar crack.

"Blue flame knows where Rim wandered off to. Good riddance anyway. Maybe he's keeping things calm at the casinos." Lachlan traced a swirl of gold paint on the scabbard. "Not that word of the prince's condition has gone public, but I imagine it's good to see members of the royal family out every now and again."

"Who's that?" Ryder asked as a black SUV pulled up in front of the mansion.

I sat up, shielding my eyes against the rain with my hand. The back door swung wide and out stepped two tall, lanky figures. I focused on Joseph first, his dark hair and shoulders hunched against the downpour, then veered to Finn who squinted up into the sky, a backpack gripped in one hand.

With a slash of my hand, the rain stopped. Lachlan and Ryder exchanged a look, but weren't far behind when I leaped to my feet. The corners of my eyes prickled, and I took one hesitant step forward. Then another.

"Sorry we're late," Finn called, trudging up the least muddy part of the sidewalk with Joseph on his heels. Both watched me warily. "The weather finally cleared, but then the computer system crashed—I won't bore you with all the details. But we're finally here."

"I don't care." I was a strung bow, an arrow notched and ready to fire. My body vibrated with tension. "It's so, so good to see you. Both of you."

"Any reason you tried to drown us on the way in?" Joseph glanced between me and Ryder before settling on the elf over my shoulder. "This storm has a distinct 'Zara' feel to it."

"I—" The words caught in my throat. I had to swallow a few times to force the lump down and finished lamely, "Things escalated."

"Come here, Z." Finn dropped his bag at my feet and yanked me into a hug. I closed my eyes as he held me close. We normally weren't touchy-feely like this, but I needed this, needed *him.* I squeezed him as tightly as he embraced me, and I remembered why I liked him so much, why I cared about him so much. Finn had my back. He was flawed in so many ways, but he had my back. He'd flown halfway around the world to prove it, hadn't he? "Ryder kept us appraised."

He had? I turned to the incubus. Even with his brother like this, and everything going on, he'd found time to keep Joseph and Finn in the loop? A corner of the incubus's mouth turned up, though there was no humor in it.

"As much as I'd love to catch up with you, I think it's best if we focus on the immediate problem at hand," Joseph said. He removed his glasses and cleaned them on his shirt. "Where is the Prince of Sin and how is he doing now?"

Lachlan tapped his cap. "He's upstairs. The curse is spreading quickly."

It tore through me, like claws ripping through a jugular, that clinical way of speaking.

Ryder cursed. Finn nodded grimly. "Let's go see him."

Chapter 36

It occurred to me, standing in the doorway with my friends behind me, I'd never seen the prince's bedroom before. Unlike the rooms I'd already been in, which were, admittedly, wonderfully furnished and weirdly formal, this place took the meaning of richness and elevated it to the moon.

Its size alone was comparable to some basketball courts, and that wasn't counting the en suite—which I assumed was through the doors at the far side of the room. In front of those doors was an office space and living area, with a massive wooden desk and fat leather chairs. Royal purple wallpaper with accents of gold the exact shade of Ryder's eyes when he was in a good mood ran the length of one wall. The rest were painted a midnight blue. In the middle of the room, commanding most of the attention, was a four-poster bed. Well, more than a bed. You could put an entire soccer team on that thing and still have room to sleep comfortably.

With his back against some massive, gold pillows, the big square ones I didn't think anyone actually owned, sat Ridley, his eyes searching as he watched me hover in the doorway. A book lay open on his lap, the glowing face of his phone visible beside it.

"Are you coming to see me or to gawk at my stuff?" he asked. "If you're gawking, then please proceed. Otherwise, I'd welcome the conversation."

"You have the most ostentatious taste." Ryder nudged me aside and strode to the side of the bed where he towered over his older brother. All external signs of vulnerability and misery he'd revealed to me were gone. "You let all those centuries with that stupid crown on your head go to your brain. Maybe you should toil a little. That will make you appreciate the finer things."

The prince fired back some glib response I missed because Lachlan pressed a hand to the small of my back. "Go on, you need to see him. Maybe it will give you some answers. I'll keep watch from here so no one disturbs you."

I surveyed him. "You want an excuse to stand there and look imposing with a sword."

He fisted the grip and winked. "TruthTeller doesn't have the same heft, you know?"

I grinned and gestured for Finn and Joseph to follow me to the side of the bed where the brothers went quiet.

"I wondered when you'd be by to see me, Water God," Ridley said. He closed the book. "And you brought company."

"There's that arrogance of yours talking again," I countered. The virus had spread quickly. Twisted veins of black wound around his throat, circling his jugular. He didn't have weeks like I'd first thought. We were down to *days*. "Not everyone is falling over themselves to see a prince."

"First prince," he corrected. "With an empire at my feet."

"Uh huh." I stepped aside, realizing I was being rude, and motioned at my friends, inviting them forward. "This is Finn, he's a kelpie who helped lead the military at the Palace of Oceans once upon a time. He's also my guardian and showed me how to use my magic."

Finn flipped a wave. He wouldn't bow to royalty because he technically served me, as the slash of the Water brand across his neck represented. He'd shed his raincoat somewhere and looked rather dashing in his tan boots, ripped skinny jeans, and black button-up shirt.

"And this is Joseph Windrunner, God of Air. The first God I stumbled upon and saved from certain death at the hands of the Order." Joseph turned a bland look on me. Before he nodded to the prince on the bed, I caught a flicker of something ugly in his eyes. A whisper of trepidation twined around the base of my spine.

"Finn, Joseph, this is Ridley Caron, Prince of Sin and head of the daemoni."

Ridley held out a hand. "A pleasure. I'd greet you properly, but the witch helping me has an awful bedside manner and would kick me if I tried to stand up." I hid my smile with the back of my hand. That definitely sounded like Lee. "You sure know how to pick 'em, Zara."

My grin was genuine this time. "She is one of a kind, isn't she?"

"Just like many of those you align yourself with."

"What have you been doing up here?" Ryder asked. I knew he wondered if I would bring up that *thing*. The connection. He would have to wait a little longer. "Besides lounging around while the rest of us do the heavy lifting."

The prince started talking and Joseph and Finn fell into the conversation, asking a million questions about how he was feeling, what he knew, how he knew it. I helped answer the questions I knew, but some questions Joseph asked were straight weird, but in a way that made sense. I should have brought him on long ago. His analytical brain worked much differently from my own.

With their questions finally exhausted, Joseph and Finn took their leave. Both promised they'd catch up with me and Ryder later. Finn, though, lingered for a moment after Joseph bolted for the library. I could tell he wanted to say much more to me with the way he fiddled with his piercings, but he took off after the God without voicing any of his thoughts.

"You'll figure it out," Ridley said, calling me back to his bedside. "I'm not counting you out yet."

"Why?" I demanded, gripping his forearm. I was sick of this. Sick of people leaning on me, staring at me like I had all the answers. Putting their faith in my fledgling abilities like I was some second coming of Kaleal or something. "Why are you so certain of that? How can you be so confident in me?"

"Because we know you," Ryder answered for his brother, his eyes molten with an intensity I'd only ever seen twice before. "Because you won't stop at anything to figure this out. You won't let anyone or anything tell you otherwise. You won't give up. You never have and you never will."

That may have been the deepest cut yet.

- - -

I wished I'd had the nerve to stay with the prince longer that afternoon.

I wished I'd talked to him about the lessons I'd learned from him.

I wished I'd asked him about the bond we shared and what he thought about it, the reason I'd tracked him down to begin with.

But I hadn't. And I regretted it.

That evening he fell into a coma from which he wouldn't wake.

Chapter 37

I spun my dagger, idly wishing for one with a thinner blade and a ninety-degree point. One that shimmered like the surface of the sea on a calm day. I glanced down at the still figure on the bed, monitoring the rise and fall of the violet sheet covering his chest.

Ridley had counted on me. They'd *all* counted on me.

Now the prince was comatose.

With a snarl, I flung the dagger on the mattress. My head dropped into my hands, and I massaged my temples. I'd spent all morning poring over Ridley, holding a tortured vigil, wishing there was something I could do. Anything.

There wasn't.

My foot twitched and a pile of books toppled over. Yeah, I'd given up on those too.

I slowly lifted my head, fingers hooked around the back of my neck, and stared into the mirror across the room. It was a full-body monstrosity propped lazily against the wall with ostentatious gold-leaf flakes pressed into the frame. But that wasn't what I disliked about it.

It was the girl reflected in the glass I could barely stand to see.

This girl was a shadow of the woman she'd become before arriving in this city of sin. This girl was gaunt and frightened, a husk of her former glory. From the hunch in her back to the smudged shadows under her eyes—the strain evident in her clenched jaw and pinched lips. A blast of wind would knock this pitiful excuse of a being over without half a thought.

I stroked the rune at my temple, not seeing what everyone else claimed to: A figure of strength and confidence. A woman smashing the barriers holding her down.

A God worthy of the title.

No. I was out of ideas. I had tried everything at my disposal, yet I kept running up against barriers.

Barriers.

The circling of my fingers stilled.

No. I hadn't tried everything.

A chill swept through me, rattling against the backs of my ribs, and I eyed the blade again. My knee bounced. Joseph didn't have any ideas. The Kraken wasn't speaking to me. Phenex refused to help.

But I did know of one more creature who might shed some light on the situation. A creature that scared me shitless.

A glance at Ridley's blue-tinged lips sealed my decision. While holding court, he'd vowed to do anything and everything in his power to save his people from this curse, *even at the loss of his own life*. If he could make that vow, then as the head of all fey, I should hold myself to those standards too.

I had not exhausted all of my options.

Kaleal had been there for me in my greatest moments of need. She'd helped me embrace my magic, she'd shown me how to manipulate water, she'd ripped the magic I needed from Finn when I lay bleeding out in the back seat of a car, she'd forced me to find hope when I'd nearly lost it all.

If there was one being left on the planet who would have an answer for me, it was Kaleal. Aside from Phenex, she was the oldest living creature I knew, one stretching all the way back to the beginning, a soul nearly as old as magic itself. She had to have answers.

I shuddered.

I would need to face her wrath to get them.

My hand remarkably didn't tremble as I lifted the weapon to my face and pressed it to the edge of the rune. One little slit was all I needed. One tiny cut. I inhaled deeply and—

"What in the blue flame do you think you're doing?"

I whirled to find Lachlan framed in the doorway, TruthTeller clasped in his white-knuckled hands. His lips were parted, his breathing quick, and his pale eyes flicked from me to the knife I'd lowered in defense. A million thoughts whirled through my head. I held up my hands.

"Lach, it's not what it looks like, I promise."

One idea, a desperate one, snapped into place.

"Care to explain? Because it sure—"

I blasted the elf with a torrent of water so hard he tumbled back into the hallway. Frost skated across the walls and floors, freezing him solid as he fell. In the doorway, I erected a wall of ice between me and my friends. I couldn't risk them getting in, and I had no time to waste. I had only seconds before Lach recovered from my attack.

"Promedis ad," I whispered, then slit the longest leg of the rune at my temple.

A thunderclap slammed me backward. I crashed into the wall as a brilliant burst of white shredded my vision. Drywall flecked the ground as I collapsed. Pain erupted, sprouting from my core and spiraling through my limbs. It was a forgotten, ugly pain that destroyed my muscles, broke my bones, flayed my skin. I wanted to scream, to roar at the agony, but instead I clawed at a pair of hands wrapped around my throat.

I flailed against the weight of Kaleal's body pressed against me, gasping and choking as I dug my useless nails into the stone of her arms, struggling to speak, struggling to breathe, struggling to *live*. It was as if we'd picked up where we'd left off, when Kaleal had nearly dropped me into the hidden depths of my own mind.

Black spots skittered across my vision.

Once Kaleal knew I was on the verge of collapse, she released me.

My gasp was a shriek as I sucked in a bellyful of air, tumbling from my back to my side as I struggled to pull oxygen into my lungs. But still I had the presence of mind to search for the dagger, my hands slapping the floor in desperation. The pointed heel of a stiletto jabbed the center of my reaching hand and I screamed, tears sliding down my face, snot dripping from my nose as I curled in on myself, bruised hand clutched at my chest. Another kick and my head snapped back. The bridge of her shoe came down, pinning my neck into place.

Despite my hacking and shaking, I glared up at the God towering above me.

Kaleal was gorgeously vicious as always with her round curves, silken skin, and classically elegant features. She might have been considered beautiful, except for the arctic set of her face—her expression one of tightly constrained boredom I imagined serial killers and sociopaths preferred. Her signature purple eyes flashed, and I imagined all the ways she wished to kill me.

Starting with her bare hands.

One slender brow arched impressively before she lifted her foot, dismissing me as I wiped drool off my chin and snot off my cheeks. I flushed hot and coiled beneath her gaze, sitting up with my arms flung out behind me.

"Good to see you, too, Kaleal," I rasped.

She brought a hand with square-tipped nails to her hip. "Petulant child."

The point of her shoe slammed into my side. I screamed as a bone cracked. Slowly she circled, lashing out with violent kicks that left thick, purple bruises and aching bones—pain that wouldn't abate. I finally grasped Air, but it wouldn't move, wouldn't listen. Maybe she'd bewitched the magic, too.

The worst part of all, even worse than the pain, was the clinical way she attacked. She was not caught up in the heat of the moment. No, she was executing a plan she'd been crafting for months. Probably ever since I'd taken that first sip of the witch's draught.

I groaned when the blows finally stopped and rolled to my knees, arm curled against my ribs as I coughed blood on Ridley's pristine floors. I'd thought she might be a figment of my imagination, but she was definitely here, a real presence in the Caron mansion. She'd never manifested like this before. I didn't know how she'd done it: How she was projecting herself or how she'd split herself from my soul.

But I knew I'd made the correct decision by sealing her away before. She was too dangerous to leave like this.

"You done?" I sputtered, glaring up at her through a curtain of blood.

Her lips curled. "Oh, dear girl, we're just getting started." She'd grabbed my dagger, one already tipped with my blood, and held it up to the light. I inched back until I hit the wall beneath the indent my body had made before. "You locked me away. You left me to rot inside your brain. And you shall pay dearly for that decision. The question is: Do I scar your face first? Or work my way there?"

Icy ribbons of fear wound around my insides, but I tamped them down, maintaining the challenge on my face.

"You're the only one who can save the world, Kaleal," I spat.

She lowered the blade, blood-red lips pursing. The God considered something, then turned to the four-poster bed, heels clicking on the dark floors as she examined the prince laying quiet and still. She was good, very good, at hiding her thoughts. But I knew her better. I knew despite herself, her curiosity was piqued.

And she'd presented me with an opening.

"You have two options. Kill me now and risk destroying all the magic in the world." I braced my hand on the ground and forced myself upright, biting back the pain radiating from my broken bones. I wouldn't allow her to look down on me any longer. "Or you can kill me later and help me save the fey—save *yourself*—from that awful fate."

The God didn't react, not to my challenge anyway.

Fire and ice warred in my veins as she leaned over the prince, reaching out to touch his face, but never making contact. One nail traced a black vein running beneath his ear. She was poised, but I sensed the energy vibrating through her. The curiosity and...

"Such interesting company you choose to keep."

Recognition.

Whether it was the curse or the prince, she definitely noticed something.

"What's your decision, Kaleal?"

"So eager to die?" She straightened. "Or maybe torture is more up your alley? I'm happy to oblige."

Despite her threat, I knew I'd hooked her. She never would have let me rise otherwise.

"Someone has cursed the daemoni. It's a brutal curse, one that destroys their magic like a plague, gnawing away until there's nothing left. Most die. Their bodies are too closely connected to their magic to sustain the loss." I gripped one of the posts holding up the canopy of Ridley's bed. "Now the Prince of Sin himself is cursed. When he dies, his people's magic goes with him."

"It sounds like you've solved your problem." Kaleal tilted her head, reminding me of a haunted doll from a horror movie I'd watched as a kid. "He dies, the curse falls. You have nothing to worry about."

"It's spreading." Gods, I hated her, hated her lack of empathy. Hated how she—wait. She knew all this; she was too clever not to. She only wanted to hear me say it. I gritted my teeth. "A witch is showing signs of the curse now. And who's to stop the perpetrators from spinning up another curse, one that targets another race? I doubt they'll stop until the magic is gone. Even if they don't wipe magic out immediately, it's a trump card they'll forever hold."

Kaleal tapped her chin, a gesture I'd unconsciously adopted. I could hate myself for it. "And why do you need me, exactly?"

I tried to stand straighter, but winced when my shattered ribs flexed. My healing abilities had yet to kick in. "You're the only being powerful enough to help me find the creatures who started this and take them down. You're the only one who can save all fey from their torment. I've gone to the best of the best, I've pulled in resources, I've traveled the world. I've even asked Phenex." Her eyes flared with interest, one brow raising. "And I've come up with nothing. I can't stop this curse, but I know you can. I know you have some trick to save us all."

Kaleal stood there, face blank as she thought it over, staring down at the too-still prince. It was agonizing to watch, like laying on a bed of coals, wondering if I'd done enough, if I'd appealed to her arrogance and vanity enough.

When she brushed Ridley's arm with one nail, I knew I had her.

"Well, hurry up."

"You'll help?"

She ignored that. "Get us to Ridley. You know how to accomplish that much, I assume." She tugged at the strings of my magic. Magic I hadn't been able to access until now. Magic that bound us together. "We need him to guide us."

Chapter 38

I'd known she would try something.

If I'd thought Kaleal kicking me to a pulp was painful, the sensation of my soul splitting in half as we tumbled through the black void of the 'in-between' was outright agonizing. My insides turned to fire, my bones to lava, as whatever bound Kaleal to me and me to her cracked.

I knew we would never be the same after this.

Moments after touching down, something tugged on my—*our*—magic. Kaleal had recovered first, and was clawing at the ribbon of gold trailing behind me, the link connecting me to my body. The ancient God was already reversing course without a glance back, scrambling back up that line to, no doubt, take over my body.

She intended to lock me in this abyss with a dying incubus forever.

She also left me with only one option.

I dug deep, searching for the connection, the golden strand...

And severed it.

Kaleal shrieked as she tumbled down, motes of static whirling around her. I thrust my forearm up to block the incoming punch.

"What did you do?" Kaleal's outraged scream shattered the hornet-like buzzing of Ridley's mind. No wailing winds this time, it seemed. "Are you out of your bloody mind?"

I snagged her second fist out of the air, dipped low, and used her momentum to toss her over my shoulder. She crashed into the muck with a satisfying slap. "Yeah, I'm fairly certain we're both in Ridley's mind now."

Amethyst eyes blazed as Kaleal floundered. She snarled and fought her way to her feet, black gunk dripping from her limbs. She flexed her hands in a method I recognized, and her face contorted again when she realized she didn't have access to magic anymore.

It had remained with me.

One magic, one God.

She was the outsider.

"What now, Zara?" She swiped uselessly at the stains on her soul. It didn't bypass me, the use of my name. She'd recognized the shift in power, her ability to adapt chameleon-like. "You destroyed your only way back to your body. Now both of us are stranded. What's the plan, hm? What's your big idea?"

I backed out of reach of her legs, not wanting a repeat session of earlier. Damage to my soul, for all I knew, was permanent. "I told you, we're going to save Ridley and put an end to the curse."

"And after that?"

I shrugged. "You were the one trying to rob me of my body. I solved the immediate problem. We'll get to the other when we get to it."

A low hiss slipped between her teeth. "Cutting that particular cord isn't something easily undone."

I pointed at her. "See, you know things. Like the bonds connecting souls to their bodies. That's exactly why you're here. Now let's find Ridley, and then you'll fill us in on exactly what happens next."

I glanced at the billowing clouds of tiny gray particles, then along the vast horizon and the layers of static preventing me from seeing the landscape. Knowing Ridley and his immense power, I imagined it had once been a beautiful place.

Kaleal gave up on scrubbing at the curse, expression thoughtful. No doubt she thought I had a fantastically wild plan to get us out of this nightmare. She turned, mouth dropping open in what I knew would be a particularly cutting remark, and hesitated before straightening to her full height.

"I believe we've solved one of our problems," she said.

"I had a feeling you'd follow me here sooner or later." The low timbre of Ridley's voice vibrated through me.

Seeing him, or at least seeing this *part* of him, alive and talking… swamped me. I wanted to launch myself at him, touch him, to assure myself he was still here, he hadn't gone. But under Kaleal's scrutiny, I settled for tossing my braid over my shoulder.

"I couldn't let you hog all the glory, could I?" I snarked.

"True. Though if you'd waited much longer…"

I squinted, recognizing the fuzziness marring the edges of Ridley's body, the slightly muted tone of his skin and clothing. It sobered me. The prince was fading into this not-reality. It was only a matter of time… and with me and my magic here…

"I'm making it worse," I admitted. The buzzing of the static increased in volume. I kicked at the muck lapping at my shoes. "My magic will destroy what's left of you faster."

His hand snagged mine, and Ridley pulled me to his side. "Nah. This is how it's supposed to be. The head of an entire clan of fey and one of the Gods tasked with protecting them all—together. Staring death in the face."

A million questions hovered on my lips as I gazed up at him, the bond linking us humming fondly. The prince's eyes darted across the planes of my face, drinking me in. His brow twitched, betraying his cool façade. It gave me the courage I needed to grab hold of the one question I finally wanted to face. "Ridley—"

"Excuse me."

The red tint in Ridley's eyes deepened. He winked, angling himself between me and Kaleal, who had her hand on her hip, chin thrust outward as she glared down her nose.

"Didn't see you there," the prince said. "And you are?"

Kaleal's eyes narrowed in acknowledgment of the insult, but she locked down her thoughts, sliding seamlessly into the graceful and manipulative being I knew her to be. "You know who I am. Princes all recognize their Gods."

"I do recognize my God." Ridley threaded his fingers between mine, lifting my hand. I gasped at the sensation of his smoky magic wrapping around me, spreading *through* me. "And she's most definitely not some pale imitation who should have moved on to the Underworld far too long ago."

His magic reluctantly slipped from mine, and I wondered what it had cost him. What putting down an Original God *would* cost him. I edged closer to him, threads of power bunched in my fist. Kaleal's face showed nothing, but there was no way she would forget this, no way she would forgive this insult.

His slight would not go unpunished.

Before things got worse, I shoved between the two. "Ridley, Kaleal may be as annoying as she is brutal, and I might not like her much as someone who shares my mind, but she's the only one who can help us stop this curse."

"Is that so?" the prince drawled, unimpressed. "This should be good."

My stomach dropped. It physically hurt to say my next words. "We have to trust her."

"I don't have to. She's the invader inside my head."

"You can't be serious." The world seemed to fade away again, leaving only me and Ridley behind. My pulse stuttered. I reached for him, not understanding why this was so important to me that he trust her.

No, I realized with a start. That wasn't it.

The dizziness clouding my thoughts cleared. "I need you to trust *me*, Ridley. Trust I know what I'm doing."

The prince's lips thinned; his chest heaved. Static buzzed in my ears, loud and unforgiving, and he inclined his head. The world dropped back into focus, and I became aware of Kaleal's sharp gaze upon us as he gripped my shoulder over the elemental brands.

"My trust is always with you," he said.

The nausea faded, and I swallowed past the lump in my throat. The relief sweeping through me was paramount, his firm support a pillar I'd never known necessary to my being. There was that question again, the one I desperately needed to get out, the one about what he thought of me, what I meant to him. But now wasn't the time.

That meant we'd have to make time.

Ridley had to survive this with his magic intact.

I squared my shoulders and eyed Kaleal, ignoring the coy curl of her lips. "What do we do?"

Kaleal smoothed her features again and shrugged. "It's simple, actually."

"Do tell," Ridley said dryly.

"We follow the curse back to the source."

I shook my head, frustration tearing at my chest. "We've already tried that. Both a friend and I tried using the runes to guide us to the witches. It doesn't work. The magic is too muddled."

"Oh, Zara. That's cute." Kaleal crooned and clicked her tongue. The stranglehold gripping my heart tightened. "You need to join the cursed, first."

Chapter 39

"I have to what?" I screeched, at the same time Ridley said, "That's not about to happen."

Was she insane? That plan risked destroying magic at its core. What was a God if not the heart of all magic?

Kaleal fluffed her hair. "I didn't say you'd like the solution."

"There has to be another way," I gasped, gripping the sides of my head. I paced in a tight circle, trying to keep from vomiting. "Anything besides succumbing to that—that—"

The God speared me with a look. "There is no other way. The spell is too complex for you or any of your *friends* to break using the regular methods. You must become one with the curse to understand it, to track it."

"'Can't beat them, join them,'" Ridley murmured drolly. He hooked an arm around my shoulders to stop my pacing. "I never particularly liked that adage. It always felt too much like surrendering."

His voice steadied me and I remembered why I was here, what was at risk if I didn't do everything in my power to stop the curse. My voice came out small. "Explain it again."

"You can't be serious," the prince snapped. His blood-orange eyes flared as he shook me lightly. "You can't seriously be entertaining this insane idea."

"'Insanity is doing the same thing over and over again, and expecting different results,'" Kaleal quoted. What was happening right now? Was this the same God who assaulted me on a regular basis? Her grin sharpened. "Which is exactly what it sounds like you've been doing."

Everything inside me seized. My skin crawled. Her casual observation wrecked me... because it was true.

Through numb lips, I asked, "What do I need to do?"

"This isn't you, Zara." Ridley shook me again. "Don't let her get inside your head like this."

"No." A snarl ripped from my throat, and I lashed at him. "We need to do this. Whatever she suggests, we have to do it. I don't see any other options." I slapped at his arm when he reached for me again. "Or have you forgotten that all of magic is at stake here?"

The incubus froze, throat working, eyes glistening, and he backed off.

"How does this work?" I asked Kaleal.

Her cheeks plumped with smug satisfaction. I had a feeling I shouldn't have let her see this side of me with Ridley. I shouldn't have allowed her to observe us for this long. There was no doubt in my mind she'd learned what he had the potential to be to me. She would use that to her advantage down the line. But what was done was done.

My world had already tilted on its axis. What was another degree or two?

The God folded her hands demurely. "Once the curse latches to your magic, it will begin destroying it. It will become one with you. Once that connection is established, your soul will have a direct line to those on the other end. That will clear up the 'muddled' quality to the magic—as you so eloquently put it earlier." Kaleal smoothed an eyebrow with her middle finger.

I bared my teeth. "So, the connection forms. What then?"

"You'll send your soul right down the line and destroy the witches responsible," she chirped. "They've basically invited you directly into their circle."

"What?"

"I get it," Ridley said blandly. He locked his hands behind his head and stared up at the cloudy waves of static. His features grew fuzzier. We were running out of time. "I mean, I don't understand *why* they're doing it, but I can see they're latching on to souls to drain them. By going to the witches yourself, you're accelerating the process." He eyed the God. "Do you think these witches were working up to pulling souls directly to them all along? It would be faster than draining them remotely."

"Most likely, though they're not at that level yet."

Ridley nodded. "And you honestly think they would have to cast a circle for this level of magic to work? I thought most covens had moved past that archaic method of spellcraft."

"Absolutely." Kaleal spoke without hesitation. "A curse this complex would require a coven to weave the spell and actively maintain it. I doubt they've left the room where they're working to pull it off. The circle would break if they left."

"How, exactly, do I fight them on the other side?" I asked, grasping at something substantial.

Kaleal wrinkled her nose. "Your soul and its magic will manifest as a physical shape, something like a ghost. You'll be able to use your magic like you normally would." She folded her arms. "I doubt they'll anticipate us taking this route, so the odds are good we'll be able to catch the witches by surprise."

"They may also be prepared for the possibility of a soul finding its way back to them," Ridley pointed out.

Kaleal's brow arched. "I didn't say it was a perfect plan. Nor did I say I could read minds."

It sounded insane, and I didn't understand enough about the magic making all this possible, but if Ridley found sound reason in her explanation, that had to be a good sign, right?

"How many witches are we talking here?" I asked.

Kaleal tipped her head from side to side. "Could be a dozen. Could be hundreds. But I'm betting three. Witches like the number three. They're superstitious."

"Three," I agreed, the fey's voice coming back to me—the one I had lost at Cura. "It's definitely three."

"So, are we in agreement then?" Kaleal asked.

"One sec." I tapped my chin and immediately wished I hadn't. "If this is your solution, why did we need to enter Ridley's mind at all? I know the curse wants me. I can feel it reaching for me when I touch other fey. All I need to do is make contact and it should meld to me if I let it."

A wide grin split Kaleal's face. "No, we didn't need to come here."

"So you wanted—" I broke off, realization dawning. "You only came here because you wanted to trap me outside of my body."

She clicked her tongue again. "And I almost succeeded, too."

I'd never wanted to murder someone so badly before—including Geoffrey, who'd ruined my life. My limbs shook with the effort it took not to launch myself at the God and claw off her face.

Ridley sidled between us. "Hold up. I'm coming with you."

"No can do, Prince." Kaleal went to touch him, and he smoothly blocked her hand. "This train can only carry one God since the curse will latch itself to her magic. Besides, she's the only one who can see the connection because she's the root of all magic. Since you don't share her abilities, that means… you're out." Kaleal knelt and smacked the muck at her feet. "You sit tight like a good little prince and let her do the heavy lifting."

"It's ok." I squeezed Ridley's arm, my insides clenching at the devastation on his gaunt face. "Have a little faith. I can save your people. I'll accept the curse, I'll kick some ass, and we'll both be back in our own bodies before you know it."

I wasn't sure how much I believed that, though.

He nodded. His expression was torn, eyes strangely hollow. I would have given anything in that moment to know what he was thinking.

I swallowed and stepped up to Kaleal, hating that once again I was turning to her for help. "What now?"

She stared at me, amethyst eyes searing a hole through me, and held out her hand. "I could explain it, but it may take longer than your friend here has. What I'll do is bind us together again so I can access your magic." She wiggled her fingers impatiently when I hesitated. "I'll get you through these next few steps, and you'll regain control on the other side."

I kept my hand against my chest. "How do I know this isn't a trick?"

"You don't." She grinned, shark-like. "It's a risk you'll have to take."

This magic was beyond me, but it sounded like it was the only shot we had at stopping this horror show. I risked a glance at Ridley, who seemed to snap back to himself, blinking rapidly as he glanced between me and Kaleal.

"Alright. Lead the way," I said as Ridley's lips moved. I couldn't hear what he said, though, because long, cool fingers circled my wrist and the static vanished.

Chapter 40

I wasn't sure what I'd expected, but emerging flat on my back, limbs splayed, staring up at a plain, white ceiling wasn't it. I attempted to move my arm and met resistance. Similar results with my other wrist and ankles. Something thick and heavy bit into my neck, preventing much movement.

My mind raced.

If a soul could sweat, I'd be laying in a pool of the stuff.

Calm yourself, Kaleal murmured. *Don't let them know you're awake.*

I thought you said we would catch them by surprise, I snapped back. Keeping my eyes closed, knowing that I should keep them closed, was proving difficult. In my panic, I wanted to see what I was up against, *who* I was up against.

I also said my plan wasn't perfect, Kaleal's voice grated. Her presence filled me like it never had before, my mind and body feeling compressed, crowded, as her weight settled against mine. *You're the one who ran with it.*

"Can you believe it?" My limbs locked at the new, excited voice. A woman that existed in the world outside of my mind. "Both the Prince of Sin *and* the God of Water? At the same time?"

I swore I blacked out for a moment in shock. *Did she say... Prince of Sin?* I asked Kaleal.

You and I share the same ears, she replied. *I wonder how he...* She paused. *My, my. He is a naughty one, isn't he?*

What did he do? I demanded, panic rising. *What did he do?*

Shhhh, she hissed.

"I don't know how you sensed them coming, Mari, but well done." A second voice, this one deeper than the first but no less frenzied. "Getting those runes in place in time was a stroke of genius."

A snort from the first woman. "Imagine telling that to my mother. She'd have laughed in your face, then told you to dunk your head in a bucket of ice water to wake your senses."

Kaleal. I attempted to get the God's attention again, but the conversation had snared her.

"Imagine when the world finds out three minor witches not only captured a God but absorbed her magic, too." I sensed movement from my left. The second woman's southern accent grew slightly more distant. Something scraped against a wooden surface. "That'll teach them for mocking us."

So they aren't *trying to destroy magic?* I asked rhetorically. *They're absorbing it?*

With your abilities, even divided three ways, they would be among the most powerful beings on the planet, Kaleal murmured. *I've always loved a good power trip. I suppose they could pull it off with the right amount of luck.*

How so? I asked.

Witches rely on runes to cast their magic, but minor witches are notoriously weak. Most can barely make water boil or heal a paper cut. Kaleal paused. *To pull off a spell this complicated would require either a high level of magic or a very simple spell warped in a very specific way. Simple is a minor witch's middle name.*

"Uh, guys." The third witch sounded meek, her voice soft yet squeaky. Floorboards creaked beside my head. "A-are you s-sure we've bound her t-tight enough? I mean, sh-she is a G-god."

She might be an evil witch bent on destroying magic, but her tone still held a tinge of awe.

"Of course I did, Liza," said Mari. "Did I doubt you when you figured out how to bind that nymph's magic to our spell? No. Even though that was a failure. But it helped when the incubus came along. Who would have guessed *giving* magic mattered more than simply taking it?" A huff. "Anyway. I didn't doubt you. Why would you doubt me now?"

Liza hesitated, and a faucet turned on. Water pinged against the base of a metal bucket. "I wa-wasn't doubting you. But I've h-heard what she can do. And him. They-they're scary."

"Of course they're scary." The second voice again. The witch I didn't have a name for. "They're some of the most powerful beings on the planet. Tossing their magic around without a care in the world? Pretending like they care? It's all smoke screens, and you know it. Only a stupid stroke of luck and a mix of good genetics gave them their abilities. It's not like they earned their power."

She hawked a loogie.

Disgusting, Kaleal muttered. I wasn't sure if she was referencing their manners or the subject.

"Iris is right." Chalk scraped the ground near my hand. I made a concerted effort not to allow my fingers to twitch. "That's why Victor gave us some of his magic, remember? He's sick of the status quo, those stupid Carons acting as if the other daemoni owe them something because they claim to be royal. What makes someone royal anyway? Blood. You know what everyone's got? Blood."

She's not wrong, I said to Kaleal. *That's why so few humans rely on monarchies. It is sort of ridiculous when you think about it.*

Humans overcomplicate everything, came the ancient God's reply.

"Now if they'd *earned* their power or their stupid titles, that would be one thing. But since they were born with it? They might as well lose it. Learn what it's like to be a little guy. It's not right some have more magic than others." Mari paused. "Do you need help with that?"

"Nah, I got it."

So, it's not merely the daemoni they're after, Kaleal purred. *It's everyone. And it's clever, really, binding another fey's magic to their spell. That's probably why your friend couldn't break it. She doesn't understand what daemoni magic is, so she couldn't defuse it.*

Something about that statement gave me pause, but before I could put my finger on what it was, a bucket of icy water splashed across my face. I gasped in shock, eyes flying open as my body went rigid under the blast, my limbs held fast by the invisible ropes tying me down.

"Time to wake up, Water God." The figure above me was blurred, and I frantically blinked water out of my eyes, still gasping from the shock of it. I never would have guessed souls could *feel* quite so much. "I want to see your face when you realize we have bested you. It's the sweetest kind of treat."

Mari. The most malicious of the bunch. As she moved aside, I made out a mass of frizzy brown hair and a tattered gray robe. Another sound of water sloshing and Ridley sucked in a gasp.

A second woman appeared at the edge of my vision. Her glasses magnified her eyes to twice their size, and a snarled bun held back her mousy hair. She blinked at me, uncertain, and opened and shut her mouth a few times, revealing a large overbite. "You—you won't be able to get away. Those r-r-runes are holding you down, spelled against the elements." Horror flooded her face. "They also b-bind your magic. That's important. If your magic weren't with you, w-we couldn't s-strip it from you."

"Shut up, Liza. Stop spilling our secrets." A large woman with a double chin and hands the size of hams cuffed the smaller woman in the side of the head. "They don't care, anyway. They'll be dead in a few minutes. Mari, did you grab the knives?"

"Of course." I startled when the first witch jumped into view, her feet planted on either side of my torso as she crouched over top of me. She had eyes the clearest of blue, too pretty to belong to a woman with such twisted motives.

Mari leered, her putrid breath fanning my face, and dipped a hand into the pouch at her middle. She grinned crookedly and drew out two ordinary-looking kitchen knives. Runes in black were scrawled across the steel blades. The only differences were the handles. She raised the one with a black grip. "This one strips away your magic. And this one," she offered the wooden one, "destroys your soul. We plan to use both on you. Don't want to take any chances."

Kaleal didn't recoil as I'd expected. Instead, she spread out, relaxing her limbs so they fit just so.

Iris appeared overhead. "We created these in case anyone traced the trails of magic back to us. Only the most powerful beings could do that. So, we were well prepared."

A trap. We'd fallen right into a trap.

And what was Ridley doing here, anyway? I thought Kaleal told him he couldn't join us.

"And you're the creme de la crème." Mari was back in my face, the French words blending strangely with her Texas accent. "If that stupid witch, Marinda, hadn't whisked you from the Water Temple during the attack, then you would have died." I blinked against the spit showering my face. "What a traitor to our race, she was. Without you, magic never woulda come back. Without you, we would have kept living our same old lives. Not been pitied and looked down upon for our lack of ability. We wouldn't be forced to take magic for our ourselves."

I knew this had to be your fault somehow, Kaleal mocked. *Creating a couple of psychotic witches seems right up your alley.*

Oh, shut up. As if you have any room to talk.

Mari spat and the glob hit my cheek, close to my eye. I wished I could free my arms and punch her in the face.

"Guys," Liza whispered, "I'm getting n-nervous. G-get on with it."

Mari dug the points of her knees into my belly, the black-handled knife flashing in her grip. "This first one will be a nick, just a little thing. But the next one... it's going right through your black, black heart."

I closed my eyes, every muscle straining, as the knife dropped.

And my skin *ripped.*

It was the only way to describe the sensation of Kaleal peeling away from me.

"Maybe later," the God hissed. The witch shrieked as Kaleal jerked upright and grabbed her by the throat, heedless of the blades that flew from her grip. Mari struggled as the other two witches screamed. A well-placed kick from Liza sent the God sprawling.

Mari scrambled up, fingers prodding her throat as she backed away. "Who are you? How did you get out?"

Kaleal was already in motion, uncaring of the useless, stupid questions, and launched herself at the offending witch. As she ripped herself up, her foot must have scrubbed away some markings pinning me down, because suddenly my right arm was free. Liza, the only witch who lingered, squeaked in terror as I reached for my throat, scrabbling at the floor, destroying more runes.

Something crashed into a wall, and bits of chair whizzed past my head. I wiped away the last of the chalk and popped upright. I was free. Sore and covered in spit, but free.

"Zara, a little help over here," Kaleal called. She stood across the room, blocking the door as Mari and Iris advanced. Mari suddenly whooped and dropped to her knees, a stick of white chalk gripped tight in one hand. "I could use some magic right about now. Water would be great."

I released the strands of blue quivering inside me while sprinting toward Ridley's side, keeping an eye out for the knives. A geyser of water erupted from Kaleal's half of the room. I heard Mari's shriek of rage as I made quick work of freeing the incubus and hauled him to his feet.

"Watch out." He pushed me down as a bucket soared past my head.

"What are you doing here?" I hissed, fisting his shirt in my hands.

"My people, my problem." He gently loosened my grip, focused on the witches. "I needed to see this one out."

I gaped. "That is such a man thing to say. Kaleal and I had this figured out. We can—"

"Can you yell at me for my sexist behavior later?" He forced my head down again as a dozen icicles flew by. "Let's survive this mess first."

"Fine," I said. Liza had worked herself into a corner and folded herself into a ball, cowering while Kaleal traded blows with Mari. Iris dug through a drawer in a small kitchenette. "But you owe me a reason for *how* you got here, too."

"I'm hoping you'll forget about that."

"Don't let them out the door," Kaleal yelled as icy spikes erupted from the ground, nearly spearing her opponent who jumped on a table at the last second. "That breaks the circle and we all vanish. We have to destroy the spell and the witches first."

"I'm going to help her with the crazy one," Ridley said, smoke curling from his nostrils. "I'm sure you can handle the big one."

A blur of black blasted across the room and smashed into the frizzy witch, but I only had eyes for Iris, who'd stuck her hand in a bag at her waist. She emerged with something that looked like pebbles. She tossed a few my way, and I realized they were, in fact, rocks covered in runes.

They exploded like demonfire.

I countered with flames of my own, a whirlwind of air saving me from the blast of extreme heat.

"Is that the best you got?" I yelled, striding through the blaze. "Because I can do one better."

The air sharpened to razor blades in my grip and I flung them, one after another, cursing as she tossed pebbles in response. The shields blocked the blasts with remarkable effectiveness. What she wasn't expecting was for me to follow up with a bellows' worth of fire, and she screamed as the flames devoured her whole.

I wished I could say I felt bad, but I didn't. Instead, I formed a spear of air and slammed it through her chest, saving her from the worst of the pain. Blood bubbled from her lips and soaked the gritty floor beneath her body as she went limp.

Across the room, Kaleal and Mari circled one another, the God whipping up spiraling balls of ice and water that hit the witch and seemed to disappear before touching her. To counter Kaleal like that… they must have already absorbed the magic they'd stolen. There was no other way the witch could have countered her power or skill.

Mari's grin grew, cracking her snarled face in half as Kaleal dropped low. Her fingers curled as I snagged the flame from the candle, a roaring inferno rising high.

"Trying to freeze my blood?" The witch waved a hand and chucked another pebble that exploded when it hit the ground at Kaleal's feet, sending her flying. Her head hit the door with a crack and she slumped to the ground.

Mari didn't have time to gloat, because Ridley launched at her, bat wings spread, and punched a hole through her rib cage. She gasped, jerked, dark blood spilling from her lips as he ripped his arm back, her heart gripped in his fist.

She fell with a crack, twitched once, and went still.

The incubus tucked his wings back, black skin fading as he turned around. He spotted the charred remains of the witch on the ground between us and bared his teeth. I tried hard not to look at the blood coating his arm past his elbow.

Instead, I scanned the room. The third witch. Liza. She had to be around here. But she wasn't in her corner. I scented the air, searching for another living being, and tensed as Ridley screamed, "Zara, no."

I whirled, realizing too late the woman had snuck up at my back. In her fist: A knife. As it swung downward, I threw up a wall of air, but the blade spliced right through it. This close, there was no way she could miss. Something soft fluttered past my face, a glimpse of gnashing wolf-teeth and gory battlefields flashed before my eyes, then a figure formed. Ridley grunted at the impact, even as he grabbed the witch's head and ripped it clean off her shoulders. Blood geysered, showering me and the incubus in red. Liza's body tumbled as he tossed her head away.

Shock. Horror.

Disbelief.

All coursed through me.

The incubus swayed, then dropped to a knee, my name on his lips. That, and only that, snapped me from my stupor.

"Ridley," I said, barely recognizing my own voice, the franticness of it. He was too still. Far too still. "Ridley, talk to me."

He turned, revealing the handle of the dagger stuck in his chest, black blood pumping down the handle. My heart stopped, and I froze in the middle of reaching for him, staring as he grabbed the knife with trembling fingers and pulled it from his soul. He cursed and dropped it as he crumbled, falling into my arms.

This wasn't the magic-severing blade. This one bore a wooden handle, the one that was much, much worse. The blade spelled to destroy souls, strip them from this plane, reduce them to nothing.

An endless stream of noes filled my ears as I crouched beside him, and I realized the person pleading was me. I pulled him close, felt him rest a cheek, sticky with blood, against my hair.

"You can't die. You can't." Tears I couldn't feel spilled down my cheeks as I patted him, pulling him tighter, my insides cracking and breaking and burning and shattering. "We'll fix this. We will. I don't know how, but we will."

He grunted a coarse sound that might have been a laugh and unwrapped my arms, leaning back to look at me. The incubus seemed strangely at peace as he traced the curve of my cheek.

"Promise me you won't hate me," he said.

"Why would I hate you?" I buried my face in his chest again, not sure if I possessed a heart anymore, because it felt as if a grenade had detonated my insides. Ridley cradled me close, his hands running down the length of my braid, then coming back up to the side of my head. "You saved me. How did you—"

"I accepted the bond. The one tying us together." He pulled back with a choked gasp. "It's how I followed you, by using the magic you shared with me. I couldn't let my people down. I couldn't—"

He coughed into his hand, body shaking.

The krav legara bond? Was that what he was talking about? What did that have to do with anything?

"We'll talk about it when we get back. Come on, let's go," I begged, tugging on his arm as he slipped down my body. "Let's get out of here and we'll figure it out."

"I'm not leaving here, Zara," he said, bringing my face close to his. "I don't have the energy. But I… I did what I came to do. I destroyed the curse, my people are safe. Killing the witches broke the spell." His lips peeled back in pain. "It's time… for a new… regime."

I grabbed the back of the hand speared in my hair. "You're coming with us. If we can get you back in your body, we can fix this, I know we can."

"So... optimistic." His lashes fluttered as he leaned heavily against me, his chest rising and falling slower, his breaths longer. "It's too late... for me." He pressed a hand to his chest, summoning a ball of smoke. "I rescind... my title. I accept my time. I leave... the queen... this choice to make."

"What's happening?" I stuttered, horrified by the ball of smoke he offered. A dribble of blood trickled from the corner of his mouth. "What is this?"

"Take it, you fool." Kaleal crouched beside me, one hand pressed to the side of her head, auburn hair matted with blood. "He's revoking his title, protecting his people. If you don't accept, then he can't rest in peace since he won't be able to pick his successor himself. He's giving that honor to *you*."

Her eyes focused on the ball hungrily.

"Ridley, I... I can't. This is too—"

"I trust you... to make the right decision." His face was intense, yet somehow warm. "Take it. Take it and make this world... a little better."

With trembling hands, I accepted the ball, feeling it cling to me in a way the ooze of the curse never had. This was soft and comforting. Somehow right.

"Thank you." He pressed his forehead to mine, blood-orange eyes alight. "I hope... someday you'll... forgive me."

"Time to break the circle." Kaleal stood, dragging on the back of my shirt. "We need to destroy the spell and get back to your body. The longer we wait, the longer we risk someone finding this place and taking the spell for their own."

I surveyed the room, the dead bodies, the broken furniture, the hundreds of chalk markings, and finally the Prince of Sin himself. "I don't know—"

"Burn it down!" Kaleal swept out her arm, indicating the room. "Set a fire so we burn it to the ground, not a floorboard can remain." Her nails pierced my shoulder as she shook me. "That will break the circle and send us back."

"But how are we—"

"Go, Zara," Ridley whispered. "You need to go."

A new kind of horror slithered through me. Starting a fire and then leaving him behind to perish in it? I dragged a rough breath into my lungs. It was like leaving my parents all over again.

"You have to," Kaleal said, purple eyes desperate as they flicked between me and the incubus. "There's no other way."

I nodded, feeling the flames twine through me until their heat grew to be too much. They spread along the perimeter of the room, crackling as they gnawed through the dry floorboards. It was the first time I'd ever created fire without using a lighter.

I was too far gone to marvel at that realization.

Ridley's lips were cool, his taste minty as he brushed them across mine. "Tell him… I'm sorry."

Then he pushed me away and Kaleal pulled me in… our magic swirling and thrashing angrily as I resisted her. But she was too strong, too desperate…

I held Ridley's eyes, his body framed by flames roaring closer and closer, my arm outreached. Tears streamed down my cheeks as we vanished back into the abyss.

Chapter 41

Kaleal let go the moment our feet touched down. I nearly tripped, but pinwheeled my arms to stay upright, dogging her steps out of pure instinct, not because I wanted to.

"Where are we?" I wheezed, muscles protesting when she took off running. We'd appeared on a long canyon path carved among the craggy, obsidian rocks of a mountain that speared the sky. The sky was smoky and gray, the air heavy and musty, like a room that badly needed airing out.

"We should have dropped in the in-between. But this clearly is not—" She cursed to herself. "That stupid fool. When he completed that bond, he must have screwed up the magic somehow. No matter. It's the same process—whether it's through the ether or his mind."

"Are you saying we're back in Ridley's head?" I glanced up again, not recognizing anything about this place. Granted, before it had been a swamp of static and ooze, but, somehow, I felt the prince's mind would have been more welcoming. The ball of smoky glass Ridley had gifted me seemed to burn in my palm, and I hugged it tighter. "How is that possible?"

"Anything is possible with magic," the ancient God snarled, dirt flying as she skidded around a corner. "When he tied your magic to his, it must have created a link. It wouldn't normally be an issue." She grunted as she scaled a boulder in the middle of our path. At some point, she had removed her shoes. "But he's dying, and if we don't get out before his mind collapses, we may never get back."

She hit the ground with another plume of white dirt and grit. As I followed, I risked a glance behind, chest thudding when I found a gaping hole of black nothingness in the distance.

"It's starting," I shouted to Kaleal. "His mind. It's closing in."

Her speed kicked up a notch. So did mine, the glass ball slippery with sweat in my palm.

A thought occurred to me, a thought that prickled at the edges of my mind and curled its talons into my intestines. "How do you know we're going in the right direction?" I demanded of Kaleal, pushing my body harder until I drew level with her. "I severed the link to my body. I didn't tell you—"

"But didn't you? When you allowed me in your head?" The God tossed a smirk over her shoulder, whipping out an arm to snag the top of a shoulder-height rock to help her swivel around one of the tighter turns. "I knew you weren't stupid enough to cut yourself off from your body completely."

She shoved me. I hadn't expected the move, and I slammed into a wall of rock, my side exploding with pain as I tumbled into the dirt. I lay there, shocked, bruises blooming, the glass ball remarkably unbroken, my thoughts a flurry of too much information being processed at once.

I reached for the blue strands of Water.

A void opened inside me when I remembered giving it away.

My plan, my hastily constructed plan built on a whole heck of a lot of luck and trust and not much else, all hinged on my connection to Water… and the elf holding firm to the other end.

I hauled myself to my feet, hurrying after Kaleal who, to my devastation, had gained a substantial lead. But she was still within sight. I could catch up if I tried. I lowered my head, legs pumping faster as I pushed myself harder, ignoring the screaming of my legs, the wheezing from my lungs.

When I'd attacked Lachlan back at the mansion, I'd done so not to keep him out, but to forge a connection with him. I'd meant to use that magic to follow it back to him if it came down to it, following the blue threads home where the glimmer of gold could no longer take me.

My vision blurred, and I slowed when my feet hit the hard, cracked earth of a dried-up lakebed. Ahead loomed the imposing side of an impossibly tall cliff, this one flecked with rose and emerald rock. On the surface, it was quite beautiful, but that wasn't what caught my attention. What did was the opening to a cave cut at the base and the figure sprinting toward it.

Kaleal must have figured out my plan when she'd re-entered my body to get into the witch's lair. She must have rooted through my thoughts and found exactly what she'd needed, that's why she'd sounded so smug. She hadn't asked for Water on a whim. No, that sneaky monster sought to lock me out of my own mind by stealing the only link I had back to myself.

But Ridley had also forged a connection with me to use my magic. With his mind still semi-intact around us, that bond must still be there. If that were the case—butterflies exploded in my chest. My magic must work as it should in this realm. I launched myself into the air, the cracks of the earth blurring as I soared across the surface, moving faster than I ever had before. I focused on Kaleal's shape, her body growing larger and larger.

I could catch her. I could.

She was only a hundred yards away. She couldn't… she wouldn't…

Amethyst eyes glowed as she turned, winked…

Then dove through the mouth of the cave.

A siren's scream ripped from my throat as the entrance disappeared.

Dust plumed as I crashed to the ground, skidding to a stop right before I collided with the bare rock face. I slammed a fist against it, pounding the ragged surface as the skin on my knuckles shredded. When it hurt too much to keep going, I slammed my shoulder into the side, screaming for it to open, to grant me access to my mind.

I couldn't end like this

I didn't want to end like this.

My back hit the wall, and I slid down, collapsing in a small, boneless lump. I picked up the ball and pulled it close to my chest, staring at my fisheye reflection on the surface. Sweat streaked through sprays of blood and dirt on my forehead and cheeks. My mouth seemed too small, my eyes too big.

And beyond the ball—the lakebed.

The flat expanse that so closely resembled another lakebed. One where I'd nearly lost my life to one of the most powerful men on the planet. How fitting I'd return to that memory now. Fitting it would end like this. Because it would.

Ridley wouldn't be able to hold on much longer.

Already, the horizon had vanished, a starless, inky sky reaching for eons beyond. The blackness engulfed the mountain and crept across the plain, closing in bit by bit.

Lachlan, if you can hear me, I'm sorry. I'm so sorry. I scraped at the ground. Dust crumbled beneath my fingernails. *Kaleal figured it out. I hope you'll find a way to contain her, to kill her, before it's too late.*

The top of my head rubbed against the rock, ripping hair from my braid as I leaned back. The void had crossed roughly a quarter of the lakebed already, taunting me with its encroaching nearness.

Ryder, I'm sorry I couldn't save your brother. I'm sorry I ran from you and our friends. I'm sorry we'll never have the time we dreamed we would have to figure out what we had between us. And after what Ridley did, which I don't understand, I don't know what impact that would have had on us. If we'd have been able to figure this out. Maybe it's for the best we'll never know.

The black crept faster now, tendrils stretching, clawing as they ripped through the ground, shattering the dirt and sending it back into the nothingness that would soon encompass this wasteland.

Defiance pulsed through me as anger set in.

What was it that Ryder had said to me?

"You won't give up. You never have and you never will."

I might be beaten. But I wouldn't go down like this. I would face my end like I faced everything else in my life—with strength and fire. If it wanted me, it could have me. But not lying down.

Red and gold threads whipped about, a firestorm of magic that pulsed and flared with heat and light. It might have been a trick of the eye, but for a moment, the blackness paused, hesitating in its feeding frenzy. Wind fluttered my hair and clothing, and the scorching burn of fire zinged through my veins.

I took one step forward. Then two more.

No. If I were going out like this… I'd meet it head-on.

Sprays of color shot from my hands as I picked up speed, narrowing the distance between me and nothingness. The fear that had consumed me so potently before was now a memory as I stared deep into that abyss. Let it take me. I dared it to…

A hawk's shriek shattered the silence, the sound cold and clear.

What the…

I tried to look over my shoulder.

… Don't slow down…

A thrill shot through me. I recognized that hollow tone. The Thunderbird? The breath ripped through my lungs and I looked straight at the abyss, looming ever closer.

I obeyed the Thunderbird's command, feet pounding the earth. I risked another glance back as a streak of golden light crested the cliff.

Wings shot with rays of sunshine flared wide, halting the Beast's trajectory as the creature opened Its cutting beak and unleashed another glass-shattering shriek.

My magic flared in response, calling to It.

Its wings pulled in again…

And the Thunderbird dove.

My arms pumped faster, my legs eating up the distance between me and the black. Almost there. Another seventy-five yards.

Is The End truly the end?

Fifty yards.

And what, precisely, marks... The End?

Twenty yards.

Bright light flared at the edges of my vision, crackling against the darkness reaching for me.

For what do you fear most? The End... or what comes After?

I reached for the black, muscles tearing, lungs screaming. A smoky tendril broke from the mass. Stretching for me, a hand, an offering.

And I knew now, I wasn't scared.

I wasn't afraid.

Whatever happened next… I would be ok.

There's always something on the other side.

Warmth pulsed through me as I connected with the smoke. A last, lingering remnant of the prince who'd cared so much. My toe left the edge of the crumbling ground and I was falling. Falling. Onto a hard back. I bounced once and snagged a handful of the golden feathers, wrapping an arm around the Thunderbird's solid neck to secure my spot on Its back.

The joints of Its wings flexed on either side of my body, long wings snapping furiously as we delved into the nothingness.

But I wasn't afraid.

Not knowing who I was. Not knowing the faith those who loved me placed in me. Not knowing there was still a place for me on this earth. Kaleal may have found one way out, but I would find another.

Why did you come? I asked the bird, pressing my nose into Its back while keeping my gaze forward, ahead. The Beast smelled warm and a little musty, like blankets pulled from the closet before the first frigid night of winter.

Some calls were not meant to be ignored.

I called you?

The bird banked left, long wings splicing through the dark. My arm tightened around Its neck. *Many call me.*

I didn't know the Beasts were spirits, too. I pulled my legs up, bracing against the Thunderbird, riding It instead of clinging to It.

We are what we need to be. Its head swung so one flat, black eye blinked at me. *Much like weakness is perception.*

Its words clung to me, washing over me and sinking in. I'd never liked riddles—this particular Beast's mode of communication. But this felt... paramount. Much like this darkness, the peacefulness that was this place. It no longer felt ominous. It was somehow right, as if it were always intended to be this way.

Are you taking my soul back to my body? I asked.

I am but a vessel.

I frowned, staring down into the blackness stretching beyond Its shimmering talons. The Thunderbird wasn't taking me back to the mansion? Then where were we going?

Its riddles and all the unspoken spaces between them rolled around my mind.

Weakness is perception.

We are what we need to be.

Me. I was guiding us. I was strong, not weak. I would beat back this nothingness because I didn't belong here. I was what I needed to be, and I was the guide bringing myself back home. Back to my friends.

Back to *myself.*

Back to Kaleal.

I straightened on the bird, sitting tall and proud. *I'm ready.*

The darkness shattered like glass. It splintered as a burst of light engulfed the black, driving it back, sweeping the abyss into nothing but a realm where I'd found myself once again. A realm not meant to be feared. Dark always came with light. Weakness came with strength.

The Thunderbird threw Its wings wide as we dropped beside a door I recognized. A door that used to connect my mind to Geoffrey's. A door I'd closed permanently in yet another show of strength.

I pressed a kiss to the nape of the Thunderbird's soft neck. *Thank you.*

I didn't wait for Its response before throwing myself from Its back, because there, at the mouth of the hallway that took me to the core of my mind, stood Kaleal.

Her lips moved, but I couldn't hear the sound. I didn't want to. Didn't care to. Now, back in my own mind, my magic swirled. All of it. Watery footprints marked my steps as flames rolled down my arms. Armor made of wind encased me, gleaming bright as a warrior's heart. A familiar, wonderful blade of ice dripped in my grip.

The Ancient God backpedaled, face slack in amazement and maybe, just maybe, a hint of fear. I peered past the crown of flames flickering along my brow, leveling my weapon, saying nothing. I didn't need to.

"I locked you out," she sputtered. "How did you get back here? How did you—"

Weakness is a perception.

"I don't know how to kill you. Not yet." I didn't recognize the ring in my voice, the unwavering authority imbibed in every syllable. I liked it. "But I will. And when I do… you'd best watch your back, Kaleal, because I'm coming for you."

The colorful mosaic of my magics twined around her arms and legs.

The ancient God snarled and screeched as she struggled against them, words from an unrecognizable language streaming from her lips.

"You have a room." I lowered the weapon. "Be glad I've given you that much."

"This isn't over, Zara," Kaleal shouted. "And I won't forget this."

I turned my back, bowing my head as she disappeared.

There were some people I needed to see.

Chapter 42

Fresh, gloriously clean air filled my lungs. My skin tingled as my soul reconnected with my body, the painful, prickly sensation of frozen limbs warming after a race home through the snow. As my body adjusted, the pain receded. I felt myself waking up, the familiar shape of my form. A hand wrapped around mine, the pressure hard but not painful. And warm.

I opened my eyes, and they collided with a pair of beautiful amber irises. "Welcome back, glowstick."

I blinked, my focus shifting beyond Ryder as Finn appeared over his shoulder, face pinched with concern, green eyes bloodshot with exhaustion and worry. Beside him, Joseph hovered awkwardly, gripping Finn's shoulder. The kelpie's chest heaved with relief when I offered a slight, sad smile, knowing exactly what was going through his mind, knowing it wasn't fair to my guardian.

How many more times would he have to see me like this? On the brink of death?

At the foot of the bed, gripping the frame, stood Lee, her bag of tattoo supplies beside my feet. She nodded once, her head dropping between her braced arms. Beside her, Rue sobbed, hands obscuring her face as gulping gasps ripped from her throat.

Against the wall leaned Lachlan—my friend, my magical connection. He braced TruthTeller at his feet when I met his pale eyes. I wondered what truths might be released if I were to fire an arrow right now. A hint of wry amusement touched the elf's lips before he ducked his head.

A heaviness pressed against my side, a weight I didn't recognize. Another person, laying too still, beside me on the bed. Cupped in my hand, clenched between our sides, was the silky ball Ridley had entrusted with my care.

It all came rushing back.

I launched myself into Ryder's arms, my own tangling around his neck as he ducked to meet me. I pressed my face into his throat; wetness trickled down my cheeks and soaked into his shirt. I wished I could stop crying. I never wanted to cry again. He cupped the back of my head as I inhaled his scent, muttering nonsensical words.

Inhale. Exhale. Inhale again.

It was all I could do to keep from shattering.

The nightmares of those selfish witches. Ridley getting stabbed. Dropping into that endless abyss. Fending off Kaleal.

It was too much.

Ryder maneuvered my body so I was wrapped around him, clutching me close as I lost my bloody mind. I selfishly took all the comfort and love he had to give. But lingering along the edges of my hysteria, like a nightmare the princes so heavily favored, was the worry about how much Ryder would hate me when he learned the truth about what had happened to Ridley.

How much they all would hate me.

Finally, my shaking receded. The buzzing in my head calmed. I scrubbed at my face with one hand and realized I still cradled the ball to my chest with the other, wondering how no one had seen it yet. Or maybe they had.

"Hey, it's ok. You're here." Ryder nudged me so I could see his face, his dark hair shot with sparks of gold, his mouth firm in a concerned line. "It's alright. I've got you. You're here."

"I'm sorry." The words spilled from me before I was ready to let them go. "I'm sorry. I'm so, so sorry."

His hand moved down my back. "What are you talking about? You have nothing to be sorry about. Whatever you did, whatever you and Ridley did—" A knife slashed through my gut, hot and sharp and oh so deep "—it worked. Rue got a call a few minutes ago from Cura. The patients are recovering. The curse, it's gone. They're all going to be ok."

I barely heard him. The pain of loss clashed sharply with the raw edge of relief.

I'd assumed our efforts to destroy the curse had worked...

But if it hadn't...

I clung to him harder, my nails digging into his back. It was too much. Too much to feel. Too much to think. I leaned back, searching for Lachlan, needing his support. His gaze flicked from my tear-stained face to the bed beside me... and lowered.

He knew.

Ryder spoke again. "Now that you're back, we just need Ridley—"

"I'm sorry." The words felt like motor oil on my tongue, cold and viscous. I choked. "He's not... he's not... he can't..."

Ryder's brows pinched as he peered past me. "What are you saying? He's taking longer to come back. Give it a minute."

"No. He's not. It's not... he's gone." I pushed against Ryder's chest.

The black beast in the corner snapped out and Rim appeared, arm curled around his sister, who must have known about Ridley already, because she didn't flinch. Her cheeks were sunken, reddish eyes narrowed to slits as mascara mingled with the tears streaking down her face. She wrung her hands so hard I feared she'd cut off the circulation. Rim's face was murderous, his eyes accusatory as he glared at me.

I blotted my cheeks, the pain squeezing my chest so hard I feared it might never let go. I held up the ball of smoke.

Ryder went still, unblinking, a thin mist wafting off his skin. Rim snarled, a hint of his beast bleeding through his features, turning them more monster than human as he dragged his sister closer. "He gave me this. Trusted me with it. Told me… you'd know what it meant."

Rue ripped herself from Rim's grip and dropped to the other side of the bed, wailing, grabbing Ridley's arm as she buried herself in his too-still chest. I couldn't look at her, couldn't face Ryder…

Lachlan gripped my shoulder. He'd crept up from behind, a steady presence like always.

And a warning.

I offered the ball to Ryder who drew away as if it were a live wasps' nest.

"What happened?" he asked.

A strange sense of calm settled over my shoulders.

Weakness is a perception.

I owed them this.

It was all I had to give.

And I told them everything.

Chapter 43

"I only knew Ridley Caron for a short time. In the grand scheme of most of your lives, it probably counted as less than a blink. But your prince was something else, something wonderful and rare, and although I didn't know him long, I'm glad I did."

Turned out, choosing the prince's successor wasn't as simple as shoving a ball of smoke into someone's hands. Like many things involving the fey court, this, too, was a ceremony within a ceremony, the conclusion of a lengthy funeral that had wrung me emotionally dry.

I squeezed my hands together behind the podium on a stage that, when I'd last seen it, housed a row of seven thrones. Seven thrones with only three fey to fill them. It was the very chamber where I'd watched Ridley hear his people out a few weeks ago. This time, instead of watching from behind a veil up above, I stood front and center. Alone. With what felt like millions of eyes fixated on me.

"He was an inspiration. Protective of his family, fiercely dedicated to his people, honest with himself." My eyes tracked up the aisle, seeking a set of vibrant amber ones. Eyes that belonged to a fey who, though he was grieving in his own way, never blamed me once for what had happened. For his brother falling in the line of duty while I survived.

Again.

"I may be a God, but I am young. I am foolish. And I am learning. Despite that, Ridley sought me out. Your prince made a bet with himself that he could find the being who would save his people from devastation. It was a bet he was willing to lay his life on the line for. And he did."

I neglected to mention the other costs that sacrifice had inflicted, costs that came at great personal expense. I'd found it difficult to sleep these past few days, kept awake by the carousel of what-ifs circling my mind. What if I hadn't waited so long to call in my friends? What if we hadn't required Kaleal's help?

What if Ridley hadn't felt so deeply bound to protect his people that he manipulated a bond considered sacred by his people… as a means to an end?

I never had asked Ridley the questions I so desperately wanted answered.

And now I never would.

His actions had saved me as much as they slayed me.

"I learned so much from him. I learned how to look inside myself in moments of doubt. I learned how to rely on others to help carry the load."

I stroked the rune on my temple, the one Lee had touched up a few nights ago. It still held, but had weakened. While this seal wouldn't hold Kaleal back for long, I knew I might stand a chance against her now. I understood myself, and I was starting to understand exactly what I was capable of.

"And Ridley taught me strength. He taught me to find strength both within and without. He taught me strength isn't necessarily facing your fears, but finding the people who will help vanquish them alongside you. He taught me strength is knowing when to show your doubts and when to rein them in. He taught me strength comes in many forms, and maybe someday, someday I will come to understand all the strengths I still have yet to discover."

I brushed my knuckles. The skin was faintly marred, almost ruddy. Lee thought the damage I'd inflicted on myself hitting that cliff had left a permanent mark on my soul.

I didn't mind.

It was another scar in a series of hard-earned lessons.

Ryder smiled now, faintly. Behind him, looking incredibly out of place with his uncovered hair and bright clothing, sat Lach. The seats on either side of him were vacant, but he didn't seem to mind. He'd tossed his newly acquired sword on one and his coat on the other.

"Today, we say goodbye to a prince I respected deeply. But this isn't necessarily a somber day." I produced the ball of smoke I'd held so close these past few days. A slight murmur fanned out around the room, fey whispering behind hands, eyes darting from me to Rue who walked up to the dais.

"It's also a day to celebrate. In his final moments, Ridley entrusted in me the power to choose your next leader, the next Prince or Princess of Sin." I turned, looking up into the crimson hue of Rue's somber gaze. "If there's anyone I've met in this city, anyone who cares about their people as much as, if not more than he, it is his sister. So today, I crown Rue Caron as the new head of the Throne of Sin."

As I pressed the ball into her chest, the daemoni rose from their chairs and knelt as one, heads bowed in supplication. Rue gasped once, eyes swirling darkly as she watched something only she was privy to, memories only for daemoni royals to see. A crown, one spun of smoke and lust, circled her head like it had Ridley's when he became incensed. Then it, too, vanished, as she collected herself once more.

"So be it," the room chanted as one.

- - -

I didn't linger in the throne room long. Rue had a laundry list of formal duties to check off before she could call it a night, and while she was clearly still suffering from pain and grief, she had told me she was prepared to shoulder the weight. Rim on the other hand...

I wasn't stupid enough to get stuck in the same room alone with him. For as much understanding and forgiveness Rue and Ryder had shown me, Rim clearly held a grudge. I wanted nothing of his retribution.

Silvery hair fluttered around my face as I gazed up at the arcing waves of water, the fountain sparkling gold in the evening light. As pretty as it was, I wouldn't miss it. This city wasn't for me. I wasn't sure if any city would be.

"Where to now, boss?" Lachlan propped a boot on the lowest rung of the railing surrounding the fountain and dropped a bag at my feet. I knew without looking he'd packed my things. He'd probably found time before the funeral to whip up some of his infamous granola bars, too. I hoped he'd thought to stir up my favorite kind.

"What makes you think I have a plan?"

He shoved his cap on his head, ruffling his hair, and leaned against the railing, lacing his fingers together. "Because you always have a plan."

"Are you going to Geneva?" Joseph threw his voice across the plaza using his magic. The God of Air had gotten much better at controlling his element. I wondered what other tricks he'd picked up these past few months. "Your note asked for six months. It's only been four, but the world needs you right now."

"You're only worried what Pyra will do if you turn up without me."

Joseph shoved his glasses up his nose as Finn grinned beside him. "You have no idea what kind of nightmare she is."

"Then I guess it's a good thing you and Finn are destined for Rome." I knew Joseph wouldn't shirk his duties fixing the Order. We'd only talked a little about subjects not related to the curse, but even those brief conversations made it clear how proud he was of the work he was doing. "That puts you out of harm's way for a week or so."

"Maybe." Joseph didn't sound convinced.

I leaned against the railing, arms spanning the top rung. Finn surveyed my attire: my black shirt, forest green jacket, dark jeans, and boots with buckles. He shook his head. I hadn't answered Joseph's question, but the kelpie knew. He knew I wasn't coming back yet.

"If things do get bad, don't hesitate to call." I met both their eyes, making sure they understood I meant what I'd said. I had changed. I wasn't doing this alone, and that came with give and take—like the tides. "I will come back, no questions asked, if you need me."

Finn hooked my pinkie with his, our promise unspoken. Some tension faded from his face, the worry lines a little shallower between his brows.

"Since neither Rome nor Geneva is on the agenda, where are you going?" Ryder pulled me against him, the railing between us. Since arriving in Vegas, he'd become fond of using his smoke-state to sneak up on me. I didn't mind. I detected the weariness in his voice, the exhaustion in his arms, even so, he was here. With me.

"I need to find someone," I said.

"Oh?" Joseph moved his bag from one shoulder to the other.

"The witches mentioned a woman, one who took me from the Palace of Oceans as it fell." I tapped my chest, right above my heart, where it panged every time I thought of her. I was still struggling to process everything that had happened that day, but this detail stood out in strange clarity against it all. It was important in a way I couldn't fathom. "I need to find her. I don't know why. I don't know what she knows or what she might say, but…"

"But she might have answers," Finn finished for me.

I'd only known one person who escaped the North Sea the day of the attack, and that was the kelpie standing by my side now. Logically, someone must have helped get me to safety. I'd known that, but I'd never really thought about it. Never allowed myself to think about it. But now that I had a name…

Marinda.

It was a name that tasted mysterious on my tongue.

"I need to know who I am." I looked at all of them, my friends, my loyal companions. The ones who'd been there for me in all the ways I'd never known I'd needed. The ones I'd help without hesitation, too. "I need to know what she knows. About me, about the items she left me with, about my destiny."

Ryder ran a finger down my fishtail braid—one lacking adornment. I couldn't bear to weave a knot into it, not while I was still so uncertain about what had happened in those final moments with Ridley… about what his choice would mean for me—for me and Ryder—down the road.

"And I'm going to need your help."

If you enjoyed part three of The Elemental Gods series, I kindly ask that you leave a review. Reviews are the lifeblood of every author's career, and every star helps.

Book Four Coming Soon

To stay up-to-date with the latest release information, sign up for my monthly newsletter! In those, I send out writing updates as well as free and exclusive content related to both The Elemental Gods series and my other work. To find out more, head to www.septemberthomas.com.

Books by September Thomas

The Elemental Gods

Walk on Water

Fan the Flame

Wind and Reign

Acknowledgements

Writing books never gets any easier. Sure, you learn the rhythm, the delightful cadence of letters and words that comes together in a glorious symphony of plot and character and discovery, but the act of writing itself remains as complicated an affair for me in my third book as it did for my first.

Fortunately, I have a wonderful team of people in my corner to help. Without their support, Zara's adventure would be a dry and dull affair—hardly deserving of a teenage God out to save the world.

First, I recognize Fiona McLaren, my brainstormer, my editor, my motivational cheerleader (remember how those witches love their threes??). As a writer, it's easy to try to cheat a story, to cheat yourself, especially when the going gets rough. Fiona never hesitates to call me out when she finds those pitfalls (and trust me, she misses nothing). She deserves as much credit for weaving Zara's story as anyone. Fiona—I hope this book gives you 'all the things' you wanted.

Second - to my cover designer, Natasha MacKenzie. I never make these covers easy for you, but once again you created an absolute work of art. You captured the soul of this book and all its nuances. Bravo.

Also, to my brother whose eagerness for these books is paralleled by none. To my mom and dad, who always fostered my love of books and writing. To my family and friends for showing up on my launch day and being more excited about my accomplishments than even I was (and let me tell you, I was ridiculously excited).

Of course, I can't leave out Josh. The man who hears all my random brainstorms, who blinks politely when I launch into a bit of Elemental God lore no one outside of my head could understand, who has almost vacated his claims on our shared office because my books and art have taken over. You are the best hugger, the greatest listener... and you make me a better person—for that I can't thank you enough. I love you.

Finally, to Sydney. You laid by my feet as I hammered out every word, every page, every book. You offer nothing but your love and support. You are my Chunkdog, my cuddly fluff, my beautiful girl. Don't ever change.

About the Author

September Thomas is the author of the Elemental Gods series. She lives in Nebraska with her boyfriend and rescued Australian Cattle Dog. She also boasts a large collection of (fake) owls that some consider amusingly ridiculous.

You can connect with me on:

- https://www.septemberthomas.com
- https://twitter.com/SeptemberAuthor
- https://www.facebook.com/SeptemberThomasAuthor
- https://www.instagram.com/september.thomas

Subscribe to my newsletter:

- https://www.septemberthomas.com

www.ingramcontent.com/pod-product-compliance
Lightning Source LLC
Chambersburg PA
CBHW021439240626
47153CB00001B/214
9781734254525